HYBRID

GREG BALLAN

Hadrosaur Productions, Mesilla Park, NM

Hybrid
Hadrosaur Productions
Second Edition: June 2021
First date of publication: November 2008
hadrosaur.com

ISBN: 1-885093-96-9
ISBN-13: 978-1-885093-96-7

To my son, Thomas.
This book would never have come to be without your encouragement and honest critique. You're the best friend a writer could have.

Acknowledgments

A special thank you to my cousin, Lieutenant Colonel Chris Ross, and every other serviceman and woman who has sacrificed so much over the past several years for our freedom and safety. Chris, you are truly an American hero.

HYBRID

Prologue

Douglas Gillespie hated the fact that he had been stuck up here in the middle of nowhere for nearly six weeks. He cursed loudly as he swatted at a swarm of annoying horseflies buzzing incessantly around his head. Doug dreamed of a 5-Star Boston restaurant, cold champagne, and attractive companionship. Spending time in this hillside forest digging an illegal mining tunnel was not his idea of a good time.

If the environmentalists or the state government discovered this little enterprise, they would be jailed, and their corporation would be facing a lawsuit of bankrupting proportions. His attention left the annoying insects when his radio beeped.

"Go ahead." He lazily keyed the mike on his radio.

"We found something, something fantastic!" the voice screamed through his receiver. "You'd better get down here."

"What do you mean 'something'? Details, man!" Gillespie continued to swat at one extremely persistent horsefly.

"We don't know! You're the expert here, so you get off your ass and get in here!" the voice answered with hostility.

* * *

Michael Gibson had been digging preliminary mining tunnels for twenty-five years. He had dug for D'Biers Consolidated in South Africa, Exxon, and several other large companies. This dig was supposed to be a cakewalk. But ever since a whisper-silent helicopter dropped him into this area four weeks ago, he knew something was not kosher with this particular operation.

There were no access roads leading up to their site, so a helicopter dropped everything in the dead of night. The choppers never had any running lights, and never made any noise. The wind from the wash of their rotors was the only evidence of their presence. Gibson knew that these were not standard cargo birds either. He had heard noisy Bell copters, and loud, clanky Huey cargo carriers. These birds were different, even their rotors were near-whisper silent.

But since the tunnel collapse during the Exxon job, he hadn't been able to find any work. Gibson knew that he wasn't to blame for the accident; he had warned the petroleum company that tunneling under water was dangerous and unpredictable. When the roof of the tunnel collapsed, millions of gallons of seawater rushed in to swallow a small fortune in equipment and dozens of lives. Exxon blamed him. He blamed the company for ignoring his warnings. The end result was that no one would hire him with that accident hanging over his head.

This job was a blessing for him, in addition to being well paying. If he could bring this tunnel in on time and on budget, he'd be set for life.

He stared nervously at the small chamber they had blindly stumbled into. They had tunneled down into the mountainside nearly one thousand feet at a forty-five-degree angle, and then gone parallel about another two hundred feet, when they broke into a small chamber roughly forty feet in diameter. The walls of this chamber were polished mirror bright and covered with strange engravings. At the far end of the chamber, directly blocking the progress of their tunnel, was a large metallic doorway with two huge gargoyle-like stone sentinels at either side. When Gibson looked at the figures, he felt his flesh crawl with a deep ice-cold chill.

"All right, Gibson, what's so all-fire? Oh my God, what the hell is this?" Gillespie stared at the chamber with awe.

"You tell me," Gibson remarked

"I don't know. I'm a geologist, not an archeologist."

"Who do you think did this?" Gibson continued, peppering Gillespie with another question.

"Elvis." He looked at Gibson with a pained expression. "How in the hell would I know. Have you tried opening the door?"

"It won't budge," Gibson replied. "We took a sounding of the door. It's at least a foot thick; the chamber behind it goes on beyond the range of our meter. Oh, and the metal in the door registers like nothing we know of. The spectrometer is giving us readings I've never seen before. Whatever it is, it's more sophisticated than titanium or any other steel alloy we're used to. Whatever culture made this chamber and whatever is beyond was fairly advanced. I'd say we stop what we're doing and get some qualified archeologists and scientists in here. This find could be priceless. Hell, it probably *is* priceless."

"That would be nice, but implausible," Gillespie replied, knowing that this operation was strictly secret and strictly illegal. "Blast it or bore through it. I don't care. Just get us through."

"Are you crazy?" Gibson shouted. "We don't know what's behind this door. We don't even know if we can blow through it safely."

"You're supposed to be one of the best in the business; that's why you're here. We're not here for some relic dig. We're here to do a job. The company doesn't care about artifacts. It cares about profits and share value; and may I remind you that our percentages are at stake if we can't do this job on time. If someone was kind enough to tunnel for us, so be it. Our orders are to get this tunnel dug and get things prepped for the second phase of the operation."

Gibson shook his head. "Fine, you're paying the bills, but I'm on the record saying that this is a bonehead maneuver. If we blast, we risk bringing the whole hilltop down on ourselves. I'm not going to be standing here while tons of dirt and rock land on my head. This section of the mountain is already geologically unstable. We knew that going into this. That's why you hired me. If this tunnel collapses, where will the corporation's precious profits be then?"

"Then drill or cut or burn through. We'll get you whatever equipment you need," Gillespie responded.

Gibson thought for a moment. "I have an idea." He turned and headed out of the dark tunnel.

Gillespie watched him briefly as he vanished up the narrow corridor. He spun his head, studying the fearsome stone statues one last time before hurrying after the contractor.

* * *

Twenty-four hours had transpired since the team entered the strange chamber. Gibson and his work crew had emerged from the tunnel and not ventured back down since the initial discovery. Gibson had requested a very specific large piece of equipment from an associate, and 'The Company' was having it flown in this evening.

Gibson's men were all whispering about the eerie feel the chamber had, and how reluctant they were to proceed any further. Gibson had to admit to himself that he too was nervous about violating the chamber without understanding what they were getting into. The massive stone gargoyles looked ominous and seemed to shriek of an unknown danger.

A large silent helicopter lowered a bulky crate from its winch. Five of his crew attacked the crate like busy worker ants once it touched the ground. The work party, followed by a curious Gillespie, ventured back into the tunnel and set up the formidable-looking device in front of the large door inside the tunnel chamber.

"What is that thing?" Gillespie asked, staring at the large device.

"This, my friend, is an argon laser," Gibson answered, patting the large emitter node. "It's one of three that have been developed for mining purposes, a by-product of the arms race of the 1990s. No explosions, no vibrations, we'll just burn clean through. I don't care what kind of metal that thing's made of, this puppy will more-than-do the job," he added. "Are we all about ready?" He placed protective goggles over his head.

All of the men stood behind the large laser platform, each one holding their breath in anticipation, anxiety, and fear.

"Fire in the hole," Gibson said as he activated the device.

A brilliant beam of reddish white impacted with the heavy door. Gillespie could smell something burning and saw the door glow with radiant heat. The weapon hummed with power as the generator increased its rhythm to accommodate the energy drain. Gibson knew the beam was having some slight effect, but wasn't cutting as effectively as he had anticipated. With trepidation, he increased the beam's intensity. The weapon chirped an octave higher. The door glowed brighter, and the circle of red molten heat increased in diameter another foot.

"We don't seem to be getting through," he shouted above the louder chirping.

"Can you increase the beam's intensity any more?" Gillespie asked.

Gibson nodded and increased the power to the unit by another twenty percent. "That's all she's got!" he shouted above the weapon's harmonic whine. "Any more and we'll fry the circuits for sure."

The laser beam was nearly blinding now, even behind the dark protective goggles. The additional power had done the job. A large section of the door literally fell away in a molten pool of metal. Gibson quickly shut the machine down and activated the liquid nitrogen cooling units.

"We'll give it some time to cool before we go in," Gibson said. "We don't need anyone getting fried by that molten slag."

* * *

Deep within the chamber, something stirred. It had been sleeping for over one-hundred centuries. A flash of light and some strange noises had disturbed its near-eternal slumber. The entity stretched itself slowly, flexing each claw, testing each muscle. It dug its claws into the rock and left four long scratch marks in the metal and granite wall. It slowly opened its eyes, which were a fluorescent blood-red and glowed like two fiery embers. The creature stood and unfurled its long serpent-like tail, whipping the tensile appendage back and forth.

It walked over to another creature next to it and affectionately stroked the large creature's hide. The second beast growled softly and moved a massive paw that was easily the size of a dinner platter. The first creature grinned, revealing large reptilian teeth.

Slowly, it made its way toward the opening, its senses alert for whatever freed it from its eternal prison. It hadn't fed for nearly ninety centuries. Those that were buried with it had been drained eons ago. Their dried remains still littered the cavern floor. It needed to feed. It smelled traces of food out beyond the opening. It relished the thought of hunting again after so long.

It approached the opening and caught the scent of primates. This was not the prey it had expected, but at this point, anything would do to satisfy its raging hunger. The primates were busily scrambling around the outside of its chamber, so it was able to step into the outer chamber unnoticed. It needed to feed. One of the primates turned, saw it and screamed. Then they all turned. It felt the waves of fear, and immediately consumed them, relishing the primitive emotions as a man in the desert would relish a canteen of cool water.

It rushed toward the closest man and caught him in a grip of iron around his throat. The flesh thing struggled and shrieked with fear. It savored each wave of terror, like a connoisseur appreciating an excellent vintage of wine. The man fainted in its grasp, providing it no more food. It casually crushed the primate's throat and tossed it aside, looking for its next victim.

* * *

Gibson's mind shrieked with terror as he heard the sickening crunch of bone. The god-forsaken thing had just killed one of his men and tossed him like a plaything. Gibson tried to reactivate the laser, but it was still in cool-down. He reached over for a pick and heard another scream. Gibson grabbed his makeshift weapon and charged the monster. He swung the pick with all his strength. His blow landed true upon the thing's massive shoulder, but simply bounced off in a shower of sparks.

Gibson felt something run him through, and he looked down, realizing the creature had just impaled him with its tail. He paused, staring at the creature's appendage in disbelief. He felt no pain when it pulled its tail free, just the taste of his own blood building up in the back of his mouth. He felt his lungs fill with blood, and tried to adjust his breathing shallower so he wouldn't cough.

"Oh, shit," he whispered as blood poured from his mouth. Gibson fell face-first into the stone floor, his eyes locked open in a dead man's gaze.

* * *

The creature quickly killed everyone else in the party and slowly made its way out into the world, a world that it hadn't seen nor walked upon in over ten thousand years. Its priority now was to continue feeding. The primates it had just killed could not satisfy its needs. It no longer felt starved, but it needed a purer form of fear. Fear was what it needed to survive. These men had that emotion, but neither strong enough nor pure enough to satisfy it or the other creature left behind.

Its primary job was to find food for itself and for the other. Its secondary goal was to destroy those who had imprisoned it and its kindred. The two creatures would gather sparse nourishment from these primates, and then, together, they would hunt down the race of non-primate beings it only knew as Espers.

Chapter 1

The Lexus SUV looked out of place among the more common automobiles as it pulled into Madame's Restaurant. A man in a suit stepped out of the car cautiously before he opened the passenger door. A short, stocky, elderly man slowly climbed down from the passenger compartment and gratefully took the cane the suited man offered. Both men approached the entrance to the restaurant and quietly entered the establishment.

A young woman in a waitress outfit approached them immediately. "Party of two?" she asked between chews of her gum.

The old man looked quickly around the immediate area, scanning booths and tables, obviously looking for someone in particular. "We're supposed to be meeting someone here: Tall, about six-foot plus, very long dark hair, blue eyes, medium build." He hoped she could place his associate on such a vague description.

"Right this way, Mr. Denton; he's expecting you." The waitress turned and proceeded to a back hallway.

Denton raised an eyebrow toward his companion and proceeded to follow the young woman. The hallway was narrow, barely wide enough for the two men to walk side by side. The hallway ended, emptying into a room the size of a master bedroom. The room was modestly decorated with certificates and a criminal justice diploma. There was a large computer suite at one corner of the small room that was sputtering paper from an ink-jet printer.

Denton quickly scanned the room. A series of personal photographs occupied a place of prominence on a small desk. He recognized his associate in a picture, and assumed the woman and child in the photograph were of some personal significance. Denton knew that people in his associate's line of work rarely had many personal affiliations. He knew that was a blatant stereotype, but it was a judgment he validated from thirty years of experience. Spooks with wives and family were seldom worth the money they charged. Denton focused on the imposing figure that sat behind a large, out of place dining table. If this man had such affiliations, he was the exception.

The man had long jet-black hair that was pulled back into a ponytail. The white V-neck T-shirt did little to hide a well-developed upper torso, and powerfully developed arms. Denton judged his associate spent a great deal of time doing some kind of serious physical training. His build was not what would be associated with a body builder by any means. He lacked the sheer massive size that weight lifters possessed. His body seemed to be the build of an athlete – lean and muscular, but without the excessive bulk that could hinder mobility.

The man studied some reports intently, his eyes riveted on whatever the page said. Denton's eyes immediately fell upon the shoulder holster that held two auto pistols and four spare clips. Denton knew this was a formidable man.

Denton continued his scrutiny of the man as he sat behind the dining table with papers and photographs spread haphazardly in front of him. The man looked up and stood to meet his guests.

"Martin, come in, have a seat." He gestured to the table covered with papers and pictures. The man in the suit stood quietly by the entryway, his face expressionless as he assumed a guard position.

"How did we make out?" Denton asked anxiously as he took a seat.

"I think I have enough for you to make our friend very, very uncomfortable, but nothing that could be totally admissible in a court of law." He paused. "But the court of public opinion may be something different."

Martin Denton let out a long sigh of relief. He knew that if anyone could infiltrate Medcorp Industries, Erik Knight would be the man for the job.

Erik Knight was in his early thirties. His eyes were sky blue, and seemed to have a haunting look that spoke of some unknown past torments and horrors. He leaned back in his chair, stretching his arms above his head and yawning. His muscles writhed and flexed as his focus returned to the matter at hand.

Knight had been referred to Denton almost two years ago when the attorney needed a special operative to penetrate a mob-operated stronghold in Chelsea. Denton was impressed with the quick, efficient manner in which the job had been done. What impressed Denton even more was how inexpensive the services had been. Denton admired skill, but knew a more seasoned man would have much higher rates. Despite his concerns, Denton continued to utilize him, and was always amazed at how effective the young man was.

Normally, Denton would never travel to meet a contractor, but he was curious about Knight, and curiosity was something that would gnaw at the old man until he could satisfy it. Something about this young investigator didn't seem to add up. Denton couldn't quite place it. Seeing a family photograph only added to the mysterious equation Denton had built up in his head.

People in Knight's line of work were all of the same paradigm: Wild and reckless, usually foolhardy with money, a taste for expensive liquor and cheap women. His study of Knight indicated that the young independent was in some dire financial straits, but nothing too extreme. From his own gatherings, he knew that Knight didn't drink and seemed relatively tame in comparison to other contractors the firm utilized in prior months. Erik Knight was an enigma, a stand-out from other independent operators.

Denton liked that for some reason. He found the private investigator to not only be deadly efficient at his work, but to possess a keen intellect and incredible instincts.

The investigator leaned forward slightly and began recounting the past events of his case. "I penetrated corporate security and got the accounting files that you requested, but couldn't find any information pertaining to the rumors we discussed," he began. "I figured that what we were looking for was in his personal safe at his compound in Weston."

"Go on," Denton remarked.

"I got in a couple of nights ago," Erik continued. "He always leaves his third story window open."

"Please elaborate," Denton urged; the older man loved details.

"I knew from a source that Hegart would be at a Political Action Committee fundraiser. I waited outside the estate until I saw his Rolls leave the gate. I waited another half hour to make sure he was actually on his way. He has a habit of leaving, and then returning five or ten minutes after leaving." Erik paused as he adjusted his position on his seat. "I can only assume that he's absent-minded and forgets something or other.

"I used a frequency blanket to interfere with the monitors as I scaled the outer wall of the estate. As far as the guards could tell, there was some momentary static in the system, just enough time for me to clear the wall."

"How did you actually get into the estate house?" Denton asked curiously.

"Your nemesis is very fond of clinging ivy. It grows up the side of his house, particularly where the open window is," Erik explained. "It was a simple matter to climb the ivy and the lattice, and then slip into the window. It took me about twenty minutes to find the safe, and another fifteen minutes to open it. I was in and out of the estate in under two hours," he remarked with minor self-gratification.

"You are very lucky, my young friend," Denton responded.

Erik gave a shark-like grin. "I believe that we make our own luck, Mr. Denton. This 'luck' was the result of careful planning and surveillance, and a disgruntled servant." Erik reached for a stack of photographs and papers. "Here's what our friend has been hiding in his bedroom safe." He pushed several photographs toward Denton.

Denton carefully studied the pictures of ledger pages, references to offshore bank accounts, bank statements and other various financial references that had been meticulously photographed.

"What are these papers?" Denton asked.

"Letters," Erik responded evasively. "Let's just say I figured you'd like another ace in the hole during your dealings with our friend."

Denton took one of the letters and started reading, then

another. He put the other letter down, digesting the information.

"This is perfect." Denton's face adopted a wolfish grin as he gathered up the photographs and letters to put them in his briefcase.

"How are you going to use that? You know you can't introduce it in court. It wasn't exactly obtained by legal means," Erik inquired. "He'll realize the letters are missing, eventually; but judging from the dates on the letters, the affair ended over a year ago."

"You're right, of course," Denton answered, "but I can mention that we have knowledge of potential evidence, both professional and personal – enough to make them nervous. Even the threat of a financial subpoena would serve our purpose in this case. Even though we can't claim enough here for a judicial decision, there's enough incriminating documentation to make them settle. Plus, if word of an extra marital affair leaked out, the negative publicity would cause more damage to his lily-white image than he could afford. It would save our clients a great deal of time and money—"

"And increase your firm's profit margin by eliminating the costs involved in a trial," Erik interrupted.

"There's that too." Denton nodded in agreement as he finished gathering his evidence.

As he opened his briefcase, he pulled out a letter-size envelope and tossed it onto the table in Erik's direction. Erik smiled slightly and placed the envelope in the duffel bag next to him.

"You're not going to count it?" Denton asked.

"Mr. Denton, I've done four contracts for you in the past eighteen months, and you've honored the terms of each one. I will not insult you by counting payment – in front of you, that is." Erik flashed another half-smile. "We should almost trust each other at this point."

The old man paused, considering Knight's words, and then laughed aloud. "Mr. Knight, I do indeed like your style." He laid down a large roll of hundred-dollar bills onto the table. "Consider this a bonus for another job well done."

* * *

Erik nodded toward Denton and escorted him to the hallway. He watched through a small window as Denton and the man accompanying him departed the diner. Erik picked up the roll of bills and counted out thirty, one hundred-dollar bills. He took twenty of the bills and tucked them into his wallet, and then palmed the other ten. He carefully removed his gun vest and placed it into a small wall safe. The detective gathered up the envelope from his contract and headed toward the main room of the diner. Erik walked up to a tall middle-aged man with wavy blond and gray hair.

The lean figure looked Erik up and down and then smiled. "I trust everything went well?"

Erik nodded and placed the ten bills from his hand on the counter next to him. "Thanks for giving me the extra time to wrap this up, Jeff. We're square for last month and this month now."

"I know you, Erik, and I know you're always true to your word."

When business in his diner had slowed two years ago, Jeff had let Erik use the back room in addition to a small one-bedroom apartment behind the restaurant. Erik paid him a modest amount in rent, and used the back room as a base of operations for his business. Erik helped cleaning dishes and sweeping during business and closing hours as thanks for paying such a small rent. Real estate, like everything else in Hopedale, was pricey, far too pricey for the investigator's limited finances.

Erik took his leather jacket off the coat rack and headed for the door.

"Make sure you're back for the dinner crowd!" Jeff barked in his motherly tone. "I could really use the extra help tonight."

"Yes, Mom," Erik replied as he made his way out the door.

* * *

Erik pulled his truck into the long driveway at the wealthier end of Hopedale. He always felt uncomfortable in this area, but his ex-wife and daughter were doing well here and his daughter received all the things he was unable to give her. He walked up the meticulously laid brick walk and rang the doorbell. A young girl opened the door and her eyes immediately lit up as she saw him.

"Daddy!" She screamed with delight as she jumped into his arms.

"Hey, Munchkin!" he answered as she settled into his arms. "Where's Mommy?"

"She's out back with Ricky. They have company – some goofy business people." The little girl rolled her eyes upward.

"Brianna!" a voice interrupted. "You know better than to talk like that."

Brianna giggled as she jumped down from her father's arms and headed out into the back yard.

"Hello, Margaret," Erik began. "You're looking beautiful, as always." He tried his best to sound pleasant.

"You still look...." She paused, letting her eyes study him for a good five seconds. "Blue collar, as always." She finished with a small tone of contempt in her voice.

Erik felt a quick pang of hurt at her remark. Margaret had never been happy with his trade, or the amount of money he earned. He was sincerely glad she finally got what she wanted. She seemed truly happy, and looked upon him as her biggest mistake.

"Easy," he said as he put his hands up. "I didn't come here to start an argument." He reached into his wallet. "I have the support payment for this month and next month." Erik pulled out six hundred dollars and handed it to her. He put his still-flush wallet back into his pocket and looked at Margaret.

"Where did you come across this much cash on such a short notice? The last time we spoke you didn't have two nickels to rub together." She studied the crisp bills.

"I just finished a case. That money was part of a bonus from my employer. You know I've been working a case for the last three weeks."

"Doing what?" she asked sarcastically. "Finding missing poodles?"

"No, I really can't discuss it," he answered evasively, deliberately ignoring the venom in her tone.

"Please!" she commented. "You're just so important that

you're working on secret cases now. I find that difficult to believe."

"What's the matter with you?" Erik said louder than he intended. He let her know she hurt him. She seemed to revel in that. "I didn't come here looking for a fight. Why are you treating me this way? I haven't done anything!"

"Is everything okay, darling?" a voice asked, thick with contempt.

"Everything is fine, Richard," Erik spat with equal loathing.

Richard walked up to Erik and stared at him momentarily. "Oh, it's you." He looked at Margaret. "I gather you've told him our intentions."

Erik noticed that Margaret's face suddenly became red, and she looked uncomfortable.

"Richard, go back to our guests. I'll be with you shortly," she whispered.

Richard, however, did not leave. "No, I should be here when you tell him. I want to see the look on his face," he insisted.

Margaret looked into Erik's eyes, and he saw the fear. He sensed something was coming – something big. He could read it in her body language, all the subtle physical indications of discomfort. He could feel his ex-wife's emotions, her sudden panic and anxiety.

"Richard wants to start proceedings to adopt Brianna," Margaret began. "His attorneys will be mailing you a form to sign over your paternal rights. Before you say anything or go on a tirade, you can see her anytime you want instead of what the old court decree says," Margaret announced softly, not looking up from the ground. "Richard really wants us to be a family."

"No," Erik said in a soft, deadly voice. He looked at Richard with hate-filled eyes. "You have my wife, you already have my daughter under your roof. The first one you can keep, but you'll never be Brianna's father. I'm her father. Me, Erik Knight, and I won't give that up, not for anything."

* * *

"No one is asking you to give that up," Margaret began. "Bio-logically, you are her father; but face it, you're very rarely here.

Richard, for all practical purposes, is Brianna's father. She's been with us for the past seven years. I wanted to talk with you about this at a more convenient time."

She gave her husband an annoyed glance. "But now that it's out in the open, I'll say my piece. Brianna deserves a father that's home every night, someone that can provide her with the finer things of life, giving her the opportunities you can't. She doesn't need someone who's only around every other weekend or off at all hours of the night playing Sherlock Holmes, or whatever it is you call what you do." Margaret paused, studying her ex-husband.

She could see the fury building up within him, she had been with Erik long enough to know that there were limits to his tolerance. Deep down, she knew doing this would emotionally cripple him. She'd crushed his spirit when she'd filed for divorce. This would be the finishing blow.

Erik's shoulders slumped and his face tilted slightly as he considered his response. He looked sharply into her eyes, and she could see the blazing intensity that burned there. "You two are really something, you know that? Your high-priced lawyers set the terms for my visitations after you smeared my reputation. I'd love to spend more time with Brianna; only you two have seen to it that I can't. I'm surprised I'm not in jail, thanks to the smear campaign you pulled at the divorce hearing.

"As it stands, I get two weekends and four nights a month. In the six years that this arrangement has been going on, I've never missed my visitation. For God's sake, Margaret, she's all I have left. You've got everything you ever wanted. Don't take the one thing I have left away from me," he said in a soft whisper. "Have you discussed this with our daughter? Is this something that she wants?"

"What she wants or doesn't want is irrelevant," Richard broke in. "It's time for us to become a real family; and quite frankly, you're getting in the way of that. Brianna mistakenly puts you on a pedestal. She doesn't understand you like I do. You have no real future. You're a blue-collar PI with no real clientele and no real experience. How long do you think you can earn a living doing surveillance and security work? You need a plan, only you're not smart enough to realize that. No one wants an investigator who works out of the back room of a low-brow diner," Richard said with a self-righteous tone.

"My personal finances are my business," Erik replied darkly. "Unlike you, I don't make money off the misery of others, you slum lord. I've already checked you out, and I know all about you. You inherited everything you have. You've earned nothing. You make money off real estate law on property that should be condemned, and you pillage land with your shady development and mining operations across the country. I may not have much, but what I have I've achieved on my own.

"As for my office space, I like where I am. I like to associate with a better class of people than I'm associating with now. I'm accessible to people. I don't hide myself in an ivory tower eighty stories above the ground, or surround myself with black iron fences and gates. I'm not afraid of regular people like you seem to be."

"Spoken like the true riffraff that you are." Richard's face adopted a smug look. "Mr. Knight, you barely make enough money to get by, you have no real address, and you have no place for your daughter to call home. My attorneys could do this in court, but I don't think that is in the child's best interest.

"If you don't want to abide by our wishes, I'll see you in court. I have enough power and influence to see that you lose all rights to your daughter. Plus, I'll personally see to it that you never have another client for your ragtag business. I buried you once before, don't force me to do it again," Richard added with an unmistakable loathing in his voice. "Do we understand each other?"

Margaret groaned inwardly, she knew her husband just made a critical mistake. Threatening Erik was not going to solve anything, except make him furious. She could see the intensity burning inside her ex-husband. She knew Erik would respond, most likely with force.

Erik responded to the threat as his ex-wife predicted. Moving with astonishing speed, he grabbed Richard by the lapel of his Italian jacket and lifted him a foot off the floor.

"Listen to me; I don't care what you try, or how many lawyers you have. You'll never, ever take my baby girl from me. Furthermore, I don't care who you are. Never threaten me again. If you cross me, I'll deal with you on my terms this time, my way; and I promise you, you won't like it. Do we understand each other?"

Richard nodded, as his legs dangled in the air helplessly. With a mighty heave, Erik tossed Richard ten feet down the marble foyer. The man landed in a heap, sliding another ten feet and crashing into a large potted fern.

Richard picked himself up and charged Erik like a wild Rhino. Erik timed his counter with deadly precision, redirecting Richard's charge into the mammoth solid oak front door. Erik grabbed his stunned opponent by the back of his jacket and forcefully threw him back to the floor, pinning Richard easily with an arm lock. Erik applied increasing pressure until Richard yelped in agony. Erik let up on the pressure and allowed Richard to return to his feet.

"Next time, rich boy, I won't be so forgiving," Erik whispered.

"Stop it!" Margaret screamed as Richard prepared for another assault. "This won't solve anything! Richard, clean yourself up and go back to our guests." She gestured toward the door.

Richard glared angrily at Erik. "This isn't over, Knight. Not by a long shot."

"For your sake, it had better be. Any time you want to continue, you know where I am," Erik remarked with hate-filled venom.

"Both of you, knock it off!" Margaret screamed. She looked at Erik. "Must it always end in fisticuffs with you?" She turned her attention to her husband. "And you! Must you act like such a pompous ass? Why must you always torment him? He's a trained fighter. You're not going to win that kind of brawl with him."

Richard brushed himself off, mumbling as he limped back to their guests. Margaret turned toward her ex-husband. She saw that the look of anger was now replaced by one of shock and actual hurt. She really didn't hate him personally, she realized, just what he chose to do with his life. Deep down, she knew she was to blame for a great many things that went wrong during their two-year marriage. All of a sudden, she felt a great pity for the man standing in front of her.

"I'm sorry, Erik. I wanted to tell you under different circumstances. Sometimes Richard can be a little condescending, but his heart is in the right place, and he really does love her."

"I'm sure he does, but can't he love her without adopting her?"

"Of course he can, but he's got this whole family thing right now. We'll discuss it later. I promise."

"I just don't want to go through what I went through seven years ago," Erik replied.

"That was a mistake. I swear I didn't know he took it to that end. I won't let that happen, I promise. We've both had enough hurt."

Erik nodded. "On that point, we can both agree."

She hesitated momentarily. "Erik, I shouldn't have been such a bitch earlier. You didn't have that coming. I'm really happy your work is picking up. I don't know what's wrong with me. I've just been snapping at everyone lately."

Erik seemed startled by this sudden change in her tone. "Well, no harm no foul," he responded lightly. "I'm sorry about the ruckus here. It shouldn't have happened. You better get back to your company. I'll see you Friday night to pick up the munchkin."

Margaret nodded, watching Erik turn away and head down the long brick walkway. She stared at the now crumpled bills in her hand and did something totally unexpected.

"Erik, take this and show our daughter a great time." She balled up the bills and casually tossed them toward him. She quickly closed the door, knowing the act she just committed was pure charity and could possibly embarrass him. She watched through the stained glass as he picked up the crumpled bills.

He looked toward the house and mouthed the words, "Thank you."

Margaret stood at the door and watched him as he drove out of their driveway and out of their gated community.

* * *

Erik had made his bank deposit and paid the remainder of his overdue bills from his bonus. It was very rare that a client paid a bonus of fifty percent of a total contract. He had enough money now to get him through the next three months – four if he was very careful. Money matters still weighed heavy on his mind as he entered the dojo for his Saturday workout.

There had to be a way he could drum up more business. Erik absently threw kicks and punches into a one-hundred-pound heavy bag as he mentally ran through his options. He had thought about joining the police force, but he was already too old. He could move his agency into a city like Boston or Worcester, possibly hook up with a law firm like Denton, Ross and Priscoli. That would guarantee him fat paychecks every month, and more than enough money for him to pay his bills and provide for his daughter.

The downside was working for somebody else – taking direction and following orders. Those were the two things he never did well. It wasn't that he couldn't follow direction – after six years in Special Forces, you learn how to take commands – Erik just didn't like the idea of not controlling his own fate. That was the key element that led Margaret to finally leave him. He had turned down a lucrative job in New York in order to start his own agency in the Metro West region of Massachusetts. Margaret was home with their baby, and he was out all hours of the night doing work.

He came home after a two-day stint to find their small apartment vacant and a note in their empty bedroom. Margaret had wasted no time finding a new man. They had both known Richard for several years. He had been a good friend of Margaret's, and had been present at their small wedding. Erik had always sensed that there was something more between the two of them, and wasn't surprised when they started seeing each other. Two weeks after they started dating, he was served the divorce papers, and just like that, he was alone.

Margaret had used Richard's hired gun attorneys during their divorce. They had done everything possible to degrade and destroy Erik's character and credibility. They had painted him as a lazy, shiftless man with no ambition or sense of responsibility. Erik had to admit, in some warped sense, Margaret was right. A more responsible man would have accepted the job offer for the sake of his family. A more mature man would have probably made some different choices.

Erik knew he couldn't blame all of this on her, but she had more than made him pay for his mistakes. He had spent all of his savings on attorney fees and wound up losing the few clients he had, thanks to the personal and professional smear campaign put out against him. It had taken him over three years to recover from the disastrous events of his divorce, and he still had the lingering debt to show for his troubles.

The more Erik recalled those bitter memories, the harder his blows struck the heavy bag. His rhythm of strikes increased, and he began sharper exhalations with each blow against the heavy canvas. He punched and kicked his way through the memories, reliving every loss and humiliation Margaret's lawyers put him through. The heavy bag flew backward against the force of his blows. The more he remembered the difficulties of his past, the harder his blows became.

After nearly an hour, he was dripping with perspiration. The bag he had been pummeling so mercilessly now had several creases and indentations caused from the impacts of exceptionally hard kicks and punches. After all his exertion and thought, he was no closer to finding a solution to his problem than when he started.

Deep down, he knew Richard was right. If Richard wanted to take Brianna, there would be nothing Erik could do. He quickly amended that thought. There were plenty of things he could do, and probably get away with, but he was above that. Richard knew all the right attorneys, had all the right connections in high society, and he had hundreds of millions of dollars behind him. Erik had done the wrong things in the past, but never out of spite. He admitted to himself that Margaret was partially justified in doing what she did, but it was still painful to him.

For all his strength, Erik felt weak and helpless. It was a feeling that he loathed. Erik walked over to the breaking blocks and began stacking them one atop another. He was still in thought before he realized that he had stacked six of the three-inch thick breaking blocks. As he looked around, he was aware of the other students and instructors staring at him.

He kept thinking about Richard and that smug expression

of superiority that he wore. Erik channeled that anger as he raised both his fists over his head. He focused his concentration, and felt his body respond by unleashing a surge of energy throughout his system. He shouted a savage cry and smashed his fists down in a hammer-like blow upon the top brick. The top four bricks exploded under the impact of his blow, while the other two split evenly at their centers and crumbled under the impact of his strike. Erik felt better, momentarily, until the pain shot up his arms and reached the neural synapses in his brain.

"Oh shit," he whispered to himself. "That was really stupid." He masked the pain and silently disposed of the fragments in the dumpster behind the training facility. Erik shook his hands in an effort to stop the stinging. He didn't hear the lead trainer come up behind him.

"I'll bet that hurt," a voice said that half startled Erik.

Erik spun around quickly, his hands instinctively raised.

"Easy, big man, I'm not looking for a fight. I just want some conversation," the man replied calmly.

"I know you," Erik began. "You own this building. This is your school."

The man nodded. "The name is Dawkens, Neal Dawkens, and you are?"

Dawkens was a man in his early fifties with short cut salt-and-pepper hair. He stood as tall as Erik, but had a much thinner build. Dawkens sported a dragon tattoo on his left forearm, and a tiger on his right. His black belt was covered in gold stripes, indicating that this man was a martial artist with decades of experience.

"Erik Knight," Erik answered as he approached the man with an open hand. The two exchanged a firm, powerful handshake, each man taking a slight measure of the other.

"My associate was right. He described you perfectly. You have some excellent talent, Mr. Knight – good techniques and fantastic power. Besides myself, I've only seen two other men go through four of those concrete blocks, and you just smashed through six. I wouldn't have thought it possible. I'm impressed, and I don't impress easily, Mr. Knight," Dawkens complimented.

"Thanks," Erik said, "but it's been some time since I did any formal training. My last pro fight was over twelve years ago."

Dawkens raised an eyebrow in surprise. "I didn't realize we had any professionals at this school. Do you mind telling me a little bit about your training background?"

"I studied Shotokan for about five years, about three years of Northern Shaolin Kung Fu when I was in junior high and high school. I studied some formal hand-to-hand and weapons training techniques at Fort Bragg with the 45th Combat Infantry after college. I owed them some time since they were kind enough to pay for my education. I went pro in the Army, fighting at different bases. There were always kick-boxing or Ultimate Fighting tournaments going on back then. The Army looked at it as good PR for recruitment – get some of the younger fit men into the service.

"After that, I hooked up with the Fighting Arts League in Chicago for almost five years. They didn't teach any forms of martial art in particular. It was more like fighting arts, lots of great hand techniques, weapons, with only basic foot applications. That's where I learned the best way to train on a heavy bag," Erik imagined his background probably paled in comparison to Dawkens'.

"I see," Dawkens remarked with genuine interest. "I'd like to discuss using your talents in a more constructive way rather than pummeling my equipment sometime. But right now, I'd like to discuss a more pressing matter with you."

"Such as?" Erik nodded, inviting the man to continue.

"Well, Mr. Knight, I've been told that you're a private investigator, and a fairly competent one. Is there any truth to this?" Dawkens gestured Erik forward.

Erik nodded as both men headed back inside

"Yeah, among other things. Do you need something?" Erik asked hopefully. Another case so soon after the last one would be the wildest stroke of luck.

"No, not me personally, but my sister could use the help of someone like yourself. Are you available for hire?" Dawkens asked intently.

"Yeah," Erik answered as calmly as he could. "What kind of trouble is your sister in?"

"Missing person," he answered. "Her daughter, my niece.

We've been to the police, but they haven't been able to do anything. Let's face it, this is a small town. There ain't a lotta crime here. The cops aren't prepared for a kidnapping case."

"Whoa!" Erik gestured. "There's quite a big difference between a kidnapping and a missing persons case. Kidnapping is one of those messy federal crimes where the guys with suits and dark sunglasses usually get involved."

"I'm aware of that. We can't actually prove she's been kidnapped, but I can't think of any other reason for a child to be missing," Dawkens replied.

Erik nodded. "Does your sister know where Madame's Restaurant is?"

Dawkens nodded. "The large diner off of Route 141, the one with all the fancy decorations."

"That's the place. Have her meet me there tomorrow afternoon for lunch, 12:00 sharp."

"12:00 sharp," Dawkens agreed.

*   *   *

Erik quickly showered and changed. As he left, he nodded toward Dawkens who was teaching a class. Dawkens returned the gesture with a half-smile, and then returned to his students.

Erik thought about the several scenarios that could possibly lead to a missing child. During his experience as an apprentice investigator, these types of cases rarely had a happy ending. Usually, the child had run away or was abducted for hideous purposes. He silently hoped that this case wouldn't evolve into something that deep. His mind kept asking questions, and each question led to another.

"Easy, Erik," he said to himself as he got in his truck. "You have no information and no idea what you're getting into just yet. Just keep cool and keep your mind open." But as he drove away, his extra sense – that little voice in the back of his head that he told very few people about – seemed to trigger a subtle warning. Erik had learned early not to ignore that warning. It had saved his life on a few occasions. Silently, he continued to wonder what he might be getting himself into.

Chapter 2

A woman of early middle years walked into the reception area of Madame's Restaurant. She looked around hesitantly. Erik recognized her from Dawkens' description.

"Mrs. Reynolds, over here." Erik gestured as he stood from his booth in the main dining hall.

"Mr. Knight, I'm Andrea Reynolds," she answered with a relieved smile as she made her way toward his booth. "Thank you for taking the time to meet with me."

"You're most welcome," Erik answered as warmly as possible.

Erik knew the one most important thing about people who came to him: They needed help. To him it wasn't about the money. It was about a chance to make a difference in somebody else's life. Erik did his best to make his clients feel special, like their problems were as important to him as they were to them.

This was one of the reasons why he liked to operate out of Madame's. The atmosphere was incredibly comfortable, and everyone was exceptionally friendly. These elements made it easier to relate to people on a more personal level than he could get in an office setting. Also, one of the best benefits was that they served the best chicken breast sandwich and beef vegetable soup in all of New England.

"Please, sit down. I've taken the liberty of ordering for us." He gestured to one of the waitresses who disappeared into the kitchen area. Erik poured her a steaming cup of coffee from the pot placed on his table and sipped his while she began her story.

"Four days ago, Lisa came to me and said she thought that something was watching her and her friends from the playground. I really didn't pay much attention because she's always had such an overactive imagination – you know, monsters in the closet, ghosts in the basement, the typical ten-year-old fears

27

and phobias. I told her not to go to the park unless she was with her older brother or going with a group of children—"

"Excuse me," Erik interrupted. "You said some*thing* and not some*one*."

"Yes," she replied quickly. "Again, you know how active a child's imagination can be, or so I thought."

As she continued her story, Erik focused on her eyes. If she were making up anything, her eyes would give her away. He had been taught the eyes were the gateway into a person's essence. If someone were lying, they could not look directly at someone for any length of time. Their eyes would look off in a different direction and dart back, only to pull away again.

If someone were creating a story, their eyes would wander to their left, as if the person was accessing the creative part of their brain. If they were remembering some detail or fact, their eyes would usually look straight up or veer off to their right, as if querying the logic centers of the brain. Erik knew that these methods were not one hundred percent reliable, but human body language was very difficult to camouflage, and he had seen these methods proven again and again.

"As I said," she continued, "I told her to stay with her friends and not wander off if she was playing there. They said she only left for a minute to use the bathroom. She just never came out. And when they went to look, all they found was her necklace behind the bathroom door." She began weeping as she concluded her story.

Erik reached over and gently took her hand.

"That was two days ago." She wiped her tears with a dinner napkin. "I would have expected something, a ransom note or a phone call, anything."

"Have the police given you anything at all?" Erik asked.

"No," she answered sadly, "they've talked with all the children, and they've all said the same thing: It got dark like the night and terribly cold. When the sun returned, she was gone."

He considered her story and analyzed it quickly: A young girl abducted amongst other children, darkness in place of the daylight, and a sudden drop in temperature. The whole story seemed more a like a bad fairy tale than an abduction. Erik knew that nobody simply vanished. The police were smarter than that. He knew, as they did, if she had not received a message from the girl's kidnappers by now, there would most likely be no message. It did not bode well. There was something about the necklace though. He felt an eerie buzzing in the back of his head.

"May I see your daughter's necklace?" he asked.

She handed him the plastic bag that contained the necklace. Erik studied it carefully: A fourteen-karat gold chain with a large heart-shaped locket. As he opened the bag, a chill went up his arms and down his spine. He caught the scent of something foul. He emptied the contents of the bag into his hand, and let the jewelry sit in his palm. The hairs on the back of his neck stood on edge as he held the gold chain. Erik struggled to maintain his composure as he carefully slipped the item back into the plastic bag.

"Mrs. Reynolds, may I borrow this for a few days? An associate of mine may be able to provide some further insight. Perhaps she and I can uncover something that was missed, assuming you want me to work for you."

She looked at him, as if trying to read his own body language. "You know something, don't you?"

"No, ma'am," he lied convincingly. "I know nothing for certain – a wild theory, maybe, or half-baked assumption. Can you meet me here in two days? I need to do some research."

"Well, that's more than the police have done," she replied. "I'll see you Tuesday afternoon, and thank you. Thank you for everything."

Erik watched her as she left. "Don't thank me just yet," he mumbled.

From what he could gather, she was telling the truth. Her body language and facial motif were all normal. He needed to start at the beginning, and that would be with the Hopedale Police Department.

He looked at the necklace again, and the feeling of dread ran through his body. There was something terribly wrong. He focused intently and detected an overwhelming sense of terror, and something else, something extremely malevolent and alien.

He had had these types of intuitions before, usually warning him of some unforeseen danger or threat. Erik never liked to discuss, or even acknowledge, the latent abilities he seemed to possess. As far back as he could remember, these intuitive abilities had always been present. It was not only the telepathy, it was an uncanny ability to sense weather changes, deal with animals or be in tune with almost anything related to nature.

Erik somehow felt more a part of the Earth than the people around him. He was more at home in the wild, almost like some modern-day mountain man. He could disappear into the wilderness for weeks at a time and live comfortably off the land, existing on native roots and berries and sleeping under the stars. He was never comfortable cooped up in an office. He liked to be out in the open, free. He knew that it was this ability that had caused him to seek his own independent path, and cost him his marriage.

* * *

It was early Monday morning when Erik walked into Veronica's Coffee Shop and sat at one of the stools near the counter. He ordered a cup of coffee and a blueberry muffin. Veronica's was right next to the Hopedale Police Department. The establishment was a frequent haunt for both on and off-duty police officers.

Erik had worked with the Hopedale Police on a few prior occasions, and he kept them well-informed of any cases he was working that may directly impact the town. He knew officers ending the graveyard shift regularly stopped here before heading home. Erik was hoping that he could find his friend Steve. Steve was a seasoned officer whom Erik had given a narcotics lead to a few years back. His tip led to the arrest of several men operating a heroin distribution center less than a half-mile from the precinct.

As if on cue, Steve walked in, spotted the detective, and sat down on the nearest stool, motioning the waitress for coffee. Steve Forrest was a seasoned Hopedale officer with nearly twenty years' experience in law enforcement.

"Look what the cat dragged in," Steve started in a humorous tone. "What's the matter? Did they run out of coffee at Madame's?"

"Nah, I was just lonesome for your ugly mug," Erik retorted as he motioned for the waitress. "Actually, Steve, this is a professional courtesy call. Does the name Lisa Reynolds mean anything to you?"

"Yeah, she's down as a missing person, last seen at the park. We have two officers investigating it. Could be a runaway." He paused momentarily. "I think it was two or three days ago. I didn't take the report or work the case, so I'm a little foggy on the exact details, some wild story about ghosts and darkness though. Why do you ask?"

Erik reached inside his leather jacket and produced the necklace inside the plastic bag. "I've been hired to find out information regarding her disappearance. The word *kidnapping* keeps popping up in my head. I know that there has been no contact with the Reynolds girl in three days since her disappearance. That can only mean one of three things: Abduction, runaway, or kidnapping." Erik paused as both men took a swig of their coffee.

He continued. "I think we can rule out kidnapping since there has been no contact with the family. She was with a group of friends when she disappeared, and this was left behind. I think it's safe to assume she didn't run away. What does that leave us with, Steve?" Erik slid the necklace toward him on the counter.

Steve grew apprehensive. Erik could see the telltale changes in his body language. He had adopted a closed, protective posture – arms folded, slightly slouched. Steve kept his eyes turned down as he considered the words Erik just said. He looked up and slid the necklace back toward Erik.

"I agree," Steve whispered softly, "but we have nothing to go on, no leads. The kids didn't see much of anything, and what they said they saw didn't make any sense."

"Would you care to elaborate?"

"They said it got dark, as dark as the middle of the night, as if somebody turned out the sun. They said it got extremely cold, and that they were scared. Each kid said the exact same thing. What the hell are we supposed to make of that?" Steve sipped the steaming beverage in front of him. "And there were only a few adults present for us to question. It's like this girl just vanished off the face of the Earth. I know it sounds bizarre, but go look for yourself. There are no specific prints to work from. The crime scene had been corrupted by dozens of other kids before anyone noticed that she was missing.

"This," he added, pointing to the necklace, "doesn't give us much to work with. There were no prints on the locket, and nothing on the chain – no blood, no nothing." He replaced his coffee mug on the counter.

"We both know a child doesn't just vanish into thin air. Somebody must have seen something. I just can't believe that a kid could be abducted in broad daylight, in the middle of a park full of children with no one – not a single soul – seeing anything," Erik stated emphatically. "It just doesn't make sense."

"I know that. All of us know that. I'm telling you; we couldn't find a thing. All we can do is wait, continue to question children who were at the park, and hope that someone does call with a ransom note. Otherwise...." Steve paused, not wanting to complete his sentence.

"Yeah." Erik sighed heavily. "And otherwise spells bad news for the Reynolds."

"On that we agree, my friend." Steve drained his coffee cup. "Look, I gotta get home and get some shut-eye. Debbie and I are supposed to be taking the kids to the movies later on. If you do, by some chance, find something, fill us in. We really need to be in the loop on this one." Steve reached into his back pocket for his wallet.

"Don't," Erik said. "This one's on me."

"Thanks, I owe you one."

Erik watched his associate climb into his car and drive off. Mrs. Reynolds was right: The police were genuinely baffled. Erik looked down at the necklace and again got that strange tingling at the back of his neck. He knew there was some connection, some element that he was not seeing in this entire puzzle. He had already determined his next course of action. He paid his tab and made his way back out to the street.

Erik knew he was being watched. He could almost feel the eyes following his motion. Erik tried to casually look behind him, but he knew any look back would be obvious. He made his way to his pickup, fired the engine, and made his way toward I-495. He noticed a black sedan had been behind him for nearly three miles.

"Well now," he muttered to himself. "It appears I've got myself a tail."

He made his way through the small suburb, being sure to take several back roads in his route to the interstate. As he had expected, the sedan was still back there, but keeping a respectable distance. Erik knew the road he was on, and he waited until he finished navigating a large turn and gunned his truck, the vehicle shuddered and leapt with acceleration. He knew that the sedan would not realize what he had done until it completed its turn around the last bend in the road.

Erik spotted what he was looking for, the Amato Farms dirt access road. With a loud screeching of rubber, he took the sharp turn and hid his truck behind the tall stalks of corn. He watched with great delight as the black sedan sped by seconds later. He backed up his truck and pulled back onto the road. It was his turn to pursue.

He knew that he had to catch the car before it made the intersection. He spotted the sedan behind four other cars at the stop sign where the road ended. He stopped his truck a good fifty yards behind the sedan. Erik took binoculars from his glove compartment and looked through them at the sedan's license plate. He said the numbers out loud to himself as he grabbed a pencil and scrap of paper. After writing the plate number down, he pulled up behind the traffic that had accumulated behind the sedan as it made a right turn into traffic.

Erik waited his turn and then followed the car onto the highway, and for nearly fifteen minutes shadowed the other vehicle. The driver of the sedan suddenly realized that he was being pursued and accelerated. Erik could hear the loud roar from the sedan's engine as it took off like a rocket. He knew instantly that his truck was no match for the car. He had gotten what he needed. He'd run the plate through his database when he returned to his office. Though in the back of his mind, he knew who was responsible for the tail.

"You need to find more competent help, Richard. That's the fourth one this month," he whispered.

Richard Pendelton liked to keep tabs on Erik, hoping to catch him in some shady underhanded business. Erik knew Pendelton thought he was lowbrow, but he couldn't recall anything that would make Richard consider him crooked or even a threat.

The fact that the wealthy industrialist nearly destroyed him with minimal effort during his divorce should have satisfied the rich businessman. Richard knew everything about him, with the possible exceptions of his dealings with a certain law firm in Boston. Erik knew, by reputation alone, nobody was stupid enough to meddle in Martin Denton's business affairs.

He pulled into a small shopping plaza in Shrewsbury. Erik parked his truck and headed into the Newbury Comics store. Instantly he felt out of place. This was a store for teenagers on the cutting edge of punk. Spiked hair, pierced noses, and multi-colored hair surrounded him, as well as girls with black lipstick and other gothic attire.

Erik approached an older woman who had on tight leather pants and a black, shiny leather vest. Her black hair had streaks of purple and light pink. She looked astonishingly beautiful, despite the unusual attire. Erik noticed she had pierced her nose since the last time he'd seen her. He felt an unusual spark of electricity run through him, as it always did whenever he was near her. He was drawn to her, pulled like metal to a magnet.

"I like the look," Erik commented.

The woman looked up and broke out into a huge smile when she spotted him. "Erik Knight, as I live and breathe. What brings Mr. Work Boots and Blue Jeans into this neck of the woods?"

"What always brings me here, Shanda, your beautiful décor and charming clientele," Erik remarked lightly while gazing at some of the more bizarre patrons.

Shanda laughed as she approached, giving him a friendly hug. She was in her early thirties, like Erik. But unlike Erik, she took a lighter view of life and enjoyed associating with the cutting edge, while it made him uncomfortable. Despite this, Erik liked her a lot and they'd dated on several occasions over the past years. Erik still felt a strong physical and emotional attraction to her, and she still carried a torch for him.

"I need you to examine something for me," Erik whispered. "I can't hold it without getting the creeps."

Shanda looked around her store and instructed a clerk to cover for a few minutes. Erik followed her into a back room up a flight of stairs. Shanda sat down on a large black chair. Next to the chair was a large crystal ball similar to what children see at carnivals. Only this was a real seer's crystal, not some cheap glass replica.

"Okay, let's see it."

Erik reached inside his jacket pocket and handed her the plastic bag. As soon as she touched it she exhaled sharply.

"Oh, God, what is that awful smell?" Her hands were trembling as she took the necklace from the plastic bag and placed it gently into her hands. Shanda's eyes became glassy, as if she were seeing something that he could not. She whispered something in a language that Erik instinctively understood, but rarely, if ever, used.

"She's frightened. She sees it. She's wondering why no one else can. She sees it coming out of the black," Shanda whispered, her eyes were focused someplace else.

"He's walking right by her playmates and all the other children. She's running, hiding. There's darkness everywhere." Tears streamed down Shanda's face.

"Oh, God!" she screamed. "All I can feel is absolute terror, the dark." She paused and threw the necklace back at him.

"That's enough. I can't take anymore." She struggled to compose herself. Shanda looked at him through tear-streaked eyes. "Where in the world did you get that?"

"It belongs to a little girl who's been missing for several days. She was kidnapped from a park in Hopedale. The necklace was found behind the park bathroom." Erik walked over to Shanda and put his hands on her shoulders. "What did you sense, exactly?"

"Fear," she answered. "In layman's terms, absolute fear. Whoever took her, terrified the crap out of her."

"Did you sense anything else?" Erik pushed.

"No, just fear, and that awful smell when you first opened the bag, kinda like sulfur. But why are you asking me? You can do this yourself. You have the gift too. I don't see why you simply won't use it," she said forcefully.

"I prefer to deal with the natural, Shanda. This kinda thing is more your cup of tea," Erik answered. "And right now, I need answers, not more questions," Erik retorted moodily. Shanda always brought up his abilities. "I have to meet with this little girl's mother in a few days, and I want to have at least some kind of definitive lead for her regarding her daughter's whereabouts."

Erik tucked the necklace into his inside jacket pocket. He looked at her more softly this time. "This little girl is only a few years younger than my own daughter. Her mother feels absolutely helpless. The police can't do anything for her." He paused, looking away. "She needs help, and I don't want to fail her as well," he whispered quietly as he looked away.

She reached over to him and gently put her arms on him, allowing her hands to touch his powerful chest and arms. "Erik, if anyone can pull a rabbit out of the hat, it's you. If there's something to find, I know that you'll find it."

He looked down into her face and smiled. Shanda always seemed to know the right words to say to make someone feel better. "For her sake, I hope you're right. Because right now, things look very bleak for that little girl."

Erik made his way back to his apartment. He'd been carefully watching for the black sedan, or any other car that followed too close, but his ride home proved to be uneventful. He pulled into Madame's parking lot and drove to the back of the building where his small apartment was located.

He glanced at his wristwatch as he opened his apartment door. He decided that he could spend some time at the Hopedale Park. Steve claimed that there was nothing there, but Erik needed to see for himself. Somebody must have missed something. He figured that he could grab a quick bowl of soup, help clean up after the lunch crowd, and be at the park by 2:00. He could look around for at least four hours before having to head back.

* * *

Carol Carlin enjoyed running in the Hopedale Town Forest. The maze of trails offered a variety of courses and challenges for her. Her objective today was to break a nine-minute mile. She knew she would never be a world-class runner, but loved running for the sake of the exercise and a chance to get away from the humdrum of daily living.

As she progressed deeper into the forest, she had the feeling she was being watched. Carol looked over her shoulder, but saw nothing. She picked up her pace along the winding trail.

She continued for another fifteen minutes, still with the uneasy feeling that someone watched her. Carol turned to look over her shoulder again, causing her to miss seeing the divot in the path. She stepped into the depression and fell heavily on her shoulder. A sharp pain shot through her leg, and she knew immediately she'd sprained her ankle.

"Damn!" she cursed aloud as her ankle throbbed with pain.

She crawled over to the edge of the path and untied her shoe. Her ankle was already swelling. There was a good chance she had broken her ankle. Carol was too deep in the forest to make it out without help. Her best chance of connecting with somebody would be to make it to a well-used walking trail.

She struggled to stand, leaning heavily against a tree she was near. She took one step forward on her good leg, and then dragged her bad leg behind her. Every motion sent a searing wave of agony through her body. Perspiration rolled down her head as she struggled to endure the pain. As she took her fourth step, her leg gave out and she collapsed on the trail. Carol screamed out in agony as more pain rocketed through her body. She stood again and tried hopping on her good leg, but after fifty yards, her other leg cramped up.

She sat beneath a large oak tree to recover some of her ebbing strength. She could imagine her boyfriend laughing at her as she told him her tale of woe when she finally made it out of the woods.

She noticed a drastic change in the light. It was as though someone put a dimmer switch on the sun. Her flesh became cold. She looked down the path and saw someone approaching her from a distance.

"Hello?" she called out. "Can you help me? I think I've broken my ankle."

The figure was silent, but kept approaching. A wave of fear swept through her body. She struggled to her feet and began hopping away from the figure. She had gone only thirty feet, when she stopped. She didn't want to look back, but her body instinctively turned her head in the direction of the dark figure. She expected to see the figure closing on her, but it was gone. She still had that creepy feeling, but at least her pursuer was gone.

Carol laughed to herself. "You wimp. You're jumping at shadows now."

She turned to head back down the path, not realizing this mistake would be the last she ever made. As she hobbled down the pathway, a dark form leapt out from behind a large pine tree, tackling her. She tried to struggle, but her attacker was too powerful. Although her attacker was on top of her and she was wrestling with him, she couldn't make out his features.

She watched in horror as a black claw reached down, grabbing her throat in a grip of iron. She grasped the arm that had her throat, astounded by the intense cold of her attacker's flesh. She felt the pressure building on her neck as her attacker closed his hand tighter around her throat.

Carol knew she was going to die the moment she hit the ground. She knew instinctively her life was over. The pressure on her throat increased, black spots hovered around the corners of her vision. Then, she felt her throat crush. Her body went mercifully numb. She tried to close her eyes, but couldn't.

Her last sight was to finally see the face of her attacker, to see the red pupiless eyes and that malicious evil grin as it squeezed the last remnants of her life. Carol's last thoughts were not of herself, but of all she was leaving behind: Her boyfriend, whom she knew intended to marry her; her family, friends. Would they find her out here? Would they anguish over never knowing, or would she turn up a half-eaten corpse somewhere?

* * *

Carol's attacker dragged her lifeless body deeper into the woods. It had fed deeply upon her fear. The fear of an adult was not nearly as satisfying as the fear of a child, but the creature still hungered and needed to feed

* * *

Erik had spent two hours carefully walking every inch of Hopedale Park. He checked out both bathroom facilities and the grounds surrounding them. Nothing – no overlooked item, no hidden shard of cloth, no mysterious footprint.

Erik spoke with some of the children that were at the park. A few had actually been there the day of the disappearance. As Stephen had claimed, they saw nothing, but spun the same elaborate fairytale he'd heard earlier.

He walked over to a park bench and sat down, pausing momentarily to adjust the holster carrying his 9mm Ruger. Erik didn't feel that he was in any danger – it was just from his training. His mentors had beat it into his head. The one time he didn't have his gun would be the one time he found himself in a situation where he needed it. He normally wore his twin Wilson Super 45s, but a shoulder harness and intimidating weapons were too much for this atmosphere. A concealed pants holster was much better for public gathering places. The last thing he needed was to cause more tight nerves.

He could sense the parents there were hyper-cautious about watching their children. He imagined Brianna on a swing or near the monkey bars, and pictured himself being just as tense and nervous.

There had to be something, he just wasn't seeing it. He reached inside his pants pocket and pulled out the plastic bag containing the child's locket. Erik was reluctant, but he took the locket out of the bag and dropped in into his open hand. He instantly felt the sense of fear and dread. He closed his eyes and allowed himself to focus only on the locket in his hand.

Erik accessed a part of himself he kept hidden from others – latent skills of telepathy and something more, a sense of nature and the supernatural. He opened himself up to all the sensations and phenomena around him, and then took that reception and focused it on the object in his hand. He began to mumble in an alien language he instinctively knew but never understood how he knew it, or where it came from. Shanda had told him that it was a Sorcerers' Tongue, inherent in all people with their specific gifts.

"C'mon, talk to me," he whispered.

He felt himself drawn, pulled toward the road, away from the park. He continued walking – crossing the street, heading up the street. He still felt that he was moving in the right direction. He was almost a quarter mile away from the park and still walking. The further he got from the park, the faster his body propelled him. The essence of absolute terror still shrieked in his mind. The child was frightened beyond all rational ability. Her fear was so strong he actually felt his own flesh crawl.

He continued to walk until he came to a protruding yellow gateway, the entry into the Hopedale Town Forest. As suddenly as he was pulled to this area, the inkling that compelled him stopped. Erik was trembling, actually shaking. The girl's terror had been so powerful that it seemed to be emblazoned upon the piece of jewelry.

He again caught the scent of something foul, a scent that was unfamiliar. Erik held up his right hand in front of his face. It still trembled. He felt lightheaded and had to sit down on the side of the road. He leaned his back against a yellow railing. He placed his face in his hands and closed his eyes, trying to rid himself of the emotions passed into him.

He slowly opened his eyes, staring into the sand and debris that accumulated on the edge of the road leading into the parklands. If he hadn't been looking down he would have missed it completely. There, half buried in the sand, were three shiny objects. Erik picked up a nearby twig and stirred up the debris.

"Damn, I was hoping this wouldn't pan out," he whispered to himself.

The objects were buttons. Clinging to one of the buttons were tatters of thread and a small piece of cloth. Erik guessed the buttons were forcefully ripped from a garment. Erik, carefully making sure he didn't touch the objects, scooped the fabric shards, thread, and buttons into a small handkerchief that he carried in his back pocket.

Erik was playing a long shot, but he would need to actually touch the objects. If this was evidence, he would have to turn it into the police immediately and he didn't want his fingerprints and body secretions corrupting a potential piece of evidence. He would have to show this to Mrs. Reynolds tomorrow. Only she could shed more light on his find.

He stood, feeling a little better, and headed back toward his truck. If the girl had been taken forcefully to this area, he had little hope for her being alive. He didn't understand how someone could abduct a child in broad daylight, force her all the way here, and no one witness a thing. People jogged, fished, and rode their bikes in the parklands constantly. Yes, there were remote sections of woodland higher up on the mountain, but there was also a maze of paths leading up to that wilderness area, usually with people on them. Somebody had to have seen something.

The more he considered the odds, the less likely he believed that what he had found had any bearing on Lisa Reynolds. Erik knew he had to play out the odds, no matter how remote. To ignore even the slightest possibility would be irresponsible. Erik was sometimes shortsighted, even reckless on occasion, but never irresponsible when it came to somebody else. He would bag the objects and have Mrs. Reynolds examine them. At this point, it was all he had.

* * *

Erik was seated at his favorite booth in the back of Madame's, nursing a glass of water and a bowl of vegetable beef soup when Shanda walked into the restaurant. She spotted him, walked over to his booth, and seated herself.

"Hi," she began. "I decided to stop by and pay a social call. Also, I'm hungry; and since you've always bragged about the food here, I figured I'd give you an opportunity to buy me dinner."

"I'm touched," Erik gestured to one of the waitresses and she immediately walked over.

"Alissa, my friend here will have a cup of vegetable beef soup, a grilled chicken breast sandwich, steamed vegetables in place of French fries, and a medium Coke, lots of ice." Erik recited the order he gave every night for his own dinner.

"Hold the veggies, keep the fries," she corrected. "Plus an extra pickle slice."

"Excellent." Alissa smiled as she headed toward the kitchen.

Shanda looked around the restaurant, admiring the unique décor of Erik's favorite haunt. "I can see why you like this place so much. It must be nice to have your office in such an interesting place."

"It puts people at ease," Erik answered.

Erik and Shanda exchanged polite, pleasant conversation for nearly half an hour, discussing a variety of topics. She was finishing off the last of her fries when Erik decided to cut through the pleasantries.

"Shanda, it's been great to see you again, and I've enjoyed the dinner conversation, but considering that I've been here for almost six years and this is the first time you've come here, I tend to think this isn't a social call," Erik gently hinted.

Shanda blushed. "No, it's not. Curiosity got the best of me. I was wondering if you had any success with your case so far. I had this hunch earlier today that you found something."

"Actually, I did," he replied. "I won't know much until I meet with my client tomorrow."

Erik reached into his pants pocket. He pulled out a small sealed plastic bag and tossed it on the table.

"I found these. I'm sort of hoping it's a bogus lead, because if it's not, things suddenly don't look very good for our missing person." He took another sip from his second glass of water.

Shanda picked up the plastic bag and studied its contents. She looked up at Erik, who seemed to be very distant. "How did you manage to find these? More importantly, what makes you think they're related to this girl's disappearance?"

"I spent over two hours combing the park area. I couldn't find anything, not a single clue," Erik began. "I was getting desperate, so I followed my instincts. I wound up at the Hopedale Town Forest, over a quarter mile down the road. I sat down by the entry gate to collect myself, and when I looked down, there they were." He pointed at the sealed plastic bag. "Can you tell me if they're hers?"

Shanda looked at the bag and whispered to herself. She clutched the bag to her chest and held it tight. Shanda looked up at him after a minute, tears welling up in her eyes.

"It's hers. The energy is the same," she muttered.

"I thought as much," Erik replied.

Erik stood and led the shaken woman to his back office. He sat on the couch next to her and placed his arm on her shoulder. She turned to him, laid her head on his shoulder and cried. Erik put his arms around her and held her in silence as she wept for several minutes. Shanda lifted her head off his shoulder and sat upright on his couch. She stared, embarrassed, at the large wet spot on the shoulder of his shirt.

"I'm sorry, it was just so overwhelming," she explained.

"Don't apologize. I was bowled over myself to the point I was trembling earlier today," Erik explained as he changed his shirt.

Shanda bolted upright. "You did it! You used your telepathy!"

"There was no other way." Erik pulled a clean T-shirt over his torso.

"I thought you swore off your abilities for good?"

"I swore them off for personal gain or the material gain of others," he explained. "Most practitioners use telepathy and the occult to get something for themselves. Then they want more and more. They delve deeper into things that are best left alone. That is what I swore I would never do." He sighed. "To pursue that course eventually leads to an abrupt, unhappy end. I've never needed to use it on cases before. This happened to be the first time."

He sat down on the couch beside her. "Besides, it's not just telepathy. It's more. I can read things, but not as well as you. I can also sense when bad events are going to happen. I feel alive when I'm in the wild, not just in an ordinary sense, but almost like I'm a living part of the forest. I know what animals are within at least a half mile of me, what people are feeling most of the time, and I can sense changes in air pressure and almost

smell different kinds of weather." He paused. "It's all very unusual, but I've learned not to ignore my instinct when it makes
itself known," Erik added in a serious tone.

"You have so many unusual gifts. You shouldn't be
ashamed of them. I thought, perhaps, you didn't believe in utilizing them anymore, or maybe using them made you uncomfortable," she whispered. "But there's more you're not telling
me," she added forcefully.

"Yes," Erik acknowledged. "Promise you won't think I'm
crazy."

"This is me, Erik." Shanda pointed to her purple hair and
wild attire.

"Okay," he released a deep breath. "There are times, when
I really focus, I can double, almost triple, my physical strength.
It's like my body has some kind of built-in overdrive or something. I feel like I've been plugged into an adrenaline high. I've
tested it before, at the gym when nobody was around." He
paused, reluctant to continue.

"And?" Shanda urged him on.

"I was able to bench-press over 750 pounds, and I weigh
just over 185 pounds – nearly four times my own body weight.
A few days ago during a martial arts workout, after an argument with my ex's husband, I got angry and pulverized six
cement blocks with my bare hands. The head instructor said
he only knew of a few men who could break four of them, and
nobody who could break six. I think I could have done more,
a lot more."

"Erik, that's fantastic. Don't be ashamed of whatever abilities you have. They're gifts, not a curse." She paused. "I always
thought you no longer believed in this kind of thing, that maybe you were turned off by them," she added, hinting at the
still unknown reason for his termination of their relationship. It
secretly hurt Shanda that Erik had not confided in her earlier.

"I still believe. How can I not when I'm reminded of it every day practically?" he replied. "It's just that if I told anybody
besides you, they'd think I'm nuts. Sometimes, I just want to fit
in and pretend I'm just like everybody else," Erik added with
a sour note.

Shanda needed to hear him say that for some reason. It

was good to know that she wasn't rejected for who she was.

Erik looked directly at her, his eyes burning with intensity. "Do you ever wonder why?" he asked in a whisper. "Have you ever been curious as to how we got these abilities in the first place, or what our lives would have been like without them?" He had a deep longing in his voice.

"Yeah, I guess, sometimes I think about it. But I've never wanted to lose the power. I accept that it's a part of who and what I am. I think it's more of a blessing than a curse," Shanda replied. "What do you think, Erik; are you blessed with these abilities, or are you cursed with them?"

"If they'll help me find Lisa Reynolds, I'll consider them a blessing. Otherwise, they haven't exactly helped me through-out my life," he retorted with a half-smile.

Erik started pacing, thinking about the case again. "There always has to be a motive, a reason. If Lisa Reynolds was abduct-ed and kept alive, something isn't making sense. Why haven't the Reynolds been contacted? If she's been murdered, where is the body? If it's in the woods, it could take weeks to recover," Erik mused as he paced back and forth. "No!" He smacked his fist into his open palm. "We don't have all the pieces yet. It's not making any sense. There's a hole in this thing big enough to drive a tank through." He turned toward Shanda. "Are you going to be okay?" Erik knelt beside her.

"Yeah, I'll be fine in a few moments. It's weird; I've touched objects before, but I've never felt such powerful feedback as I've gotten from those two objects. Strong emotion leaves re-sidual energy that can be sensed, but usually its only one emo-tion. I felt fear from that necklace like I've never known. What I sensed from the other package was the same fear with a trace of something else. Something I still can't place, but I know that it's not good. If I had to describe it with one word, I would have to say malevolent, or maybe even evil."

Erik walked over to his phone. "I need to get a hold of somebody. If this is really Lisa Reynolds', I need to turn it over to the police once it's been properly identified." Erik dialed a series of numbers and waited patiently.

"Hi, Steve, how are you? How was the movie?" Erik asked. "Look, I'm sorry to call you at home. I wouldn't do this normally, but you said you wanted to be informed if I found anything." Erik paused as the officer responded.

"Yeah, it's physical evidence, bagged and tagged according to procedure. Listen, I'm meeting my client at noon tomorrow in my office for a positive I.D. on this. I'd like for one of you to be here to take this if the I.D. is positive." Erik's face turned sour as he was listening to the voice on the other end. "Yeah, I'm starting to get that 'otherwise' feeling as well," Erik commented dismally into the phone receiver.

"Steve," Erik began in a serious tone. "I know it's asking a lot, but can you handle this one? It's probably going to get a little uncomfortable emotionally, and you seem to be one of the better officers in that kind of situation."

Shanda could hear the voice on the other line but was unable to make out what was being said.

"Thanks, I'll see you at 11:30 sharp." Erik looked relieved as he hung up the telephone.

Shanda was staring at some photographs on his table in an open album. He placed his hand gently on her shoulder and she rubbed her cheek against his forearm.

"How did it go?" she asked.

"Steve said he'd come by himself tomorrow after his shift. He's done this for me before, so he's familiar with the drill. This case isn't going to go away. The Reynolds family has money and influence. They could keep this ongoing for quite a long time if they wanted to, at least until...."

Shanda had known Erik for many years. She knew he had seen things and done things that would cause most people to soil themselves. She knew that he didn't know the meaning of the word fear, but it was always difficult for him when he was dealing with a child. Children were innocent, completely undeserving of the terrible things often done to them in modern society. She knew that if this were an adult missing person there would be less intensity and less emotion. A question popped into her head.

"Erik, don't take this the wrong way, but why do you think they hired you for this investigation? If this family is as wealthy as you say, and has as much influence, why hire a small agency with one man? Why not hire a team of investigators with unlimited resources? Don't get me wrong; I mean, you're good, but you're only one man with limited assets and very limited resources." Shanda regretted the question as soon as she said it. She could read the hurt and offense in his eyes. He turned away from her and walked toward the other sofa in his office and plopped down on it.

"I really don't know, Shanda, but I'll be sure and ask tomorrow," he said with all the contempt he could muster.

She rose from the couch and walked over to where Erik sat. She put her hand over his and smiled. "You know that's not what I mean. You're probably the most dedicated professional I know. I'm simply saying there are a lot of big guns out there. What possessed them to hire a small independent operator? I mean, think about it. If Brianna were kidnapped, wouldn't Margaret and Richard hire dozens of investigators to look for her?"

"Yeah, I'm sure they would, but they wouldn't hire me." Erik looked at her and knew she was confused. "My darling ex-wife and her husband are serving me papers to sign over paternal custody of Brianna to Richard so he can adopt her. They want to become a *real* family. Richard has already threatened me with high-powered attorneys and court costs I never could afford." When he looked at her, there was a deep tortured agony in his eyes. "I'm going to lose my baby, Shanda. That bastard is going to see to it that I can never see her again. What kills me is that I brought this about; I caused this, my stupid need to be my own man."

She tenderly embraced him, allowing him to pull her close. They held each other in silence for several minutes.

The telephone rang, breaking their moment. They both looked toward the machine. Shanda tried to get up to hand him the phone, but Erik was reluctant to give up his hold on her.

"Let it ring," he whispered.

"I'd like to," she said as she leaned over and kissed his forehead. "But that phone is killing the mood," she added as she felt his arms unwrap.

Erik walked over to the telephone and picked up the receiver. "Knight Investigations, how can I help you?"

"Yes, Mrs. Reynolds." Erik's face took on a very pained expression and his shoulders suddenly slumped. Shanda walked toward him, concerned. Her ability already told her what was occurring. Erik was off the case.

"I understand, Mrs. Reynolds, no need to apologize. They are an excellent agency and have a lot of good men. But, I really need to see you tomorrow afternoon. I've found something that may or may not belong to Lisa. I need you to identify it for the police." Erik nodded and grunted a few times in answer to some questions.

"Yes, it would be a good idea to bring representatives from there to this meeting. That'll let me brief both you and them as to where I am in the investigation. There's no need to be sorry, I understand. I'll see you tomorrow at noon," Erik said politely as he hung up the phone. He looked at Shanda.

"Well, you really are psychic. It appears that Mr. Reynolds had the same idea you did. They've hired Halls Investigations from New York. They're probably the best private detective agency in the country. Three men are flying in on the shuttle tomorrow morning, plus two mobile crime labs are already en route. They'll be here to take over the investigation. It seems I'm out of a job."

Erik sat back on the chair in front of his desk and sighed heavily. He started shaking his head.

"I don't know," he began. "Maybe this was for the best." He laughed as he looked at Shanda. "Maybe I can come work for you."

"No, you're a private investigator. That's what you do. It's what you are supposed to do. The Reynolds are just concerned for their daughter. Look, you found a lead that no one else did, or ever could have. You're going to provide them solid physical evidence tomorrow. They'll know that you're good, the best. You have nothing to be ashamed of, Erik," she answered.

"Thanks."

"You need to get out of here for a while, Erik," Shanda took his hand and led him toward the hallway.

"Where are we going?" he asked.

"There's nothing like a good movie and some fattening popcorn to take your mind off your troubles," she answered.

"That's fine by me, but let's go eat our dinner first. It's probably getting cold," he answered as they headed back to the dining area of Madame's.

Chapter 3

Erik had finished his workout at Dawkens' Gym and was preparing to head back home when Neal Dawkens called him into his office. He gestured Erik toward a chair and sat himself behind his large desk. Erik noticed several awards, trophies, and photographs of the man with several well-known martial artists-turned-actors, movie stars and politicians. Dawkens noticed him staring at the photographs and other paraphernalia that decorated his office.

"I've been very fortunate," Dawkens commented.

"Indeed," Erik agreed.

Dawkens leaned over the desk and looked directly at him. "I know my sister took you off the case; I'm sorry. I feel somehow responsible, seeing that I sent her to you. Please understand, she was impressed with you; it's just that they feel that the more people looking for my niece, the better." Dawkens paused. "And, you are only one person," he added, looking as though he wished that he could have taken the words he just spoke back when Erik flinched.

"I understand," Erik answered. "I'm seeing her and her new-hires at noon. I've gathered some information that I'm hoping will be useful to them," he responded in a neutral tone. Erik didn't blame Dawkens for anything, and he really understood the Reynolds' reasoning for going with a bigger agency.

"Neal, I understand, really. Don't blame yourself. Your sister and her husband have nothing to apologize for. Actually, I really can't blame them. If my daughter were missing, I'd want lots of qualified people with lots of resources on her case along with the police," he said as he stood, offering the older man his hand. "I need to get back and prepare for this meeting."

Both men clasped hands, and then Erik headed back home.

He needed to pick up the clutter in his office and make it look as presentable as possible.

* * *

Steve arrived at Erik's now pristine office and seated himself on the couch against the far wall. Erik had ordered a pot of coffee for the two men as they prepared to discuss the items Erik found earlier.

"Okay, Erik, what have you got?" Steve asked.

Erik walked over to his desk and took the sealed plastic bag from its resting place and tossed it to his police counterpart. Steve caught the bag and carefully studied the objects sealed within the plastic. Erik could see Steve scrutinizing the evidence, examining each button and fiber.

After five silent minutes, he looked up. "They could be buttons from a child's shirt, or it could be anything. What makes you so sure that they're from the Reynolds girl?"

"Call it a hunch, my friend. I have it on good authority that they are."

"That's not much of an answer, Erik," Steve chided his friend.

"I know, but right now it's all I have." Erik then remembered something: "Oh, by the way, the Reynolds have hired Halls Investigation Agency from New York yesterday. Some of their investigators will be joining the couple this morning. Before you bite my head off, I didn't find out till just yesterday, so save the speech. I just figured that you guys should know that it's no longer just an investigation within our own community. The Reynolds have brought in the big guns now."

"Oh, bloody marvelous." Steve sighed heavily. "You realize what's going to happen next, don't you?"

"Yeah", Erik answered. "Publicity and exposure, just what this investigation doesn't need."

Steve hesitated momentarily, weighing something in his mind. "Erik, I'm breaking procedure by saying this, but I know you'll probably find out eventually. I took a missing persons report last night. This will be the second one in a week. A woman in her thirties never came home from her afternoon jog."

Erik's extra senses suddenly triggered; intuitively he knew. "Let me guess." He took the bag of evidence from Steve. "She was jogging in the town forest."

Steve stared dumbfoundedly at his friend. "Yes, that's what her boyfriend claimed when he and her parents filed the report. How the hell did you know that, Erik?"

Erik looked at him, his eyes alight with fire. "I found these buttons and fabric outside the gateway into the town forest," he answered in a low and deadly tone. "Steve, I think we may have a problem, and I have a feeling it's just beginning."

"Now, hold on. Let's not jump to conclusions just yet. Let's investigate all avenues before we cry 'wolf,'" Steve countered.

"That's why you're here, Steve. That's why you're here," Erik answered as calmly as possible. Erik's heightened senses were buzzing in his head like an angry wasp. It told him that there was a connection, as remote and unlikely, the two events were connected. Unfortunately, he was off this case, unemployed.

* * *

Mr. and Mrs. Reynolds arrived promptly at noon, escorted by three men dressed in business suits and tan overcoats. Two of the three men were in their early fifties, the other in his mid-twenties, Erik guessed. All three had short-cut hair and wore identical sunglasses. He could tell by the barely noticeable bulges on the sides of their overcoats that each man was armed. There was another man with them. He wore a blue suit that didn't fit him well.

Alissa escorted the party into Erik's back office. She stared at him with something akin to awe as he introduced them to Steve. Alissa continued to stare as everyone seated themselves around his overcrowded office. Erik walked over to Alissa and gestured for her to follow him out to the hall.

"Quite a crowd," he began.

"Really!" the young girl agreed, nodding her head and looking up at him.

"Can you take an order for me?" he asked.

Alissa nodded and smiled. Erik ordered three pots of

coffee, an assorted cold-cut platter, some sliced pickles, and an assortment of dessert pastries. He gave the young girl a hundred-dollar bill and told her to keep the change. Her big smile was appreciated, as was all of her service when Erik had guests.

When Erik returned to his office, he noticed that there was a flurry of activity. The three detectives were busily talking with Steve, while the Reynolds talked to their attorney, the man in the bad suit. He walked back over to his seat and everyone ceased their activity.

"Thanks for coming, everyone," Erik began. "I spent several hours combing the park area, but like my colleagues in the police force, was unable to uncover anything. So, I played a hunch, if you will, and I found these." Erik produced his findings and slid them on the table toward the Reynolds. "Do you recognize the contents of this bag, Mrs. Reynolds?"

Both Mr. and Mrs. Reynolds stared at the buttons and tattered cloth. The woman intently focused on the objects and then began to weep.

Mr. Reynolds held his wife, whispering small words of comfort. He looked over at the other men. "Those buttons came from my daughter's shirt," he answered, barely suppressing his sob.

"Are you sure?" Erik gently pushed.

"Yes. I bought her that shirt only a week ago. She loved the shiny silver buttons because of the red hearts embedded in each one. Where did you find them?"

"I found them outside the town forest," Erik answered as he took the bag from Mr. Reynolds and handed it over to the detectives to examine. Each investigator examined the evidence, and then the last of them handed it over to Steve.

"Officer Forrest will catalogue this evidence and submit it for analysis," Erik muttered as he tried to filter out the poor woman's cries of despair.

"We'd like to get a copy of the report as soon as possible," one of the investigators said.

"And a copy of any other documentation pertaining to this case," another added.

"We'll provide you with all the information that we have

up to this point. May I remind you, any other physical evidence or leads must, by law, be channeled through Hopedale's department," Steve replied firmly as he pocketed the evidence.

"I assure you, Officer," the third investigator spoke, "that we'll abide by the law. Just make sure your people don't interfere with our work, and we'll wrap this up for you in a couple of days," he responded, prompting laughter from the other two.

Steve was about to respond, when there was a light tapping on the door. Erik stood up and opened the door. Alissa walked in carrying a large platter with cold cuts, pastries and coffee. Erik cleared a space on the table for the young girl to set the tray down. The detectives dug into the food hungrily while Alissa poured coffee for everyone.

"Will there be anything else, Mr. Knight?" she whispered shyly.

Erik stood and placed an arm on her shoulder. "This is my receptionist, Alissa." He introduced the young girl to the others. "If it wasn't for her, I'd probably die from starvation. She's probably the best receptionist anybody could ask for."

Alissa smiled at his guests then turned her appreciative smile toward Erik before leaving the office.

Mr. and Mrs. Reynolds were quiet for the rest of the meeting. Erik spent another twenty minutes over lunch discussing possible leads and theories with the investigators, and the possible tie-in to the latest missing person. He was surprised at how easy it was to discuss theory and analysis with these men. Erik was secretly proud of himself to be able to hold his own with men of such high caliber.

"Of course, we're going to have to conduct a complete search of the parklands, possibly the entire forest," one of the investigators commented as he studied the map of Hopedale Park and the town forest that Erik had provided.

"That's a lot of ground to cover, dozens and dozens of square miles, and a good deal of it has no trails or markers. You're talking about thousands of acres of virgin woodlands. It would be very easy to get lost in there," Steve commented. "You city slickers don't seem the type best suited to a rustic environment. You may wrinkle those expensive clothes," he added, returning the slight that he took earlier.

"We'll do just fine, Officer. Just go back to your doughnuts, coffee, and traffic tickets, and leave the real work to the professionals," the youngest of the investigators countered.

Steve was about to retaliate, but Erik cut him off. "Gentlemen, let's leave our personal prejudices about our trades aside. We all serve justice, only in a different way. Steve is a uniformed professional. You three are expert corporate investigators. As for me...." He paused and laughed. "I'm just trying to pay the rent." All four men laughed at his self-deprecating remark, and the tension seemed to evaporate slightly.

"Mr. Knight makes a valid point. However, I think he underplays his own capabilities," one of the investigators commented. "I suggest we use Mr. Knight as our mediator between authorities. Mr. Knight, I want you on our payroll for this – working for us, of course. Do you have knowledge of the area in question?"

"Yes," Erik replied, struggling to keep down the excitement in his voice. "I know the area very well."

"That's an understatement," Steve replied. "Nobody around here knows those woods, or more about the woods, than Mr. Knight."

"Excellent, we'll let you scout the deeper, unmarked woodlands. We'll start off where you found the buttons and cloth and stick to the trails and water area here." He pointed to a particular section of land on the map. "Your friend is right about one thing. We're not familiar with deep wooded environments, but you are. We'll let you handle the rougher terrain. We'll start bright and early, say 7:00 a.m. tomorrow. That gives us time to appropriate the proper woodland attire and set up our mobile units. We'll meet at the point where the evidence was found and proceed to explore each path in sequence. We can't cover all this terrain in one day, but we'll do as much as we can. The longer we wait, the less likely it is we'll find anything, and the trail is far from being hot. We can only hope that one of us gets lucky." The detective stared at the Hopedale cop. "Can we get any additional support from your people?"

"I'll see what I can do," Steve answered coolly.

"Fair enough," the detective replied. "Let's get things moving then."

The other two investigators nodded, and then stood, signaling the conclusion of the meeting. Two of the investigators led the Reynolds out to their car, while the third, which had done the majority of the speaking, stayed behind.

"Mr. Knight," he began.

"Mr. Nelson," Erik answered.

"I have an envelope for you from the Reynolds covering your services rendered up to this point in time. I'm sure the thousand dollars in here should more-than-cover your time spent. Your rate of compensation working for our organization will be three hundred dollars per day, as long as we require you," Nelson stated bluntly.

"Fair enough," Erik answered.

Nelson extended his hand with the envelope, and Erik took it. Without saying another word, Nelson headed for the doorway. As he approached the narrow hallway, he suddenly turned. "Oh, Mr. Knight, welcome aboard," he remarked, then quickly vanished down the hall.

Erik stared at the envelope in his hand, still trying to recover from the sudden twist of good fortune that fell upon him.

"Well, my friend, you certainly came out of that encounter under par," Steve commented from the couch where he was still sitting.

"So it would seem," Erik answered. "Thanks for the support."

"Don't mention it, but I wasn't bullshitting. Nobody spends more time up in those woods than you, or knows more about the wilderness in general. That's an asset we need to exploit right now," Steve replied as Erik wrinkled his brow. "Something's bothering you."

"Yeah, that missing person report you spoke of earlier. It's no coincidence that they're both around that particular area. This could be the beginning of a pattern."

"Erik, for Christ's sake, you're worse than an old lady. Worry about one case at a time. I'll review the statements tomorrow on my break and let you know if there's anything unusual. Take my advice and relax for the rest of the day. You're going

to be an indentured servant to these people for the next week
or two, so take the time to enjoy your last breaths of freedom,"
Steve said as he headed out of the office.

He stopped at the door. "One more thing, be careful. The
woodlands higher up can be very dangerous and inhospitable;
so, watch yourself, and keep me informed, please. I don't have
much faith in those corporate suits. They'll probably all get a
nasty case of poison ivy out there."

"Always. Now who's being the old lady?" Erik retorted.

Erik waited until he was by himself before he opened the
envelope from the Reynolds. He looked at the check for one
thousand dollars and started to feel some guilt. He knew he
needed money – everybody did – but taking money from a
grieving family somehow didn't seem right. Erik struggled
with his conscience for a few minutes and decided that he did
work for them and he did find a lead. He placed the check in
his wallet and headed out the door.

"How did it go?" Alissa asked as he entered the main area
of the restaurant.

"It went very well. Better than I'd hoped, actually. Everyone enjoyed the food. Thank you very much," he answered,
causing Alissa to smile again.

"If the door is unlocked, I'll get the dishes," she offered.

Erik considered her offer. It was obvious that she was trying to establish a friendship and that she had chosen him. She
usually was amazingly shy and kept to herself. Erik wondered
how long she had been trying to get his attention.

"That would be a big help. Jeff has a spare key. Tell him I
said it's okay for you to go in there and get the stuff."

Alissa smiled again and turned away quickly.

* * *

Erik deposited the check and took two hundred in cash. Shanda had showed him a good time last night and he felt like returning the favor. He stopped at a florist and picked out a doz-
en long stem roses, and headed toward her store.

As he walked in, he drew the gaze of many customers.
He spotted Shanda at the cashier counter, heatedly discussing

something with two large men. Erik could tell from Shanda's body language that she was angry. Erik was stunned when one of the men reached across the counter and grabbed her forcefully by the collar of her shirt. He dropped his flowers and quickly made his way to her.

"I said Mr. Decinto would appreciate it if you would move some of his merchandise in your establishment," the larger of the two men said as he tightened his grip on Shanda's blouse.

Erik could clearly see the look of terror in her eyes. He quickly made his way toward the pair, pushing astonished employees and customers out of his way. He was directly behind the men now, and they were unaware of his presence.

"Release her, now!" he commanded in a voice seething with anger. The smaller of the two men, who Erik quickly sized up at two inches taller than himself, turned and looked down at him. Erik knew the man had quickly determined that he was no real threat.

"This doesn't concern you. Go away, punk, before you get hurt. Go be a Good Samaritan someplace else," he responded as the larger of the two men tossed Shanda back behind the counter and turned to face Erik.

"I can't do that," Erik answered flatly.

"Finally," the big man commented, "one of these punks found a pair."

Erik guessed that the larger of the two men was at least six feet nine inches tall, and had to outweigh him by a hundred pounds easily. Erik knew there would be no way of talking himself out of this. The two men had already assumed offensive postures.

"Take him down, Tank." the smaller man commented.

Tank, as Erik quickly surmised, was aptly named. He was gigantic. His body was built like an oil barrel, thick and solid, with a large midsection and a bloated stomach that, Erik guessed, was from a love of beer. His arms were nearly the size of Erik's legs. There was no clear muscle definition, just massive bulk of flesh and tissue. Erik would have to take Tank apart piece by piece, knowing that he would need a step-ladder to land a blow on the man's jaw.

Tank moved with surprising speed for such a large man.

He rushed toward Erik with his arms outstretched in an effort to simply tear his smaller opponent apart. As Tank's arms went to close, Erik ducked and, pushing off his back foot, met Tank's charge with a swift uppercut into the man's sternum. Erik heard the breath escape from Tank's lungs. He gasped as the air was forcefully expelled from his body. Erik jumped back as his foe stumbled forward, trying to catch his breath.

Tank collected himself and threw another series of blows. There was no finesse in his fighting style, just brute force. Erik easily avoided the series of punches and countered with a solid right cross to the man's large paunch. Erik felt his fist sink deep into the man's soft midsection. Tank buckled slightly but quickly righted himself. Erik ruled out hitting him in the gut again, there was too much fat cushioning that area. Tank lunged forward unexpectedly and caught Erik's leading arm. Erik felt the sheer power of the larger man's grip. Tank smiled, revealing large, uneven teeth.

"You're meat now, shrimp," he grunted as he tried to force Erik to the ground.

Erik took a quick step back and pulled on his arm, causing the big man to step forward. He suddenly twisted his arm and applied pressure to several specific points on the larger man's forearm. As Erik found the desired locations, he dug his fingers into the man's flesh. Tank's face quickly went from a smile to a grimace of pain and discomfort. He tried to pull back, but Erik applied even more pressure on the arm, which was still clamped on to his.

"I'll bet that hurts," Erik commented as he doubled the amount of pressure he was applying. He felt the grip on his arm suddenly weaken and let go. He took this opportunity to slam a back fist into the side of Tank's face with his other hand. The resounding impact sounded like a thunderclap. Tank fell back, stunned by the force of the blow. Erik stepped in quickly and put all his strength into a solid right cross into his opponent's chest cavity. The force of his blow threw the large man off his feet and landed him, posterior first, on the floor. Erik stopped his attack, hoping that he had made his point to the two men.

"Are we finished?" he asked while Tank still sat dazed on the floor.

Tank picked himself up and shook off the impact. He reminded Erik of a gigantic Bull Elephant emerging from a mud pit. "Nobody knocks down the Tank and gits away with it," he answered, preparing to charge again.

Erik summoned his latent gift of enhanced strength. His whole body tingled with vitality and energy. He wanted to end this fight as quickly as possible and was no longer in the mood to simply exchange blows with the large gorilla standing in front of him.

* * *

Shanda quietly watched the battle, waiting for her moment. She watched Erik intently. His face was set like stone, his eyes narrowed like a predatory cat.

She sensed an almost inhuman quality about him; something in his aura that wasn't always present suddenly appeared around him. It was almost comical to watch the large portly man try to catch his more agile opponent. Every time the fat man tried to attack, Erik skipped out of the way and punished the man for his efforts. Shanda could see that the large man was getting frustrated and angry. The man nearest to her began to look concerned.

Shanda slowly stepped back. She saw her objective, a small red button underneath the sales counter. She silently reached underneath the counter and quickly pressed the button. Soon, the police would respond to the silent alarm and this nightmare would be over.

Tank gasped as he took another rock-solid blow to his midsection, causing him to fall back several steps. He looked up at his opponent, amazed at the force of the blow he just absorbed. He managed to straighten up and raise his fists in a defensive posture.

Erik stepped in and threw a blistering roundhouse kick, which impacted with the outside of Tank's knee joint. There was a loud crack as the joint splintered. Tank roared with agony as he lunged forward in an effort to grasp his smaller foe again. Erik leapt, and, twisting in mid-air, smashed his back foot against the man's face with a spinning back kick, which drove Tank backward. Tank stumbled back and hit the floor with a resounding *thud*. He did not get up. He lay on the ground, holding his broken leg and moaning as blood poured from his broken nose.

"You're a tricky bastard," Tank's colleague remarked as he slipped off his jacket. "But you'll find me a more skilled opponent." He raised his hands and approached Erik.

Erik didn't return the taunt. He just waited, crouching low, like a Tiger, waiting for his new opponent to strike.

The man was right; he was more skilled than Erik's previous opponent. He didn't lunge forward like Tank, but carefully threw well-aimed jabs and punches in an attempt to distract Erik. Shanda noticed that Erik was able to adjust to this man just as he had adapted to Tank. Erik didn't avoid this opponent. He met each blow with a block and counter strike. There was no mistaking the other man's skill, however, and at times both men were blocking and punching with amazing speed, neither man striking a clean blow.

Erik surprised his opponent by changing his tactics, suddenly throwing a sharp side-thrust kick that caught his opponent completely off guard. The kick forced the man backwards, causing him to crash into a display shelf, knocking him and the shelf over. He slowly picked himself up, holding his left side with his hand. Erik again did something unexpected, he leapt across the eight feet separating them, crashing into him like a freight train and sending both men to the floor, colliding with the fallen shelf and display items.

As they stood, Erik began peppering the man with jabs of his own. His left hand struck like a serpent, at times, only visible as a blur of motion. Each time he struck a blow, there was a resounding crack. The thug's face became very puffy and swollen. He tried to counter, but could not establish any defense. Erik brushed aside his attempts at punches, and disdainfully blocked an attempt at a front kick. Erik threw combinations, left jabs, followed by quick rights, left hooks, and spinning back-fists. The larger man's eyes had that telltale glazed look, which indicated that he was on the verge of blacking out, and his legs were visibly buckling.

The sound of sirens made both men pause. Erik smiled, while his opponent looked very scared.

"Time's up," Erik commented as he backed away. "You lose."

Both men looked out the large display window and saw several patrons and customers waving to the oncoming police car. The thug shook his head to clear away the dizziness caused by Erik's blows. He took a step forward, and stumbled as he nearly lost his balance. He slowly walked over to where Tank had fallen, and sat beside him.

"Hang on, Tank, we'll get you to a hospital." He looked up at Erik. "You didn't gain anything. We'll be out before you know it," he remarked as the police entered the store.

"But you won't be back here," Erik retorted, "if you know what's good for you."

* * *

Two employees had cleaned the broken items, and replaced the fallen display case. Things had returned to normal. Shanda had filed a report with the police and an ambulance had taken Tank off to the Milford-Whitinsville Hospital. The other antagonist had been handcuffed and was on his way to the police station.

Shanda escorted Erik to her office on the second floor where he had presented her with the somewhat ruffled rose bouquet. She placed the roses in a large vase that was now serving as a centerpiece on her small desk.

Shanda had explained to Erik and the police that for the past few months the same two thugs would come in weekly urging her to sell particular items that were not in line with her Newberry franchise. Today, however, her visitors were more insistent. Erik and the police wisely concluded that the goods were just packaging for narcotics or some other illegal substances. The products confiscated by law enforcement would be carefully examined. The two officers assured Shanda there would be careful surveillance of her store in the near future.

Now the two sat in her office, suddenly unsure of what to

say next. Erik began recapping what had occurred during his meeting with the Reynolds and their hired professionals.

Erik had finished describing the events of the afternoon, recounting his excitement of working with a large agency and not being removed from the Lisa Reynolds case.

"I knew those things belonged to her," Shanda boasted.

Erik nodded. "Yeah, deep down, I knew too. Though I kinda wish we were both wrong. Every day that passes, the odds of finding that little girl, alive or otherwise, decreases drastically."

There was a moment of awkward silence as Shanda stared at her roses and then back at Erik. "In all the six years I've known you, I've never seen you in a fight. I mean, I knew you were a fighter, I know you train. I've just never seen you in that light before." She stood up and plucked a rose from the vase and inhaled the elegant fragrance.

"When I saw that guy grabbing you, I was afraid he was really going to hurt you," he confessed. "I didn't want that to happen. I still—" Erik stopped himself.

Shanda smiled. "I'm glad you were here. You saved me from a probable beating, and most likely from having to file a large damages claim with my insurance policy."

Please, Erik, just say it. She had already read his feelings for her, and she knew of his self-doubt. If he would only come out and say something, she could tell him how she felt about him.

"I'm glad I was too." He turned toward the door. "I have to go," Erik added quickly as he headed out of her office.

Shanda watched him through the second story window as he headed for his truck and drove out of the parking lot.

You poor soul. They took everything from you, including your self-confidence. I don't care about how much you earn, Erik. I only care about you. Why can't you just let go of the hurt? Shanda decided that if she wanted something permanent from Erik Knight, she'd have to make the first move. She smiled as an idea came to her.

* * *

It was close to 9:00 p.m. Erik was preparing the equipment he would need for tomorrow's expedition into the woods. He had sharpened his Jim Bowie hunting blade and chosen his LED compass, as well as other assorted hiking gear.

The Hopedale Forest surrounded a large hill. Some people called it a mountain because it was one of the highest elevation points in Central Massachusetts. There were no other large hills or peaks near it. It stood alone as a geological oddity. The woodlands surrounding this vast hilltop numbered in the thousands of square acres. Unlike other woodlands, some small dirt roads had been laid through various sections of the forest. Otherwise, the pathless wilderness was as secluded and isolated as any other wild land in North America.

Erik was busy rinsing a canteen with water when he heard footsteps coming down the hallway to his apartment. He instinctively grabbed one of his Wilson 45s in the left chamber of his shoulder holster and listened intently as the footfalls approached his doorway. To his recollection, the other tenant who had the adjoining apartment was away on vacation. Nobody should be here at this hour, yet his instincts were not alarmed by the footsteps. His door rattled with a light tapping.

"Erik? It's me, Shanda. Are you there?"

He flipped the safety back on the weapon and placed it back inside its holster. "Just a minute." He unlocked the door and opened it.

Erik was shocked. There was Shanda, but without the leather pants or wild make-up, and her hair was all one color. The ring was missing from her nose, as were several other pairs that she wore in her earlobes.

"Well," she asked, "are you going to stand there gawking at me or invite me in?"

Erik stepped back and gestured for her to enter. He did his best not to stare, but the change was so drastic from how he was used to seeing her. She had on simple blue jeans, worn black leather boots, a blue Van Halen concert shirt, and a faded, black leather jacket.

"You look great," he marveled.

"I look like how you'd expect a normal person to look," she retorted lightly. "This is who I really am. The other Shanda, the owner of Newberry, has to dress like that. That's part of my business. I put on a costume to go to work, the same way you wear that funky *Miami Vice* shoulder holster and those two hand cannons. That's part of your costume for your trade. This is who I am, Erik Knight. Who are you?"

She reached up behind his head and undid the clasp that held his long hair in place. She gently let it fall over his shoulders. She undid the buckles of his double holster and slid it down his arms and around his torso. She held up the heavy weapons package of two guns and four clips, and tossed it onto his couch. "That's not you."

Shanda knelt down and lifted the right leg of his jeans and reached inside his faded Frye Cowboy boot, pulling out a leather sheath, which contained two throwing knives, which she knew that he kept there. "This isn't you either," she added. "Nor is this," she continued as she tugged the 45th Battalion combat ring from his finger. "There." She smiled. "Now you don't have a costume on either."

"What's all this for?" Erik asked.

"I wanted you to see the real me, and I figured if I was going to do that, I deserved to see the real you, not the costume you put on for the rest of the world." She twirled around in front of him like a ballerina. "Well, what do you think?"

Erik had always known that Shanda was beautiful, but dressed as she was now, no fancy make-up and no costume jewelry, he could really see her and appreciate her for the first time. Even the times that they had dated, she always wore her punk attire.

"Do you know what I see when I look at you?" she asked. "I don't see the fearsome gun-toting PI that you want everybody to see. I see a person who's in pain, so much pain that he's hiding from the rest of the world, afraid to let who he really is show through, so afraid of getting hurt again. I see fear, Erik. I sense a fear of just letting go and enjoying life again. Why are you still punishing yourself for something that happened over seven years ago? She's moved on with her life. It's okay for you to do the same."

Erik shook his head strongly in disagreement. "No, you're wrong. I'm not afraid of anything, and I like my life the way it is – simple and uncomplicated."

"Bullshit!" she snapped. "That's a bunch of macho crap and you know it. You're afraid of being hurt. You're afraid of me. I'm telepathic, Erik; I can sense your fear. You're afraid of the feelings that you have for me, afraid that I'll hurt you like Margaret hurt you, but you're wrong. I'm not like Margaret. I like the man inside the costume. I like the man standing before me. I've always seen through your costume, Erik. I see you as you are right now. You tried to tell me earlier, in my office. Why did you stop?"

Erik could feel that Shanda was being sincere. He, too, had unusual gifts, though he hid his capability. He felt her warmth and affection for him, and he knew that he was holding back his true feelings for her.

She reached out her hand toward him. "Touch me, Erik. Let me know how you feel. You don't have to hide it anymore. Stop fighting it and share it with me. Show me how you feel. It's okay to like me." She touched his hand. Shanda relaxed her mental guard. "I'll go first."

* * *

She guided him through happy memories of her mother and father, family and friends. He shared her joy at her first puppy, her sorrow at the death of her grandmother. She shared various strong, happy images of her life, and then the not so happy ones.

She relived the tragic death of her father in an automobile accident and how it hurt her to see her mother in such grief. She showed him the development of her gift and how her mother taught her to utilize it to its full potential. She took Erik back to the first moment they met.

Her car had broken down in the parking lot outside of her store. After waiting for over an hour, Erik pulled up in his truck, with Brianna. She remembered his first smile and how friendly he was toward her. She also remembered how he did his best to put her at ease.

She recalled their first date, how nervous she was about dating him. She took him through their first kiss, and how much she enjoyed being with him. She also shared her hurt that he never made any efforts to pursue their relationship further than occasional dating. She took him to the episode at the store, the fear and helplessness she felt when the large men attacked her, and how grateful she was when Erik suddenly appeared as if answering her silent prayer. Shanda heard his mind respond to that image with force.

"*I'll always be there,*" he projected to her.

"Now you; will you open up to me?" She gently probed the outer boundaries of his mind, but stopped when she came across a vast sheet of gray. Erik had erected a mental barrier to protect his thoughts. She probed the wall gently, but then backed off as she felt the obstacle get stronger.

"I won't pry," she swore. "Please, Erik, open up to me. Trust me. I won't judge.," she whispered as she placed her other hand against his temple to enhance their connection. Without warning, she felt his mental wall vanish. She gasped at the onslaught of powerful emotions he had been withholding.

She saw a much younger Erik Knight dressed in battle fatigues on a training ground at Fort Bragg as Erik recalled the training exercise that took the life of his best friend. Erik was next to him when he was hit during the live fire drill. He caught his friend as he fell. She saw his scream of pain and sorrow as he held the dead body, cradling the head of his lifeless friend.

She was then transported deep into the jungles of Columbia, on a covert anti-drug mission. She saw him pinned down with his unit taking heavy casualties. She heard his scream as a bullet tore through his leg and felt his anger as he fired his M-61 auto-rifle, killing dozens of enemy soldiers. She was with him as he buried his dead platoon members and she shared every tear cried for each soldier entombed on the foreign soil.

He took her into a world of covert operations in jungle after jungle. She saw the horrors of pain and death that had marked his years in the military. For all the pain he had endured, Erik Knight still took pride in the uniform he wore and looked on his service as the key to the man he was.

He didn't have many memories of family, only foster home after foster home. She saw flashbacks to the images he remembered from the car accident that claimed all of his family, but he was barely four years old, and had no real cohesive memories of the event. She saw images of distant men, and women whom she knew were images of various foster parents. She saw pictures of a little boy watching *Dragnet* on television; that same boy in a bedroom, reading Sherlock Holmes mysteries and fantasizing about being the world's greatest detective.

Shanda experienced Erik's discovery of his latent gifts. He was at a local zoo on a field trip with his classmates. She saw an image of a young girl who had fallen into the large recessed lion pit, and saw the image of a fourteen-year-old Erik Knight leap in to help her. Shanda shuddered as the huge male lion approached Erik and the young girl. Erik, however, stood his ground. His eyes were filled with a deep intensity as he stared at the large predator. Erik pointed his finger back toward the man-made rocks and told the creature that they were not food.

The great beast growled curiously, but turned away back toward the grass and rocks of its man-made home. Erik knelt by the girl, warning off several other curious cats until the animal handlers made their way into the pit. Instead of finding acceptance for his heroics, Erik was shunned by the other students for being different. They called him names like 'Tarzan' and 'Jungle Boy,' claiming that he, like the lions, belonged in a zoo.

Shanda relived another episode where his inhuman strength first manifested itself. Several boys were teasing Erik after school. The taunts had angered him. She saw the shocking image of the sixteen-year-old easily overpowering the three older boys and then challenging the other onlookers. Even though he had defeated his tormentors, he had only succeeded in further isolating himself from his peers. She saw the images of his foster parents urging him not to utilize the gifts he had because he would never fit in. Erik, with all of his abilities, was alone in the world with no one to guide him or mentor him.

The only happy times Shanda witnessed occurred at a local martial arts studio. In this arena, Erik seemed to excel and found acceptance and friendship. According to the trainers at the school, he was gifted. Erik eagerly learned all they had to teach.

She now knew he enlisted only for the chance to get an education and chase his dream, becoming a private investigator.

She saw images of his marriage and felt the pain caused by all the problems he had with work and his wife's dissatisfaction with his income. Shanda quickly realized how fortunate she was compared to him. Through their link, she felt the fear and anger he experienced at his ex-wife's house, she felt the pain of coming home to an empty apartment, and the pain of being rejected by someone he loved more than anything.

Shanda now understood why he wore the costume that he wore, lived the way he now lived: It was to keep people from ever hurting him again. She experienced the joy he felt being with his daughter, and also the pain of not seeing her as often as he'd like. Then she experienced the guilt that he felt over his role in the breakup of his relationship. She shared his realization that he drove his family away with his blind pursuit of his dream. He had achieved his dream, but lost everything else in the process. She experienced all of Erik's financial worries.

Shanda wasn't prepared for the unchecked emotion that he felt when he walked into her store to give her the flowers. Through him, she relived the experience in his mind. She felt his panic when he saw the man holding her. She also felt his rage and unbridled power as he destroyed a man nearly twice his size to protect her. To her it was euphoric to experience combat through someone else's mind.

She marveled at how precise and focused his mind and body were during each phase of the fight, and was amazed when he simply willed his body to become stronger. He was fighting to protect someone that he loved and was afraid to lose.

Erik was opening up to her completely. It was only then Shanda realized how deeply he cared for her and how much he had longed to tell her how he felt. She felt his conflict over telling her his feelings and his fear of being rejected by another potential romantic interest.

Erik regained control and quickly pulled her hand away. "I'm sorry. Once it started, I couldn't stop it." He stared at the floor. Shanda noticed drops of water on the floor. She quickly realized they were tears. She wondered if she had pushed too far, and in doing so, hurt him further.

"As you can see, there's not too much happiness in there," he whispered.

She noticed that he was struggling to control his emotions. Shanda had pushed too far. The memories that he recalled had been buried. Now each hurt was fresh and new in his mind. Erik sat down on the couch and hid his face in his hands. A grief-wracked sob escaped him.

"God, Mark! I'm so sorry," he cried out.

Shanda went over to him and wrapped her arms around him as he grieved again for the tragic loss of his best friend in the Army Special Forces. "It's all right, Erik," she whispered as she held him tighter. "You're not alone anymore."

"He was my best friend back then. We helped each other through basic, and then we went through Libya, Columbia, and Panama together, dozens of covert ops. One hundred jumps, and he fucking buys it in a training accident." Erik stood up, wiping the tears from his eyes as he paced back and forth.

Shanda sensed Erik's efforts to calm himself. When he turned back toward her, his face no longer grieved, but his eyes still had the haunted look of a man who's known too much pain. Shanda now understood why. There was very little happiness or love in Erik Knight's life. The only time he had ever loved someone, he had been rejected.

Erik looked puzzled for a second, and then turned to her. "I can still feel you. I can sense your presence in here." He pointed to his head.

"I know," she answered. "And I can feel you. We're telepaths. We can share feelings and experience things that most people can only imagine. But your gifts are greater than mine. You can sense all of nature and the world around us, and your enhanced strength, it's mind boggling!" Only now, through her sharing of his mind, could she understand the unique abilities he kept in check.

Erik turned to her. "I'm sorry. I wanted to say something. I just didn't know how. I was—"

"None of that matters now. You know how I feel and I know how you feel. Let's work from there," she said affectionately. She could sense that he was emotionally drained from the experience. Erik had relived a great deal of pain and he would have to re-bury the feelings back into the recesses of his mind.

They spent the next two hours cuddled on his small couch in quiet conversation. Erik went into greater detail describing some of the memories that the two shared, entertaining her with stories of Army life. Shanda listened intently, asking question upon question, trying to learn more about him. Erik answered each question, and more, revealing to her the lighter side of his nature.

He paused as a giant yawn escaped from him. "Wow, I'm really beat."

"That's normal for what we've just experienced. I'm wiped out as well. What we both need now is sleep. You have a long day ahead of you and you need to recharge your batteries," she added as she escorted him into his bedroom. Erik didn't argue. He was exhausted. He climbed onto his bed and stretched his limbs, then exhaled deeply.

"Do you mind if I take the couch?" she asked. She waited for an answer, but Erik had already fallen into the beginnings of a deep sleep. "I'll take that as a 'no'!" she said with a soft laugh. Shanda took a pillow from his bed, found a blanket, and settled in on the couch in his living room. She held on to his presence in her mind and slowly let herself drift off to sleep.

Chapter 4

The sound of birdsong awoke Erik from his sleep. He lifted his head to see the time on his alarm clock read 5:30. Erik sat up, knowing that he just had time to stretch, shower, and gather his gear before he had to be at the Hopedale Town Forest gate. He looked through his bedroom door over at Shanda who was still fast asleep on his futon in the living room.

Erik stretched his muscles methodically and then stepped into his small shower stall. He set the water for as hot as he could withstand it, causing his blood to more freely circulate into his tissues. He quickly washed and stepped out of the shower. He towel-dried his long hair, and quickly ran a brush through the black locks.

Erik paused and stared at his own reflection. Was Shanda right? He wondered: Did he wear a mask as she claimed? She had made a convincing argument and she had gotten in. No, he amended, he chose to let her in; and once she was in, he couldn't stop his mind from revealing everything he was to her. She, in turn, allowed him to see deep inside her. She looked deeper into his being than anyone else ever had before. She saw what he was, truly, and still accepted him for all his internal issues.

Only two telepaths could accomplish what they achieved last night. He focused his ability for a moment and called up the memories she imbedded upon his mind. She had placed her memories into his mind, to be there forever. It was the most intimate gift that one person could give another.

Erik quietly crept back into his room and slipped into his camo hunting pants and black T-shirt. He went into the living room and picked up his guns from the place where Shanda had deposited them last night, and put the intricate garment around his torso. He picked up the sheath containing the throwing knives and tucked them into his right hiking boot. Erik picked up a large pack that strapped around his waist with a thick nylon web belt and clip. Through the belt, he had placed his large Jim Bowie hunting knife, a Velcro pouch that contained a compass, and a small igniter for lighting fires.

He knew this was only a day search, but his survival training in the military had taught him to always carry certain essentials, and his PI training had always taught him to carry his guns while working. Today, he used the teachings of both.

He heard Shanda stirring behind him. "Good morning," he whispered as he brushed his lips against her cheek.

She responded by gently wrapping her arms around him. "What time is it?" She sat up.

"Nearly 6:30; I've got to get rolling in a few minutes."

"Can I borrow your truck?" she asked. "I don't feel like waiting around for another cab."

"Sure thing. What happened to your car?"

"Back in the shop," she replied as she yawned.

"So how did you plan on getting home last night?" Erik inquired.

"Who says I planned on going home?" She had a coy look on her face.

Erik raised his eyebrow and she responded by laughing at him.

* * *

Erik pulled his truck over to the side of the road by Hopedale Park. Shanda noticed two large vans and several town police cars already parked on either side of the road. She saw Erik shake his head and roll his eyes upward as he killed the ignition.

"What's wrong?" Shanda slid over to the driver's seat.

"Nothing like being subtle," Erik replied in disbelief. "Why don't they just phone the local paper?"

Shanda giggled as he stepped out of the vehicle. "I'll meet you at Madame's for dinner?" she asked hopefully. "My treat this time."

Erik nodded in approval.

"Erik?" she said softly.

"Yeah?"

"Please be careful. Something's not right. I can sense it."

"That's why I carry these." He lightly gestured to the twin 45s hanging within quick reach inside his shoulder holster.

She wrinkled her nose. "Just promise me you'll be cautious."

"I will."

"Good." Shanda reached over to him and kissed him deeply. The kiss caught him by surprise but he returned the affection eagerly. "For luck." She smiled.

"Thanks. I think we'll need it today. We're looking for a needle in a haystack." Erik gently stroked her cheek and turned away.

Shanda watched him walk toward the vans and police cars. She noticed how he really did seem to stand out from the others around him. She realized his rogue quality was what made him unique and special, and what attracted her to him so strongly.

* * *

"Mr. Knight, right on time, excellent," Nelson remarked. "We're about to kick off our little jaunt into this jolly green paradise you have here."

Nelson led Erik over to where the other two operatives and three police officers were reviewing a map of the forest. There were several pins and marks strategically placed around the map, locating possible points of investigation. The younger Halls operative gave Erik a brief smile of acknowledgment, which he quickly returned. The operative went back to staring at the map when Nelson began speaking.

"Good morning, gentlemen," he began. "We will be conducting a three-stage operation this morning – our agency, in cooperation with the local police and a local experienced investigator." He looked over at Erik. "My people will start at these points here." He pointed to specific points of the map. "The Hopedale officers have graciously agreed to patrol this area here, while another officer will divert the human traffic from the areas we'll be searching.

"Another thing to keep in mind, we have another missing person report filed. A female jogger never made it home a few nights ago. The odds are she's in here somewhere too. Keep your eyes open, all of you. The last thing we need are injuries. Each man will take one radio and one linear chip. The chip emits a microwave signal that we can track from the computers in this van. Our Command Control Van will know where you are at all times. Keep in touch. The search effort will be coordinated from here." He handed out the equipment to each man.

"Mr. Knight is the only man here with knowledge of the unmarked woodlands in this area. He gets the thankless job of heading out into that deeper scrub. Mr. Knight, you especially keep in touch. We wouldn't want you to wind up as dinner for a pack of wild dogs or a cougar, or whatever else may be living up there. I expect call-ins from everyone on the mark, each quarter hour," Nelson ordered.

The equipment was all dispensed and Erik took the chip and placed it in one of the bullet clip pouches on his gun holster, and fastened the radio to his belt.

"Everyone, be careful. We've got a job to do, so let's do it," he concluded.

Erik was about to head off when the senior Halls operative, Nelson, pulled him aside.

"Mr. Knight, keep your eyes open. If anyone has a chance at finding anything, odds are it will be you. These radios have a range of about five to eight miles, so you should be able to contact us no matter how deep you get into those woods. Good luck."

"Thanks," Erik replied as he turned to enter the parklands with the other men.

* * *

Erik had assisted the youngest of the Halls agents, Henderson, on his search of one of the outer-most trails until he reached the designated area that led to the deepest trail and into the wild areas of the parklands. He could tell that the young man was uncomfortable in these surroundings. Erik told him which trails led back across the lake, and which trails would take him deeper into the forest. The two parted ways and Erik began his walk on the outmost path to the woods.

Extra senses automatically kicked in. He became aware of wind patterns; sounds increased in clarity, as did his awareness of everything around him. He clearly smelled the various scents of different flowers and plants. He had to stop momentarily and allow his mind a few extra seconds to process the increase in sensory information.

His vision became far more acute, as if somebody placed magnifying lenses inside his eyes. He could see more detail, and focus on objects in the distance and see them clearly. Once his brain adjusted to the increased stimulus, he continued on his way, his mind analyzing the extended sensory information at incredible speed. Up ahead, he noticed some disturbances in the path.

Erik walked another fifty yards, when he came across a set of footprints. He knelt down and studied the tread pattern of the shoes. The exaggerated tread pattern indicated he was looking at the print of a cross-country running shoe of some type. He moved ahead cautiously, spotting more footprints. He could tell, by the general size and shape, that they were most likely female. He reached over to his radio and keyed the transmitter.

"Knight to base. Over," Erik called, using his designated call sign.

"Go, Knight. Over," the reply came with slight static.

"I've got footprints, on the outer-most white path. Size and shape indicate female. The track was made by some type of cross-country shoe. These tracks are no more than a day old. Over." There were a few seconds of silence before the response came.

"Noted; proceed with caution. Over."

"Gee, now why didn't I think of that?" He shook his head.

Erik slowly covered more ground, and then suddenly stopped when he observed the footprints were haphazardly placed all over the trail. He cautiously moved forward, careful not to disturb any potential evidence, and then followed the set of footprints deeper into the trails.

His eyes quickly spotted another set of single tracks over-laying some of the others, but going in the opposite direction. He went another fifty yards, when those tracks came to an abrupt halt. Erik knelt, studying one track in particular. It was half in and half out of a sharp depression in the trail. He looked over and saw that the leaves beyond the track were disturbed. Erik studied the scene for several moments, trying to put the entire thing together in his mind. The tracks told a story, but he wasn't sure what. Suddenly, it dawned on him.

He noted that the right foot on one set of tracks left a scuff-ing trail. He also saw other various depressions in the soil. He knelt down and followed the line of the tracks to a large tree off of the trail. He followed that set over to the tree, careful not to disturb any of the tracks with his own.

"Okay." Erik sighed. "She was running. She tripped, possi-bly injuring her right leg. She hobbled over to this tree, possibly crawled. That would explain the weird depressions."

Something caught his eye under some fresh leaf fall. He walked over to the object and knew exactly what it was, a run-ning shoe – a running shoe that probably belonged to the miss-ing person.

"Oh crap!" he whispered under his breath. He reached into the pack he was carrying and pulled out a large Ziploc bag. He placed the open bag over the shoe and scooped it in, along with the few leaves and debris that were around it.

"Knight to Command. Over."

"Command, go ahead. Over."

"I've got more tracks, and a single women's running shoe, bagged and tagged. From the pattern of the tracks so far, it looks like our missing jogger had an accident, possibly a fall leading to an ankle fracture. We may want to send more men out here. Over."

"Noted; we'll have a few uniforms head up there. We have you locked at grid 7, quadrant 9. Over."

"I'm going to look for some more tracks. There's no way in hell she just walked out of here on her own!" Erik exclaimed. "Please, God, let me find her alive," Erik whispered.

"We didn't copy that last part. Over," the radio responded.

"Just mumbling. Over." Erik replaced the transmitter. "All

right, lady, where the hell did you hobble off to?" Erik muttered. Something felt wrong. His eyes narrowed and his senses locked in combat alert. The detective sampled the air; no unusual scent. He walked slowly back down the path toward the edge of the trail. He spotted a series of broken bushes, disturbed leaves, and upturned dirt on the pathway. He had been focusing so intently on the footprints that he walked right by without even noticing.

He knew something was dragged through here, and he got that uneasy feeling in the pit of his stomach. Erik noticed more small footprints, and some other unusual tracks he didn't recognize. He knelt by the strange track, studying the depth and indentations. They were the same age as the footprints, but much larger and deeper.

"What the hell made these?" he whispered, examining the print more closely. "This guy's gotta be huge." Erik knew he wouldn't find the missing jogger alive. Somebody attacked her, and with all probability it was the same person that had abducted Lisa Reynolds. The Reynolds girl's body was out here somewhere as well. He reached into his pack and pulled out some bright orange marker tape and tied a large, ungainly bow tie knot onto a broken limb. He reached over to his radio and activated the unit.

"This is Knight. I'm getting a bad feeling. Get those uniforms up here now. I've found a drag trail that shouldn't be here, and there are two sets of footprints all around it. I think something very bad happened to 'Jane Doe' up here. I've marked the discovery with trail tape. I'm proceeding in, weapons unlocked. Over." He freed both Wilson Super 45s from their holsters.

Erik made his way into the woods, every instinct in his body on full alert. It took no real skill to follow this trail. It was easily marked with dug-up leaves, dirt, and broken saplings. The detective's hyper senses were scanning every minute detail as he walked deeper into the unmarked forest. Both Wilson auto pistols reflected the tree-filtered sunlight off their muted stainless steel barrel slides. He smelled the faint odor of decay. It grew stronger the deeper he went into the woods.

Erik heard a low growling sound coming from his right

side. He pivoted and adopted a defensive combat stance. From out of the brush came the largest cougar he had ever seen. Erik leveled the barrels of both weapons at the cat. The cat sensed the threat and stopped its approach.

"Nice kitty," Erik whispered. "Nice kitty with the big fangs and sharp claws," he added with a nervous chuckle.

Erik had been in these woods for years, and had never encountered feline predators this close to the main trails before. The larger cats and coyotes usually stayed higher up on the mountain.

"Don't make me shoot you, cat."

Erik could sense the animal's feelings. It felt threatened by his presence. The detective looked directly into the big cat's eyes and didn't blink. He focused his telepathic abilities on the animal, crouching down to the cat's eye level and slowly placing one pistol back into his harness.

"We're not going to fight today. I'm not looking to encroach on your territory. I'm just passing through, big fella." The detective held his hand straight out and lightly exhaled in the cat's direction.

The animal quickly caught his scent as the air carried his spoor. The cat sensed no fear, and did not smell any standard prey scent. Without warning, the cat crouched down low – it felt something. At the same instant, a feeling of dread passed through Erik. Somehow, the sun seemed imminently darker. The cougar howled and hissed as it backed away from something unseen. Erik stared hard into the woods in the direction that the cat was staring, but could not see anything. The cat slowly retreated, and then broke into a full run in the opposite direction.

Erik's body began to tingle, and he felt goose bumps run up and down his arms and back. He was being watched. Someone was out there, in the darkness. Now that the distraction of the cougar was gone, his heightened abilities could sense it. He turned back to where the cat had looked and knew the source was there. As he made the realization, the surrounding woodlands became even darker. He saw some movement, coming toward him, quickly.

"That's far enough, friend," Erik shouted loud enough to be

heard by the figure. It still advanced. Erik's senses were shrieking. It was the same feeling he had when he was led to the park earlier. His senses all sprang into full combat alert. Bioelectric impulses sent signals to all parts of his body. Erik's involuntary nervous system responded, as trained, to the potential threat. Erik quickly tugged the other pistol from its holster and both Wilson's locked on the intruder, following every movement, adjusting to every action. Every muscle fiber was prepared for action, but relaxed, not tense as most in this situation would be.

"I said that's far enough!" he warned again.

The figure was like an animated shadow, all black in appearance. It didn't move so much as it seemed to hover over the ground. Erik momentarily stared at it and admired the graceful, fluid movements it possessed. The creature passed into Erik's red zone. He warned one last time, and was ignored. It was then he saw the thing's blood-red eyes and spiked tail whipping back and forth.

Both Super 45s roared to life, spewing hot metal-jacketed slugs at near supersonic speed and illuminating the darkness with the muzzle flare from both gun barrels. Eight bullets impacted against the intruder, causing a dazzling display of sparks as the slugs collided with its hide. The thing cried in pain and surprise. The shriek was something so loud and terrible it sent shivers down Erik's back. Erik stopped firing, but kept his guns aimed directly at the target.

The thing was bleeding some type of blue ichor. It touched a wound with its hand, and held up the stuff in front of its vacant blood-red eyes. Those eyes looked at Erik with absolute contempt and malice. Erik felt hate and the desire to kill emanating from it.

"What in God's green earth are you?" Erik whispered, staring at the hideous dark figure.

As sudden as the creature appeared, it simply vanished, evaporating into the darkness. The sun once again was normal, and the eerie chill was gone from the early fall air. Erik slowly approached its position, guns ready to fire at the slightest hint of danger. The repugnant scent of decaying flesh even stronger, he advanced further and spotted the lacerated body of Carol Carlin, minus the jogging shoe he had in his pack.

"Good Lord, what the hell happened to you?" he whispered.

He heard the shouts of several voices in his radio responding to the sound of weapons discharge.

"Knight to base, I found our Jane Doe number two, deceased. We need a coroner team up here, and someone better notify her family."

"Knight, this is Patrol Two, closing on your position. We heard gunfire. Over."

"Knight to all parties, we've got something out here besides animals. Over," he began reluctantly, knowing the other people would think he was crazy.

"Base to Knight, would you care to elaborate? Over."

"I wish I could. Something came at me. It was hovering near the body. Just make sure everybody is hot!" he urged. "There's something out here and it is a hostile, I repeat, hostile! Over."

"Hey!" a voice came back over the radio. "Did our local 'Grizzly Adams' see a Bigfoot in the woods?"

"Just get up here and help me with this body. And for God sakes, watch your ass!" Erik responded into the radio.

"Don't wet yourself, local. We're almost there. Patrol Two out," one of the Halls investigators replied

* * *

Agent Henderson cursed as he looked at the map. He wondered how he had gotten turned around. The agent decided to cut through the woods, hoping to get to the adjacent path and save time. He'd been monitoring the radio and knew a body was found. He also heard Knight panic over seeing something hostile.

Amateur. The worst thing you could get out here is a case of poison ivy.

He waved his hands at the swarms of flies buzzing around his head incessantly since he began his foray into the forest. "Or maybe a billion mosquito bites," he mumbled, amending his prior thought. He quickly realized that one should not wear cheap aftershave in the woods. It drew every blood-sucking insect for miles. To Henderson's misfortune, it also attracted something else.

The young agent fumbled his way through the thick scrub, sounding like a stampede of buffalo as he tripped and stumbled his way over fallen trees and saplings.

"Damn woods," he muttered as he lifted his radio. "Henderson to base. Over"

"Base here."

"Base, where the hell am I? Give me a direction to the target. Over." Henderson heard stifled laughter over the static on his radio.

"Base to Henderson, proceed north at 278 degrees, for 200 yards. That should take you to the next path, follow that path west. Belechek says that you can't miss the orange marker on the trail."

"Thanks."

"Base to Henderson," his radio called.

"Go, Base."

"Henderson, we have a girl scout here willing to go out and be your guide. Over."

Henderson heard the laughs of the men who were at the Command Control Van. He keyed his radio. "Ha, ha, ha. Why don't you come out here and do this, smart ass." He took a compass reading and headed in the given direction.

As Henderson plodded through the woods, he noticed the temperature had dropped. He looked up at the sky, and the sun seemed dimmer than it had been moments before. As he continued on his way, he caught scent of something foul.

"Oh, God, what the hell died out here?" He spotted some strange blue stains on the ground, and knelt closer to examine the fluid. He quickly determined this was the source of the foul smell. He touched the stained leaves with his finger and brought the substance closer to his face to study.

"Sulfur base. What is this shit?" he asked aloud.

He heard a twig snap, then footsteps. Henderson looked up in time to see claws rake across his face. The force of the impact knocked him end over end. The agent got up quickly and felt his own warm blood flowing down his face. He looked into the face of something that wasn't human. The fear spread through him like wild fire. He went to draw his gun, but the thing slapped the weapon away with its long tail.

"What are you?" the agent shrieked in a voice filled with panic.

Silence was the thing's only response. It attacked again, moving with incredible speed as it jumped upon its intended victim. Henderson fought back with the ferocity of a man fighting for his life. He slammed a right cross into its face only to feel his hand crack as it hit a surface much harder than flesh and bone.

"Oh my God! You're not human. Get back," he screamed in panic.

The creature grabbed the agent by the throat and held him in the air with one hand. Henderson responded by driving his left foot into the creature's midsection. The creature felt the blow, but shrugged it off easily. Henderson grabbed the creature's arm that had his throat to avoid being choked as his neck supported his whole body weight. He tried again, kicking at the thing, but his blows had little effect. He felt the blood supply being cut off from his brain, and it was becoming harder to breathe. He saw black specs begin to appear in his vision. He was blacking out, having his life literally squeezed from him.

* * *

It felt the human struggle against its iron grip. It savored every ounce of his sheer terror. The creature squeezed the primate's neck harder, and was rewarded with a sickening crack. The man no longer struggled. It hung at the end of its arm with limbs dangling lifelessly.

It dropped the bloody corpse and withdrew deeper into the woods. It needed time to finish healing. The other man had caused it intense pain. It knew the primate's scent. It would find him, make him fear, and feast on that fear. It would not kill that man – not for a while. These soft, fleshy primates were fun to play with and they scared so easily.

* * *

Erik stood over the body of the young woman, a gun in each hand. The adrenaline still coursed through his body from the previous encounter. He heard voices of other men converging on his location.

"Over here," he shouted.

The two Halls operatives Nelson and Belechek arrived and made their way over to the body. They were accompanied by two uniformed police officers.

"There's an ambulance unit on the way with a team to take the body. Did you touch anything?" one of the officers asked.

"No," Erik answered. He reached into his pack and handed the officer the sneaker he bagged earlier. "She's wearing the other one." Erik walked away from the body as the others voiced their astonishment at the condition of the corpse.

* * *

Erik sat alone on a large rock while the once-quiet woodlands were now buzzing with activity. The medical team had removed the body by stretcher, and the police were combing the surrounding area for more clues. Nelson, the lead Halls operative, was speaking via radio to the van operatives. His face looked pale as he placed the receiver back into his coat. He looked toward Erik and walked to the shaken detective. Erik stood up and met the operative in a small clear area.

"All right, Erik, I need to know what you saw."

"It was weird," Erik began. "It was like somebody put a filter over the sun, then seemingly right out of nowhere this ... this thing shows up. I called out to it twice, warned it off. It kept coming faster. As it got closer, I saw its eyes, they were red, almost a blood-red. Its skin was black, not black like an African-American, I mean freakin' Crayola Crayon Black. That's when I saw it." He sighed.

"Saw what?"

"Its tail," Erik replied. "I emptied eight rounds into the thing as it continued to charge me. It gave off a moan that sent shudders down my spine. Then, almost as fast as it appeared, it simply vanished." He cursed, looking at the other man. "I know what you probably think, but I'm not nuts. I saw what I saw. Go look at those weird tracks, that blue shit it bled is still decorating the ground. I didn't imagine that," he added defensively.

"I believe you. I also believe Henderson encountered it too, although he wasn't as quick to react as you were."

"What do you mean?" Erik demanded.

"Something attacked Henderson. His radio was locked on transmit. The boys at the van recorded the whole encounter. Whatever attacked him, he didn't think that it was human either. We got that much from the recording." The older man sighed, and his shoulders seemed to slouch. "Henderson is overdue. He hasn't checked in for half an hour, I'm hoping you're not too shaken by your encounter to help me look for him." He handed Erik a map with the missing man's last location.

"What about that chip thing we each got this morning. Can't you find him with that?"

"It's no longer functioning. We're going to the last location lock we had."

Erik stared at the map, visualizing the marked location. It was very close by – only a fifteen or twenty-minute walk through a thicket, a little under a mile. Erik paused momentarily and swapped the clips from each weapon with two others. These clips had blue bumper stops on them. Erik loaded each weapon and re-holstered the guns.

He looked at Nelson. "45 supers – more 'knock down' power. Next time, it's not getting away," he remarked, heading toward the woods. "Let's go find our missing man."

Nelson nodded and followed him. The two broke away from the rest of the group and headed into the woods toward the marked location. This particular section of woods was dense with saplings and undergrowth. Erik had drawn both his weapons. Nelson responded by drawing his Glock 9mm. Erik stopped abruptly, his eyes closed. He opened his eyes, then looked back toward Nelson. Erik gestured with his head and both men continued forward.

Erik spotted Henderson's body first and pointed it out to Nelson. Both men approached cautiously.

"Check him out," Erik said quietly. "I've got your six."

Nelson nodded and approached his associate. Henderson's face looked as if it had been slashed by razor blades. His head was lying in a pool of blood. Insects and flies circled around the corpse. Nelson noted the awkward angle of Henderson's head in relation to his shoulders. The elder detective looked back at Erik, his face betraying sorrow. "His neck's been broken."

"Look for strangulation marks, like our Jane Doe," Erik suggested as he studied the surroundings.

"Same thing," Nelson replied after examining his fallen colleague.

"We have ourselves a problem," Erik commented, approaching Henderson's body. Erik stared at the man's corpse. The left side of his face was literally sliced to shreds. "Sleep peacefully. May your final journey take you to a better place."

"God-fearing?" Nelson asked.

"Not like you think, probably; not in the typical sense anyway," Erik answered evasively. "Somebody should say something though. No one deserves to die unmourned."

Nelson activated his transmitter and made the call. "They're sending the coroner's team back up here. You can head back if you want. I'll stay with him," Nelson offered.

"No," Erik answered. "You're not staying here alone, not with that thing out here. I don't feel like getting ambushed on the way out of this mosquito farm either. We're better off if we stick together."

"Touché," Nelson replied. He paused as he sniffed the air. "Do you smell that?"

"Yeah," Erik replied as he continued to scan the area. "Just like the other site." He took several steps away from Henderson and spotted a patch of blue-stained leaves about six yards from the body. He knelt down and examined the substance. The stuff had a foul sulfur-like odor and had partially dried to several leaves. He took another bag from his pack and placed all of the stained leaves into it. He sealed the bag and placed it back into his pack. "At least we have something," he remarked making his way back to Nelson.

"What is it?" the detective asked.

"I think it's more blood from the thing I shot at earlier. The color is the same and so is the smell. Henderson definitely saw the same thing that I saw. Now I know I wasn't seeing things," he concluded. "I'll bet there are other patches of this further out," he guessed, itching to investigate.

"Remember what you just told me about sticking together?" Nelson reminded the younger man.

"You're right, of course," Erik replied. He had to admit, if only to himself, that he didn't welcome another encounter with the strange thing again.

"Whatever it was, do you think it's still in the area?"

"I don't know, Nelson." Erik looked around, his guns following his line of sight. "I drew down on that and hit it with eight rounds. No man could have walked away from that, a bear wouldn't have walked away from that, yet it lived and still had the strength to do this. What the hell are we dealing with?"

"You tell me. You saw it, I didn't. All I know is that Henderson was terrified. I heard it in his voice while the tape was played. Henderson was not one to scare easily, but whatever it was scared the shit out of him."

Erik shook his head. "You know she's out here, somewhere."

"Who?" Nelson asked somewhat bitterly. The loss of his man seemed to wear on him.

"Who!" Erik snapped. "Lisa Reynolds!"

"Sorry, this whole thing made me lose focus for a moment. If she is out here, I don't give her very good odds at being alive."

"Nor do I," Erik replied as he finished another quick scan of his surroundings. "Let's warn the team coming back up here to bring an armed officer for escort. Let's not lose any more people today."

* * *

Erik and Nelson walked out of the woods on either side of the medic team, carrying the stretcher containing Henderson's body. Erik had never been uncomfortable in these woods before, but he was glad to leave the forest. He walked over to the van with Nelson and paused to take a long drink of water from his canteen.

Nelson and Belechek were conferring with the command staff in the two vans. They had replayed the tape over and over again, trying to extract some clue as to the events leading to Henderson's untimely end. They all shuddered as they heard the muffled sound of the man's neck being broken.

"What the hell happened out there?" Nelson asked no one in particular.

"We just lost a good man, and I just lost a good friend," Belechek replied with a belligerent undertone.

"You," Belechek began, pointing at Erik. "You saw something out there. What was it? What killed him?"

"I honestly don't know," Erik answered. "It was...." He paused, looking for the right word. "Different. That's all I can say for sure. It walked like a person, but looked like no man I've ever seen before."

"I don't care what it is," Belechek answered. "When I get my hands on it, it'll be dead."

"Let's not get off the subject," Nelson commented, heading off his angry colleague. "Something is out there, gentlemen, something that in all probability is wounded. We're having our lab geeks examine the sample brought in. We should have some answers in a day or two. The question that remains is: Do we go back in and continue the search for our main objective, Lisa Reynolds, or do we back off until we know what we're dealing with?"

"I say we carry on the search," Belechek answered quickly. "We know it's out there, and we know it can be hurt. We weren't prepared before, now we are. We were hired to do a job. I say we do it."

"Erik, your position on this?" Nelson asked.

"If Belechek is in, I'm in as well." He looked at Belechek who now gave him a nod of approval.

"Fine, if we're going in, we need a plan." Nelson pointed to a map taped to the open door of the Command Center Van. Nelson circled the areas where Carol Carlin's body was located, and where Henderson was found. "This is the logical area in which to start. I'll tell the boys in blue we're heading back in, and to keep everyone out of the area until further notice. We'll see if they can pull together a team for deep recon as well. Keep your radios on Channel C. It's the highest frequency and will carry the strongest signal.

"Belechek, get the 30-06 from the other van. There's a box of shells on the bottom of the shelf. If we're going in, we're going in with some real fire power." Nelson looked at Erik. "Do you feel comfortable with those 45s, or do you have something that will pack more of a punch?"

"I do, but let's not waste the daylight. Belechek and I should stick together. He doesn't know the area. We'll use his big gun and my tracking. I don't think going in solo is the best idea."

"Agreed. Take an hour to rest. We go back in at 1400 hours." Nelson turned to study the map. "Can you coordinate our effort with the uniforms, and see if they can pull a team together?"

"Consider it done," Erik answered as he headed toward the police cars parked in a group several meters from the Halls' vans.

Erik gave a quick sigh of relief as he spotted Steve talking with two other officers. "Steve?"

"Erik. How are you?" He walked toward him.

"I'm hanging in there. How are you?"

"I'm okay. I heard you had some kind of encounter out there? Are you going to give us a report? Those suits are being awfully quiet since their guy went down."

"It's not good, Steve," Erik gestured his friend away from the others. "Here's the lowdown. There's something out there and it came after me. I put eight rounds into it, and it quite literally vanished into thin air. It was in the same area as the jogger. In fact, I think it's what killed the jogger. The same thing whacked the Halls operative, Henderson. They both had their necks broken and wind pipes crushed in the same way. Whatever's out there has killed two people, and possibly killed Lisa Reynolds."

Steve shook his head in disbelief. "You're kidding, right?"

"I wish I was. It looks like those kids at the playground weren't fantasizing. Nelson and I brought back a fluid sample for the Halls techs to evaluate. My guess is we brought in blood from this thing. I'll make sure that you guys get a copy of the lab report when it comes in," Erik replied. "Look, we're going back in at 1400 hours. Can your people put together a team to coordinate a search with us?"

"Yeah, we'll go in, but we're not taking directives from them. We'll pattern our own search in the designated area. Give us the location and the frequency you're working with, and we'll coordinate from the field," Steve responded coolly.

"Steve, I know they didn't treat you too well before, but they just lost a man. Try to cut them some slack. They really are good. Let's all try to play nice in the sandbox."

Steve smirked and nodded. "We'll head in with you at 1400 hours."

* * *

Wednesday afternoon. 1:49 p.m.

Steve and two officers walked over to the Halls portable crime labs.

"Are we ready?" Steve asked.

"As will ever be," Nelson replied, placing a full clip into his Glock pistol.

The two groups of men entered the town forest, each individual nervously looking around for any slight thing that was out of the ordinary. Their destination was the point where Carol Carlin's body was discovered. From there, they would go to where the body of Henderson was discovered. At that point, Erik would look for tracks from whatever caused the death of both people.

They walked the forty-five minutes to their first objective in total silence. Belechek held the 30-06 scoped rifle at the ready, his finger never far from the trigger. The man was wired, coiled like a snake and ready to strike out at the slightest thing. Erik knew those emotions often were self-destructive. Belechek wanted revenge. Finding a missing person was second on his list right now, no matter what he said to Nelson.

Erik looked over at Steve, and both men exchanged uncomfortable glances. Steve shook his head. He was clearly concerned about the detective's motives for being out there as well.

The six men converged on the location of the jogger. Everyone instinctively drew his weapon. The woods were suddenly alive with chambers cycling live rounds and clicks that signified the removal of safety levers.

"There's the marker." Erik pointed out the trail tape to Belechek and the others. "If no one objects, I'll take lead. Belechek, you've got the real firepower. You cover our six. Steve, you and your partner watch my ass in case I miss something. Let's move out."

Of all the men there, Erik had the most knowledge and experience in the wilderness. The others would be relying on his knowledge and expertise.

The six men cautiously made their way into the small clearing, all weapons at the ready. They approached the position where the Carlin body had been found. Erik and Steve spotted another patch of blue fluid. This fluid had dried completely and lost its repugnant odor. The other uniform bagged the substance and tucked it into his side pocket.

"We move this way." Erik gestured, following the path he and Nelson had taken earlier.

After a cautious twenty-minute walk, the men came to the area where Henderson had been found. Erik approached the spot where he'd taken the blood sample, and moved out to where he had seen some disturbances earlier. He spotted more of the dried blue substance, and gestured to the other men. They all fell in behind him silently. With precision, Erik scanned over the carpet of leaves, low-lying branches, and shrubs. His heightened senses easily picked up sign on the leaf-covered forest floor. They had been following a blood trail for at least a half-mile.

Erik examined his compass and realized that they were heading due west in an almost perfectly straight line. He looked up. "It's heading back up the hill. If we keep going, we'll be up into the higher elevations."

"Could this thing live up there?" Steve asked.

"I don't know," Nelson responded as he gave the officer a friendly look. "Are you game for an extended hike?"

"Certainly," Steve replied.

"Let's think about this for a minute," Erik countered. "If we venture too far off the trails and up the hill, we'll be traveling back in total darkness. I say we go forward for another two hours, and then head back. If we do that, we'll just make it out before sunset." He paused. "Unless you don't mind being out here in the dark."

The five other men looked at each other uncomfortably.

"Point taken," Belechek conceded.

"Another two hours," Nelson confirmed.

The police officers nodded in unison. They continued their journey in silence. They had been walking for fifty minutes, when Erik paused. He raised his pistols and assumed a low crouch. The other men took his lead and responded in kind. Erik stood stone still, his eyes distant, but his ears straining to pick up the slightest sound.

"What is it?" Belechek whispered.

"Don't you hear it?" Erik asked.

"Hear what?"

"Listen," Erik whispered softly.

"I still can't hear anything."

"Exactly, where are we?"

"In the fucking woods, where do you think!"

"And what does one hear in the woods, genius?" Erik retorted.

Belechek was silent as he considered Erik's words.

"Ya know, you're right. I don't even hear a bird chirping or anything."

"Do you hear or see any insects?" Erik asked.

The insects plaguing them most of the hike had simply vanished. Belechek became very nervous. "Oh shit! What's goin' on?"

"I don't know," Erik answered. "But everyone keep sharp."

They were walking steadily uphill now. The incline began to take its toll on the older Halls detectives, and the other officers were also suffering from their lack of conditioning. Soon, Erik and Steve had put several meters between themselves and the others. The two men decided that they would proceed up the incline and keep in contact by radio while the others scouted the lower regions in a northwesterly direction.

They had been hiking for nearly half an hour when Erik

suddenly paused. The inside of his head began to buzz, the hair on his arms stood up, and he felt a tingling sensation race up and down his spine.

"Steve, it's here," he whispered.

"Where?" The officer crouched down in an effort to lay low.

"Close."

Steve radioed the others in their party for backup as they proceeded forward. The two moved slowly upward, when both experienced a sudden drop in temperature, noting the disappearing sun.

"Oh my God, Erik, what on earth is that!" he exclaimed at the approaching wall of black.

Erik looked in the direction his friend indicated and saw an encroaching mass of darkness that seemed to be growing and expanding with every passing second. "Oh shit."

"It wants me. I can feel it!" Steve exclaimed in a voice thick with fear. "Oh, God, whatever's causing this can't be human, it can't."

"Easy, Steve, let's not lose our cool just yet," Erik replied, straining to see the being that he shot at earlier.

Erik focused his breathing, and concentrated. He looked in the direction of the encroaching blackness again and stared, focusing his enhanced vision, urging his eyes to see what they normally couldn't. Slowly, something began to materialize. It moved within a shroud of darkness, closer to the two men. The entity paused as if studying the two men, unsure of how to react to their intrusion.

"It's the same thing as before," Erik whispered. "How in God's name could it still be alive? Not after eight rounds," Erik marveled as he whispered to the near-terrified Steve.

The thing suddenly rushed forward. Erik squeezed off four shots into the shape before it struck him and sent him flying backward, knocking his weapons from his hands. The creature then tackled Steve, sending his radio flying into the nearby bushes. Erik heard the shouts of panic from his friend. As he shook off the daze, he saw the black thing holding Steve in midair with one arm. Steve was struggling, pummeling the creature with his fists, but Erik could tell he was getting weaker.

Erik leapt up and charged. He ran toward the creature and slammed into its back with both his feet. The impact drove the creature forward, causing it to drop Steve, who lay on the ground, not moving.

The black creature spun toward Erik. Again, Erik was awash in the creature's fury and hate. It reached out with its large razor claws, but Erik ducked and responded with a front kick into its face. He followed that kick with a roundhouse, and then a spinning back kick, followed by an open-palm strike to the thing's chest area. When his hand struck it, Erik felt the cold. This thing was not alive as he understood it. It had no real body heat and its skin was more like armor than flesh.

Erik's flurry of blows had managed to drive the creature back, and it hissed with fury. It charged at him again, flailing with its arms in an attempt to slice his flesh open.

Erik retreated slightly, avoiding the creature's knife-like hands. He threw a quick series of left jabs into the creature's face. Erik knew that the blows had no real effect. He felt sharp impact pains in his fists each time they struck the thing's iron-hard hide. His weaker human flesh ripped and tore with each impact. Erik paused and took one step back. He could feel those red eyes studying him. He could feel wave upon wave of maliciousness emanating from the black armored monster in front of him. Erik sensed it was going to do something, but he didn't know what. At that instant, the creature struck.

Erik saw the tail swing at him, but it was moving too fast for him to avoid. He rolled his body in the direction the tail was moving in order to absorb most of the impact. The tail struck him like a pile driver, knocking him over in somersaults. When he finally stopped, the thing was above him and was reaching down toward his throat.

Erik grabbed its claw with both hands, and bent it sideways with all his strength. He heard a snap like a lobster shell cracking and the thing roared in pain. It struck at him with its other hand, lifting him three feet off the ground and backward. Erik stood up and slowly came to his senses. As he tried to gather his strength, he felt fingers closing around his throat like a vice. He felt himself being lifted off the ground.

The thing simply held him there as if waiting for something.

Erik could read confusion upon the creature's face as it held him nearly two feet off the ground. Erik heard it make a sniffing sound, and then he saw a look of puzzlement come over the creature as it slowly studied him.

The creature seemed to recognize or acknowledge something. Its face contorted with rage and anger. Slowly, it began to squeeze. Erik gasped as he struggled for air. He felt himself losing consciousness. He knew he only had seconds to break the thing's iron grip.

Erik lifted both his legs and drove them heel first into the thing's blood-red eyes. He felt the grip loosen slightly, and he quickly inhaled a much-needed breath of air. He took his right arm and slammed it in an upward motion into the arm holding him, where the elbow joint would be on a man. He was rewarded by another cracking noise as the creature dropped him.

As the detective hit the earth, his opponent kicked him solidly, propelling him several feet across the ground. The creature looked back toward Steve and slowly approached him. Erik crawled over to where his 45s had fallen. He grabbed one of the pistols and turned it on the creature. It was heading toward Steve who was still out cold. Erik grabbed his other 45 and shouted as he emptied each clip of high-powered slugs into the dark entity standing before him.

A shower of sparks appeared where each bullet either impacted or bounced off the creature's hide. Erik could see that at least four of the shots had pierced the thick skin, causing the creature to bleed again. Erik quickly reloaded, and continued to fire into the thing's back as it approached his friend.

When his 45s were emptied, he pulled his hunting knife from its sheath. He raced toward the thing, remembering the motion he used at the gym earlier. He shouted and leapt into the air, raising the large blade above his head. As he came down, he drove the Jim Bowie knife, point first, into the creature's shoulder plate. The blade penetrated about three inches, then snapped at the hilt from the excess forces applied on the metal, leaving a nine-inch section of steel protruding from the creature's dark, armored body. The creature spun around quickly and smashed Erik's face with its claws.

Erik was thrown back ten feet, but absorbed the force of the blow and rolled with the impact of the ground. He could feel blood flowing down the left side of his face. The creature quickly turned back toward Erik, and he prepared himself for combat. He crouched down, ready to strike out with all his fury against this seemingly unbeatable opponent. The creature closed in toward him, and Erik exploded with another series of complicated kicks. His heavy boots struck the creature's face with deadly precision. It swung its tail at him, but Erik anticipated its attack and dove over the appendage. He rolled sideways and came up in a guarded stance again.

Erik knew his blows were only glancing. Hitting the creature was like hitting a suit of metal armor. His hands were throbbing with pain. He willed his body to become stronger, but doubted that even then he would have enough sheer muscle to harm this inhuman juggernaut.

The creature paused to look at Steve who was still out cold, and then at Erik again. It rushed forward, reaching out to grab Erik with its razor-sharp claws. Erik grabbed each claw, and rolled himself backward, moving with the creature's momentum. He tucked his right foot into the creature's midsection and launched it eight feet into the air as he rolled over on his back. It landed with a loud thud against the forest floor, but quickly stood up and faced him again. The thing looked beyond Erik, to where Steve was laying. It wanted its victim.

Erik knew he needed to distract the creature, get it to focus on him, and not his unconscious friend. Erik took a step forward. The creature responded by swinging its arm toward him. Erik raised his left forearm and met the blow with a standard martial arts block. Erik nearly buckled under the force of its blow. If not for his greatly enhanced strength, his arm would have splintered. However, he felt a wave of pain travel through his arm and shoulder. The creature swung with the other hand, and Erik used a similar method to block this strike as well.

"Steve! Wake up, damn it. I can't keep this up forever," Erik shouted to his friend.

Erik leapt into the air and launched a flying sidekick into the creature's midsection. The blow was solid, and caused it to fall backward several steps. "C'mon, you bastard," he swore at it as he peppered its face with hard jabs, ignoring the pain already there from his previous punches.

The creature swung its arm again, but Erik swiftly ducked the blow. The creature moved its other arm unexpectedly, raking its claws across his chest. Erik responded by slamming both his open palms into each side of the creature's head, causing it to step back momentarily.

Erik's adrenaline was pumping through his body. He ignored the deep gashes cut into his flesh. Something inside him was pushing, giving him even more stamina and strength to attack this monstrosity. Erik's fingers began to swell from colliding with the thing's rock-hard hide.

"You can't have him!" Erik screamed as he pummeled the creature's armored hide. He succeeded in forcing the monstrosity back, but his hands were now bleeding from several cuts, and his fingers and joints were swollen. He crouched in a low defensive posture, preparing himself for the creature's next attack.

"Fall back," a voice commanded.

Erik turned to see Steve pointing his 44-magnum revolver at the black creature. The weapon erupted, spitting slug after slug into the creature. Erik retreated as he saw the sparks, and then bright blue blood flowing from the creature's torso. Steve paused as he emptied the spent brass and dropped in a speed loader with six fresh shells. He held the weapon head high, his eyes angrily locking on the creature that had struck him down.

"Get away from my friend, you bastard!" Steve shouted as he fired two more rounds into the thing.

The creature screamed with rage and anger as the jacketed hollow points burned into its armored flesh. The sound echoed throughout the forest for miles.

Erik sensed it, another presence. He turned, retreating behind Steve. Erik reached inside his boot and withdrew the two throwing knives he kept hidden there. He stepped up beside his friend as he peered into the forest depths.

"Something's coming," Erik whispered to Steve.

"Just fucking great," Steve replied hoarsely. "Inside my left pant leg, I have a 32 auto. I'd rather you use that than those," he said, glancing at Erik's throwing knives.

"So would I," Erik replied as he quickly retrieved the weapon.

The forest became even darker, as if some great hand completely blocked out the afternoon sun. The two stood their ground, staring at the creature before them, waiting for something to appear. They heard a low rumbling, and heard branches snap as something approached their position – something big. A loud screech broke the silence, more deafening than any sound Erik had ever heard before. Each man felt a shiver go through his spine. The expectation hung in the air.

Then Erik saw it. He spotted the bright green eyes that were easily twelve feet above the ground. Erik realized that it was now as black as the darkest night around them. The creature they had fought dissipated into nothingness, to be replaced with a larger, spookier horror. Erik could feel the tremors of terror emanating off his friend. A flash of lightning illuminated the forest. Erik could see a large feline-like creature looking down upon them.

"Yikes!" Erik whispered. "What in God's name are you?"

"What do you see, Erik?" Steve asked.

"Nothing you'd particularly want to look at," Erik whispered.

"I can't see a damn thing in this darkness." Steve cussed. "Are you sure it's out there?"

An ear-shattering roar answered the officer's question.

"Did you hear that?" Erik asked.

"Oh yeah, may I suggest a strategic withdrawal?" his friend asked.

"The question is: Will they allow us to retreat?" Erik whispered as the men began a cautious withdrawal.

The two men retreated back down the hill. The large creature held its ground. Erik felt a second presence. He looked up into the trees near the feline creature. The first creature crouched on a branch watching with hate-filled eyes.

"Our other friend is watching us leave," Erik observed, pointing it out to his friend.

"I don't see it now," Steve replied. "How is it that you can?"

"I don't know. Let's just focus on hooking up with our team members," Erik answered.

Erik had lost a great deal of blood. He was still bleeding from the deep gashes in his chest and face. The two men walked in silence down the sloping ground for nearly half an hour. Steve had continually tried to make radio contact with the rest of their party, but only received static through his radio.

"Damn it," Steve swore. "What the hell is wrong with this piece of junk? Where are they?"

Erik's head began to spin. His enhanced strength had long expired and the adrenaline rush that allowed him to hold off the monstrosity was long past. His body was wracked with pain. His hands had swollen and were bleeding from several places where the flesh had literally peeled away. He could no longer hold the 32.

"Steve," Erik whispered, "I think I'm going to black out."

* * *

Steve turned and helped Erik off his feet. He instructed his friend to drink deeply from his canteen. Steve looked overhead, relieved to see sunlight. He looked at Erik. The investigator was in bad shape. His hands and forearms were a bloody mess, and his shirt was in shreds. Blood was still seeping from the deep wounds across his chest. There was no way Erik was going to be able to make it out of the forest on his own.

"Nelson, Belechek, Hooper, Ramirez," Steve shouted into his radio, "I need help!" Steve looked over at his friend. He appeared to be going into shock. "Hang in there, Knight. Don't fizzle out on me."

"Steve, this is Hooper. Over," a voice crackled through the radio.

"Hooper, where the hell are you guys? I need help here, quick."

"We're heading up. Hang in there. We're on our way. Hooper out."

Steve sat with Erik who was in and out of consciousness. It seemed like endless moments waiting for the rest of their party to arrive. After fifteen minutes, he heard footsteps, and quickly reached for his weapon. He sighed in relief as he recognized the voices. "Hooper, over here," he called out.

* * *

The four other men quickly arrived and were horrified to see the condition of both men. Nelson took out a first aid kit and began to work on Erik. He was very concerned about the flesh tears on Erik's upper torso. He applied a disinfectant and wrapped his chest in bandages as best he could, while the two other police officers applied cold packs to his swollen hands.

"Didn't you hear us trying to contact you?" Nelson asked.

"Nothing," Steve answered. "All we got on our end was static."

"We saw the darkness approaching our position and fell back. We tried to contact you, but couldn't get through. This veritable wall of darkness just kept expanding, then it seemed to shrink back and slowly fade." He paused. "Then we heard the weirdest sound. It seemed to shake the forest," he added as he turned his attention back to Erik.

"Nelson to base. Over," he said into his radio.

"Base, go ahead. Over."

"Base, I need an ambulance and a med team to meet us at Grid 07-01. We have a man with multiple deep lacerations and impact wounds." He reached inside Erik's shirt and scanned his dog tags. "We need some type-B positive blood and equipment for immediate transfusion," Nelson concluded.

"Roger that, B positive for transfusion."

"Erik? Do you think you can walk?" Nelson asked.

"Yeah," he replied weakly. "Just help me up."

Erik was leaning heavily against Steve and Hooper as the six men made their way down the hill and through the woods. The third Hopedale officer, Ramirez, had his weapon drawn, providing cover for the group as they made their way down the mountain. Steve told Nelson of the events that transpired, and how Erik had fought the strange creature off while he was knocked out.

"Erik said that something else was coming. The next thing I knew, it was as dark as midnight, and I heard a shriek that shook the ground and echoed throughout the woods. I nearly peed my pants. We heard tree limbs breaking and a weird growling. At that point, we didn't think our weapons were going to do much good. I had four shots left in the Magnum and Erik had the five in the 32 auto. We felt a cautious retreat was in order. After that, I couldn't see the things anymore, just darkness. Erik claimed that our sparring partner was perched on a tree limb next to the other thing, watching us go," Steve reported. "I'll be damned if I know why they let us leave, but I'm not going to question our good fortune too closely."

"We saw the patch of darkness," Nelson confirmed. "Almost as if somebody just turned out the sun like a light bulb. As I said before, we heard the same sounds you did; and I'll be honest, it made my skin crawl. Somehow, we got turned around. We tried calling you two on the wireless, but only got static. We're not equipped to deal with whatever's going on up here," Nelson exclaimed, reinforcing his earlier remarks.

Erik was coming in and out of consciousness. Steve and Hooper were dragging him through the trails when he passed out, and helping him walk when he awoke. The trip out of the deep woods seemed to last forever. They finally met the med team at the designated grid and placed Erik on a stretcher. The paramedics started a transfusion immediately, and were busy tending to the other injuries he sustained.

"Cripes," one medic exclaimed. "Did he pick a fight with a tiger? His chest is torn up with claw marks. What the hell's living up there?"

"Just fix him," Nelson answered moodily.

That was the second man on his team down in one day. Nelson was not a man used to setbacks. Nelson took a hard look at the detective's battered body and torn flesh. He wondered how Knight was able to take such a beating and, according to the Hopedale cop, dispense physical punishment as good as he got.

Something didn't add up in his mind. Why kill Henderson and not kill Knight and Forrest? Was Knight that much better at defending himself, or just luckier? Nelson was grateful the two men survived their ordeal, but wondered why they were spared while his employee wasn't as fortunate.

Chapter 5

Erik sat up on the stretcher as the medics finished bandaging his chest. He had stubbornly refused to be taken to a hospital, wanting nothing to do with any more blood transfusions. He finished the half-gallon of orange juice Nelson provided, and paused to stare at the other men staring at him with some concern.

"I'll be fine," he reassured Nelson and the others. "They said it looked a lot worse than it actually was."

"You're starting to get some color back, anyway," Steve replied. "You had me spooked, my friend."

"We all got spooked," he replied seriously. "Gentlemen, I've been in these woods for nearly eight years and I've never, ever seen anything like we saw earlier today. Steve, you saw it. I saw it up close and personal. Nelson and Belechek, you saw what it did to Henderson and our 'Jane Doe,' Carol Carlin. Can we all agree that we're not dealing with an animal?"

They all nodded in agreement.

"If it's not a man and it's not an animal, then what the hell are we dealing with?" Nelson asked.

"I don't know," Steve answered. "All I know is that I put enough forty-four lead into that thing to stop an elephant, and it simply walked away. It picked me up like I was a rag doll. I can still feel its icy cold grip around my neck." The officer had a tone of dread and a hint of fear in his voice.

"It's obvious that it has some kind of armored covering." Erik held up his skinned knuckles. "But, I do think we hurt it. We just need something with some more firepower. Like maybe Belechek's rifle, which we should have taken with us. As for the thing's larger friend out there, I just don't have the answers." He sighed heavily, shifting the position of his heavily bandaged torso.

"Bottom line, gentlemen," Nelson remarked. "We just got our asses kicked. Steve, from what you and Erik said, this larger thing could have had you, but it let you withdraw. I think they were just making a point, saying 'you can't hurt us, so stay away.'"

"I don't follow you," Erik said.

"I'm just applying logic, Erik," Nelson replied. "Let's look at the facts. You put eight rounds into it earlier, then capped off the rest of your four clips. So that's eight rounds times four clips. I've looked at those peashooters of yours. They're not exactly stock. It took thirty-two rounds from you alone, and six or eight rounds from Steve. Plus, you said you buried the blade of that big pig-sticker you were carrying earlier into its shoulder. Nothing human could live through that," the detective stated firmly.

He continued. "You were both beaten up there. It could have killed you like it killed Henderson. I'll admit that you may have caused it some measure of difficulty, Erik, but face it; we had to carry you out of the woods. If this thing wanted, it could have killed all of us at any time as we were heading back to the main trails, but it didn't."

"Maybe you're on to something." Belechek nodded in agreement. "Think about it, Erik. What better way to discourage trespassers than by spooking the hell out of some of them and then letting them escape? The trespassers won't return and they'll warn everyone else off the area. And let's face it; we're going to do exactly that." He continued looking at the Hopedale cop. "You know as well as the rest of us that the police will cordon off these trails and keep everyone out of the woods. We'll never tell the public that there are monsters up there. You'll blame it on some wild animals or some other cover story. Whatever it is, it wants to be left alone. It used today to make that point, I think."

"Maybe," Erik conceded, "but it seemed determined to get a hold of Steve."

"Or," Steve countered, "maybe it only wanted one of us to get out alive. Maybe it figured that since you weren't going to let it get me, it would settle for you and let me live. Either way, its mission is served," Steve commented, as he weighed the points of discussion.

"We're still missing one important piece of the puzzle, which puts a hole in this theory," Erik commented. "Lisa Reynolds. I think that this thing took Lisa Reynolds, and she was nowhere near the woods. Why would it go out of its way to abduct a child? She doesn't fit into this equation we're building," Erik countered. "Also, if it did take the child, where is her body? If this thing is following the same pattern, we should have found her somewhere in there. The jogger wasn't too far off a path, and Henderson was left right where he was murdered.

"This ... this *thing* abducted a child right under the noses of several people and carried her off to the parklands without being seen by a single hiker or a jogger. That doesn't match anything we've experienced and puts a damper on our working theory," the detective observed. "I still think we're missing an important piece of the puzzle." Erik looked at the five other men for their comments.

"Maybe the girl is the key," one of the other Hopedale officers responded.

"The key to what?" Belechek asked as he took a long drink of water. "Let's look at the score card: We've lost Henderson. We almost lost Knight and the cop. We have something that can block out the sun and make things as dark as midnight, as well as interfere with radio transmissions. Sometimes it can be seen, and sometimes it's invisible. This creature has an armored hide and seemingly impervious to small arms fire." He paused, wiping his mouth.

"The question we need to ask now is what do we do about all of this? We can't give a factual report of what occurred up there because nobody will believe us. Hell, I was there and I still don't believe it," he concluded, staring at Nelson.

"What are you going to tell the Reynolds?" Steve asked. "They footed the bill for this debacle, and you boys came up with a big fat goose egg."

"We found your missing person," Erik countered somewhat bitterly. "And we found out what's doing it. What the police choose to tell the public is your bailiwick. I only deal with what is, and 'what is' is very disturbing." Erik didn't appreciate

Steve taking a cheap shot, considering the dire circumstances. Now was not the time to resort to blame.

"I'll speak with the Reynolds," Nelson responded to the Hopedale cop. "That's my responsibility. You deal with the local crap; that's your hassle. Whatever you do, just keep people out of these woods. Let's not piss this thing off any more than we've already managed to. I've got a report to file, and a family back in Manhattan that I owe a phone call. We've succeeded in one thing, gentlemen: We've made a very nice young woman a widow."

Nelson stepped out of the van and walked to his car. Belechek followed closely behind him. Erik stepped down from the van and followed. He said a quick goodbye to Steve and headed toward Nelson's car.

"Look, Knight, we're wrapping it up for today. We're taking Henderson's body back to New York tonight. I'll be flying back Saturday or Sunday to continue the search. Take a few days to get your strength back because we're going back in. There's a little girl's body that needs to be recovered. Can I count you in?"

"I'm part of the team," Erik replied. "I'll be here, you just tell me when."

Nelson nodded as he opened the car door. "Get in, the least we can do is give you a ride."

* * *

Erik walked in the back door of Madame's and went up the basement stairway that led to his office. He didn't want any of Jeff's customers seeing him in this condition. Erik was sore and tired. There wasn't a muscle in his body that didn't ache. He entered the hall through a side door and quickly went into his office. He removed his heavy gun holster and tossed it on the table. He removed what was left of his shirt and casually tossed it into a wastebasket. The knock on the door startled him.

"It's open," he responded.

"You're just in time for the dinner crowd," Jeff's voice began. He suddenly paused as he looked at the condition of the man standing before him. "Good Lord! What the hell happened to you?" He studied the cuts on Erik's face, hands, and torso.

"Did you know that there are cougars up on the Hopedale Hill?" Erik asked evasively.

Jeff shook his head.

"Well, they're awfully big," he continued. "Let me get a quick shower and I'll help Alissa set the tables." Erik took three steps and then stumbled slightly. He was feeling lightheaded again. He knew it was from the loss of blood and that he needed to give his body time to recover.

"You're not doing anything except going back to your room and getting some rest. You're not doing any good to anybody right now," Jeff ordered, taking his motherly tone. "I'll have Alissa bring you something later. Now, go on, get out of here. You'll scare my customers if they see you like this," Jeff added as he lightly pushed Erik out of his office and through the side door in the hallway.

Erik made his way back through the small passage into the building's large basement. He went up a staircase on the opposite side and entered the foyer where his apartment was located. He entered his apartment and eased himself down on his bed. Sleep overcame his body as soon as his head hit his pillow.

* * *

A jet-black helicopter flew swiftly and silently through the dark of night. There were no running lights on this vehicle or significant markings of any type. The chopper was flying dangerously low, below the conventional radar-tracking ceiling for aircraft. Its destination was Hopedale Mountain. It flew silently over the sleeping town, and made its way toward the lone peak.

"Spectre 1 on final approach," the pilot said into his headset. He was carefully studying his infrared scanner and night flying instrumentation. The view outside his cockpit was nothing but midnight black.

The helicopter reached its designated target and slowly circled the area. He activated the FLIR pod on the belly of the helicopter and slowly scanned the entire area. He saw several heat signatures from animals, but nothing that fit a human pattern.

"Spectre 1, report," a voice sounded through the pilot's radio.

"Spectre 1, no sign of them. I'm setting her down at the landing site. Our team will head for the tunnel." The pilot circled the area one final time before setting the chopper down on the makeshift landing pad.

Five men disembarked from the helicopter and began a quick equipment check. Two of the men had camera equipment and other communication gear. One man carried a high intensity spotlight, while the other four wore head-mounted light straps. The two other men were busy checking over their various monitors and geological equipment.

The plan was for the five men to investigate the surrounding area and then the tunnel. The camera and radio equipment would relay continuous signals to the helicopter, and the helicopter would bounce the signal off a satellite to their corporate headquarters in Boston.

The last report that they had received before losing contact was that the tunneling team had found some kind of chamber. The site foreman was going down to investigate and evaluate the situation. The foreman on the site had requested some very expensive equipment to bore into the chamber, but never reported back. The suits at the corporate headquarters assumed that a cave-in had occurred, but needed to send a team in for a positive assessment. It had taken some time to compile a list of trustworthy, yet expendable, resources willing to do the job with no questions asked.

The five men finished their equipment check and activated the lights upon their helmets. Each individual sounded off to the pilot inside the helicopter who would be forwarding their transmissions.

"Anderson, testing."

"Rogers, testing."

"Phillips, testing."

"Takei, testing."

"Harris, testing."

The pilot acknowledged each transmission and responded as he fine-tuned the communications array in his cockpit.

"Spectre 1 to team, video and audio transmissions are

positive, proceed to target," the pilot responded to the team.

"Harris, you have the main video, you're up with Rogers and his flood light. Takei, stay with me. Phillips, you have the point," Anderson said as he took charge of the mission. The team proceeded through the thick darkness of the campsite, checking each individual tent and piece of abandoned equipment in their vicinity.

"No sign of anything out of the ordinary." Harris picked up a half empty Pepsi bottle resting on a small table.

"How far away are we from the tunnel entrance?" Anderson asked.

"Maybe 150 meters or so that way," Takei answered, pointing into the darkness.

Anderson took a deep breath and exhaled loudly. "Let's go, people."

The five men moved cautiously through the woods toward the location of the tunnel entrance, the large spotlight did little to illuminate the heavy darkness of the forest lying before them.

* * *

The pilot was busy in his cockpit, aligning the ship's communications array with the designated orbital satellite while simultaneously monitoring the digital feed to make any fine adjustments to the signal bandwidth as the team descended into the tunnel. He wasn't used to serving as a relay tech, but they could not afford the weight of a seventh man on this operation.

He carefully adjusted controls and dials as instructed, and was rewarded with a clear signal from the team's camera unit. The pilot flicked a switch, which would activate the broadcast to the satellite. He was rewarded with a flashing green light that signified a transmission.

"Spectre 1 to base, can you confirm transmission?"

"Spectre 1, we have satellite feed," a voice over the radio set confirmed.

The pilot sat back in his chair and studied the images. There was nothing else for him to do until it was time for extraction.

* * *

The team performed a complete sweep of the area and found nothing. The five men headed toward the opening of the tunnel and began the long slow walk down into the bowels of the mountain. The powerful floodlight did little to illuminate the tunnel depths, and the men were huddled close together.

"What the hell happened to the overhead lighting?" Anderson wondered aloud.

"The generator probably ran out of fuel," Harris answered.

The party proceeded through the 500 feet in relative silence, pausing to double check equipment readings.

"I'm getting a different reading up ahead, almost like an echo of a larger opening," Takei reported as he paused, studying the readout. "The tunnel seems to open up after this leg."

The group of men moved forward, straining to make out details ahead of them in the darkness.

"How much further?" Anderson inquired.

"I'd guess another 150 feet or so. I'm getting some weird readings on the spectrometer. There's definitely some kind of metallic structure ahead, but it's like nothing I've ever seen before." He paused momentarily, adjusting the gain to its highest sensitivity. "Base, are you getting these readings?"

"We're getting it," a voice on the radio replied. "Proceed."

"Yeah, proceed, let them fumble around in this darkness," Phillips mumbled.

"Typical bureaucrat," another of their party answered.

The party continued their way forward and entered the large opening. They stood in awe as their lights reflected off the polished stone walls. Then their lights fell on the bodies of the tunnel party. They cautiously made their way toward the bodies.

"Can you see this, base?" Anderson asked in a voice filled with panic. "Some of them have been literally torn apart. They were murdered, butchered."

"But by what?" Takei asked as he studied the body of Gillespie. Gillespie's body was laying in a large dried pool of blood.

"How the hell should I know? I wasn't here," Anderson answered.

"Focus on the objective!" a firm voice called over their headset.

"Fuck you, pal," one of the party answered. "It's easy being calm behind a freakin' desk."

"Hello?" Phillips screamed into his headset. "Five men have been murdered here, five of your employees. Guys, let's bug out of here before what happened to them happens to us."

"We're paying you to do the job," the voice over the headset answered firmly. "If you wish to terminate your contract, you can leave now. Of course, you'll have to walk down the mountain. You will not be allowed back in the corporate helicopter. If you don't complete the job, all of you, I'll order the chopper back, right now."

"Asshole," all five men whispered simultaneously. They each paused and shared a nervous chuckle.

"Okay, guys, let's pull it together. Whatever happened here is history now. Let's do what we came to do and get out of here," Anderson remarked, trying to calm the men under him.

There was dead silence among the five men for nearly 30 seconds.

"Let's get back to work," Anderson commanded. "Phillips, see if you can get the generator back on, let's get some more light in here."

The party continued their observation of the uncovered chamber, recording images of the symbols on the wall and the huge gargoyle statues.

"What kind of symbols are these?" Anderson asked Takei, the team geologist.

"It looks similar to writings I've seen at ancient Aztec pyramids. This other stuff, I can't make out. It's like nothing I've ever seen," he responded as he ran his fingers over several of the carved runes. Takei raised his small digital camera and sent several images to the chopper to be relayed back to the company. He instructed Harris to shoot several seconds of the walls with the larger camera system. "We'll need to bring in a team of archeologists to study this."

Phillips had little success with the generator, as they had

expected. Its fuel supply was exhausted. He did, however, manage to retrofit power connections to the generator's back-up battery, supplying some sparse overhead light for the team to work with. With the new light source activated, the men spent nearly twenty minutes photographing and taking instrument readings on the external chamber, and did their best to ignore the corpses and blood scattered throughout the cavern. Anderson examined the large Argon laser. He studied the controls, trying to reconstruct what could have possibly happened.

"It looks like they used this device to break through the door into this other chamber," Anderson commented absently.

Harris had been studying the stone figures at the entrance to the main chamber. Each member of the team was reluctant to enter. Something inside each one of them was warning them away. Silently, they all lined up behind Harris outside the chamber, each man peeking inside the doorway as their small halogen headlamp beams were swallowed by the vast darkness beyond.

"This chamber, it's huge," Harris added as he aimed the large spotlight into the unexplored cavern. Even the powerful five million-candle power beam seemed pale in comparison to the dark void that lay before them. Harris took a deep breath, held it, and slowly entered the unexplored area.

The other men reluctantly followed him into the large chamber.

"Let's move further on," the cameraman replied, his curiosity slowly began to replace his fear. "Base, are you getting all of this?"

"The images are coming through, proceed further," the monotone voice replied.

"Holy shit!" Takei swore. "According to the scanner, this cavern is nearly a half mile from end to end! Who on Earth could have made this?"

"I don't know, but this is the archeological find of the millennium. It's bigger than the pyramids!" Anderson replied.

The party swept the entire area around them with the floodlight, noting the unusual architecture and tablets with alien symbols emblazoned on them.

"This looks like some sort of control panel," Takei observed, "but to what? The surfaces in here aren't rock, or any geological substance that should be in this strata of surface crust," he added in utter amazement. "There's trace granite almost like a tiling layer, but we seem to be in some sort of metallic chamber. I'm reading traces of granite, shale and quartz, almost as if there are pockets of earth or maybe gaps in the chamber." Takei continued to sweep his scanner back and forth into the abyss.

They had covered a scant fifty meters, pausing to record and transmit as much data as possible. As they proceeded forward, it became more difficult to establish a solid footing. It felt as if they were walking on dried twigs. One of the men turned his light down toward the ground. He spotted a grayish mass protruding from the ground, walked over to it, and gently grabbed the object. As he tugged it, it snapped in his grasp. He studied the broken section carefully. Suddenly, it dawned on him.

"Bone, this is a bone fragment," Rogers observed.

"What?" another of the party asked in disbelief.

"Bones," he repeated. "We're stepping on bones."

The party carefully swept away several layers of dust and debris and began to unearth several other bone segments. Suddenly, one in the party gasped and jumped back. The other four men rushed over to him. He was staring at the remains of a skeleton, remarkably preserved. The bone structure, however, was not human.

"Base, please tell me that you're seeing this," Harris asked as they all turned their lights on the discovery.

"We see it," the voice answered.

"Damn," Anderson began. "Is it just me or is it getting cold in here?" He rubbed his arms in an effort to warm them.

"Yeah, it is getting chilly."

"We're hundreds of feet underground in a tunnel, it's not going to be warm and balmy," Takei replied.

"Truly, but it does seem remarkably cooler," Anderson noted. "Let's break up into two groups, we can cover more ground that way."

The two groups separated and headed deeper into the chamber, slowly and carefully photographing and measuring. The large light swept back and forth, illuminating several parts of the massive cavern. The powerful beam passed over a stone-like monument, illuminating it for several seconds. On the monument, a set of ruby-red eyes opened then quickly closed. The team of Harris, Rogers, and Phillips made their way toward it. They walked up to it and bathed it in the spotlight.

"What a fantastic statue," Harris commented as he studied the monument.

They filmed it and proceeded deeper into the cavern. As they were walking, Rogers heard the sound of footsteps behind him. He stopped short, alerting the others. Soon, all the men heard the footfalls. Rogers slowly turned his powerful light behind them. They saw nothing. The beam reached out to where they had studied the magnificent statue, only the statue was no longer there.

"Oh shit!" Harris scanned the area they had just covered. There were fresh prints – prints that were not human – leading away from the statue's makeshift pedestal. Each man felt a wave of fear course through his spine. Harris' head was tingling with primal fear. He knew something was out there, and that something wasn't human.

"Everyone stay together, head back toward the opening. Base, did you see that? The statue walked away! It's alive! Something is alive down here!" Harris shrieked into his headset.

From out of the darkness, something struck the heavy floodlight, the glass lens shattered under the impact, destroying the krypton bulb inside. The cavern became more ominous and oppressive as only the three halogen beams remained to light the darkness.

"What the hell was that?" one of the men screamed.

"I don't know," another replied. "Stay together."

In the darkness, just outside of the circle of light, something moved. The men heard the crunching of footsteps on dried bones and stone.

"It's circling us," Rogers whispered.

"When I say three, make a break for the door," Harris whispered.

"One, two, three!"

The three men broke in a panicked sprint toward the door

to the outer chamber. They could barely see without the aid of their powerful floodlight. They were stumbling over objects as they scrambled toward the pale light source that marked the outer chamber. To their surprise, the light source vanished, replaced by two large malicious green eyes. The three men froze in their tracks, slowly backing away. They didn't realize that their other tormenter was scarcely three feet behind them. They were only aware of the two large green eyes rapidly closing in on them and cutting them off from their only possible escape.

They were trapped. Both creatures closed in on the small party, circling them in tighter and tighter like dolphins corralling a school of herring into a tight food ball that could easily be devoured. One by one, they screamed an agonizing wail that announced each death, their video and audio equipment recording and transmitting every sight and sound to the helicopter outside and through the satellite relay to the base corporation miles away.

* * *

Anderson and Takei heard the shouts of panic, and rushed toward the voices of their companions. When they arrived, they discovered three severely mutilated corpses.

"Anderson to Base, we lost three men, there's something alive down here," he shouted in panic into his headset. "We're out of here. Keep that chopper waiting for us, we're leaving now." Both men quietly stalked their way through the darkness toward the faint light of the outer chamber.

"Did you hear that?" Takei whispered.

"I didn't hear anything. Just keep moving."

As they moved, Takei heard faint footsteps directly behind them. He swung around suddenly. His light illuminated a being with searing red eyes. Takei had no time to scream, no time to react. He felt his body being run through by something. He tried to scream, but managed only to cough up blood and saliva.

The creature grabbed him by the throat and held him two feet off the ground. The last thing Takei heard was Anderson's screams of horror as he witnessed the occurrence. Anderson tried to run, but panic held him frozen in place. The creature pressed its face eyeball to eyeball with the man. Anderson lost control of his bladder and felt himself trembling. The creature placed an icy hand around his neck, never once taking its blood-red eyes off the man's face.

"Please, please, please don't kill me," Anderson whispered as the creature turned his head from side to side. The creature suddenly released Anderson from its icy grip. It slowly backed away from the terrified man and disappeared into the darkness.

"Thank you, God, thank you, thank you," he whispered as he headed toward the door to the outside chamber.

Anderson wasn't aware of the creature stalking him. When the massive tooth-filled jaws snapped his torso in half, he was completely stunned and surprised. Anderson had felt no pain, only a numbing coldness. He looked around into the darkness, his headlamp still functioning. The last sight he saw was a large feline-shaped head with green luminous eyes devouring what was once the lower part of his body. Mercifully, Anderson closed his eyes and expired.

* * *

The pilot of the helicopter was in a state of total terror. He warmed up the twin turbine engines on his ship and counted the agonizing seconds as the rotors slowly turned. He watched the continuing video stream from the fallen camera, he saw as the two creatures made their way outside of the cavern after brutally devouring the expedition team. He knew they were coming. Somehow, he knew that the creatures were coming to claim the last member of the reconnaissance party.

"C'mon, damn you!" the pilot swore at his machine.

More agonizing seconds passed as the rotors increased in intensity, he knew that in another few seconds those things would be outside. He checked his gauges one last time. He had enough RPMs for a lift-off.

He jammed the control yoke back and depressed the throttle forward. The helicopter shot up in the air as though fired from a cannon. At 100 feet above tree level, the pilot felt safe.

He turned the craft around, circling the area.

He then felt his skin go cold. He glanced down over his passenger side console and saw a set of large green eyes staring up at him from the treetops. He wanted to pull his craft back, but something about those eyes was hypnotic, he had to see more. He reached down and activated the chopper's forward floodlights, bathing the creature in eight million-candle power of halogen light. The beast roared up at the helicopter in savage anger. The pilot stared in amazement at a creature that was a cross between a cat and some mythical fairytale dragon.

There was something else, something sitting on the thing's broad back, a creature that was slightly bigger than a man, the pilot judged. Its hideous blood-red eyes looked right up at him. Looking through the intense floodlight, through the dark midnight, through the aluminum hull and Plexiglas of his ship, straight into his soul.

The pilot felt an uncontrollable wave of fear and nausea as he felt it probing him through the distance that separated them. He pulled the yoke back, raising his craft higher and higher into the night sky. At 3000 feet, he felt safe, and banked the craft away from the quiet town. He didn't give a shit about radar at this point. He wasn't going near the ground until he reached the helipad in Boston. He had witnessed the death of five men at the hands of something out of a horror movie. If not for the footage that was transmitted back to the corporation, no one would believe a word he said.

"Spectre 1 to base. Over."

"Base, go ahead, Spectre 1," a subdued voice responded.

"The entire recon team's been slaughtered! Did you see it?" the pilot screamed into his headset. "They were murdered by these ... these creatures. Oh, God, it was horrible." The pilot wept into his headset.

"Did you see anything else? Was anyone else there?" the voice over the radio asked.

"Who the hell would be out there? Of course no one saw," the pilot answered.

"Spectre 1, are you operating below surveillance altitude?"

"Yeah," the pilot lied. "I'm at 650 feet, in whisper mode and holding course southeast until check-point delta."

"Affirmative, Spectre 1, hold course and speed until checkpoint delta. Base out."

* * *

There were six men seated at the conference table, 80 floors above the Boston skyline overlooking Logan Airport and the waterfront. The man seated at the head of the table stood and walked over to a small wet bar. He poured himself a double scotch, inhaling the drink with one swallow. He paused momentarily as the booze burned its way down his throat and sat like acid in his stomach.

"Gentlemen, it appears we have ourselves a problem. I want every available resource we have studying the recordings we made tonight. Did we get the images from the pod cameras we put by the FLIR?" he asked.

"Yes, Mr. Pendelton, we have the visuals from the chopper as it circled away. The heat signatures didn't register on the Infrared FLIR though."

Richard Pendelton smiled a sadistic smile and walked over to a wall control panel. He took a card key from his suit pocket and slid it through the locking mechanism. A door panel opened revealing a flashing red button. "Contact the chopper."

"Spectre 1, come in," a man at the table called out.

"This is Spectre 1."

"Spectre 1, give us a detailed systems and equipment check," Pendelton ordered.

The pilot responded with various technical readings while Richard pressed the red button. The pilot's voice was suddenly panicked. He radioed that the aircraft was deviating from course, heading out toward the Atlantic.

"One less loose end for us to worry about," Richard remarked as he poured himself a brandy. "Okay, gentlemen, let's get down to business. We need to remove all traces from the site that could implicate us without getting anymore men killed. There are only so many disposable assets available."

* * *

The pilot struggled with the controls of his ship for almost forty minutes. He gave up trying to radio for help, the communications system board went black shortly after he'd lost control of the ship. The helicopter's dual turbine boosters had been engaged for nearly half an hour, moving the craft through the air at nearly 300 miles per hour, all but exhausting the craft's fuel supply.

The helicopter's sophisticated guidance chip relayed its position to a satellite in low orbit. The helicopter was now nearly eighty miles out over the vacant Atlantic Ocean. The pilot noticed that a red light on the navigational board began glowing.

A small pulse of energy traveled through the navigational console to a small package on the ship's underside fuel tank. The package was two bricks of C-4 explosive. The electric current contacted the charge. The ensuing detonation of C-4 and fuel vapor spewed bits of helicopter and pilot throughout the icy Atlantic Ocean.

Chapter 6

The phone woke Erik from his sleep. He was still groggy as he answered with a gravelly voiced hello.

Shanda was calling to check on him. She had come by Wednesday night for their dinner and was informed of the accident. Alissa escorted her to Erik's apartment where she had knocked several times to no avail. She then tried calling on Thursday.

"I'm so sorry," Erik exclaimed. "I cannot believe I slept through an entire freaking day! I only meant to sleep for a few hours, I didn't hear a thing."

He listened to her for a few moments, but was itchy to get out of bed and take a hot shower. His entire body was one big knotted muscle. Groggy eyes studied a small alarm clock.

"Can I make it up to you with lunch?" he asked. "It'll have to be for three, today is my day with Brianna. How about lunch here and gourmet ice cream for dessert, my treat of course."

"Excellent, I'll see you at my booth at noon."

Erik slowly made his way to the shower. He studied his body and face in the bathroom mirror. Eight deep claw marks ran across both pectoral muscles, and three deep cuts scarred his left cheek. Erik examined his battered hands. The skinned knuckles had scabbed over, and the swelling diminished in his fingers. Massive bruises covered both forearms from deflecting the creature's blows.

"What the hell were those things?" He stepped into the comforting stream of hot water. The steam and heat from the shower helped relieve the soreness and tightness in his muscles. He felt much better as he toweled himself off. Erik slipped into a faded pair of jeans and a V-neck T-shirt. He put on comfortable sneakers, grabbed his keys, and headed out for a light breakfast and a cup of coffee.

All through breakfast he brooded about Wednesday's confrontation. He battled something inhuman, possibly not even of this world. How could something so abnormal exist for so long undiscovered? If these creatures had been around for any great length of time, people would have known something. At the very least, there would be several missing persons reports or unsolved murder cases, based upon the creature's aggressive behavior. Once again, Erik felt there were missing facts. It was as if he were trying to solve a picture puzzle and several key pieces were missing.

No! These things were definitely predators. If they'd been around for any period of time, the police would have numerous missing persons reports and several grisly murders in the parklands. Erik had hunted and explored those woods for nearly a decade, and had never experienced an encounter like yesterday. Something happened in those woods, something recent. The answer was up there, on the mountain top, somewhere, waiting to be discovered.

The only problem was getting up the mountain without getting killed by the creatures that now inhabited the forest there. If these things were linked to Lisa Reynolds, they were not content staying in their little woodland habitat. If they fed on humans, they would come to where the humans are. Nobody would be safe. He knew these threats had to be destroyed before more people wound up missing or worse.

"How are you feeling?" a voice broke Erik from his deep thought.

Alissa stood over him with a steaming pot of coffee. She smiled shyly as she refilled his cup.

"I'm better, thank you."

She stared at the wound on his face, and then at the damage to his hands. "How does the other guy look?"

"I think I gave as good as I got," he answered evasively.

"I'll bet you did." Alissa reached over and gently touched his cheek where his flesh had been cut, and touched the large greenish-blue bruises on his forearms. "Be more careful next time, Erik, we can't afford to lose you."

Erik felt an unusual spark of electricity as she gently touched his cheek. "I will be." He watched her walk away, wondering exactly what she meant.

He gathered his keys and headed out toward his truck to pick up his daughter. He glanced back over at Alissa as she was busily gathering dishes as he headed out the door. She caught his look and smiled.

* * *

Erik pulled into the palatial gated community where his ex-wife and daughter lived. He always felt awkward here. His old Chevy 4X4 seemed out of place in a neighborhood littered with Mercedes, BMWs, and Jaguars. He parked his truck as close to the end of the driveway as possible and made the 100-foot walk to the front door. To his surprise, Margaret met him at the door.

"What on Earth happened to you?" she asked, studying his face and arms.

"Hazards of the woods," he relayed jokingly.

"She's running behind schedule," she announced, gesturing him inside.

"Nothing unusual about that," Erik answered.

"Erik, I hate to do this to you, but Brianna was invited to a pizza party at the park this afternoon."

"Oh?" Erik replied, waiting for the bomb to drop.

"It's her best friend Peggy's party and she really wants to go. Would it terribly ruin your time if she spent some time there today?"

The park, the place where Lisa Reynolds was abducted. Erik was reluctant to agree, and Margaret sensed it. "You realize that a girl is missing, and she was last seen at the park?"

"Yes," she replied quickly. "I read about it in the paper and it was on the local radio station. But, there'll be several parents there, other kids, and she'll have her father to watch her."

Erik smiled slightly at her. "I have some plans for the day. Bri and I will be having lunch and dessert with a friend of mine. If she really wants to go to her friend's shindig, I'll see if we can stop by later."

"Fair enough," Margaret replied.

As if on cue, Brianna sauntered down the stairs with her small suitcase. Erik was amazed at how much his daughter had grown over the past six months. She had her mother's rich tan skin, combined with his light blue eyes. She was truly becoming a beautiful young girl. He experienced a few guilt pangs about not seeing her as often as he'd like.

"Hi, Daddy!" she said with a beaming smile. She stopped and stared at the wounds on his face and arms. She wrinkled her face and commented. "I'll bet that hurts." She hugged him.

"Hey, Munchkin, are you all set?"

"Ready to go," she answered, already heading out the door.

Erik turned to Margaret, smiled, and followed his daughter out the door. "We'll see you tomorrow morning after breakfast."

* * *

Erik and Brianna spent two hours at the mall. Erik heeded Margaret's advice and took his daughter on a shopping spree with the money she'd returned to him. They were headed back to Madame's for lunch, when Brianna began hinting about her friend's gathering at the park.

"Did Mom tell you about the party this afternoon?" she asked in her best innocent little girl voice. Erik recognized the tone.

"Yes, your mother has done her best to lobby on your behalf."

Her face turned red and she grinned sheepishly.

"What time does the party start?" he asked.

"Around 3:30 or 4:00. But all the cool kids are going to show up earlier," she answered eagerly.

"Oh! I suppose that you'll want to be one of the cool kids."

"Daaaad," she whined in perfect teenage girl pitch.

"Fine, we'll go at three. Your mother expects me to be a doting parent, so I'll be loitering discretely." He paused momentarily. "I know it's not cool to have your parents hanging around, so I'll stay in the background as much as possible, but your mother wants me there."

"Okay," she agreed. "Just try not to embarrass me too much."

"Just for that, I'm going to wear a pink shirt and bow tie,"

Erik replied lightly.

"Yuck! Gross! Big fashion faux pas, Dad."

* * *

Erik and Brianna seated themselves in his usual booth in the back of the restaurant. They just settled themselves when Shanda walked in. Brianna greeted her with great enthusiasm. The two met several times and got along well. Brianna was discussing the party with Shanda and they rifled through her bags of new clothes. Shanda carefully studied each article of clothing and put together an outfit that the young girl hadn't considered. Both women disappeared into the ladies' room, Brianna talking excitedly as they walked, carrying her bags.

Erik smiled as he watched his daughter talk excitedly to Shanda. The fact that his daughter and his new romantic interest got along would make things easier. Erik took the liberty of ordering for everybody and casually sipped a glass of water.

Fifteen minutes passed. Brianna and Shanda still were not back from the ladies' room. Erik got up and headed toward his office in the back room. He went to his desk and unlocked a drawer. He took out a pistol case and placed it on his desk. The case contained his Ruger P-89 9mm auto pistol and leather holster.

Erik loaded one of the weapon's 15-round clips and slid it into the receiver on the weapon. He slid the barrel assembly back and let the spring-loaded action jump forward. The action grabbed the top bullet from the clip as it was propelled forward and loaded it into the weapon's muzzle. He activated the weapon's safety and slipped it into the leather holster. Erik clipped the holster onto the back of his jeans and belt.

He untucked his T-shirt and let it fall freely. The loose shirt hid the weapon effectively. He loaded the remaining clip and slipped in into his back pocket.

Erik figured he was overreacting, but Lisa Reynolds was taken from the park and he was unable to stop the creatures in their prior encounter. He wouldn't take any chances when it came to his daughter's safety. But deep down, he wondered if even 30 rounds would be enough against the things he had encountered. The detective hoped he wouldn't have to find out.

He walked back to his booth and had a surprise waiting for him. His pre-teen daughter had been transformed into a six-teen-year-old-looking cover girl. Shanda used her fashion sense to give his daughter a pre-party makeover. He sat across from the two, and they waited with anticipation for his comments.

"What happened to my baby girl?" he whispered. Brianna had been magically transformed from a little girl into a young woman. Erik peered behind the subtle make-up and clothing ensemble to see the little girl he knew behind this flashy new image.

"Do you like it, Daddy?" she asked.

"I like it, but I think it may be just a little too old for you just yet."

"Can I please keep it for the party? Everyone will flip when they see it."

"Right, and your mother will have my hide," Erik retorted lightly.

"Pleeeaaaaase," Brianna replied, using all the little girl charm she could muster.

Erik looked at Shanda momentarily. She gave him a quick wink and nod. "Fine, but right after the party, you get cleaned up, okay?"

"Deal! Daddy, you're the best," she gushed.

"Yeah, yeah, until your mother finds out and you sell me up the river," Erik replied as both Shanda and Brianna laughed.

* * *

The three arrived at the Hopedale Park at three o'clock sharp. Erik was amazed to see several ponies, two tables of catered food, and three people in clown attire.

"How the other half lives," he whispered to Shanda.

"Behave yourself, young man," she whispered back lightly.

They crossed the street and Brianna ran over to where her friends were gathering. Erik and Shanda could hear the other girls' screams of enthusiasm regarding Brianna's new look.

Erik chuckled. "You're a hit!"

"Her friends obviously have good taste," Shanda replied with no trace of modesty.

"Clearly," Erik agreed, trying not to laugh.

The two sat on a wooden bench on the opposite side of the park, Erik watching over his daughter like a brooding hawk watching a mouse in a field.

"Are you going to tell me what happened out there?" Shanda asked.

Erik took his gaze off his daughter and looked at her. "I'm not really sure. Even now it seems so farfetched I can hardly believe it."

"What, Erik? What happened?"

"Something's out there, up in those woods. I saw it, Steve saw it, something that isn't human, nor is it animal."

"Can you describe it?" Shanda asked intently.

"You can't really see it, not at first, it can hide itself somehow. But when it's close, the sun seems to fade and it gets chilly. It's black. Its body is as black as the darkest night. It's cold, and hard, almost like iron on a cold day. I ruined my knuckles exchanging pleasantries with it." He held up his hand. "I got the bruises on my forearms from blocking its punches. All I can say for sure is that it's sentient. When it held me, I could feel it looking at me, evaluating me for something. I could feel its hate and anger."

He paused, looking back over at his daughter who was playing happily with her friends. "I can only describe it as sentient evil."

"Can I share your experience?" she asked.

"No," he said firmly. "Believe me, you don't want those memories." He paused. "I don't want these memories." Erik stood and stretched.

He looked back at her with fear-filled eyes. "I hit that thing with dozens of rounds, punched and kicked it harder than I've ever hit anyone, even with my alternative strength, it still wasn't enough. Steve put eight rounds into it with that portable hand cannon he carries and it's still out there. Whether we hurt it or not, I really can't say for sure. I only know that we managed to piss it off a great deal, not like that's an accomplishment to brag about. That thing killed Andrew Henderson, a young jogger named Carol Carlin, and it could have killed us too if it wanted, picked us off as we retreated, but they just let us go."

"They?" she asked.

"Yeah, there was the one that I fought, and then there was this really big thing that arrived as we were heading back down the mountain. I think...." He paused and then turned away.

"You think what? Don't hold back, say what's on your mind," Shanda insisted.

"All right," Erik agreed reluctantly. "I have no proof, and no real rationale, but I believe that the creature we fought has something to do with the disappearance of Lisa Reynolds. I think that she's up there somewhere." He pointed to the large mountain that loomed in the background.

"I think that thing came here, using its cloaking ability and simply carried her off, and I have no clue as to why. There are too many unanswered questions, too many pieces of the puzzle still missing. Something happened up there that drew these things out. The answer is up there, somewhere. The key is getting there without those things interfering." Erik sat himself back down.

"Are you going back up there?"

"Nelson is coming back from New York in a few days. I'll meet with him and we'll decide the next course of action with the local authorities. I'm sure, after Steve's report, the police will want to be involved in the next step and probably the town officials. We need to keep people out of that area. There's no need to antagonize these creatures more than we already have at this point. These things have to be neutralized," he replied.

Erik and Shanda walked around the park hand in hand, enjoying each other's company and watching the girls take turns riding the ponies.

"She's really growing up," Erik commented as he watched his daughter riding one of the horses. "It seems like only yesterday, she was just a baby and now she's into makeup, fashionable clothes, and being embarrassed to be seen with her father," Erik observed with a note of sadness tinged in his voice.

"I think you're being pretty hard on yourself. She bragged about you non-stop while we were in the ladies' room. She thinks you're wonderful, Erik. She was bragging about how most of her friends have a dad who is always too busy with 'boring stuff,' but her dad is a real-life PI, doing exciting things, always there when she calls, and has an office less than ten minutes from her house.

"She sees all the good in you that you don't see in yourself. Brianna knows she can always talk to you and that you'll always be there for her no matter what. She knows that her dad loves her unconditionally, and that's very comforting for a kid," Shanda remarked.

"Thanks, I want her to have what I didn't growing up," Erik replied.

The couple continued watching Brianna and her friends for the next hour and a half, stealing an occasional kiss when the mood struck them. The ponies were getting restless, whinnying nervously. He watched with minor concern as the owner was struggling to control them.

"Erik!" Shanda whispered in alarm. "Something's here, stalking the girls. I can't see it, but I can sense it."

Erik looked throughout the park grounds, focusing his vision, but couldn't see anything. Fifty yards away, children played, unaware of anything but their innocent fun. Erik walked quickly over to the party, Shanda following close behind. As he closed the distance, he noticed his daughter staring at something and pointing. Erik looked in the direction she was pointing and saw a patch of darkness. His mind shrieked with panic and he ran toward his daughter, screaming for the other girls to leave the park area. The girls looked at the direction Brianna was pointing and froze. They were terrified, frozen into inaction.

After a quick sprint, Erik was beside his daughter. Several of the other mothers had gone to their children as they all pointed out the closing patch of darkness.

"Get your children back!" Erik commanded. "It wants your children."

Mothers and children were panicking. Children were crying with fright as the afternoon sun dimmed and the temperature dropped twenty degrees. Brianna hadn't moved since Erik came by her side.

"What do you see, honey?" he whispered.

Brianna's eyes were transfixed on the corner of the park, her finger still pointed in that direction. "It's a tall man, I think. I can tell he wants me. He's calling to me, Daddy. I'm scared. Please don't let him take me. I can tell he wants to take me." She screamed in mindless terror.

Erik reached behind his back and pulled his Ruger from its place of concealment. He wrapped both arms protectively around his daughter, his gun pointing in the direction of her finger.

"Bri, point me in the right direction. I won't let it hurt you. No one is taking you anywhere."

She gently guided his hands so that the pistol was aiming at the heart of the dark anomaly.

"Daddy," she whispered, "it's coming right for us."

"Go back with Shanda and the others, now!"

"Daddy, I don't want to leave you."

"Go, honey! Please," he whispered. "Shanda!" Erik shouted, breaking the eerie silence. "Take Brianna."

Shanda came up quickly and took Brianna. "I can just barely see it, Erik. It's just like you described. It stopped when you pulled the gun. All the children can see it, but the parents can't. All they can see is the darkness, and they can feel the cold."

From behind them, the ponies were shrieking in panic.

"All right, you two, get back!" Erik stood up. He holstered his weapon and began walking toward the darkness.

"I know you're there!" Erik called out to the inky darkness. "Maybe you can hide from them, but you can't hide from me!" Erik focused his eyes, concentrating his extra senses on the darkness as he continued forward. Slowly, he saw the man-like figure materialize. The figure stopped its approach and assumed an aggressive stance. Erik paused a scant twenty feet from it and assumed a basic combat stance he used in Kung Fu.

"You can't have the children!" he shouted, his voice booming above the silence, challenging the being of darkness. "You can't have my daughter or any other child here."

The thing responded with silence. Erik finally saw the blood-red eyes looking right through him. He could feel the hatred, the sheer malevolence. Yet, now he also felt desperation, a hunger beyond his ability to define. The hostility threatened to overwhelm him. Erik fought his own emotions, fought down his own fear and doubt. He knew he couldn't defeat this thing physically, but he would not let it have his daughter or any other child there, not while he drew breath.

It was then he felt another presence, something bigger. He glanced up into one of the massive oak trees and spotted the large creature he'd seen earlier. He slowly stepped back. Without warning, the red-eyed creature attacked. Erik barely had time to avoid the oncoming creature. He tucked his body low, dropping his center of gravity. As the creature collided with him, he used his leverage and the thing's forward momentum against it. Erik sprang up. His sudden action lifted the creature off the ground.

He utilized all of his strength and hefted the monster's bulk high into the air. He let the creature's momentum drive them both backward. At the last moment, before they both would topple over, he turned his body and slammed the creature into the ground as hard as he possibly could. The thing impacted the ground with a loud, sickening crunch. The momentum forced Erik forward. He dove over the creature and executed a forward roll, righting himself quickly.

Erik heard parents and children shrieking in raving terror and panic. He prepared himself for another onslaught. The creature stood, but very slowly.

The dark being shook off the powerful impact and gathered itself for another attack. It charged. Erik waited as the thing closed the gap between them. At the last moment, he leapt into the air, spinning his body and propelling his back leg forward with the motion of his upper torso. Erik roared like a lion as he utilized his enhanced strength, his rear leg shot forward as he finished his rotation and his foot collided with the creature's face. The impact was like a giant whip cracking. Erik fell back and landed on the soft sand. The force of his blow knocked the creature off of its feet, driving it several feet backward.

Erik looked over at his fallen adversary. Bright blue fluid flowed from its face. It picked itself up again, hissing angrily. Erik shook his head and began to rise as well. A wave of pain burned through his leg and he knew he'd strained his hamstring with that last maneuver. Erik knew his body was already overworked and stressed. His body ached from their earlier encounter. He was limping now, favoring his good leg.

The creature lumbered over to a section of broken chain link fence. It grabbed a steel post and with a primal screech, ripped the post from the earth and held the eight-foot steel pillar like a club.

Erik retreated slowly, freeing the Ruger auto pistol as he withdrew. He took careful aim at the creature's head, waiting for it to take another step forward.

"C'mon, you bastard, show me those eyes so I can park a bullet in each one of 'em," he whispered, locking the pistol's sights on the creature's head.

Erik spotted the other giant creature drop from the trees. Again, he heard loud shrieks and screams from the mothers and children behind him. The cloak of invisibility was finally lifted. Both of the monsters started to stalk him. Erik could see other spectators beyond the creature that could catch a stray bullet if he missed his targets. Erik adjusted his aim and fired a warning shot at the foot of the red-eyed creature. The sand in front of it exploded as the metal-jacketed slug impacted with the playground sand. The creatures paused, the larger one sniffed at the crater caused by the bullet's impact.

The larger creature stepped forward aggressively. Erik responded by emptying half of his clip into the creature. The beast roared in agony as bullets tore into its hide. This horror didn't have the armor plating the small one did. The larger creature stepped backward slowly, dripping a bright purple ichor where the bullets had embedded. It growled and hissed at him angrily, destroying a nearby steel slide with one swipe of its massive paw, but ceased its advance.

Erik could hear the whimpering of the children and mothers behind him. There was no possible way he could defeat both of these creatures alone. Oddly, he felt no fear. His body was calm, his thoughts extremely acute. His mind was calculating different tactics based on his remaining ammunition, potential vulnerable points and hand-to-hand techniques that could be applied in this no-win situation. He tried to formulate some kind of strategy, allowing most of the children to escape.

The sound of sirens caused the three combatants to pause. Erik stared at the creatures. He knew they could hear the sounds, whether or not they knew the significance of sirens remained to be seen.

"Here comes the calvary!" he shouted to the creatures as he continued pointing the barrel of his weapon at his inhuman adversaries.

Erik glanced toward the street and saw several officers heading toward the area from the parked squad cars. The smaller creature adjusted its hold on the steel post and hurled it toward him like a speeding missile. Erik couldn't simply duck the object because it could easily kill someone behind him. The detective dropped his gun and quickly side-stepped the speeding post. Before the steel and concrete missile could speed by him and strike a mother or child, he reached out and grabbed it with both his hands. The friction from grabbing the speeding object burned his palms. Erik leaned into the object and deflected it into the ground. He winced in pain from the friction burn as the searing heat shocked his body.

He quickly retrieved his weapon, and again looked at his inhuman adversaries. The creature stared at him long and hard, Erik felt hostility and hatred directed solely at him. This battle just became personal. His opponent was bigger than him, stronger than he was, and nearly unstoppable. Erik knew that he should be afraid, but for some reason, as he looked into himself, he found no fear. He'd meet these things again. Somehow, he was a part of something much older than himself or his species.

With a sudden icy gale, the two creatures dissipated into nothingness, absorbed by the blackness that brought them to the park. The police closed in on the area, weapons drawn. Erik quickly holstered his gun. He turned and saw Shanda and Brianna. The child was huddling inside her arms. Erik could see the tear streaks running down her face, ruining her makeup. She ran into her father's arms, weeping. Erik caught her, ignoring the pain in his leg while he held his daughter tight.

"It's okay, Munchkin, it's okay. They're gone now," he whispered into his daughter's ear as he held her tight, rocking her body as she continued to cry.

Erik looked over at Shanda, he could feel the tears flowing from his eyes, and could see her crying as well. Erik gently lifted Brianna, again ignoring the pain in his leg and walked over to Shanda. He gave the child one more hug, grateful they all pulled through unscathed. Shanda looked up at him, her own eyes wet with tears.

"You were absolutely incredible." She wrapped her arms around them both. "I've never been so scared in all my life," she whispered.

Before Shanda could say another word, grateful parents and children surrounded them. Erik accepted all the platitudes from the mothers and children, but wanted to get out of the park and to the relative security of his small apartment.

"Hey, hero! We need a statement," a familiar voice called out.

Erik turned and saw Steve making his way past the party guests. "Let's say that this was round two," Erik replied moodily as he shifted his daughter's weight to his other arm.

"Same thing as yesterday?" Steve asked.

"Yeah," Erik replied.

"How can you be so sure?" Steve pressed.

"One was tall, black armored flesh, bad attitude. The other was big, cat-like with green eyes," he replied. "I think that you've met the pair." Erik stared at the officer.

Steve nodded as he wrote things down in his notepad. "I just had to follow procedure, no need to get huffy."

"Those fucking things came for my daughter!" he swore angrily. "You'll excuse me if I take it a little personal and get a little pissed off!" Erik shot back in a voice seething with anger.

Shanda gently rubbed Erik's back, while he and the Hopedale officer continued to stare at each other.

"I'm sorry, Steve," Erik apologized. "I shouldn't be snapping at you. This one just hit a little too close to home."

"There's no need for an apology, my poor attempt at humor notwithstanding," Steve replied. "There's more to this, isn't there, Erik?" Steve probed. "They're not confining themselves simply to the woodlands. You were speculating earlier. I'm betting that you already have a working theory."

Erik wasn't in the mood for questions. "Breakfast tomorrow

at Madame's; you buy for all of us, and maybe we'll talk. Nelson will be back from New York in a day or two and we can plan our next step. I'd really like to know what they saw." Erik gestured toward the other mothers and children talking to the police.

"We've gotten several different stories, but they all have the same things in common: Darkness, a large cat-like dragon, and you fighting another man shrouded in black clothing." Steve paused. "The children, however, added something totally different, and their stories are all the same. They saw two monsters, with glowing eyes coming out of the darkness, coming to take them, and then you and one of the monsters squaring off in a fistfight and you shooting the larger thing." Steve paused. "With the exception of the feelings regarding abduction, the parents and children generally all say the same thing. It gives them a great deal of credibility."

"And what did you see?" Erik pressed the officer.

"Dissipating darkness, with two dark forms in the center. I'm afraid we arrived too late. Thank God one of the mothers had a cell phone. We were right on the next block."

"Amen to that," Erik replied. "There wasn't much more I could have done, Steve. You got here just in time."

"Don't sell yourself short, Erik. You saved a lot of people today, including your own daughter. We're a team. Nobody I know is keeping score, that's not why we both do what we do."

Erik gently put his daughter down. "You're right about that. We'll talk tomorrow. Right now, we're going home," Erik said as he put his arms around his daughter and Shanda, and painfully limped toward his truck.

Chapter 7

Erik, Brianna, and Shanda sat quietly in his booth at Madame's. Brianna sat between the two adults. There were lingering traces of fear in her eyes. Shanda could see that Erik was also disturbed. She sensed he wanted to talk, but not in front of Brianna. The young waitress that had brought her to Erik's apartment the other night was carefully watching them from behind the cash counter. Shanda met her stare, and the young girl simply smiled and turned back to her job at the counter.

She looked back over at Erik. He was slowly flexing his left hand. She noticed the big blister that had formed on his palm.

"Are you all right?" she whispered to Erik.

"Yeah, I'm just in some pain. I'm in no condition to go back into those woods. I personally don't think that anyone should go there anymore until we know what we're up against," he said moodily as he sipped a glass of water.

"I think you're right."

"The ironic thing is that the answers are up there. Eventually, one has to go where the answers are. We can't keep floundering around, reacting to these things. A way must be found to stop them." He rubbed the glass of ice water against the burn on his hand.

The dish of ice cream in front of Brianna had turned into a soupy mess. She had been very quiet since the events of the party. She continually leaned against her father's shoulder, and Erik would give her an assuring pat or hug.

"Erik, why don't we go back to your apartment? You look like you need to unwind."

Erik nodded as he and Brianna slid out of the booth. Erik was limping badly and Shanda could see blood soaking through his shirt. She knew that he had reopened his other wounds during his confrontation. As they headed out the door to his apartment, Shanda noticed that the young waitress was again watching Erik as he made his way out the door.

* * *

Erik sat on his couch, Brianna next to him. Shanda sat on the remaining small chair directly across from them. Brianna began asking her father several questions concerning the things she had seen. Erik was having a great deal of difficulty answering his daughter's questions.

"I really don't know, Munchkin," he began. "I really can't say what they were. I do think they live up on the mountain somewhere. I'm sure the authorities will take care of it. I don't think that they'll be popping up in the park anymore."

"Especially after the beating you gave it, Daddy." Her innocent voice beamed with pride.

"Nobody monkeys around with Daddy's little girl." He lightly kissed the top of her head. However, the look he gave Shanda was not nearly as convincing as his voice.

The three spent the evening playing several board games while watching Erik's small television. By the time the evening had come to a close and Erik had put Brianna to sleep in his room, she seemed to have recovered from her ordeal. It was very important for her to keep repeating that her father stopped the monsters.

"I hope she doesn't have any nightmares about that party, I know that I will," Erik said as he closed the door to his bedroom and sat back down on the couch.

"I still can't believe things such as that actually exist." Shanda moved over to the couch next to him. She gently lifted his shirt off his body to examine the cuts on his chest.

"We have to clean and redress these wounds before you get an infection." She helped him up and escorted him into the bathroom. She gathered some body wrap that Erik had in his medicine cabinet and some alcohol. "Run yourself a hot tub and soak for a while. You need to stretch your muscles."

Erik started the tub and grabbed a clean pair of sweat pants from a laundry bin. He walked back into the bathroom, which was filling with steam. Shanda had gathered bandages and burn cream and placed them on the small counter. Erik walked in behind her and kissed her gently on the cheek. She melted against him, resting her head back on his shoulder.

"I have never been so scared in all my life," she whispered as she held his arms tighter.

Erik looked down at her and smiled. "I'll let you in on a little secret, so was I."

"Yes, but you fought it to a stand-still and saved ten children including your own. You saved my life as well. I don't know how I can repay you for that. That's the second time you've saved my bacon from the frying pan."

"You're here with me now, that's all the payment I need," he whispered as he kissed her deeply.

* * *

Shanda sat in Erik's small living room watching television. Erik had been soaking in the tub for almost twenty minutes. She knew that soaking in the hot water was the best thing for him. She too was tired, emotionally drained from the afternoon. She had seen something truly horrible and her mind was having difficulty accepting it. She recalled how calm Erik had seemed. She remembered him addressing the darkness in a defiant tone.

You can't have my daughter!

She remembered Brianna whispering a continuous mantra as she held her.

It wants me, it wants me, it wants me.

She had repeated those words over and over, while her body convulsed with tremors of stark terror.

Erik emerged from the bathroom looking refreshed. He had re-wrapped his chest, and had another wrap around his right arm covering the large burn on his palm.

"Well." Erik seated himself on the sofa. "I almost feel human again." He looked at Shanda and adopted a serious expression. "Now you know what we faced up on the mountainside." He adjusted the tie on his black sweatpants.

"I'm still trying to get over the creepies," she responded with an involuntary shudder. "I don't know what to say, or even think. I've heard some of my customers talk about things like that existing ages ago, but I thought they were reading too many fairy tales."

"What worries me," Erik responded, "are there any more of these creatures up there? We can barely deal with the two we have now; say there were four, or six of those things running around up there. What if there are more of these things scattered around the countryside? We could be facing some real danger to the general populace." Erik leaned forward and reached inside a drawer on the small table at his side. He produced a small topographic map and unfolded it on the table surface. He was intently studying the Hopedale Mountain and surrounding areas.

"What are you looking for?" Shanda asked as she studied the map's details alongside him.

"A pattern, a clue – anything that might give me some rhyme or reason as to what triggered these things. I'm convinced that something happened high up on the mountain. Something had to change to draw these things down. The questions are what, why, and how? Anybody foolish enough to attempt going back up there will need the answers to those questions."

Before Shanda could reply, the telephone rang. Erik walked over to the phone in his kitchen and answered. Shanda tried not to eavesdrop, but it was impossible not to overhear the conversation in his small apartment. She could tell by his half of the dialogue that the caller was his ex-wife. Shanda knew that word of what had occurred must have made its way to her. She could imagine the woman's panic over not seeing her daughter, not knowing that she was safe.

"No, Margaret, that's not necessary. She's fast asleep now," Erik answered.

"Tell Richard not to come over here," Erik said forcefully.

"I'm not angry, I'm just tired. Look, she's sleeping. Picking her up now is crazy. Sleep is the best thing for her. I'm not going to wake her up." Erik paused.

"I don't know what they were. I'm working on that with the police. No, I'm not mad at you for suggesting the party. It's not your fault, Margaret, so don't go there. No one could possibly foresee something like this." Erik was silent for a few moments, grunting in agreement periodically. He looked over at Shanda and shrugged his shoulders. "Fine, I'll see you in the morning, about nine-thirty is fine. Good enough, goodbye." Erik hung up the phone and walked back to the couch and the map he had been studying.

"She just heard from one of the mothers at the party," Erik explained.

"I'm sure she was probably freaking out," Shanda replied.

"She blames herself for not being there," Erik said, studying the map intently.

"What could she have done if she had been there?"

Erik's eyes burned with intensity. "Probably die, along with everyone else, but I couldn't tell her that. I can't tell her this thing wanted our daughter for God only knows what. I've been lucky, twice, so far dealing with those things. If the police hadn't shown up when they did, we'd probably all be dead." Erik looked up at her, a flash of fear in his expression. "I can't watch over her twenty-four hours a day. If they come for her again, and I'm not there..." Erik hedged. "I don't know if lady luck will smile upon the same fool three times."

"What are you saying?" Shanda asked. "You came out on top out there. You saved all those people."

"This time, perhaps," he added moodily as he flexed the bicep in his right arm. "I got lucky. Even with my enhanced strength, it would have walked through me, given enough time."

"Erik, people make their own luck. Your skill and ability have been a counter for its super strength and rage. You were handicapped earlier. Would you have fought them the same way if Brianna and the other children weren't there?" Shanda asked.

Erik was silent, considering her words. He straightened up. His eyes opened wider. "No! I could have ducked that pole, and I would have emptied the other clip into the big thing, possibly killing it, but there were too many bystanders. I couldn't risk a full assault." He was silent again, and then smiled a half smile at her. "You're amazing, you know that? I never would have looked at it that way."

"That's because you're a male. Men think differently than women do. You're always so pessimistic," she added lightly as she kissed him. "You have a self-esteem problem, Mr. Knight. You need me more than you think." She giggled as she playfully tapped the side of his head.

"I guess I can live with that," he answered as he kissed her again.

* * *

Erik and Shanda said their goodnights at his door. Normally, he would walk her to her car, but the thought of leaving his sleeping daughter alone, even for a second, was unthinkable. He made his way back into his bedroom to check on Brianna. She was sleeping soundly. Erik quietly stepped out the door, leaving it wide open, should she awaken. He slowly eased his battered body down on his couch and quickly fell asleep.

* * *

He was floating in a purple mist, surrounded by dozens of strange beings. He knew he was on a battlefield. He could see beings fighting all around and above him. They were not human. The group he was with had shiny metallic skin, with blue pupiless eyes. The beings they were fighting were charcoal in color. He saw one approach where he was standing, and attack.

He raised his weapon to defend himself, and was stunned to see that he, too, had the silvery flesh of those around him. He fought almost without thought, as if his body were being controlled by something outside of himself. He was a passive observer, only watching his body perform as some other power controlled his every move. He fought with extreme skill and confidence of purpose, performing feats of skill and strength that he knew were humanly impossible.

His weapon was a long silvery staff. It seemed to be alive, knowing his every thought and intention. The weapon seemed to purr and moan during the combat, almost relishing the feel and heat of battle.

Then, the battle was over. Hundreds of dead on both sides littered the battlefield beneath the great mountain. The dark-skinned warriors were defeated. The survivors of their race were gathered and herded together like cattle.

He saw himself guarding one of the prisoners. He could experience the conflicting emotions that the creature he shared a body with was experiencing: Pain, sorrow, regret, and grim determination. The emotion was something so pure, so intense, that he knew it was beyond human capability.

The remnants of the defeated army were being forced into a large cave, they were shrieking in terror. He caught a glimpse of something already inside the cave, he could sense the thing was not happy being where it was. It wanted desperately to escape. The captives pleaded with their captors for mercy, the fear and dread so powerful that it registered overwhelmingly on his heightened senses.

As the last of the losing army was marshaled into the cave, he heard the screams grow louder, then the thundering boom of a gigantic door closing. As he walked away with the others, he felt the concussion of a cave in. The defeated army was entombed, alive, with some unspeakable horror that terrified them greatly.

* * *

He stood on the edge of a great cliff, overlooking a large newly-forged canyon, with others of his kind. The smell of the air was different to him, sweeter, less tainted. He was one among a sparse handful, the last of his race, he knew. They were all saddened by what they had done, and even sadder by what they must now do. They arrived to this world filled with hope, only to pollute it with their very existence. They did not belong. This world had made its own race. They were interfering in the natural progression. It could not be allowed.

It was then he noticed the device blinking several yards away from them. It began to blink faster and faster. He felt the fear and hesitation, then the searing heat and concussion of an explosion. The cliff they were standing on was blown apart. Those closest to the blast were killed by the force of the explosion, those further back plummeted into the depths of the great abyss to be buried by thousands of tons of dirt and rock, to remain an unknown, their passing marked by only one last act of great sacrifice.

Even as he fell to his death, he knew what they were doing was right. It was not their planet, their time had passed, it belonged to those others now, those things who hunted with sticks and spears, He knew they would evolve over the next million years, they were the rightful inheritors of this world. Interference from outside influence would destroy the natural progression. The germs they carried were deadly to his kind, and the diseases that his kind carried had destroyed several scores of native tribes. There was no way for the species to live together.

The Earth had planted her seed, and that seed bore fruit in these ape-like beings, not from their kind. They had left something of them-selves within that seed, among a few select primitives. A gift from one dying, aged race to another young race on the beginning of its journey, a gift out of necessity to assure that race's future and survival.

He felt somewhat better. 20,000 years was a short life, but long enough to witness the end of his home world and the end of his species. More than enough, he thought to himself, and as his body struck the rock floor, it was the last thought he would ever have.

* * *

Erik jumped up, wide-awake. His body was covered with sweat and he could feel his heart pounding inside his chest. He tried to recall the powerful images that had disturbed his slumber. He could only remember bits and pieces. He remembered the sensation of falling, of war, but little else. The vivid images from his subconscious dissipated from his waking mind like morn-ing dew under a summer sun. He shook his head, not compre-hending the eons-old genetic message placed there.

"Same stupid dream all the time," Erik muttered, falling back to sleep.

Chapter 8

Shanda walked into Madame's and spotted Erik, Brianna, and a police officer from yesterday afternoon seated at Erik's booth in the back of the restaurant. Erik looked tired, and she could sense, even from this distance, he was stressing over the events of the past week. Brianna spotted her at the door and waved. Erik looked up, saw her, and gestured for her to come over. She walked over and seated herself in the chair at the end of the booth table.

"We were expecting you," Erik said as she took off her jacket and draped it over the chair.

"I never miss a free meal," she commented in Steve's direction.

Steve laughed at her jibe. "Just don't drain my wallet too much. I'm a working stiff just like you guys."

Shanda placed her order and settled back in her chair. She felt something, a presence watching her. The same waitress from last night staring at her from the cash counter. When their eyes met, the young girl turned her head away.

"What's the deal with that girl at the counter?" Shanda asked, somewhat annoyed.

Erik looked over and saw Alissa. "Oh, that's Alissa. She's a special friend of mine. She waits on my clients and helps me out with miscellaneous things around the office. She's very shy and usually keeps pretty much to herself," Erik replied. "Why do you ask?"

"That's the second time I've caught her glaring in my direction."

"Don't worry about it, she's just curious." Erik placed his hand over hers. "She's really very nice, once you get to know her."

It was obvious they all met to discuss the events of yesterday

145

afternoon, but held off in the presence of Brianna. The young girl was busy with her favorite breakfast of blueberry pancakes and hickory smoked bacon. Jeff had fussily poured the pancake batter to resemble the outline of a kitten, and had arranged the bacon strips to form a bow tie. Brianna was carefully eating each ear piece in between nibbles of the bacon tie.

She was still very clingy, constantly looking up at Erik. The four sat exchanging mild conversation for the next fifteen minutes when Erik noticed Margaret and Richard enter the main dining area of the restaurant.

"Okay, Bri, Mom's here to pick you up. Should we have Alissa pack the rest for you to take home?" Erik asked.

"I don't wanna go, Dad," she exclaimed, her voice trembling. "I wanna stay with you."

"Honey, everything will be all right, I promise," Erik whispered into her ear. "I'll even stop by tonight to check on you."

"Do you promise?" she asked intently.

"Of course, silly. I'll be there, you just call me and let me know what time."

"All right," she answered reluctantly.

Alissa escorted Richard and Margaret over to his booth. Margaret rushed over and gave her daughter a huge hug. Her face spoke volumes of relief as she finally got the chance to hold her daughter.

"Oh, baby, I was so worried about you," Margaret said.

"I'm fine, Daddy took care of me an' my friends," Brianna answered.

Margaret looked up at her ex-husband with an expression of gratitude.

"What exactly happened, Erik? I've gotten three different accounts from three different mothers. Each story was more bizarre than the one before."

Erik glanced over at Steve, and he nodded his head. Alissa caught the signal and quickly distracted Brianna, leading the young girl toward the cash register and a variety of books and magazines that were always there.

Margaret and Richard pulled up chairs as Erik began his story. He went through some limited background of his earlier encounter at the Hopedale Mountain, and then described, in chilling detail, yesterday's encounter at the parklands. Margaret's face turned pale and she began trembling. Richard looked sick, but his eyes had an unusual fascinated, analytical look, almost as if he were making mental computations or notes to himself.

"That's it; I really don't know anything more. All I can tell you is that this battle between the two of us appeared to get personal yesterday. I could feel it with every fiber of my being. These things have some unknown agenda and we keep getting in the way," Erik commented sourly. "We're going to square off again, that thing and I," he stated ominously. "I don't know how I know that, but I just do, and the next time only one of us will be walking away. That much I know for sure." He flexed his bandaged hand. As he moved his fingers, the muscles in his forearm rippled.

"Brianna doesn't need a hero, she needs a father," Margaret commented. "Don't do anything else that will put you in more jeopardy, if not for your sake, then for your daughter's. Look at what that thing's done to you already. You look as though you've been through a war."

"It's because of Erik being involved, a hero, as you say, that your daughter is alive today, and nine other daughters and mothers as well," Shanda remarked with a tone that cracked like a whip.

Margaret looked as if the words were a slap in her face. She studied Shanda intently and Shanda returned her gaze with a look that could freeze a summer day.

"You're right, of course," Margaret admitted sheepishly. "I simply mean to say that it would be wise if Erik avoided that monstrosity in the future. If it's that hostile, then it's better to let the authorities deal with it, or somebody who's more qualified in this area."

"Right now, Mrs. Pendelton, your ex-husband is the expert. He's the only one who's been able to survive an encounter with these things, two encounters, actually. Somehow, he can see them and track them while we can't. He also has extensive knowledge of the woodlands in question. Nobody I know of has spent more time on the mountain than Erik. He is the qualified person in this area, the one that the local authorities will consult to handle this matter," Steve interjected.

"You're not helping me here, Steve," Erik groaned.

Margaret shook her head, and smiled a disarming smile. "Well, Erik, you are just the indispensable man today. You saved our daughter, Richard and I are grateful for that, but will your new friends be around for your daughter after you're six feet under the ground from playing hero with those godforsaken things?" she responded loud enough to silence the entire restaurant. She looked quickly around as the normal background conversation ceased. She became aware of the spectacle she was causing.

"You're making our own case for Richard being her legal guardian. You're still too wrapped up with being the hotshot and not the parent. Your male ego is writing checks your body can't cash. I know you all too well, you can't let this thing go unchallenged. You'll go out of your way looking for a rematch!" she added forcefully. "Reckless," she whispered angrily in a voice they could just barely hear.

Erik's face was red with anger. Shanda could see his muscles trembling. His grip on his water glass had increased drastically and she could hear the glass creak under the intense pressure. The glass shattered, spraying them with water. Erik looked up, his eyes filled with contempt.

"That's quite enough, lady. You've said your piece. You're making an ass of yourself, and embarrassing all of us to boot. Don't you ever judge me about the kind of parent I am or the work that I do. You lost that right when you walked out on me several years ago. Take your attitude and opinion out of my sight, right now," he spat with a voice thick with quiet rage.

Margaret was suddenly unsure of herself. She quietly grabbed her purse and headed out the door, taking their daughter as she left.

Richard looked at them uncomfortably, "I'd like to hear more, really." He glanced toward the door and then back at them. "Perhaps some other time." He quickly walked out the front door after his wife and step-daughter.

"Charming," Shanda commented to no one in particular, though in her mind she agreed with Erik's ex. He was in no shape to face these things again anytime soon.

"A pleasant way to start the morning off," Steve remarked as he dabbed at the stream of water with his cloth napkin.

"She is a beaut," Erik sighed as Alissa came over with a fresh glass of water and a sponge.

"Is she coming back?" Alissa whispered as she mopped up the water and carefully picked up the shards of broken glass.

"No, I don't think so. Hurricane Margaret only blows through once in a great while. Hopefully, she'll cool off in a little bit." Erik sat back down.

Steve picked at his eggs while Erik and Shanda stared into their food. No one could think of anything to say to move out of the awkward moment that occurred earlier. People were still staring and whispering at the three as they sat in relative silence.

"Have you heard anything from Nelson or Belechek?" Steve asked.

"No, not since he left for New York. I really can't plan anything until we can coordinate operations. What's the word with the local officials?" Erik responded.

"About what you'd expect: Argue, delay, cover up, and keep people out of the parklands. The Selectmen want a team of heavily armed police to sweep the area where we were attacked. They will have the 'Shoot to Kill' directive. Our town fathers want this threat eliminated as quickly and as quietly as possible, and before the fall elections," Steve replied heavily.

"So, basically, the Selectman are going on a 'fishing' expedition into the Hopedale Mountain, hoping to use officers as bait to draw these things out," Erik observed.

"Well," Steve answered defensively, "they didn't quite state it that way, but that's what it pretty much boils down to. I think they're hoping that we'll have enough combined firepower to put these things down for good."

"I don't think handguns are going to do the trick," Erik observed.

"Nor do I," Steve agreed. "We'll be breaking into the heavier weapons for this little foray."

"Just make sure you guys don't blow each other to kingdom come with your toys," Erik replied as he sipped from his fresh glass of water.

"That would sort of spoil the day, wouldn't it?" Steve stood up from the booth. "I'd love to share more of your charming company, my friend, but I have things to do today." He pulled a twenty and a ten from his wallet. "This should cover things here, let me know when you hear from the boys from Halls. I'm sure they're going to want in on the little upcoming trek back into the great outdoors." Steve turned and headed out the door.

Erik sighed heavily as he stacked the empty breakfast dishes and placed them at the corner of the table.

Shanda watched him. She could tell the confrontation with his ex-wife bothered him. She was reluctant to admit that she found herself in agreement with Margaret. Erik was a father, he had a responsibility to his daughter, more than the mere financial obligations, but an obligation to keep himself alive and reasonably out of harm's way. Shanda understood the risk associated with his profession, but the inherent risk of going back into those woods after what had happened earlier was more than risky – it bordered on foolhardy. She wanted to say something to him, but she was afraid of even broaching the subject.

"I'm sorry you had to sit through all that. Was it as ugly as it seemed to be?"

"Well, Erik, it's not often that you see dirty laundry aired like that in public."

"She doesn't understand," Erik said. "There's a certain amount of responsibility that comes with this job. My clients expect me to go to the edge for them; that's what they pay me for. If I start thinking about personal safety, I'll start hesitating and second-guessing myself. I'll lose my edge. I can't let that happen, not now, not ever."

Shanda didn't agree with him, but she had not come here to argue, just the opposite, in fact. She gently leaned over and kissed him deeply and took him by the hand. "We can discuss all of that later. Right now, I'm up for a little exercise, and you need a diversion from all this gloom."

"What did you have in mind?" Erik asked.

Shanda responded with a raised eyebrow. They walked out of Madame's arm and arm, heading toward his apartment, neither one noticing Alissa's intense stare burning into their backs as they left.

* * *

Erik awoke several hours later, feeling better than he had in quite a while. He could hear the even breathing next to him, which told him that Shanda was still in a deep sleep. He kissed the nape of her neck, gently untangled their arms from each other, and quietly got out of bed. He tiptoed from his bedroom and carefully closed the door behind him. After a quick shower, he put on some comfortable jeans and a T-shirt. He sat on the couch in his living room and began disassembling and cleaning his pistol. The weapon was in several pieces when he heard a knock on his door.

"Erik, it's me, Jeff. Are you in there?"

Erik opened the door. "Jeff, is something wrong?"

"I just need to talk to you, can I come in?"

Erik stepped back and gestured toward the chair in his living room. "Sure, have a seat, what's on your mind?"

Jeff leaned himself forward and took a deep breath. "Erik, I've known you for almost seven years now. In all these years that you've lived here and run your business here, I've never interfered or questioned anything that you've done." Jeff exhaled and took another deep breath. "I'm breaking that today. I heard about what happened to you yesterday. Two of the women were in here from the party a few hours ago. They told me what happened, rather their daughters did."

Jeff paused, as if expecting Erik to reply. Erik was silent, so Jeff continued.

"Now I can understand why Margaret was so angry. Please tell me you don't actually plan on tangling with those devils again?"

"Actually, I had planned on going back in with the police and two agents from New York as soon as we can coordinate an operation," Erik answered in a flat tone.

"What are you thinking, man?" Jeff exploded. "Do you have a death wish?"

"I'm doing my job!" Erik responded forcefully.

"Your first job is to be 'Daddy' to that little ray of sunshine who comes in here every other Friday night and on Saturdays. She's your top priority, mister," Jeff shouted.

Erik stood up quickly, a storm of anger flashed across his face and his fists clenched tightly. "All right, Jeff, you just crossed the line, friend or no."

* * *

"Erik! No!" Shanda screamed as Erik made his way toward Jeff. Her words brought him to a sudden stop. "He's right," she whispered as she quickly stood between the two men. "Can't you see that we don't want you to get hurt any further? They won't care if you die up there. The only legacy you'll leave behind is a grieving daughter. Is that what you want?"

Tears flowed down her cheeks. "Margaret was right. I want more mornings like we just had, I want great nights and great days with you, for lots and lots of years to come. I want to see you grow old, watch Brianna grow up with you, not see a little girl placing flowers over a grave."

Shanda could sense Erik's thoughts, read his anger, sense the warrior's pride burning within him – the pride which compelled him to continue to fight no matter what the odds, the pride that would ultimately lead him to his death if unchecked.

"Let your love for Brianna, your love for me, be stronger than your warrior's pride," she whispered. "I know what you're feeling, Erik. I can feel it burning inside you. Your spirit demands satisfaction, it screams for a rematch despite the odds being so much against you. You know what we've shared, you can't hide your feelings from me." She stood by Jeff. "Let it go for once, Erik, walk away. Pride isn't worth dying for, not when you have so much to live for and lots of people who care about you."

Erik turned away and sat on the couch. He was quiet. Shanda could read the conflicting emotions coming from his mind as he came to grips with his ego. Erik Knight was a modern-day warrior, not only in is mind but in his actions. His body seemed to be bred for combat, it was what he excelled at above all else. The detective's whole life had been one continual battle; first for acceptance, then for survival in the military, and now for his very life and livelihood. Shanda knew what she was asking of him was contrary to his nature.

"Think about it, babe, is this worth dying over and leaving Brianna and me alone?" she asked softly.

Erik was silent for several seconds. He looked up at her, his face calmer. "You guys are right, of course. I guess I got carried away with being the center of attention, the 'Go to guy.' I forgot what was really important. I'll tell Nelson I'm not going back up there. I've done all that I can do. I have my daughter, a new love in my life, and good friends." He looked over at Jeff. "Besides, I'm not that anxious to tangle with those things anyway, I'll let Steve and the boys in blue blast them with their heavy artillery, I've got better things to do."

Shanda sat next to him and enfolded him in a tender embrace. "I know what that took and I'll reward you later," she whispered as she kissed his lips tenderly.

"I apologize, Erik," Jeff began. "I didn't realize you had company. I'll let myself out."

"Jeff!" Erik called out.

The older man turned.

"Thank you," Erik said plainly, but with a deep tone.

"Someone's gotta make sure you keep that head screwed on right," he said, chuckling as he closed the door behind him.

* * *

Several more hours had passed when Erik and Shanda made their way into Madame's. The couple was still all smiles and arm in arm. Jeff assumed the young woman had given him his reward for abandoning the notion of pursuing the creatures.

Erik wordlessly grabbed a busboy cart and started clearing three nearby tables. He looked over at Jeff and nodded as he emptied the dirty dishes on the carousel. Jeff definitely saw a spring in Erik's step that had been missing for quite a long time. Erik walked back over to his booth and sat next to his new girlfriend. Jeff continued to watch the two from his hidden vantage point. They were laughing, holding hands, and staring into each other's eyes, too busy to notice the stares from the young waitress by the cash register.

* * *

Jeff walked over to the counter where Alissa was eyeballing Erik and Shanda. "They make a cute couple, don't you think?" Jeff commented as Alissa broke her gaze.

"I suppose so," she remarked, "but she'll distract him from what he has to do," she concluded mysteriously.

"And what, pray tell, would that be?" Jeff asked, suddenly curious.

Alissa looked directly into his eyes, her dark blue eyes flashing momentarily. "It's not the right time yet, but when it is, he'll know what to do, I hope." She shrugged, and then quietly went back to her work at the counter.

"You're spookin' me, little lady, and we've had enough of that in this town for quite a while," Jeff remarked as he walked away.

Alissa watched Jeff disappear into the back room. "You're wrong, the real horror hasn't even begun," she whispered looking back over at Erik and Shanda.

"I never expected to meet all my family in one place. They were very smart in their planning. How could they have known and planned so well?" Alissa remarked as she continued to gaze at the couple.

* * *

Erik pulled into his ex-wife's driveway and made his way to the door. He rang the bell and waited. Margaret opened the door, her jaw dropped with surprise and she immediately began to look uncomfortable. Erik decided his best course of action was to head her off before she could start again.

"Before you say anything, you were right this morning and I was wrong." Erik knew the best way to head Margaret off was by conceding defeat immediately. "Brianna comes first. They'll be going in without me, whenever they decide to go back," he blurted out quickly.

Margaret took a step back and motioned him inside. "I'm glad you reconsidered." She paused and cleared her throat. "Erik, let me apologize for causing such a scene this morning. I don't know what came over me. The thought of you back out there, possibly dying...." She hesitated. "Even though we're divorced, well, it doesn't mean that I don't...." She faltered again, struggling to get her words out.

"I understand," Erik replied. "And thank you."

Margaret blushed and hugged him awkwardly. "Again, I'm sorry for causing a scene in front of your friends," she said as she pulled herself back. "Can I ask what changed your mind? You seemed dead set to go ahead this morning."

Erik smiled at her, a genuine smile of warmth. "My friends convinced me they would rather have me around than visit my headstone at a cemetery. They also suggested the Munchkin deserved to have her dad around, living, even though he can be pig-headed at times."

"It's good you have friends that care. Listen to them, you'll probably live longer," she added lightly.

"Indeed," Erik remarked, staring up the large wooden staircase.

"Go on up, she's been expecting you," Margaret remarked as she looked up the spacious stairwell.

Erik nodded and quickly headed up the stairs. He walked down the 40-foot foyer, noting the second-floor hallway had more square footage than his entire apartment. He heard the sound of a radio blaring, and knocked on the last doorway.

"Coming," a voice answered.

The door opened slowly and Brianna popped her head outside. When she saw her father, her eyes opened wide with delight.

"Hi, Daddy!" she exclaimed, jumping into his arms.

"Hey, Munchkin, whatcha' doin?" he asked as he carried her back into her room.

"Just hangin' around, listening to some music," she answered as she jumped from his arms and turned off her radio.

Erik took a few seconds to study his daughter's room. It was palatial. There were stuffed animals covering a queen-sized bed with brass head and footboards. Sitting on her desk was a state-of-the-art computer that put the one he used in his business to shame. Erik had to admit his daughter truly did have the best of everything here. Richard and Margaret provided her with anything a little girl could possibly dream of, and everything a blue-collar PI couldn't. He again felt a pang of guilt.

"Are you going to stake the house out tonight?" she asked eagerly. "Can I stay up with you?"

"I don't think a stakeout is needed, Bri, I came to tuck you in and make sure that the alarm is working," he answered as his eyes carefully surveyed the locks on her bedroom windows.

"But, Daddy, I don't want to sleep by myself, what if it comes back?" Her voice was suddenly laden with fear.

"It won't, honey, not here anyway."

"But I'm scared," she whispered.

Erik reached inside his shirt and pulled off his dog tags. "I'm going to tell you a little secret, about a time when I was scared. It was before you were born, I was in the jungles of Columbia and I got separated from my unit after a firefight. I was terrified. I squeezed these tags so tight, that I put a dent in this one. See the dent right here?" He held up the dented tag for her to inspect. "Whenever I felt the fear creeping back up on me, I would squeeze the tags and the fear would pass. After a few days, I found my unit and everything was all right again. But from then on, even today, whenever I get the chills, I squeeze these tags, just like I did years ago, and the fear goes away." He placed the tags over her neck. "If you feel afraid, just squeeze the tags and your fear will go away too, just like it did for me."

Brianna held the tags in her hands and looked at them as if they were more precious than gold. She squeezed the tags and smiled. "I think it's working," she whispered.

"Excellent, I knew it would."

"But, Daddy?" she asked suddenly. "What will you use?"

"Daddy will get by for a few nights without it, you need them more than I do right now."

Her little smile was like a warm ray of sunshine.

Erik spent another thirty minutes with his daughter and then headed back home. He performed one quick sweep of the home's perimeter before he left. Hopefully, his daughter would sleep and not be plagued by nightmares from the hideous ordeals of the day before. Those kinds of horrors were for adults to deal with, not children. All that remained was to tell Nelson that he was off the case, and he couldn't do that until he was contacted. Until then, he had an entire evening to devote to Shanda, and he intended to make the most of it.

Chapter 9

Erik yawned as he bussed the dishes from another table. Shanda had reluctantly left early in the morning to get a fresh change of clothes and check on her business. They had been out late and stayed up even later. He was paying for it now. He had been bussing and waiting tables for almost five hours, and was literally dead on his feet. What he needed more than anything now was a long sleep. Erik discarded his apron and hair net and headed back into his office. He was about to lie down on his couch and sleep, when he heard a knock on his door.

"Who is it?" he asked wearily.

"Alissa."

"Alissa, what's up?" he asked, not bothering to get up from the couch.

"A Mr. Nelson is here to see you. Should I have him come back later?"

Erik stood and opened the door. "No, I'll deal with this now. Could you please have him come back here? And could I impose on you for a fresh pot of coffee? My eyes feel like they're made of sand paper right now."

"I'll take care of it," she assured him.

Erik did his best to snap himself out of the fog he was in. He knew Nelson would be angry with him for pulling out now, but there was no more choice for him in the matter.

Erik heard Nelson and Alissa walking down the hallway. Nelson followed her in and sat on the small couch opposite where Erik was now sitting. Alissa silently poured each man a cup of coffee.

"Will there be anything else?" she asked Erik in a professional manner.

"No, Alissa, that should do, and thank you again."

159

Alissa smiled and nodded, closing the door behind her as she stepped into the hallway.

Erik studied the older man sitting across from him. He too looked tired, but there was something more. Nelson looked defeated. Erik had seen that look in men before. It didn't fit with Nelson's character.

"I take it you have news," Erik began.

"Yes, and none of it good." Nelson sighed. "I spoke with the Reynolds yesterday. They've decided to let the local authorities take the lead in the investigation. We've been side-lined. I spoke with the chief of police and three town officials this morning and they're leading a force into the woods tomorrow with some local police and reservists from the National Guard. They're bringing in some pretty heavy weapons, M-16s, M-60s, and some other munitions. They're on a mission to exterminate those things, and they said civilians would only be in the way," Nelson remarked as he sipped the steaming mug of coffee.

"Where does that leave us?" Erik asked, doing his best to hide his relief.

"It leaves us running the command post if you're up for being out of the action," Nelson answered.

"Being out of the action is just what I want right now," Erik answered.

"I figured as much, considering what I was told you encountered a few days ago," Nelson replied.

"You heard!" Erik said, surprised.

"Yeah, I got the low down from that cop you're friendly with this morning. He was kind enough to let me read the report he filed," Nelson answered. "That was pretty gutsy, Erik."

"That thing wanted my daughter, that was only going to happen over my dead body." Erik took another sip from his coffee cup. "I do know one thing: These creatures are intelligent and sentient. That one with the red eyes, there's a malevolence there that I've never felt. It's beyond human. They're a part of something that happened here that we can't even begin to understand," he added moodily. Erik suddenly changed his tone. "But, with any luck, by the end of the day tomorrow, they'll be scattered in little pieces across the forest floor."

"Let's hope so," Nelson agreed. "So, I'll see you around

9:00 sharp at the same place as before?"

Erik nodded. "Yeah, I'll be there. We'll see if we can't keep these guys from blowing a hole in each other's head." Erik drained the last of his coffee.

"One thing has been confirmed though, which you were right about all along, I might add," Nelson grumbled as he headed to the door.

"And that is?" Erik replied.

"Based on the events at the park, those things took Lisa Reynolds, and they're after other children for some reason. Whatever the reason is, it can't be anything good." The elder detective adjusted his long trench coat. He paused, reaching inside for a folded binder of papers. He casually tossed the papers on the nearby table, "Here's some light reading."

"What is this?" Erik asked as he eyeballed the documents.

"It's your copy of the lab report on the blood samples we took," Nelson answered. "I turned a copy over to the boys in blue. It makes for some good reading, if you like science fiction."

"Give me the *Readers Digest* version," Erik walked over to pick up the papers.

"Sulfur-based bio-organic compounds, unconventional DNA helicons, and a whole bunch of other tech jargon right outta *Star Trek*. The bottom line is, these things are contradictory to every other natural life form that's developed on this planet," he remarked.

Erik picked up the papers and began scanning the report. "If this is accurate, one must assume that these life forms originated elsewhere, or took a completely different evolutionary path, right down to the basic fundamental building blocks of life as we understand them," Erik observed. "I think it highly unlikely that a sulfur-based life form could have developed in a carbon-based environment such as we have on Earth," he added, scratching an unshaven cheek. "This could possibly be a reason that our weapons weren't completely effective. Our bullet weapons are designed to kill life as we know it, based on high-impact shock on a central nervous system, they may not be effective against these creatures, no matter how much power the projectiles have.

"Look at lobsters, they're exoskeleton creatures and they have a simple, almost primitive, nervous system. They don't register pain and shock like we do. What if that black creature is similar to a lobster?" Erik asked while already contemplating the question. "If these things don't have a highly developed nervous system that transmits pain or shock, guns would be of little use. Our weapons certainly didn't do too much to stop them."

Nelson nodded in agreement. "If these things can't be harmed by conventional means, somebody had better find something unconventional and pretty damn fast," Nelson added as he turned toward the door. "Our friends may be in for a nasty surprise when they tangle with these creatures, but they can't say I didn't warn 'em." Nelson headed down the hallway.

Erik closed the door and locked it. He headed toward his long couch and flopped down on the oversized cushion. A slight wave of discomfort shot from his hamstring, and there was a sudden tightness in his chest from his wounds. His body was quickly approaching the end of its endurance. He wanted to study the lab report in greater detail, but was simply too tired. Erik closed his eyes, and blissfully surrendered to the onrush of blackness that overtook him.

"When I wake up," he mumbled to himself as the report fell from his hands to the floor.

* * *

It was early Sunday afternoon, and Richard Pendelton found himself sitting in his boardroom facing his Board of Directors and Corporate Officers. He talked to them early yesterday afternoon and called this emergency meeting. He needed to share what he learned of the events that had transpired Friday, and more importantly, they needed to discuss how to deal with the investigation being conducted tomorrow around their tunnel site. If anyone made it to the site, especially law enforcement officials, they could link Pendelcorp to those creatures due to the hardware and tunneling equipment now abandoned there. Richard had spent an hour briefing the board and officers about his per chance run in with Erik Knight and what he'd learned from that conversation, plus he passed on the operation plans for Monday morning, which he received from his paid mole in the police department.

"The bottom line, gentlemen," Richard concluded, "is this: Do we try to get up there today and remove all traces of our equipment, both inside and outside of the tunnel?"

A board member squirmed. "We've tried that already and it's cost us five more specialists," he reminded the men. "If we send more men and more equipment, we risk incriminating ourselves even further, and leaving behind more bodies. Each of those men that died up there had some sort of identification on their persons. In order to assure a complete cover up, each body would have to be checked and all forms of identification removed." He paused, sipping his glass of imported sherry. "But then there is still the possibility of dental record identification or other means such as finger printing or any of the other dozen means, which we're probably not even aware," he concluded. "Or," the board member amended, "we dispose of the bodies completely, incinerate them, leaving only the hardware issues."

"Excellent points, Conrad," Richard remarked. He realized Conrad was probably the slickest operator of all the men here, and Richard needed to utilize those qualities if he wanted to keep his company afloat for more than the next forty-eight hours. "I assume you have a deeper insight to this ugly predicament in which we find ourselves?"

Conrad smiled a Cheshire Cat smile as he placed his drink back on the table. "That's what you pay me for." He produced a thin bound document from his briefcase and placed it on the large conference table. "We've managed to translate some small portion of the writing that our recon team photographed. Most of it is unlike anything we've ever seen before, but our computers could translate small pieces. The rest, we will probably never be able to interpret." He handed the report to Pendelton. "It seems we inadvertently opened a prison vault and freed, what I can only assume, were the jail keepers." The room broke into silence as Conrad began the story that was told in the ancient writings that the doomed expedition recorded and sent back for analysis.

"We broke into some kind of prison, near as we can interpret. The skeletons we saw in the pictures were remnants of those being jailed." He sipped his sherry. "What we freed were the creatures used to keep those jailed in their confinement. There were two dominant symbols. We can only assume that these symbols represented two races. From what we can gather, there was some sort of war, although we couldn't translate the phrase used correctly. Conflict is the synonym our computer chose. The losers of that war were imprisoned. We have no idea what happened to the winners of the conflict. I'm sure the data is there, we just lack the capability to interpret it. As far as our scientists can tell, what we translated was left in a language we could decipher, based on elementary mathematics, intentionally, as a deliberate warning not to tamper." Conrad drew in a deep breath. "Now, for some bad news. The metallic readings our initial instrument surveys detected were simply the vault that imprisoned them. The instrument readings the team recorded matched the recordings of our preliminary readings almost 100 percent. Simply put, there are no vast mineral deposits, no fortune in gold, or deposits of rare elements. The only value that exists is the metal used in that massive tomb."

Richard felt his heart sink. "But all those readings our geologists swore were precious metals, how could they be wrong?"

"The metals and minerals are there," Conrad answered with an ironic lilt to his voice. "They're all incorporated into the shell of the tomb, part of its alloy, the other parts our instruments can't decipher. Other mineral readings could be false echoes or from metallic objects inside the tomb itself, we just don't know at this point. The instruments picked up what they were programmed to pick up. They weren't programmed to detect alien metals, so they only picked up the native metallic compounds within the alloy and whatever was inside the tomb itself.

"The bottom line is simple: We can't mine the prison vault. We don't have that capability to extract the metals from the alien alloy. Even if we could, any attempt to remove pieces of the chamber would most likely cause a cave in nearly half a mile long which would change the landscape, not to mention kill any miners inside the tunnel. This would no doubt attract undue attention. We've wasted hundreds of thousands of dollars in shareholder equity undertaking this effort, and several lives, not to mention a multi-million-dollar argon laser platform that we can't afford to replace, and at present have no way to recover. This project is a debacle, gentlemen."

The room was silent as each board member and officer digested the contents of what was just said. Richard detected several hostile glares from other members of the board and corporate officers. He met their gazes, each one of them. Richard had to respond, quickly.

"Now is not the time to assign blame, gentlemen, all of our signatures were on the approval documents for this undertaking. No one man alone can shoulder all the responsibility for this. We are all at fault, just as we would all have shared in the profits had this undertaking borne fruit. What's imperative now is a decisive course of action to limit the damage already done," he cautioned his staff. "You still haven't given us a solution, Mr. Conrad. You have the look of a man with a scheme, would you care to share with the rest of us?"

Conrad stood and placed both his hands on the table. "Gentlemen, the solution to this problem is already in place, up on that mountain. The very monsters themselves," he said in an amused tone. "We don't have to do anything. Those poor bastards will never make it to the tunnel site. From what we've seen in the police reports, only Mr. Knight can detect these creatures, the other people who've encountered these things could neither see nor hear them until it was too late, again, according to the reports that were filed. Richard, you yourself said that your wife and Knight's friends convinced him not to venture back up onto the mountain. I imagine the young girl you say he's hooked up with did some fair convincing of her own."

The board sneered and chuckled as Conrad continued.

"All we do is sit back and watch the impending disaster unfold before us," he added. "The cops and the jarheads won't have any more luck than Knight and the operatives from Halls Agency did. These creatures have staked out that territory, according to the data we have from Knight and the police. Monday's excursion into that area is nothing short of a suicide run.

All they'll succeed in doing is adding to the body count," he concluded.

"What if you're wrong, Conrad? If we do nothing and they manage to get up there, we're all done for," a board member challenged.

"If they make it up there, we deny everything, we can bottleneck any litigation for years. We'll claim these men did what they did of their own volition. It's easy to blame a corpse." The man snickered. "They never have too much to say in their own defense," Conrad added with a voice that chilled every person in the room. "We'll monitor the frequencies they're utilizing. Our stooge on the force can give us that information. All we have to do is sit by and listen to the massacre as it happens. It should be quite entertaining."

"I still say that we should do something!" Pendelton's CFO remarked, "If there's even the slightest possibility that tomorrow's mission has any chance of success, we need to have some plan of action in place."

Conrad shook his head in disagreement. "C'mon, man, you've seen the footage we shot of those things, read the reports and analysis from our technicians. You've been given copies of the police reports from the Hopedale Mountain incident and the encounter at the park. The people going out there tomorrow have no chance. The only ones who don't believe that will be dead by the end of the day tomorrow." He drained his glass of sherry. "Besides, there isn't enough time to do anything anyway. Any attempts to infiltrate our campsite would probably end in the same kind of disaster."

The room intensified with debate as board members and corporate officers began arguing and debating amongst themselves. Conrad's opinion had clearly polarized the group. Richard allowed the discussion to continue for another twenty minutes, allowing his executives time to voice their concerns, or add insight to this situation. As the discussion evolved, more and more members were swayed to the 'Do Nothing/ Deny Everything' option proposed by Conrad. Richard had to privately agree, that was the only viable alternative at the moment. They could, in fact, do nothing. Eighteen hours was not enough time to put together a reconnaissance team and gather the additional equipment that a team would need. "Okay, gentlemen, it's time for a decision. Do we adopt plan D.N.D.E?" he asked the people in the room. Richard watched as, one by one, each member agreed to the proposed Do Nothing option.

"Good," he began. "We sit back and hope for the worst. I'll have my administrative assistant prepare a list of items that are up at the sight, and we'll prepare a bogus back dated theft report to submit, just in case. It will give us some more concrete 'Plausible Deniability' and allow us to recoup the bulk of our hardware losses through our insurance binder. If we're going to play this game, we may as well play it right," Richard added as he concluded the meeting.

The board members and officers gathered their materials and began leaving the room. Richard motioned for Conrad to stay behind. Conrad nodded and sat on a large well-padded chair facing the picture window overlooking the scenic Boston waterfront. Richard poured himself another drink and sat next to Conrad.

"Do you really think this option will pan out?" Richard asked.

"With Knight out of the picture, I have no doubt tomorrow will prove to be a complete disaster," Conrad replied in a voice booming with confidence. "Based on the video of these things, there's no way to see or hear them, unless they want to be seen or heard. Knight has some sixth sense or something that allowed him to detect these things. Without that equalizer, the men going into the woodlands will be both deaf and blind."

Richard nodded as both men watched a 757 jetliner land at Logan Airport through the large plate glass window on the high rise. "Have our people learned anything more about Knight, who his employers are? Whom he associates with?" Richard asked.

"It's different than it was six years ago. Knight keeps a very low profile. We know he's done some work for a high-powered law firm in Boston, Denton, Marks & Priscoli, but our operatives can't get anywhere near the firm. We know Knight has dealt specifically with Denton, the senior-most partner in the firm. We can only assume that Knight is privy to some heavy casework based on that relationship. Denton is a dangerous foe, nobody who goes up against him ever walks away unscathed. I strongly advise that we not poke around this particular relationship. They have some very experienced talent in that firm. It'd be too risky to pursue any one individual. They're all corporate players. If we try to press one, they'll know about it that same day. The last thing we need is a lawsuit or a confrontation, and the bad press that would come from it.

"Most of his other case work is strictly small time, but totally on the level. It would be difficult to conduct any kind of smear campaign with what little we've gathered. Our friend Mr. Knight has been helping the poor and downtrodden for the past six years, barely making enough to get by. He has a history of paying bills late, but they do get paid. All of his clients, those which we spoke to, were very satisfied with the work he did. The only gray area is the Denton law firm, and that's a nut I don't think we'll ever be able to crack without serious repercussions," he added.

"Are we still tailing him?" Richard asked.

"We're trying," Conrad answered. "He has a knack for knowing when he's being followed. I've got to give the bastard credit, he's damn good at what he does," he said admiringly.

"Praise, from you, Conrad?"

"Know your enemy, Mr. Pendelton," Conrad countered quickly. "This isn't the same Erik Knight we tailed six years ago. The novice investigator is now a seasoned journeyman. He survived two encounters with those Hell-Beasts. That alone merits admiration. I can admire and respect my opponent, understanding Knight's strengths will help us find his weakness." Conrad chuckled. "We can partially blame ourselves for that, we helped forge the steel that made him what he is today," he added with an ironic lilt in his voice.

"What about the girl? What's he doing with her? I wouldn't think she'd be his type," Richard inquired.

"There's no real mystery there. She owns and operates a Newberry Comics franchise, does a marginal business. It appeals to the punk and off-beat, catering to the building counter-culture in today's youth. Her name is Shanda Kerwick, 31 years of age, born in Lancaster, Pennsylvania. She dropped out of college, B.U., her sophomore year to manage the store she now owns. Her academic performance was less than stellar. Someone close to her said that she'd been dating Knight on and off again, and then it went cold for some reason. An incident in her store several days ago pulled them together as a couple." Conrad studied a photograph of the young woman in question. "Despite the punk attire, she is quite good looking," he added with a dark tone to his voice.

Richard sat up suddenly. "Do you know what happened?"

"Yes," Conrad responded. "Two thugs accosted her, trying to force her to sell some questionable merchandise. She refused and things were beginning to get interesting. Mr. Knight was there, with a bouquet of expensive roses, our source claims. Knight eliminated the two men in a rather impressive display of physical unfriendliness. One of the men is still in the hospital with a shattered tibia and femur bone, as well as a broken nose."

Richard nodded as Conrad concluded his quick report. "Interesting, Mr. Knight has a steady girlfriend. That alone is a weakness we can exploit if needed. If we can't keep Mr. Knight out of my plans, I can use his relationship with Ms. Kerwick as leverage."

Conrad was confused. "I thought we just agreed that Mr. Knight was out of the picture?"

"He is," Richard replied. "I'm thinking of a more personal conflict I have with Mr. Knight. He and I share some things in common and I wish to put an end to that common tie," he said with a malicious grin. "But," he added, "one problem at a time, Mr. Conrad, one problem at a time." Richard looked over at his associate. Conrad was busy reviewing another stack of reports. "Something catch your interest?"

Conrad looked up from the bound document. "Yes, a theory from one of our younger scientists. I didn't have the time to read it earlier. His peers haven't clouded his thinking. He has a different theory about the prison we've unearthed. Based on his interpretation of the data and the correlated readings he presents here, he suggests that what we originally interpreted as a vast prison is actually a massive spacecraft. He claims that the sonar echoes give the tomb an almost perfect circular shape, with a flattened end. Which he proposes

houses the ship's propulsion systems. It's an interesting theory, based on what little data we've actually been able to interpret. Our readings on the metallic shell are dubious at best,
but there are definite traces of non-terran elements. Shit, we
can't translate ninety percent of the writing we've recorded.
It has no relation to any phonetic language in our known history." Conrad paused as he took a long drag from a cigarette.
"Could it be alien? Yes. Could it be a tomb? Yes. It could also
be both, or neither. We just don't have enough information,
and based on the events of the past few days, we're in no
position to gather any more."

Richard began to speculate, if this were in fact a ship, the
technological wonders inside its mineral-rich hull could advance science by hundreds of years. "If only we could find some
way to eliminate those things, or divert them long enough to
get a recon team in there," he speculated aloud.

"A difficult task," Conrad replied. "We're in a conservation
area to begin with, which will soon have police and soldiers
wandering through it, we have two unknown creatures that
have little to no regard for human life. We can only assume
that, once these creatures exterminate tomorrow's band of mer-
ry men, the area will be sealed off and quarantined." His eyes
lit up, as if something clicked inside of his mind. "We will eventually have to go back up there. Despite our bravado during
our meeting, there is, for all practical purposes, enough concrete evidence up there to implicate us. No matter how much
we deny or delay, if law enforcement officials make it to the site
we will be implicated.

"I'm sure those morons have dozens of papers and folders
with enough written documentation to build a credible case
against us. Those scientific types love to keep written journals. We're undoubtedly mentioned on some piece of paper
somewhere. When they fail tomorrow, a larger team of heavily
armed men will most likely descend upon the area. They will
have armor-piercing explosive weapons with the ability to destroy those creatures. Even if we deny and delay, the amount of
negative press the liberal *Boston Globe* would give us will cause
a certain amount of discomfort with our majority sharehold-
ers," Conrad remarked. "And, if any damaging documentation

is unearthed, we'll have a difficult time trying to spin or deflect blame off the corporation."

Richard nodded. "We need to keep our ears open. I want to know, by the minute, what happens tomorrow. If they do all get slaughtered, we need to prepare." A thought suddenly struck him, as if by divine inspiration. "I've got it." He slammed his fist down on the conference table. "We'll have to time it perfectly, assuming another wave goes in." Richard described his plan in great detail to Conrad. As Conrad heard the details, his shark-like grin grew and grew.

"I like it," Conrad complimented. "We may just be able to pull this off. Timing will be crucial, but it can be done. It all depends upon them failing tomorrow, and I assure you they will."

"Make the arrangements," Richard instructed.

* * *

Hopedale Mountain
Sunday night, 9:45 p.m.

The creature had tried feeding on the young girl again, but could get nothing more from her. It held her in its black claw, waiting for the traces of fear and panic, but they never came. It sensed her life signs, heard her shallow breathing, but instinctively knew she was no longer aware. It placed her back down in the corner where she had crawled earlier. It checked the bowl of murky water and observed some of the fetid liquid had been consumed. It knew that these ape-like things needed water and certain organic nutrients to live, as it needed strong emotions. It looked over at its large companion and communicated telepathically with its larger ally. The large felinoid creature growled. One could almost interpret the frustration and hunger in its primeval roar.

They would need to hunt again, they needed more of the small ones or they would be forced back into hibernation. They would hunt tomorrow night. The black-armored creature considered the human it fought earlier. He was different from the others. It sensed the presence of its ancient enemy, beings it fought eons ago. The creature also detected the same presence on the female that was with him. She too would be disposed of at the right time.

The creature remembered the great war 10,000 years ago; how they were created by the Seelak to eliminate the Esper race during the latter part of their war. The Seelak lost the war and they were ironically trapped with their own horrible creations. It remembered a bountiful feed for almost 50 years, and then eons of hibernation and imprisonment underneath millions of tons of rock and dirt, only to be freed into a different world, a world where simians were the dominant species, a food species they needed to prey upon in order to survive. If they could feed sufficiently, they would both return to their full strength, and then none of the strange things that spit fire could harm them. They would be untouchable, and they would reign supreme on an entire planet full of food, not the food they preferred, but food enough to keep them alive and strong.

It walked over to its nesting area and gently parted some of the debris used in its shelter. It gazed with some affection at the three onyx-colored stones that were its eggs. It could bring its offspring up in a world full of food. They would never know hunger or forced hibernation. The Espers were gone; the Seelak, their food source during their entombment, were gone. Now, there were only primates, and the Primate/Esper hybrid it fought earlier. The creature knew it would have to destroy that primate.

It absently brushed over an area on its chest cavity where a bullet hole was still healing. It would take the Espers' little one, draw it out into its territory, then rip the thing apart one piece at a time. True to its engineered genetic programming, the two creatures hated Espers. The creatures would make this new Esper hybrid pay for that hate. It carefully climbed into its nest. The felinoid came over and curled itself around the nest to keep it warm. The black-armored creature gently stroked the large cat creature and closed its blood-red eyes. Tomorrow, they would hunt and feed. Then they would be strong and the Esper would die, and this world would belong to them.

* * *

Madame's Restaurant
Monday Morning

Erik awoke early, he showered and changed quickly. He walked to his office and accessed his computer. The database queries he ran from the Smithsonian Historical Archives last night revealed no mention of any type of phenomenon remotely related to what was occurring now in Hopedale, or in the town's history. Erik figured these creatures just didn't magically appear. He felt that they had always been here but were dormant. Something triggered them, but he had no idea what. Again, the answers were up on the mountainside, not down here in the small town of Hopedale.

The detective picked up the lab report and glanced over the chemical breakdown of the blue liquid. Sulfur base with trace elements of salt, copper, and other substances that were unknown. The lab report really didn't tell them much of anything. It only confirmed what they had already surmised. These were two very unique creatures that probably didn't originate on this planet. How they got here, and more importantly, why they were here, were questions that needed to be answered. He realized they were questions that were going to be answered by somebody else. Erik wondered how the government officials were going to hush this up. The widespread panic that could ensue if this information was leaked to the public would be disastrous.

He wouldn't be a major player in the events occurring today, but somehow that no longer bothered him. Jeff and Shanda made him realize he had bigger responsibilities. He stared at the gun holster containing his twin 45 autos hanging inside his closet, and then reached for the Ruger P-89. He tucked the 9mm pistol in its small holster and placed it carefully on the back of his pants, and then let the tail of his jersey cover the weapon. He knew he wouldn't need the weapon. The only danger he'd be facing in the Command-and-Control Van would be the possibility of getting a paper cut. Still, Erik was a creature of habit, and this particular habit had been drilled into him for many years.

* * *

He finished his first cup of coffee when Alissa escorted Nelson and Belechek to his booth.

"Good morning, gentlemen," Erik greeted them as they sat themselves in the spacious booth.

"Good morning, Erik," Nelson replied.

Belechek grunted as he motioned for Alissa to pour him a cup of coffee.

"Belechek is not much of a morning person, as you can tell," Nelson remarked, covering for his associate's lack of grace.

"Who is, really?" Erik drained the last bit of cranberry juice from his glass.

"Did you get a chance to read over the lab reports?" Nelson inquired.

"Yes," Erik answered. "I studied them last night. There really isn't much there to draw conclusions upon. Sulfur-based organic compounds, unrecognizable DNA pattern, with only six pairs of chromosomes: It's almost as if these things are a genetically engineered combination from some nightmare. Without resorting to the little green men from Mars theory, I would say what we have is a non-terran life-form. How it got here, I have no idea. I'd also venture to guess that they've been dormant for a number of years, or else there would have been reports of such things within the history of this town. There isn't, of that much I'm sure." Erik paused, sipping from his coffee cup. "I'm going to assume these things have been dormant for several decades. I've run a database check into the earlier history of this town, back to Native American folklore, and nothing came up to match what we've experienced this past week. I'll keep looking. Maybe there are Indian legends or myths that may be similar. I'll also cross reference and index my search on a wider base, just in case this kind of thing is happening someplace else we don't know about."

"How do you have access to that kind of information so quickly?" Belechek asked.

Erik grinned. "My clients in Boston have access to several data sources. They have been kind enough to give me access to those sources whether I'm in their employ or not."

Nelson laughed as Belechek rolled his eyes upward. "Keep us up to date on whatever turns up. We'll be sending the Reynolds a bill for services rendered, and then the firm will cut you a check. You should have it by the middle of next week," the elder detective said with a note of finality.

"Fair enough." Erik glanced at his watch. "We've got 30 minutes before they go in. We may as well head to the vans and get set up."

Nelson nodded in agreement and the three men departed.

* * *

Monday morning 9:15 a.m.

The normally quiet road outside the Hopedale Park gate buzzed with activity. Three police officers and six men with automatic rifles were studying topographic maps laid out on the hood of a squad car. Erik, Nelson, and Belechek approached the men after a quick consultation inside the Halls mobile base of operations.

"Gentlemen," one soldier began, "I'm Captain Robinson. I'll be leading today's expedition into the target area."

The captain was a wiry man with a thin mustache. He stood just slightly under six feet, but had the typical military demeanor that made him appear to be at least six feet four inches or taller. The captain quickly made introductions to the other party members and began to outline his plan.

"We've highlighted the spots where the targets have been sighted earlier on the map here." The officer gestured toward three red circles on the map. "We'll move through these areas using a three-meter spread. I want the local officers on point with one of my men. They're carrying the heavy firepower, so stick with them, *close*. We have the benefit of a command-and-control van, synch up our frequencies with them and we'll each pick up a tracking chip, they'll be able to track each man electronically in case the worst occurs." Robinson looked up at Nelson. "Will somebody from your group be coming along?" Everyone glanced over at Erik.

"No, we'll let you gentlemen handle this one," Nelson

answered for him.

Robinson nodded. "All right, ten minutes, people. Let's get set up and loaded."

The group dispersed, the reservists huddled in one group, the police in another, and Erik with the Halls investigators. Erik was quick to note that Steve was among the officers heading back up the mountain. He made his way over to his friend.

"Good morning."

"And to you," Steve replied as he finished up his equipment check. "I see you're skipping out on the fun this time around. I really can't say I blame you."

"And what about you?" Erik replied. "You have two kids, a mortgage, car payments. Is this a risk you really want to take?" he asked quietly.

"No, it's not, but I chose to wear this badge, and I have to take everything that comes with it, both good and bad. I don't have to tell you, I know you understand that."

Erik felt a sharp pang of guilt, like he was abandoning his friend. Steve instantly read it on his face.

"Look, you did more than anyone can expect. You're not in the military anymore and you're not a cop. You don't even have to be here now. Erik, you've got more cuts and bruises on your body than any man should have. Let's face it, you're not up for another confrontation with these things. I won't lie to you though. I'd feel a hell of a lot better if you were up there covering my ass. You seem to be able to sniff these things out before they can get close. That would be a real asset," Steve commented.

"Be sensitive to noise, or the lack of it, and the temperature. If it starts to get cold, you know you're getting close," Erik advised his friend.

"How does that happen, how can they make the temperature drop?" Steve asked.

"Your guess is as good as mine, Steve. Just be careful," Erik cautioned.

"Don't worry, I plan to make it home this afternoon," Steve answered in a lighter tone. Both men clasped hands in a firm handshake and walked toward the small command post.

The group had assembled, all the equipment was dispersed,

and all radio frequencies checked and calibrated with the Halls control van. Erik watched with mixed emotion as Steve and the others dispersed into the Hopedale Parklands.

Erik studied the nine electronic blips superimposed on the large computerized satellite map of the Hopedale Parklands. Each blip represented one of the team members. He carefully marked and noted each section of parkland that the team covered, holding his breath as each report came in. He could hear the occasional radio chatter between each man as the group went beyond the marked park trails into the vast, unmarked forest.

"Base to Steve," Erik began utilizing Steve's unique radio frequency.

"Go ahead, Erik. Over," Steve replied.

"How does it look out there?" he questioned his friend.

* * *

Steve paused as he looked up at the forest canopy and heard the endless chatter of birds, squirrels, and insects. "It looks normal. We still have plenty of signs of wildlife, so I'm reasonably confident they're not in the immediate area. We're proceeding due west to the area where we had our last encounter. Over." Steve took one more look around, then paused to stare at the heavily armed man next to him. The M-60 he was carrying with the long feed clip of three-inch shells made the officer feel more confident about being out here than before.

The party continued to move due west, covering an eighteen-meter swatch of woods as they proceeded. Each police officer was paired with a more heavily armed reservist.

"Sir?" the reservist beside Steve began. "What were these things like, really?"

Steve studied his younger escort. He quickly noted that his companion was barely over nineteen years old, twenty-one maybe. His youthful face was unmarked by the lines and creases that affected his own features not too many years ago. Steve nodded and began to describe the creatures as best he could.

"It's a little difficult to say, the one I'm most familiar with is about seven feet tall, completely black, like the ink from a black

marker. Its eyes are red, a dark, almost blood-red. I don't think
it had any eyelids, because the whole time I was looking at it, it
never blinked, not even a single time. But there was something
in those eyes – wisdom, hatred, and a hunger that seemed to
just burn right through me. It's incredibly strong, stronger than
any man. It picked me up with one hand and held me immo-
bile, and I weigh in around 210 pounds. I remember Erik was
shooting at it continuously. I shot at it with my forty-four, and
it still lived. I'll never forget the icy grip of its claws around my
neck. I've never felt anything so blood-curdling in all my life. If
we find it, I hope we send them both to Hell.

"My friend fought it, hand to hand, both in here and at
the playground. Erik is probably the deadliest fighter I've ever
known, and he barely escaped with his life. He could tell you
more about them than me. The freakiest thing is, you can't really see them until they're right on top of you; and the cold – it
gets so damn cold whenever they're near." Steve shuddered.

"Boo!" a nearby voice shouted, causing Steve and the
young reservist to jump a good two feet.

The other men shared a good laugh at their expense as
they proceeded toward the foothills of the Hopedale Mountain.

"All right, people, can it. This ain't no picnic. Close it up
now, we can't afford to get our asses jumped by these things
out here. I want a two-by-two pattern," Robinson barked amidst
the laughter.

"Kaulfax," Robinson barked to one of his men.

"Sir!" the soldier responded crisply.

"You and Billy go ahead and do a 150-meter sweep. Keep
your radio keyed at all times. If you so much as see a fucking
mosquito flying the way it shouldn't, you let out a holler! Am I
clear, soldier?"

"Clear, sir," Kaulfax replied.

The group waited until the two soldiers took a lead 150
meters ahead. There was visible tension among the men until
Kaulfax radioed the all clear fifteen minutes later. The group
proceeded ahead carefully to rendezvous with the scouting
party.

The men proceeded this way for another two hours,
working their way through the woods and foothills, 150

meters at a time, with Kaulfax and Billy running a search sweep, then providing long-range cover as the rest of the group traversed the distance. It was not the most efficient way to travel, but it was the safest. Robinson knew Kaulfax felt at home in any kind of wilderness area, and Billy had spent two years in the South American jungles doing covert anti-drug operations. They were the two most experienced men, and seemed naturals to scout ahead for anything unusual.

Steve studied the area intently. He recognized a particular tree as the spot where Erik collapsed after his first battle with the creature. He walked over to the tree and could see traces of blood staining the bark.

"We were here," Steve pointed out. "Our first encounter was a half mile or so due west, up the mountain." He gestured up the gradually sloping incline.

Robinson studied the area carefully then motioned Steve to follow him. Both men walked a small distance from the others who were either drinking from their canteens or adjusting various belts and buckles on their gear.

"Can you take us to the spot where you two squared off with these things?" Robinson asked.

"I believe so. It's almost perfectly due west up the mountain. If we continue in a reasonably straight line, we should end up there in a little under thirty minutes or so," Steve answered.

He had to admit, deep down, that he really didn't want to go back up there. The horrors of that encounter were still too fresh in his mind. Robinson informed the command-and-control van of their intentions.

"Command Control, come in," Robinson said into his portable radio.

"Go ahead," Nelson answered.

"We're heading toward the hot spot up here. Do you have a positive fix on us?"

There were several seconds of silence before Nelson answered. "Affirmative, we have you all locked in." Nelson released an audible sigh. "Be damn careful up there, Captain."

"Roger that. Robinson out." He tucked his radio in his belt

pouch and walked back toward his men. Steve followed quietly behind.

"Okay, men, here's where it gets interesting. We're a scant half mile from the hot spot, everyone keep your eyes open. Billy, unlock the safety on that M-60. You see anything at all out of the ordinary, a dark shadow, a funny shape, unload at your discretion," Robinson instructed.

Billy nodded, quickly unlatched the safety from the large automatic rifle, and double-checked the bullet feed from the pouch on his back. "All hot, sir." he reported crisply.

Next to Billy, the remaining soldiers were getting themselves ready, going over their weapons one last time. Steve nervously checked the cylinder of his forty-four magnum, which seemed to pale in significance with the other heavy weaponry in his company. He spun the cylinder and quickly assured himself that each chamber had a good round. He flipped the cylinder back into the large pistol frame, placed the weapon back in its holster, and deliberately did not set the thumb break snap. If something happened, he would need every precious second. Steve glanced down at his left hip, assuring himself that the four Bianchi speed loaders were still on his equipment belt. He was as ready as he would ever be.

"Let's get to it," Robinson bellowed, causing the reservists to quickly fall in.

Steve watched apprehensively as Kaulfax and Billy melted into the woods for their next 150-meter scouting trip. Steve marveled at how the two men were able to move through the dense forest with barely a sound.

* * *

Phil Kaulfax stepped carefully around some briar patches, his eyes peeled for any unusual motion or phenomenon. He quickly glanced over at Billy, and gestured for him to proceed forward. Billy cautiously moved himself forward another twenty-five meters, scanning for any unusual disturbances. He found nothing. Billy motioned for Kaulfax to move forward to cover the next section. He would then follow to that point, which would finish the next twenty-five meters. He saw Kaulfax, moving like a forest ghost, making his way up and beyond his point. After they had completed 150 meters, they would radio back to Robinson, and the rest of the group would proceed forward while the two front men provided cover.

Kaulfax reached his position and suddenly froze. Billy watched, stunned, as a patch of darkness, darker than the deepest night, descended upon his partner from the trees above. The patch of darkness was nearly impenetrable and all consuming, covering everything as it fell from the treetops. Billy shouted out a warning as the spreading patch of inky-black darkness was swallowing up his partner.

Kaulfax raised his automatic rifle into the blackness and fired off several rounds. Billy screamed as he ran toward his partner, that was when he saw the giant feline head reach down from behind the cloud of darkness, and with a quick snap of its jaws, remove Kaulfax's rifle and both arms from his body. Kaulfax's shriek of pain and terror rang through the forest, which had suddenly become deathly silent. Billy took aim with his M-60 and unleashed an armor-piercing hailstorm upon the monstrosity inside the black. The M-60's muzzle spit fire and bullets, tearing into the creature, causing it to roar with distress and disappear back into the darkness. Billy continued firing into the inky blackness as he closed on Kaulfax's position.

When Billy arrived seconds later, the blackness was gone, along with his friend's weapon and upper limbs. Kaulfax's body was hemorrhaging blood, and he was already in shock. Billy screamed for assistance as he tried in vain to stop his friend from bleeding to death.

"Hang on, man, hang on," Billy whispered to his partner.

"Not like this," Kaulfax whimpered. "I don't want to go out like this."

* * *

The sound of heavy arms fire caused Robinson and the rest of his group to move forward quickly. He saw one of the soldiers firing his weapon into the forest, but he was too far away to make out the target. All he could see was the fiery muzzle flash from the M-60 as it sprayed hundreds of bullets into the forest.

It took the group 30 seconds to traverse the fifty yards. No one was prepared for the sight. Billy was sitting on the forest floor, covered in blood, holding the now dead body of Kaulfax, rocking the corpse back and forth.

"Five-meter defensive circle," Robinson barked.

Each man responded, forming a rough five-meter circle around Billy, their backs to him, weapons facing out, covering a full 360 degrees.

"Billy, what the fuck happened?" Robinson demanded.

Billy sat, staring down at the lifeless body of his friend, as the blood continued to pour from the tears in the body.

"Damn it, soldier, I asked you a question," the captain hollered, using his deepest military tone.

Billy gazed up at his CO through tear filled eyes. "Something came out of the darkness, and ate his gun and ate his arms. Snap! Just like that, and his arms were gone. He fired at it. He must've hit it. I let loose a hundred rounds into the darkness before it disappeared. It has to be dead, it has to be," Billy whispered staring back down at the body of his friend.

"Sir?" a soldier cried out in a sickened voice. "I think we've found his arms, sir."

Robinson closed his eyes for a moment, and then turned toward the soldier. The soldier was pointing some twenty meters out. He handed Robinson the binoculars, and Robinson panned the general area. Sure enough, he spotted both arms within a scant few feet of each other. Robinson felt the bile build up in his stomach, and quickly put the field glasses down. He pulled out a plastic trash bag from his pack and walked out of the defensive circle toward the limbs. He knelt over them and gently scooped the severed arms into the bag. Robinson looked out, peering into the woods.

"What in God's name could do this to a man?"

Robinson tucked the bag under his arm and lifted the muzzle of his M-16 as he stood. He carefully backed up toward his circle of waiting men, shifting the muzzle of his weapon from side to side, covering his retreat. Once back in the circle, Robinson placed the severed arms next to Kaulfax's body. Billy carefully placed the body and limbs in a thin body bag that was to be used for one of the creatures. He covered the bag with leaves and brush, and emptied a vial of sterile alcohol around the makeshift tomb to ward off any nosey animals until they could come back and move the body.

"I'll be back for you, bro, as soon as I put another hundred rounds into whatever killed you," Billy said to his departed friend. He cycled the M-60's firing chamber and re-activated the unit's battery pack. "Time to go hunting," he growled, heading back toward the other men.

Robinson had been conferring with the Halls Command-and-Control Van, and informed them of the loss of Kaulfax.

* * *

Erik was saddened to hear of the loss of the man, but relieved it wasn't Steve. Nelson and Erik pleaded with Robinson to withdraw, but the soldier insisted on continuing. Erik emphasized what anomalies to be aware of that would announce the creatures' presence.

"Be careful, Robinson, you don't know what you're dealing with," Erik urged.

"Pity you're not out here with us, expert!" Robinson chided Erik. "Maybe we could have saved the life of one of our men if you were here to sense these things!"

Erik's shoulders slumped, and Nelson saw the injured look in his eyes. Erik slowly keyed the mike. "I'm sorry, just be careful," he whispered

"We will," Robinson replied. "Robinson out."

Nelson stared at Erik, wanting to say something, anything to ease him through this difficult moment. "It's not your fault, Erik. Robinson's just letting off steam, he just lost a man. He didn't mean what he said, he spoke out of anger."

"Maybe so," Erik answered. "But he is right though, if I was out there, I could probably sense these things, maybe that man would still be alive."

"And maybe you'd be dead along with him," Nelson argued. "We don't have time for self-pity now. You're not at fault, believe it and move on. We need to monitor the situation even more closely. If you have any inkling of where these things could possibly be up there, you need to let these men know. Think, man!" Nelson urged.

Something struck Erik, something he saw all along, but just put into the front of his mind.

"Steve, come in. Over." Erik called.

"Yeah, Erik, go ahead."

"Steve, if you were a wild feline predator, where would you most likely be in order to ambush your prey, where would you hide, hoping not to be seen?" Erik asked.

There was a long silence as Steve considered the question.

"Look around you," Erik urged. "What's the best position to be in for an ambush?"

"Son of a bitch!" Steve swore, as he finally understood. "Thanks for the tip."

"No charge, amigo, just watch your butt!"

"Will do, out."

Erik looked over at Nelson. The older detective looked puzzled. Erik grinned. "The trees. Our feline creature is using the trees to hunt, just like any wild cat. It came down from the trees at the parkland, they came and went with Lisa Reynolds by utilizing the large oak trees," he guessed. "They have a screening capability, but the only way to carry somebody that distance without being seen, or seeing a disturbance, would have to be the trees. There's a complete network of 100 plus-foot trees between here and the Hopedale Park. Those trees could easily support a creature of that mass and magnitude. They took Lisa Reynolds from the park, carried her up the nearest tree, and carried her from the park utilizing those fucking massive oak trees. That's probably how her buttons fell off her shirt, the fabric got caught on a limb or branch and ripped off, and why nobody saw the darkness or the creatures or the girl after she was taken.

"We never look up. We don't expect anything to come at us from the trees. The cat is hunting us the same way we would hunt a deer; ambush from above, where your prey doesn't expect a threat to come from. There are hundreds, thousands, of those massive old oaks, a literal superhighway all throughout the town and in that mountain. They could travel virtually anywhere in town above the public fray," Erik guessed, not fully understanding the nature of the creatures or how they moved.

* * *

Billy took the lead, sweeping the barrel of his M-60 in a wide arc. Each man carefully looked above into the treetops, fearful of some black creature ambushing them from above.

After twenty minutes of travel, Billy paused. He knelt down and picked up a shiny object.

"Brass casing from a 45, they're all over the place. The ground's been kicked up in quite a few places," he radioed to Robinson who was still several meters back with the main body of men.

"That's where the initial contact was made with the creatures," Steve remarked, "He'll find some .44 casings as well. The .45s are from Knight's Wilson pistols," he added, recalling the events that took place the last time he'd been here.

The group approached the area and carefully studied the forest floor, looking for more indications of the earlier conflict.

"We have more of that sulfur-based fluid on the leaves," a soldier reported. "And this…." He held up the handle and one inch of broken blade from a large hunting knife.

"Just like they reported," Robinson whispered as he examined the broken blade.

He casually tossed the blade and handle back onto the ground and carefully continued his examination of the area, studying the upturned earth. He easily read the signs of conflict and studied the different foot patterns in the upturned earth. Robinson knelt down before a set of prints he quickly ascertained weren't human. He studied the prints intently, trying to estimate size and weight from the deep impressions in the soil.

"This thing's gotta weigh at least three hundred pounds, maybe four," he said aloud as he concluded his analysis. "What the hell are we dealing with?" Robinson scanned the area intently, looking for any unusual signs of movement. "Okay, soldiers, let's keep moving due west. These things are out here. Let's find them."

"And hope they don't find us," a police officer mumbled as the group proceeded up the sloping terrain.

* * *

The party ascended another quarter mile up the mountain. Steve didn't really know when he noticed the silence, but he felt a deep shiver run down his back.

"They're near," he called out.

Everybody stopped and began peering into the depths of the woods. It was only then that Robinson noticed the absolute silence.

"Aw shit," Robinson cursed as he panned the treescape surrounding them.

Billy hefted the massive M-60 rifle and adjusted his grip in the firing mechanism. "Come on out, you bastards!" he screamed. "Come on out and face me like a man!"

"Billy," Steve whispered harshly, "shut up!" Steve radioed Command and Control, and locked the transmitter key down on his radio. The folks at C&C would be able to hear everything that would occur.

"Over there!" a soldier whispered excitedly. "I saw something moving, over there!" He pointed.

"Where? I don't see anything." Steve raised his forty-four magnum and assumed a combat stance.

"What the hell happened to the sunlight?" Robinson asked as it grew as dark as night in the forest surrounding them. "Switch to Starlight and activate IR scopes!" Robinson barked as the darkness around them intensified. "Find me a target, soldiers."

"I thought they were in the trees!" Billy said. "This blackness came out of nowhere, right in front of us!"

"Sir, I've got a silhouette, big and moving right at us," a soldier announced

"Oh, God, help us all," Steve whispered.

All Hell broke loose.

A large black figure appeared from the darkness and impaled the nearest soldier. The man fell, vomiting and coughing up bile and blood. Billy spun around, screaming as he fired his

rifle. The flame from the muzzle lit up the darkness, and illuminated the dark figure briefly. Then it was gone. The forest was
deathly quiet and dark as the deepest, starless night.

"Hudson!" Robinson screamed. "Activate the spotlight.
Find me a target, damn it."

The young soldier fumbled with his pack, reaching for the
desired item. He didn't see the long whip-like tail that dropped
from the trees and coiled around his neck like a noose until
it had begun strangling him. Hudson gasped and wheezed,
choking as he was lifted into the treetops by the silent abductor.

"Hudson!" Billy screamed as he fired into the trees. The
remaining men heard a roar that was louder than any African
lion, and caused the ground around them to vibrate. Hudson's
body fell limply from the trees landing with a sickening thump
on the forest floor. A Hopedale police officer panicked and
began running. In his mindless terror, he ran further up the
mountain, instead of down. He didn't see the creature until it
reached out and grabbed him, lifting him clear off the ground
holding him aloft with one hand. The officer screamed, a shriek
of pure unmitigated terror, as the creature's icy grip slowly
squeezed his life away.

Steve heard his fellow officer scream in terror, but there
was nothing he could do. He was totally blinded by the darkness. He heard gunfire all around him, and Robinson barking
orders to his remaining men. Steve felt a cool shiver race down
his spine. He slowly glanced up into the tree nearest him. Two
large green cat-like eyes returned his gaze.

Steve raised his revolver and squeezed off three rounds
before a large leg, the thickness of a heavy tree limb, swatted
him, lifting him nearly fifteen feet into the air. Steve was carried
backward, slamming his back into a large tree. Steve heard his
back break, shattering like glass from the forceful impact. He
tried to move, but couldn't, losing all sensation below his neck.
He looked up and saw the large cat-like creature approaching
him. He tried to scream for help, but his voice was drowned by
the sound of gunfire.

He watched, paralyzed and helpless, as the creature vin-
dictively tore the arms and legs from his body. Mercifully, his
broken back prevented him from feeling the pain, but it also

prevented him from losing consciousness from the pain and shock. Steve Forrest was forced to watch himself being torn apart, only to eventually die from severe blood loss. Steve watched, as the remaining men continued to fight. Steve saw the last of his brother officers fall. He placed a picture of his wife and children into his mind.

"Erik, I don't know if you can hear me. We're being butchered. We've lost three men already. It's not just the trees, it's something else, too, they came right out of nowhere," he shouted, hoping that his radio was still active. "I'm dying, Erik. I'm not going to make it back. Please, tell my wife how much I love her, tell her how sorry I am. I only wish…" Steve felt his grip on consciousness fade. "I only wish…" He tried to continue speaking, but found he could no longer talk. He took comfort in the images of his wife and children, surrendering himself to the oncoming blackness.

* * *

Billy continued to lay down a pulse of bullets. He knew he'd hit his quarry several times. He could see glowing blue and purple fluids spilled on the dark forest floor and in the trees above. The remaining men had gathered, huddling back-to-back, their weapons held at the ready, and senses alert, listening for the slightest disturbance. The soft hum of IR scopes and Starlight lenses was the only sound that could be heard in the darkness.

Robinson gave the order for them to fall back, and as a group, they prepared to descend the mountainside in the darkness.

"Does anyone have their light?" Robinson whispered.

Billy carefully reached into his pack and activated his 50,000-candlepower Mag-lite. The usually powerful beam seemed wan and weak in comparison to the surrounding darkness. Billy moved the beam in several directions, looking for their adversaries. He saw nothing.

Gradually, the forest grew brighter. Sunlight filtered through the tree limbs illuminating the forest floor. The remaining three men paused when they were once again bathed in radiance. The sunlight also illuminated the destruction and carnage of their fellow soldiers and police officers. Robinson walked over to the broken corpse of Steven Forrest. Although a battle-hardened veteran, Robinson threw up violently as he saw what remained of the large Hopedale cop.

In the distance, Robinson heard the songs of birds and other wildlife. Now, a scant three minutes later, the forest seemed as harmless as a fairy tale.

"What the fuck just happened?" he asked to no one in particular.

"We just had our asses handed to us," Billy answered bitterly as he surveyed the broken bodies around them. "What the hell are those things?"

"What do we do now?" the other soldier asked.

"We gather our dead, and get the hell out of here. Billy, how many bags you got?"

"Not nearly enough," he whispered. "Not nearly enough."

"Then we improvise," Robinson replied bitterly

* * *

Robinson radioed a report to C&C, and began the gruesome task of gathering body parts of his men and the police officers into separate plastic bags. It was not a job he relished, but no one was going to be left here, no matter what was out there. He steeled himself for the messy task ahead.

The three remaining men constructed a makeshift sled out of small trees and their shirts. There were too many casualties for the three men to carry down without the construct. Billy took the lead with two M-60 rifles plugged into his battery pack, while Robinson and the other soldier, Reese, pulled the sled of casualties behind them. It seemed like an eternity that they walked down the mountainside. No one spoke, each man was lost in his own thoughts about the horrors they had witnessed.

* * *

Erik and Nelson sat outside the control van. Erik's eyes were red and bloodshot, and his body still shook with grief. Both men heard the carnage. The final message from Steve put Erik over the edge.

"I should have been up there, Nelson," Erik whispered as he stared at the ground.

"That wouldn't have made any difference and you know it. We'd just have another body to add to the count," Nelson replied sadly.

"We'll never know, now, will we," Erik replied bitterly.

"No," Nelson agreed. "We never will. Did you know the other two officers?"

"Not very well. Steve was my focal point with the police. I was comfortable dealing with him. He's one of the few officers who actually gave me any amount of professional courtesy."

"He seemed like a good man, I liked him," Nelson replied softly.

"We've lost a lot of good men to these things, and one young woman, and possibly a child." Erik adjusted his position on the van's rear bumper. "I can't stop thinking about Steve's wife, his children. We've succeeded in making another widow, Nelson, and I can only assume that the other soldiers were married or had some family ties."

"True," Nelson agreed. "But that's how it always is though. Death doesn't only affect the one that died, it affects all the people that knew or cared for the deceased. It's always been that way. It's what makes us human, I think, grieving for those we lost."

"I'd rather keep my friends alive, around me," Erik whispered.

Nelson smiled a sad smile and gently patted Erik on his shoulder. "So would I, son, so would I."

Both men turned to see several officers escorting what was left of the original scouting party out of the parklands.

Erik and Nelson were not allowed at the debriefing of the three remaining soldiers. Scant minutes after they arrived at the Hopedale Police Station, an armored military transport arrived with several Army brass. After an hour behind closed doors, the brass collected the three officers and the remains, and quietly departed. Erik and Nelson waited at the Hopedale Police Headquarters for nearly three hours in order to give a written transcript and verbal account of what they heard over the radio.

Erik answered some brief questions and other formalities, and then was free to go. He didn't know what to do with himself. He felt deeply saddened, guilty, and angry. Three powerful emotions that made him feel powerless over the control of the events surrounding his life.

He headed toward his truck, fired the engine, and drove toward the restaurant he called home. He needed to smell the scents of fresh brewed coffee, bacon, sausage and eggs that would be coming from Madame's kitchen. He needed to see the friendly faces of the waiters and waitresses as he sat at his favorite booth. Erik didn't have much material wealth, but he liked where he was and the people he called friends. Today, he lost a friend, and needed the comfort and companionship of other friends to help him through his loss.

Erik walked into the restaurant and silently made his way to his favorite booth. Alissa quickly poured him a cup of coffee. She studied his face intently, as if reading his expression like a book.

"I'm sorry, Erik," she whispered.

Erik looked up at her. "What are you sorry for?"

"Your loss, your grief, and your pain," she answered bluntly.

Erik struggled with his emotions. He would not allow himself to break down, not here, in front of people. "How do you know?" he asked, fighting back the tears.

"The same way she knows," Alissa added, pointing toward the front door.

* * *

Shanda walked through the front door, moving hastily to Erik's booth. She had a look of concern that was broadcast across the entire restaurant. Alissa smiled at her and walked away. Erik looked up and she could read the emotional agony he was experiencing.

"You need to get out of here." She helped him up.

Erik didn't argue, and allowed her to guide him to his

apartment. Once there, he sat on his bed. "How did you know?"

"I don't know the what, I only knew you were in pain, intense emotional pain. I felt it earlier. I knew something terrible was happening."

"Steve is dead, along with the other two cops and three soldiers," Erik said with surprising calm.

Shanda gasped with horror as she recalled the jovial officer who paid for her breakfast earlier.

"Those things tore him apart, and I wasn't there, I wasn't there to help him." Erik's voice wavered. "My God, his body, it was in pieces. Those things literally tore him limb from limb."

Shanda embraced him, and gently touched him telepathically. She could now share his grief and experience his emotions. She saw him screaming into the radio as he heard the sound of gunfire. She felt the sharp pangs of guilt and horror as he heard his friend's final words over the radio.

Erik lay silently in her arms. His mind reeled in spasms of agony as his body tried to cleanse itself from the experience. Shanda refused to let go of her link. She wept with him and held him, doing what little she could to ease his burden.

"It's okay, honey, I've got you. I've got you," she whispered repeatedly as she gently rocked his body.

* * *

Shanda was sitting on Erik's sofa. Erik was in a dead sleep in his room. He had been sleeping for nearly two hours when there was a knock on his door. Shanda opened the door, but there was nobody there. She looked down and saw a large platter of food and four iced beverages. She picked up the tray and placed it on a table. She nibbled on a turkey sandwich and took a deep drink of ginger ale while she continued thumbing through old gun magazines and detective trade journals scattered on a coffee table. After another half hour of reading, she decided her boyfriend needed better leisure reading material. She heard Erik stir from his bed, and heard his footsteps as he entered the room.

"How long?" he asked

"A little over two hours." She gestured for him to sit by her side.

"When did this get here?" Erik picked up a chicken club sandwich from the platter.

"About a half hour ago, somebody knocked on the door, and when I opened it, this was there." Shanda looked deep into his eyes. She could see the haunted expression – the look of a man who's known too much pain and too much loss. "How are you?"

"I'm numb. I still can't believe this happened. I've lost one of the few friends I have," he answered sadly.

"I'm so sorry about this, Erik. How far back do you two go?" Shanda asked.

"About four or five years, there was this narcotics case," Erik began and spent the next hour recalling some of the cases that he and Steve crossed paths on. Recalling the happier memories seemed to soothe the hurt, so Erik continued with more stories, remembering events and episodes from the handful of cases that he had worked on with the Hopedale Police Department.

"Then," he concluded, "we come to the Lisa Reynolds missing persons case." Erik paused and sighed heavily. "You already know how that one ends," he said sadly. "I can't help thinking that if I had been up there, maybe I could have made a difference, somehow."

"Erik, is it worth the risk of Brianna grieving for her father too? What if you were brought out in pieces, what would be going through her mind at this very moment?"

Erik was silent. He stood up and began pacing back and forth. "It still doesn't make me feel better, but it is a consolation that she's spared that."

"You have to remember that there are people here that love you, and want you around. You're not alone, what you do does affect other people's lives." She walked toward him and put her arms around him.

"You'll just have to keep reminding me," he whispered as he looked down at her.

"I can do more than that," she whispered and then kissed him.

* * *

Richard Pendelton sat alone in his spacious board room, listening to the bootleg tapes that were intercepted by his man at the Hopedale Police Department. As he heard the sounds of men screaming and dying, he drained his glass of scotch.

Richard was filled with remorse and regret. What had they done? What manner of creatures had they freed from slumber? How much more blood would have to be on his hands before this was all over? Richard could no longer sleep at night. He barely spoke to his wife, or her daughter. It was so easy to plan these things – manipulate the fates of men from a distance, to hear that they were dead from some impassive piece of paper, or disinterested business associate – but to hear the actual screams of men dying, the sound of gunfire, and the hideous roar of some weird creatures brought it all home for him.

He had caused the deaths of those men, the first research team, and the recon team. All of that blood was on his hands, and his alone. The 'buck' stopped with him, at his desk. He knew he could not deflect any blame to anybody else.

He poured another glass of scotch from the decanter, emptying the contents. He had gone too far to turn back now. He'd have to play the game to its conclusion and hope he was smarter and more efficient than those investigating the goings on in Hopedale. Richard was confident the Hopedale Police would do their usual standard investigation. His people could easily mislead and derail that, what concerned him was the Erik Knight factor.

Knight had been convinced to stay out of the action, but that didn't mean he wouldn't be looking at things from the sidelines. Conrad was right. Knight had become a very formidable man, not only physically, but also intellectually. He had read some of Knight's work in the police files. He was able to come up with leads and clues the police were seemingly oblivious to. Knight was the only person to discover any actual physical evidence in the Lisa Reynolds missing person case. How he was able to pull that off was something Pendelton was very interested in discovering. His company, his wealth, and most assuredly his personal freedom relied on him playing this through to the bitter end, reluctant or not. He would not lose his family fortune or spend time in any federal or state penal institution.

Richard drained his second glass of scotch and studied the plans he'd drafted for his next operation. He reached over to the telephone and punched four keys.

"Conrad?"

A voice responded through the headset

"Have the packages arrived at our private hangar yet?"

The voice responded.

"Well, let me know as soon as they arrive. We need to be ready to move out within the week. All hell is going to break loose in that mountain pretty soon, and we need to be ready."

Chapter 10

Conrad and the two technicians studied the Apache helicopter Pendelcorp had appropriated, meticulously. The contractors who had given the airship the army-olive paint job were well worth the additional expense. The helicopter looked flawless, right down to the bogus white registration lettering and army star on the ship's tail section.

Conrad examined the two weapons pods and two hard contacts that were mounted on the ship's small wing sections. He spotted the ship's armaments stockpiled in one corner of the security hangar.

Carefully stacked in wooden crates were two typhoon air-to-ground missiles. The warheads of each missile contained as much concentrated high explosive as fifteen tons of TNT. The coordinates of the Hopedale excavation tunnel had already been preprogrammed into the Apache's tactical computer. These coordinates could quickly be fed into the missile's internal guidance system and fired with lethal accuracy, but the aircraft had to be within the typhoons' limited operational range. The solid rocket fuel engines of this missile type were extremely limited. It would be necessary to be inside of a half mile of the site before the weapon could be effectively utilized. In another large packing crate were sixteen rockets that would be loaded into the two launchers under each wing of the craft.

The two technicians spent twenty minutes studying the ship, examining the flight control system computers and the navigation consoles specifically.

Conrad watched them impatiently. "Well, can you do it?"

"Yeah," one of the technicians answered. "It's quite a bit more complicated than the other bird we wired, but it can be done." He paused, glancing at his partner. "For an added cost. The time involved is substantially more than before, and the

197

electronics needed will be more sophisticated. Plus, we'll need a bigger charge to rupture the fuel tank. That makes it tougher to hide." The technician paused then added, "Do you want to use the same frequency?"

Conrad nodded, staring at them as they continued to survey the chopper.

"You'll be well compensated for your efforts. Begin the work immediately, and remember, gentlemen, confidentiality is the key word," he emphasized in a dangerous tone.

"No worries, mate," the other technician responded in a deep Australian accent. "We won't bite the hand that feeds us – poor business." He tipped his hat slightly.

"Excellent, I'm glad we understand each other. Contact me when the work is completed," Conrad replied as he departed the hangar.

Conrad walked toward the awaiting company car. The chauffeur opened the passenger door for him and closed it as he made himself comfortable in the car's spacious seat. He picked up the Nexus phone, keying the transmitter.

"Richard, are you there?"

"Go ahead," Pendleton's distinctive voice answered.

"The package has arrived and is being prepared for service. All is going according to plan."

"Conrad," Pendleton answered after a moment's silence. "We can have no loose ends."

Conrad was puzzled for a second, then understood the meaning of his employer's last words. He approved of Richard's thinking, and chastised himself for not realizing the potential breach himself.

"I'll see to it personally," he answered. "Conrad out"

He picked up the phone in the car and dialed, the phone rang three times before it was picked up, and a synthesized voice answered.

"It's me," Conrad began. "Reference number 5862-31." He paused while the party on the other end input his account number into a database. After a few quick seconds, the voice on the other end of the line gave Conrad the clearance to continue.

"I have a contract for you, two marks. I'll send you the details in the usual manner."

Conrad listened to the voice on the other end for almost thirty seconds before responding.

"The fee is acceptable," he replied. The connection was then severed.

Conrad reached into the portable bar and poured himself a large glass of iced scotch. It had been a busy day, and there was still much to do. Conrad looked out the window as, suddenly, the lead-gray skies unleashed a torrent of rain upon the city. This was the part of his job he disliked, he had no problem with embezzlement or other white-collar crimes, but he never fancied himself as a contract killer.

* * *

Rolling Hills Cemetery, Hopedale

The honor guard of seven officers fired three volleys into the air, while the priest recited scripture from his Bible.

Mrs. Stephen Forrest wept uncontrollably, while next to her, her two young children looked up at the casket that contained what was left of their father. The fifty uniformed officers, many from several nearby towns, lined up in a procession, to offer their final condolences to the grieving widow and her extended family. As the procession continued, the skies that had been threatening rain all morning unleashed a downpour. People began to scurry toward their awaiting cars to avoid the downpour, while others opened umbrellas while escorting the widow and her children back to the long black limousine.

A lone figure stood upon the hillside, watching the ceremony from a respectful distance. Rain rolled off the long black leather jacket that he pulled tighter around his upper torso to ward off the sudden chill. A gust of wind flared and caught the insides of the garment, causing it to billow like the cape of some dark specter.

He watched quietly as the last of them departed. Once he was sure he would be alone, he slowly walked down the hillside toward the covered casket, ignoring the increasing torrents of rain, which was accompanied by violent thunder and lightning. The man stopped by the casket, produced a single flower from inside the jacket and laid it gently on top of the casket along with the other flowers already there.

"I'm sorry, Steve," he spoke aloud. "I'll never be able to forgive myself for not being along for the ride. I'm sorry for all that you're going to miss: Your children growing up, being a grandfather, the spring bass fishing, fall deer hunting, the taste of your wife's kiss, the warmth of her touch, the laughter from your kids." He paused as he placed his hand on the metalwork of the casket, the rain pelting his back and exposed head. "Forgive me, Steve, I wish I could have prevented this. Everyone keeps telling me that if I were there, I'd be in one of these boxes too, that I should be thankful that I'm alive, and count my blessings. The truth is, old friend, I feel like a big part of me died that day too. It's funny, everyone I care about seems to die: My parents, my military buddies, and now my friend on the force."

Erik continued to stare at the coffin in silence. His face contorted, the grief he'd been carrying bubbling up to the surface.

"Damn you!" he swore. "Why did you have to go? Why did he have to die?" He looked up to the heavens. "Why?" he whispered.

Then his teardrops fell, plentiful as the rain, for almost ten minutes. Erik stood by his friend, weeping at his passing, ignoring the violence of the storm that seemed to be a reflection of his own grief and sorrow. He placed his hand gently on the casket, one last time.

"Goodbye, may this last journey be pleasant and bring you to a better place." He quickly spun around. The bottom of his jacket whirled, spraying rivulets of water in a circle. Erik headed back to his tiny apartment in the back of a small diner, to the place he called home.

Erik walked into his small office and tossed his waterlogged jacket on the coat rack in the corner of his office. He sat down at his desk thumbing through a stack of mail with his feet resting upon the desktop. For the first time in over a week, there was nothing for him to do. He had no desire for company, friend or female. And no real particular urge to do anything except cope with the loss and take the rest of the week to pick himself back up. His mind, however, would not let him rest. His thoughts kept wandering back to Lisa Reynolds. She was still out there, somewhere. More than likely, the girl had expired.

Erik felt that the inability to locate the child was a personal failure on his part. He knew there was no possible way that she could be alive at this point. Undoubtedly, her corpse would turn up somewhere once a way was found to contain the creatures. Erik was certain there would be a massive assault on the mountain. The Army wouldn't accept the loss of three of its soldiers without knowing what had happened, and then dealing with the threat. It was obvious this problem could no longer be kept at a local level. He expected State and Federal officials to become embroiled with the problems occurring in Hopedale, and the inevitable media circus was sure to follow. A light tapping on his door pulled Erik from his thoughts.

"Yes."

"Erik, Mr. Nelson is here to see you," Alissa replied through the closed door.

"Please send him in, the door is unlocked."

Scant moments later, the Halls detective was escorted into Erik's office and seated himself on one of the couches.

"Belechek and I are on our way back to corporate," he announced.

"I figured as much," Erik answered. "There doesn't seem anything else that we can do here."

"No, there isn't." Nelson nodded his head in agreement. The older man seemed suddenly uncomfortable. "Look, Erik, I know Forrest's funeral was today and, judging by the pool of water under your jacket hanging in the corner, I can only assume that you were there—"

"He was my friend," Erik interrupted. "I had to say good-bye."

"That's commendable, but stop blaming yourself for what happened up there. You're wearing your guilt on your sleeve, young man. There's no need to seek penance or absolution. You are in no way responsible. Death is also a part of the job we do as investigators. Mourn his loss, keep him alive in your memories, but move on. Don't allow yourself to be hamstrung by this," Nelson warned Erik. "I've seen this kind of guilt tear people apart."

"You don't feel somewhat responsible for Henderson, and what happened to him?" Erik countered.

"Different circumstances, but yes, I do feel, in a way, responsible." Nelson replied. "Henderson was on my team and he died on my watch. I feel terrible about that, but I won't let it eat me alive. He was a good man, but he's gone, there was nothing I could have done to prevent what happened to him. We've both lost people this past week, son. It's a part of what we do. We may not face it as often as cops, but it is fairly commonplace in our particular line of work. We grieve, then we move on. It may sound cold and callous, but if we tore our hearts out every time an associate met an untimely end, we'd spend all of our time mourning and none of our time living. If you want to remember your friend, and honor his memory, be there for his wife, and kids. They're feeling the hurt a hell of a lot more than you or I ever will, and they're the ones who need the sympathy, not us." Nelson stood up and extended his hand toward Erik. "It's been a pleasure working with you, Erik. I sincerely hope we can meet again under better circumstances."

Erik clasped Nelson's hand. "Thanks, Nelson, have a safe trip home. I'll keep you in the loop as to how this thing finally plays out."

"Do that," Nelson answered as he turned and headed into the hallway.

Erik watched Nelson as he walked out into the parking lot and stepped into the large Sedan. He watched the car leave the parking lot and speed away.

Erik walked over to his computer and did a quick check on the database searches he had run earlier. As he had expected, every source of data he tapped came up with nothing. He walked back to his window and looked out at Hopedale Mountain that loomed like a lone sentinel against the gray, stormy skies.

"You've got a secret," he whispered, "and two unwelcome guests."

He turned away from the window and sat down on his long couch. He was exhausted. He lay down, intending to only rest his eyes momentarily, but quickly fell into a deep sleep.

* * *

Bill Wentworth, known to his customers only as Mr. Smith, swore as the night rain continued to fall on him as he perched on the rooftop of the Worcester office building. Breaking into the building had been relatively easy. The hardest part of the job he was doing now: The seemingly endless waiting game.

He had tailed his targets from the moment they left the Pendelton hangar late in the afternoon up to now. There was no feasible perch near the expensive restaurant where they dined, nor could he eliminate them while they were in their car. Bombs were too messy, and the mark of an amateur, he thought. Killing, to him, was an art form. There was a right way and a wrong way to proceed about the business of ending a life. Ideally, he preferred the knife. It was an intimate weapon that brought him into direct contact with his victim. It was a rush seeing the look of fear, shock, and panic as they felt the icy cold touch of steel against their heart. He relished the last look on his victim's face, their last breath, last words gurgled as their lungs filled with blood. The knife allowed him all these wonderful moments.

But tonight, it had to be quick and lethal, before his marks could say something potentially wrong to a potentially wrong person. Tonight belonged to the rifle, the high, out of the way spot, the kill from a distance, death by airmail.

Wentworth didn't consider himself an evil man, just a businessman like any other, except he dealt in death the way others dealt with stocks, bonds, goods or services. He figured the government had spent millions on training him and using his talents during the Cold War, and it would be a shame to let these expensive skills go to waste since he was no longer employed by the Federal Government. It was far more lucrative to set up his own business and provide a service to a public willing to use him.

His client had given him the go ahead to carry out the contract, and that was all the motivation required for him to terminate the marks. The pair he was hunting had wound up at a rundown bar just outside of North Avenue, not the most affluent part of the city, he absently noted.

Wentworth spotted several men he knew were part of several narcotics organizations, a few police narks, and several other shady-looking men of questionable character. He glanced down at his Rolex briefly. It was almost 11:00 p.m. They had been in there for nearly three hours now, probably celebrating the completion of their work.

Wentworth had a curvy blonde waiting back at his apartment for him, which was his form of celebration after each job. He wanted to close this deal as soon as possible before she got tired of waiting. He adjusted the position of his Kimber .243, and ran another quick check on the Night Site scope. He peered through the scope's amber lens and refocused the scope's reticle on the tavern door.

"Just step outside, boys, that's all I ask."

Almost as if responding to his request, his two targets stumbled out of the bar. He could tell they were completely intoxicated. Wentworth placed the reticle on the man with the funny hat, took a shallow breath, exhaled partially, then slowly, in a fluid motion, caressed the trigger. A muffled pop sounded as the Marenko Silencer dampened the concussion. He didn't wait to see the target fall. He smoothly worked the rifle's bolt action and chambered another round.

The other mark had turned, facing away from him, completely oblivious to his companion's fate. Wentworth locked on to the specific area of the man's back where he knew an impact would shatter the spine and rupture the heart. He tapped the trigger again, this time watching the second man stumble forward as the jacketed hollow point impacted with his body. He looked through the scope quickly. The first target's head was shattered, hemorrhaging blood and brain matter on the dirty sidewalk. Wentworth picked up the spent brass, broke down his weapon, and disappeared within two minutes of his work's completion.

He drove by the bar to admire his work. A crowd was already gathering around the bodies. He congratulated himself, two clean kills. He also smiled as the rain continued to pour down, washing away any residual gunpowder and ballistic residue from his perch. He didn't worry about the police running any ballistics on the bullets they would extract from the corpses. The rifle barrel was double grooved, one of his own inventions. Ballistics specialists would never be able to trace the noncommercial rifling on the rifle slugs back to any source.

* * *

It was nearly three in the morning when Wentworth finished his own private celebration for a job well done. The blonde he had appropriated for the evening dressed herself and prepared to depart. He watched her carefully as she applied a fresh coat of lipstick and makeup. He wondered why the woman was wasting her time with all the cosmetics. It was still pouring outside, and the rain would only make her painstaking efforts futile.

When she had finished, she looked over towards his direction. He gestured toward a small nightstand where he had placed four fresh, crisp one-hundred-dollar bills. She walked over, scooped up the money, and tucked the cash inside her shirt.

"Will you be calling again soon, Mr. Smith?" she asked.

"That depends, my dear, not that I don't enjoy your company, because I do greatly, but it all depends on business." He paused. "I'm sure you understand."

The young woman nodded. "I think I do."

Wentworth walked over to her and pressed his lips against her forehead, and allowed himself one last inhalation of her expensive perfume. "I'm glad." He pulled another hundred from his wallet. "This is strictly for you, not to be shared with the house. Buy yourself something special." He tucked the bill inside her shirt.

She smiled up at him, grabbed her coat, and left quickly. Wentworth watched her from his window as she disappeared around the corner and into the darkness of the early morning. He stared for several extra minutes into the darkness, watching the rain spill from a noisy gutter across the street.

Wentworth snapped back to attention. He looked over the contract for the two marks, entered their termination in his database, and smiled to himself. The payment for these two would allow him to retire early, much earlier than he had planned. Once he informed his client of the completion of his work, the remaining balance of the half million dollars would be deposited in his Fiji account, and he would be off to the Caribbean forever.

* * *

The young blonde walked two more blocks, the pelting rain ruined her hair and makeup. She spotted the large black limousine and approached the car. The rear door was opened for her, and she quickly entered the vehicle. The man inside gave her a rich warm towel to dry herself and poured her a warm cup of delicious-smelling hot coffee.

"I didn't realize it would be raining this hard," the man apologized as he handed her the warm mug.

"I've been through worse," she added as she studied her face in a compact mirror. "Shit, I look terrible."

"Do you know if he completed the job?" the man asked intently.

"He did, he always uses me after a successful contract, it's the same routine every time." She casually combed her long, wet hair. She took a long swig of the warm beverage, allowing herself to heat her hands on the mug. "Mmm, this is really good, thank you."

"Excellent, and you're most welcome, enjoy," the man answered as he tapped the tinted Plexiglas partition that separated the passenger compartment from the driver's area.

"How did you know about our relationship, anyway?" she asked, suddenly curious.

"It's my job to know everything about all our subcontractors. It was a small matter to trace the cellular electronics our friend uses and track their specific signals back to its source. Then," he continued after another sip of his drink, "a simple matter to place a tap on his lines, pull phone records, research numbers, bribe phone company employees, match calls to your employer, and cross reference them with work he has done for us in the past. This is the electronic age, there are no secrets, and no one can hide who uses computers or gadgetry. Information is power. The ability to utilize information is the ability to wield that power. Anyone who thinks they can hide in this age is a fool." The man poured himself another scotch on the rocks. "Did you place the device like we discussed?"

"Yeah, I kept him too preoccupied to notice what I was doing." She took another long drink from her cup.

He nodded and handed her an envelope. She quickly opened it and counted out the ten hundred dollar bills. Her eyes were shining with delight as she folded the bills and tucked them inside her shirt.

"It's getting crowded in there." She giggled as she adjusted herself to accommodate the extra cash. Her face began to look flush. She gasped for air, struggling for each breath. She felt a sharp pang in her stomach, like she swallowed acid.

"I ... I don't feel so good," she curled up in pain.

"Really?" The man took another swig of his scotch.

"What's happening to me?" she asked as she began choking and convulsing.

The man reached toward her and took the cup from her shaking hands. "Haven't you guessed, my dear? You've just been poisoned. You're dying," Conrad placed the cup on the nearby tray.

The blonde gathered the last of her strength and swung at him as hard as she could. She felt satisfaction as her knuckles connected with the front of his face with a loud resounding crack. "You bastard." She winced as the poison finally shut down her central nervous system and involuntary synapses. Her final word was: "Why?" She stopped breathing, her heart stopped beating, and she silently fell over, dead, into his lap.

The man carefully unbuttoned her blouse, reached inside her bra, and removed the money she had carefully placed there. "Sorry about this, Miss," he whispered as he carefully buttoned her blouse back up and used his gloved hands to push her against the other side of the passenger compartment.

He stared at her dead body. The full weight of what he had done came crashing down upon him. He had just committed a homicide. Murder, cold, premeditated murder. He was used to discussing the termination of people, numbers or names on a sheet of paper, but this was the first time he actually sullied his hands.

Her dead eyes kept staring back at him, looking through the coarse exterior of the man, into his vulnerable side, the small remaining piece of his soul that hadn't been totally tarnished by the greed and corruption of his occupation.

"I'm sorry, Miss, you were just in the wrong place at the wrong time, an unwitting pawn in a grander game of chess. Please don't hold it against me. It's just that I'm in too deep now, we all are. It wasn't supposed to play out like this. We were supposed to make easy millions on this operation," he whispered as her dead eyes continued to bore through him. He tapped twice against the tinted glass, and it slid down into the wall partition separating the passenger and driver compartments. "Dispose of that, quickly." He pointed to the body.

The driver pulled the car over into the abandoned area he was informed of earlier. The single tap on the glass was his cue to begin moving the car toward its destination. The driver got out of the car and opened the rear passenger door, and let the corpse fall out into a deep, large puddle of rainwater.

"Move her to that dry corner of the alley, please," he instructed the driver. He would not give her the indignity of being found in a mud puddle. He felt he at least owed her that much.

The man walked over to inspect the body. He adjusted her arms, gently folding them across her chest with his gloved hands. He pulled a small black booklet from his coat pocket and mumbled something. The driver looked at him oddly as he made a sign of the cross over their victim. The driver escorted the man back into the car and they proceeded toward Mr. Smith's townhouse.

The large car parked a block away, while the man studied the control nestled inside his palm. He flipped a switch, and a red button activated and began blinking. He looked out the window and stared at the distant townhouse.

"No loose ends." He pressed the glowing button and the explosive that had been placed under the assassin's mattress went off with a satisfying pyrotechnic display.

Mr. Conrad smirked at the irony of the whole situation that just unfolded. The explosive and detonator were prepared earlier that day by the two men the assassin had murdered earlier. Conrad had personally paid them a cash bonus for the extra work once they had completed modifying their army helicopter.

Pendelton Corporation had an understanding with the organization that controlled the blue light district in Worcester. This organization provided 'companionship' for visiting executives and important clients that did business with the large corporation. Once it was discovered their hitman had a fondness for a particular female inside that organization, it was easy to utilize that business relationship to tie up that loose end. The organization was paid a hefty price for the loss of their call girl. All tidy, with no loose ends, everybody was happy.

Conrad poured himself another scotch on the rocks as the limousine headed back toward Boston. Deep down, he had to admit, he wasn't really happy. "More blood on my hands," he whispered.

The game was getting too severe, the stakes too deep. He wasn't sure that he had the stomach for it any longer. He had just committed two murders. His company had illegally tunneled in a wildlife preserve area, and unleashed some unspeakable horrors upon innocent people. He had literally participated in dozens of other unethical, bordering on illegal, business actions earlier in his career with little to no effect on his conscience. But what he had done in the past two weeks had been more than he ever bargained for.

He thought about Erik Knight momentarily, how seven years ago he had participated in the literal destruction and character assassination of what he judged to be a fairly likeable fellow. Fortunately, Erik Knight was resilient. Despite all odds, the detective bounced back from the edge of oblivion. Conrad remembered the dozens of other poor souls who weren't so lucky. And lately, they numbered in the many – too many for his tastes.

He knew if he tried to walk away, he too would become a loose end and most likely share in the fates of the two people he just had a hand in eliminating. He took a long drink from his glass, and settled into the heated leather seat. He could only escape this in sleep, and right now, he was extremely tired.

* * *

Friday morning 8:00 a.m.

Erik was sitting at his booth, staring down at his breakfast. Normally he enjoyed a hearty meal first thing in the morning, but today all he could stomach was a blueberry muffin and some coffee. There was still a big knot in his stomach from the events of the past few days.

Erik did admit to himself, after much soul searching, he couldn't have prevented his friend's death. Nelson's words got through. It didn't lessen the loss, but it alleviated the guilt, some of it anyway. There would always be that small piece of self-doubt, the never-ending 'what if' that plagued men of good conscience and character.

Erik was deep in thought, when the sound of a newspaper landing on his table snapped him from his stupor.

"I figured you'd want to see this," Jeff remarked as he sat across from him.

Erik picked up the paper and studied the headline: "Monsters on Murderous Rampage in Sleepy Suburb."

"Oh, just marvelous," he whispered as he scanned the story quickly.

Erik noted his name in several paragraphs, as well as the officers who died on the mountain. The story of the Reynolds saga, his involvement, the involvement of Halls and the police were all described in remarkable detail. Somebody on the Hopedale police force couldn't keep his or her mouth shut. What particularly caught his interest was the reporting that another team of heavily armed men and equipment was being organized to hunt down and kill these creatures.

Erik looked up at his friend. "It seems our little township will become very busy over the next week or two." He folded up the paper and placed it on the corner of the table.

"The Town Fathers wanted to be on the 'Map,'" Jeff remarked ironically. "But I assume this isn't what they had in mind."

"I'm sure it's not." Erik nodded in agreement as he took a sip of his coffee.

"They're going to come looking for you, you know that," Jeff said suddenly. "'The only man to successfully defeat the creatures in two consecutive conflicts is a private investigator named Erik Knight, who runs a small informal operation out of a local dining establishment,'" Jeff recited, quoting the *Globe* verbatim. "You think they could have at least mentioned the name of the place," he added lightly.

"Do you really want to play host for a bunch of reporters, photo hounds, and political officials, half of them who will try to pawn you for a free meal?" Erik asked.

"No, not really," Jeff answered. "But a little publicity never hurts."

"There's no such thing as a little publicity," Erik responded.

"No," Jeff said softly. "I suppose you're right about that. What will you do if they come looking for you? Are you going to go up there this time?" Jeff asked, pushing the issue.

Erik looked at his friend, his eyes becoming unreadable, blazing with some unknown fiery determination. "I won't go back there with another group of men, but I do have a score to settle, somehow. I don't know how or why I know this, Jeff, but these things won't just go away, armed soldiers are not the answer. If these creatures feel like they're in danger, they'll just disappear like they've done before, and reappear somewhere else. We have to learn more about them before we can decide on the best way of coping with them. They can appear and disappear like a genie in a lamp, like some type of ghost."

Erik thought about all the encounters with the creatures up to now. "All we'll gain from another assault on that mountain will be more dead bodies. I'm going to have to get involved sooner or later. I don't know why, it's just a feeling I've had ever since that day at the park. The way that thing looked at me, I could tell there was something more there, an anger – a hunger and a hate like I've never experienced. It knows something we don't, those creatures seem as though they have a score to settle with us. But, for the life of me, I can't figure out with who or with what or why." He added moodily as he finished his coffee.

"Just be careful," his friend cautioned. "Don't let yourself be 'guilted' into anything," Jeff added as he stood up.

"I won't," Erik assured his friend.

Erik watched Jeff leave and turned back toward the newspaper, skimming through the last few paragraphs of the article. He thought more about the strange creatures. They seemed to be utilizing more than the trees, they seemed to have the ability to pop in and out of areas like people would use a doorway to go through one room to another. He wondered if the intense darkness that accompanied their appearance was related to their ability to jump in and out of spaces. He also pondered the extreme drops in temperature that marked their arrivals.

Erik thought about it for several more minutes before dismissing any wild theories. He was no longer involved in the investigation. With any luck, the military would catch up with these things and scatter their bodies across the hillside with some heavy artillery. That instinct in the back of his mind, the one that usually warned him of danger, whispered that the next military expedition would fare no better against these horrors than he had when he encountered them. Erik casually leafed through the paper, getting himself caught up on current events.

Alissa quietly strolled over and refilled his coffee cup, and then cleared away the half-eaten muffin and unused butter. "You seem to be healing quickly," she commented, studying the scars on the side of his face.

Erik looked up, and then rubbed his right hand across the side of his cheek. "Yeah, I sometimes forget that they're there, until I look at myself in the mirror, that is." He let out a slight chuckle.

Alissa smiled briefly and walked back toward the kitchen, while Erik continued thumbing through the newspaper.

Erik's thoughts turned back toward work. He had made enough money on the events of the past to carry him through the next few months. He decided to call Martin Denton the first thing Monday morning and see if there was any freelance work his firm needed done. Denton was always willing to utilize his capabilities, and he admitted to himself that, at this point in time, he had no other options.

He drank half of his second cup of coffee, gathered the rest of his dishes, and deposited them on the carousel outside the kitchen. He had to be at the elementary school to pick up Brianna by 2:30. He had enough time to catch up on some paper work and start his quarterly tax forms, as well as place the call to Denton before he would have to get his daughter. But first, there was something that he had to do.

* * *

It was nearly ten in the morning when the Chevrolet 4x4 pulled up alongside the curb in front of a blue split-level house. The neighborhood was full of well-kept yards and impeccably trimmed bushes and hedges. Erik stared at the Forrest name-plate on the mailbox. He took a deep breath and made his way toward the front door, his stomach filling with butterflies. He rang the bell and heard activity inside the house. The door opened and an older gentleman answered. Erik saw a distinct similarity between this man and his departed friend. He knew that this was Steve's father.

"Hello, sir," Erik began nervously. "I was wondering if I could speak to Carol for a moment."

"Who are you?" the older man asked, his tone somewhat challenging. "Are you another reporter? If so, we have nothing to say."

"No, sir, my name is Erik Knight. I was...." He paused. "I worked with Steve, I considered him among my friends."

The old man looked him up and down, as if assessing him as a potential threat. Erik knew that Steve's father must also have been a police officer. He detected the manner and demeanor of a law enforcement official.

"How many years?" Erik asked, attempting to break the ice.

"What?"

"How many years were you a cop?" Erik asked quietly.

"I put in 35 years in Boston," the old man answered. "How did you know that?"

"You have the same look and manner that Steve had when he was studying something, the look all good cops have, the awareness, the alertness. I respected that in him,"

Erik answered softly.

The man studied Erik closely, then stepped aside and gestured him into the house. "Come in, please. I didn't mean to be harsh, but there have been several reporters snooping around here the past few days; damn vultures, anything for a story," he cursed as Erik followed the man into a modest living room.

"Carol," he shouted toward the hallway, "you have a visitor."

Carol Forrest slowly walked down the hallway. Erik wondered if she would recognize him. He'd only been to the house on three occasions, the last such occurrence had been over two years ago. Erik noted the haunted look in her eyes. She was carrying her youngest daughter, whom Erik knew to be only twelve or fourteen months old.

"Erik Knight," she said as she put the baby in a playpen. "It's been a while, almost three years." She sat in a chair next to her child. "I saw you at the funeral, up on that ridge. Why didn't you come down?"

"You were with family, I didn't want to intrude," he answered. "I said my goodbye once everyone else had departed."

"Steve would have been glad that you came. Thank you"

"Mrs. Forrest—"

"Carol, please," she interrupted.

"Carol," Erik corrected himself, "I can't begin to tell you how sorry I am. Steve was a good friend to me, at a time when I didn't have too many. I was fortunate to know him. He always spoke highly of you and the kids, always showing off his 'wallet-sized' whenever he had the chance." Erik adjusted his position on the couch. "I just wanted to come by and see if there was anything that I could do to help out."

The baby started to cry as Carol was about to reply. She bent over, picked the child up, and carefully placed her over her shoulder, gently patting the little girl's back. "Do you really mean that?"

"Yes, I do." Erik answered.

"Talk to Collin, he's having all kinds of problems with this. He worshipped his father. He can't understand how his daddy could be gone. Steve talked to me a little about your past. I know you're an orphan, so you can probably relate to what the boy is feeling. It may help him if he can talk to someone who's been through it. Lord knows I don't know what to say to the boy."

"I will," Erik promised, but not really knowing what he could say to a young boy who had just lost his father.

"And one last thing," she added as her voice began to waiver.

"Yes, anything," Erik replied.

"Kill them. Avenge my husband's death. If he was a friend to you, hunt those cursed things down and kill them. They tore my husband apart, piece by piece, left me with nothing but pieces to put in the ground, and I want them dead for that!" She wept uncontrollably.

Steve's father escorted her back into one of the bedrooms, leaving Erik by himself. After a few minutes, the elder Mr. Forrest returned.

"I'm sorry you had to see that, Mr. Knight," he apologized. "The pain is still too fresh, the hurt too deep." His own eyes became tearful. "He was a good boy, my son. She's a good woman," he added in a wavering voice. "They didn't deserve this."

"No, sir," Erik agreed. "They certainly don't. I'm so sorry for your loss."

The two men exchanged a firm handshake and Erik headed toward the front door. He left the house and made his way back to his apartment. The memories of his friend, and the voice over the radio as he met his untimely end, played over and over in his mind. He'd try and say something to Steve's son, but at this point, what does one say to a young boy who just lost his father.

Erik thought back, trying to remember the scant memories of his parents. He had vague memories of the accident that killed his parents and grandparents. His father had shielded his small body, taking several jagged pieces of glass into his torso and head. He remembered waking up in a hospital room, and the agony when he finally learned that all the adults in his life had been killed in one tragic accident. But they seemed like fragments from another life and another time. Erik had just turned four years old, but he still could recall vivid flashbacks of that fateful day. He was glad that the boy still had a father figure in Steve's father, and a mother.

He arrived back at his office and checked his phone for messages. As usual, there were none. He stared at the pile of waiting paper work with distaste. He walked over to his couch and sat down. A dull pain shot through his hamstring. He hadn't fully recovered from the ordeals he'd put his body through the past week. He leaned back against a throw pillow and slowly closed his eyes. He didn't want to fall asleep, and he tried to fight the oncoming blackness, but was soon in a deep slumber.

* * *

Friday afternoon, 1:38 p.m.

Richard Pendelton sat at his large Mahogany desk, staring out over the scenic Boston Bay. He enjoyed watching the jet liners departing and arriving at Logan International.

Sitting on his desk were several confidential memos from his most trusted staff, keeping him abreast of the various activities within his large conglomerate. He read the memo from Conrad with great interest. It was simple and to the point. "All the loose ends have been cut." Richard exhaled heavily – one less thing to be concerned about.

The whole Hopedale Mountain dig had been a giant disaster. He assumed the project would go off without any complications. The mountain was desolate, never patrolled by game wardens or any other personage of official status. It seemed the perfect site to conduct a mining operation. He cursed himself for being too greedy.

It was too late in the game for self-pity. He made his choices and decisions. All he could do now was follow them through. The game had to be played out to its conclusion. He planned carefully. Once completed, there would be nothing left to implicate his firm. The tunnel would be filled in, and there would be nothing left of their campsite but smoky ruins and several impact craters. Everything now depended on timing.

They needed to know when the next team was going to storm the mountain. Undoubtedly, the Army would send in helicopters and heavy equipment plus dozens of armed soldiers into the area to flush these things out. When this occurred, their helicopter would mix in with the group, break off to the target site, and obliterate everything with the Typhoon missiles and high explosive rockets. The pilot would then bank away, utilizing the enhanced boosters, and then as before, the helicopter's programming would send it out to sea to self-destruct in the middle of the icy Atlantic, eliminating the final loose ends and hopefully burying Pendelcorp's mistakes forever.

There would be no one left to tell the tale. The military would get the blame for any loss of life, and Pendelcorp would remain untouched by any scandal. There would no doubt be an intense military investigation, and the military would be able to account for all its hardware, but there would be enough witnesses to the destruction to impede any actual progress for years to come. It would be another of many unsolved mysteries to be filed away and forgotten.

* * *

Deep in the tunnel within Hopedale Mountain, the creatures stirred, they expended the last of their energy reserves healing, were extremely hungry – desperately hungry. They had sampled the sweet meats of the small, primitive creatures, and desired more. There would be no more interference, the black entity vowed to itself. They would move in quickly and quietly, and bring their prey here to feed.

It secretly wished to encounter the Simian-Esper hybrid. Its genetic programming commanded it to destroy all Espers, there was something familiar about this one, something it remembered from long ago, before its long sleep. For what little independent thought the creature was capable of, it wanted to kill the Simian-Esper as slowly and painfully as possible, play with this victim like a cat would play with a mouse. When this Esper had finally tired and could offer no more amusement, the creature would snap its neck as easily as it had broken the others. In its own limited way, it wanted vengeance for the prior encounters.

Both creatures left their nest area and headed through the

tunnel to the outdoors. They casually passed by the now-abandoned Pendelcorp campsite, taking no notice of the boxes, crates, and scattered materials that had been abandoned. The large catlike creature took two large sniffs of air, tasting and sampling each molecule, looking for the particular scent of their prey. It found none and growled in distress. The other stroked its large flank gently, telepathically sending out calming messages to its large ally.

It climbed upon the creature's broad back, gesturing with its right claw. The massive beast took two steps, and then paused as if waiting for something. The creature emitted a high-pitch tone, and the space in front of it parted into blackness. The darkness spread throughout the woods, blanketing everything in a thick black veil. Both disappeared into the dark that filled the woods as if they'd never been there. The blackness fell in upon itself and sunlight once again filled the forest. The sudden chirp of a sparrow broke the silence, and the woods around the dig site again seemed peaceful and undaunting.

* * *

Erik looked up at the clock in his office. "Crud."

He had been wrestling with paperwork for almost two hours, and was no further along than when he'd started. It was time for him to pick up Brianna from school. This was special time for them, they had Friday and the weekend together this time, instead of just the one evening. He figured that Brianna would have plenty of things to do, and would keep both of them well occupied.

Erik stared down at the tax forms, and decided that some of his money would be well spent on an accountant. Finances were never his strong point.

He stood up from his desk, grabbed his gun, and started for the door. He suddenly stopped himself, remembering that he was entering a school zone. Firearms were forbidden, for any reason. He quickly shed the weapon and deposited it in his wall safe, grabbed his jacket and headed out to his truck.

* * *

The children at Hopedale Middle School played happily at the playground under the watchful eyes of three teachers. They were not aware of the darkness encroaching upon them until it was too late.

The darkness spilled into the middle of their play area, eradicating the sunlight. The two creatures emerged from the heart of the darkness and casually chose their prey. The large felinoid scooped up a child and tossed him into a sack-like fold of skin on its massive underside. The child was too scared to scream or even struggle. Both creatures savored the child's terror as a gourmet appetizer before a fine meal. Wave upon wave of terror emanated from the screaming masses as they were chased and corralled into an ever-tightening mass of bodies, similar to dolphins herding a school of herring before they fed on the tight mass of food. One of the young teachers tried to escape and get help, her neck was snapped and her lifeless body casually tossed aside as an example for the others.

The waves of fear continued to nourish the creatures until they had at long last reached their full strength. The traces of past bullet holes disappeared from their bodies. The felinoid's skin, which had been peppered with bullet holes and scars, was now almost liquid black in appearance, barely distinguishable from the surrounding darkness. The large creature purred with sadistic satisfaction over its feed.

The children were all shrieking and crying, and both remaining teachers were terrified into inactivity. The smaller of the beings began wading through the mass of tiny bodies, similar to a person bargain-shopping, comparing items for a particular value. It picked up a screaming girl and carefully, almost gently, placed the crying child into the larger creature's skin pouch. The pouch seemed to flow around the child and simply engulf her struggling form.

"Stop it." One of the remaining teachers boldly stepped into the path of the seven-foot monstrosity. "You can't have these children. Let them go."

The creature paused momentarily to regard the apelike female who dared to challenge it. It was about to do something permanent to her when it caught the scent, the feel of something, someone familiar. The large felinoid smelled the air, issuing a great whistling sound as it inhaled and expelled air through its gigantic nostrils. It growled savagely, looking around warily for the source of the disturbance, its roar echoing for over a mile.

Both creatures spotted a form walking toward them, into the darkness. It was Human, but it was also Esper. The hybrid had appeared. They sensed no fear from the hybrid. In fact, they sensed no emotion from it at all. He walked closer to the circle of children then stopped, never taking his eyes off them. The hybrid's apish eyes were burning with a deep intensity. They did not fluctuate nor blink, they simply moved back and forth, studying the two creatures, waiting.

* * *

Erik swore to himself when he saw the darkness; he had run right into the creatures' feeding frenzy. He had no chance against both creatures, but somehow, he wasn't afraid. Something inside him welcomed the opportunity for another chance at combat despite the poor odds of survival. Both creatures noticed him and quickly turned to face him. Erik ceased his approach, hoping his presence would pull the creatures toward him and away from the children.

"*C'mon*," he projected, using his telepathy, toward the seven-foot monstrosity. "*We have unfinished business, you and I.*"

He realized that though they could hear his thoughts, they would not understand his language. Erik adopted a simpler strategy. He calmly pointed his right index finger toward both creatures, and gestured for them to approach him. He shot them a look of absolute disdain and contempt, which required no translation and would be easily deciphered in any language.

Erik willed his body stronger, and gasped as increased strength flowed throughout his system. His mind roared at the approaching combat, warning him of the danger. But there was something else, some unknown part of him that urged him on, that seemed to welcome this no-win combat situation.

* * *

The felinoid paused, remembering the painful injuries it incurred from the hybrid at their earlier encounter. It glanced over at its companion who was already moving toward its adversary, forgetting the children that were its prey. It rushed forward in blind fury, wanting to tear its enemy to pieces, its genetic programming screamed for it to kill.

The creature's attack was met with a heavy kick to its face and a strike to the midsection. It stepped back and whipped its tail around with blinding speed. The tail struck the hybrid, but as in their previous encounter, the enhanced being rolled with the force of the blow and came up unscathed. It attacked again, unleashing a frenzied rain of blows and strikes of razor-sharp claws and whip-like cracks of its tail. Nothing connected. The Human-Esper warrior stayed outside of its reach. He had learned from their encounters and adapted.

The black-armored creature grew furious. It was stronger now, it had fed, but it still could not overcome the hybrid's speed and agility. It suddenly realized how it could defeat its foe, and realization spurred it to action.

It turned back to the group of children, wading into them. It picked up another child and approached the large felinoid. The hybrid attacked, running toward it and leaping high into the air. His feet impacted with the armored creature, causing the creature to lose its footing and stumble forward. It dropped the child, and headed back toward the group of children. The creature turned, and was attacked again by the hybrid. As it attacked, the felinoid scooped up the other child its partner had dropped.

The hybrid now stood between the monster and the children, exactly where the creature wanted him. He could no longer use his agility. He would be forced to fight and protect the children simultaneously. The hybrid's greatest weapon was now taken away. The creature walked slowly toward him and the children, waiting for the hybrid to attack. The attack came with swift precision, kicks and punches, dozens of types of strikes against its armored hide. The creature had the advantage in close quarters. Its freshly enhanced strength was more than enough to absorb the impacts of blows from the hybrid.

It swung its arm and hit the hybrid hard across the face.

The blow cracked like thunder, its second blow was blocked, as was its third, but it managed to whip its serpent-like tail and catch the hybrid off-guard. Its tail slammed into his soft flesh, tossing the hybrid five feet into the air. As it expected, the hybrid came back attacking again.

The hybrid landed a solid sidekick into its leg, actually causing a slight crack in the creature's black exo-skeleton. The creature responded by slamming its fist into the hybrid's face. It heard a crack, and felt something warm upon its icy shell. Blood. Blood was pouring from the hybrid. He was hurt. The blood caused the creature to attack furiously. Several of his blows connected with ear-shattering thumps, while the creature sustained minor cracks in its facial plate from kicks and punches as the hybrid retaliated.

The human warrior still stood between the creature and its prey, but he was panting now, having difficulty breathing. Each breath the hybrid took was labored. The creature sensed this and walked toward the children again.

The hybrid still stood directly in its path, deliberately blocking its progress. This time, the creature did not wait to be attacked. It charged its foe, quickly closing the distance. The hybrid tried to react, but he was weakening, his reaction time was too slow. The impact sent the humanoid flying backward several feet, landing on his back.

The creature picked up another screaming child and turned toward its ally. After several steps, it felt a sharp stab of pain as something shattered the armored shell on its shoulder. It fell forward, face-first, into the playground sand. The child squirmed free and ran away screaming. As it got up, the creature was again slammed in the face by another powerful concussion. Its own blood was flowing freely down its face as the force of this powerful blow threw it back.

The hybrid held a large round object in both hands. The object was now covered with bright blue blood – its blood. The creature hissed savagely, and went over to a large wooden structure. It tore at the structure until a fair sized piece came off in its hands. It turned to face the hybrid, and was stunned as the round object his opponent had been holding collided with the front of its face.

The creature tossed the bundle it had torn from the object, not at the hybrid, but at the prey. The hybrid intervened, absorbing the impact himself by shattering the object with a massive blow from his arm, saving the small creatures. The impact, however, damaged the hybrid further. The arm it used to destroy the debris now dangled uselessly at an awkward angle from his body.

He was stumbling, shouting at the prey-things. At his voice, they began to scatter. The creature grabbed one more before they could all get away and tossed it toward the felinoid. It watched happily as the small thing was absorbed. Something had fallen from the little creature's neck, some kind of metallic chain. The creature paid no further attention to it, but instead focused on its victim. As it had hoped, the hybrid was unable to fight further. It rained blow after blow upon its victim, screeching with delight as it heard the sound of a bone breaking or the spillage of fresh blood.

The hybrid tried to fight back, actually landing two solid blows with his good arm. The hybrid was screaming something, shouting at the top of his lungs. He tried to approach the felinoid, but the cat backed away. The black-armored creature pummeled him again and again, but still the humanoid warrior crawled toward the felinoid, ignoring the dreadful beatings. The black-armored creature stopped, it looked toward the felinoid ally. It gestured to its companion, whose pouch was swollen with four stolen children.

The cat creature approached, and with one casual swipe of its huge paw, sent the sprawled hybrid crashing into a wall twenty feet from where he was kneeling. The hybrid did not get up. He no longer moved. Both creatures turned back into the darkness, disappearing.

* * *

Sunlight gradually filtered back into the schoolyard. Teachers and police made their way into the playground area. It was a scene of carnage.

The broken body of a schoolteacher lay sprawled on the ground, her head turned in an unnatural manner. Red blood and bluish fluid stained the sand everywhere. A play fort was ruined, scattered across the grounds. In the corner, slumped against the side of the school building, his body cut, bruised, broken, and bleeding, lay Erik Knight.

Police and panic-stricken teachers swarmed out into the playground area. The scene that greeted them was straight out of a horror movie. Teachers did their best to keep the other students who had escaped the creatures' wrath away from the area. The police carefully checked the area, and the fallen teacher for vital signs.

"She's dead," the officer whispered as he nervously caressed the grip on his service revolver.

They both made their way to where Erik Knight lay, gasping in horror as they saw his lacerated body lying in an ever-growing pool of his own blood.

"Damn!" one of the officers swore as he checked the fallen man for a pulse. "He's been through a meat grinder."

"He's been beaten to a pulp," one of the surviving teachers whispered. "He tried to save the children, his daughter."

One of the other officers picked up something from the sand. "Dog tags – Erik Knight's dog tags."

"He's still alive, barely," the officer who stood over his lifeless body remarked. "We need an ambulance and we need it now," he instructed the teacher.

"Whatever it was, Knight got a good piece of it before he fell," one of the officers remarked. "There's blue shit all over the place, and I found a large rock that has to be at least fifty pounds, covered with the stuff."

"I want statements from both teachers. Tape off this entire area. Nobody comes in without official authorization," the officer instructed as he knelt down at Erik's side. "Hang on, Knight, help is coming. Don't you die out here, you ornery son of a bitch, don't you die on us."

Chapter 11

He was in a hospital bed, several tubes and machines violating his body. A machine assisted his breathing. One of his lungs had collapsed, punctured by several broken ribs. His right arm was in a full-length cast, broken in three places. His skull was wrapped in an attempt to set his severely broken jaw. He had broken six fingers and crushed three knuckles in his fight. The doctors had sewn over two hundred stitches into various cuts and lacerations upon his tattered body and removed almost a pint of blood from his lung that hadn't collapsed, but was still partially skewered when one of his ribs cut through the delicate life-giving tissue. Mercifully, the doctors had pumped him full of sedatives. The pain from so many injuries inflicted would be more than a human nervous system could tolerate.

Several people sat in a waiting room outside the intensive care wing of Massachusetts General Hospital. One woman, in particular, seemed excessively agitated. She paced back and forth, her leather pants making a harsh scraping sound as her legs abraded the fabric. Her hair had a slight tint of purple and she wore dark eyeliner and lipstick. A man sat on an uncomfortable seat, watching her pace. He was older, with iron gray hair. He still had on a cooking apron and a grease-stained T-shirt, not even allowing himself time to change when he had heard that his friend had fallen. The third was a young woman, who sat slightly apart from the others. She, too, was concerned, but for more reasons than those who were with her at this point.

Another woman appeared, walking swiftly down the crowded corridor toward the waiting room. She was adorned in an expensive Italian leather overcoat and expensive shoes. She radiated wealth and importance with every step. Her face, however, radiated fear and concern as she made her way to join the others in their waiting vigil. She walked into the room and Jeff immediately stood.

"Mrs. Pendelton, is there any word about your daughter?"

"No," she whispered, "the police are still searching, but it's dark, and they really have no leads. Those things, those godforsaken creatures just vanished. How is he?" she asked suddenly, deliberately changing the subject. She had cried too many tears today, and didn't want another breakdown here.

"We're still waiting for a report," Shanda answered as tears ran down her face. "He was beaten pretty badly."

Margaret Pendelton sat down with Shanda and took her hand gently. "Listen to me," she began gently, "I've known our boy in there for too many years. He's a fighter. He has the uncanny ability to always bounce back. He'll bounce back from this too, you'll see."

"I hope you're right," Shanda answered. "If only they'd tell us something, anything."

"Excuse me," a voice interrupted. "Are you relatives of Mr. Knight?"

"Yes," Margaret answered, her tone becoming suddenly powerful, the voice of an influential woman of high society.

The doctor sat down on a nearby couch, thumbing through several medical charts.

"Mr. Knight is in extreme critical care at this time," he began. "His condition is terminal. I'm so sorry, but there's nothing more we can do for him. Both of his lungs have been punctured, one completely collapsed. We've put in almost three hundred sutures to sew him back together. His right arm is shattered, along with several fingers. His left leg has two fractures that should be set, along with a severely broken jaw. His nasal passages are destroyed and his nose shattered. A fragment of nose cartilage has been lodged into his cerebral cavity. We don't know the extent of the brain damage, if any."

The physician paused as there were several gasps of shock and astonishment. "The most serious matter of all is that his heart has been damaged. It can't sustain a normal beat without machine assistance. We believe two of the primary valves or chambers have ruptured from repeated heavy concussions. In his present condition, he wouldn't survive any intensive surgery, and there is no donor heart available."

"What exactly are you saying?" Margaret pushed.

"I'm saying there's nothing further we can do. Mr. Knight will, in all probability, expire before this evening is over. All we can do is keep him comfortable and pain-free during this time until his heart finally shuts down. Mr. Knight has a standing DNR on his medical files. We can't place him on further life support, and without life support, he will die. Even with life support, his chances of recovery are non-existent. There's just too much damage to his body. One problem alone is serious, he has three major life-threatening conditions, plus several serious non-life-threatening conditions. Even if we wanted to, we couldn't put him under the knife without killing him. His heart couldn't take the strain of the anesthesia. Technically speaking, we've violated the DNR order by doing what we've done. We didn't see the request until after most of the emergency room surgery was already performed," the doctor replied sadly. "Again, I'm sincerely sorry. I wish we could do more, but we can't. In all my thirty years in trauma, I've never seen such carnage done to a body before."

Shanda began to weep, a silent heart-wrenching cry of despair. Margaret's face turned pale as she shook her head in disbelief. Jeff simply placed his head down into his hands and sobbed. Alissa picked up a large duffel bag she had been carrying and quietly departed the waiting room.

* * *

Massachusetts General Hospital, Critical Care Unit, Room 7-B1

The three entered the room quietly. It was dark, almost pitch black. They heard the whir and buzzing of medical equipment and focused their attention on the body lying in the hospital bed, illuminated only from the faint glow of several pieces of machinery. They all slowly walked over to the bed and stared at the lifeless form. Shanda turned on a tiny lamp and was shocked to see the condition of her lover. She barely recognized his battered face. His cheeks were black and blue, and there were large dark rings under his eyes.

"Oh, Erik," she whispered, "what did they do to you?" Tears rolled down her face. "We were supposed to be together, my love. I really wanted to have a life with you. We were finally together, for such a short time. The doctors say you're going to die. They say you're not going to make it through the night. I don't want to believe them, but look at you, hooked up to machines to do your breathing, keeping your heart beating. Oh God! Don't leave me, not now, not after we've finally found each other." She broke down into tears.

"Erik," Jeff whispered as he grasped a battered hand. "I don't know what to say. You've been a blessing in my life. I know you think that I was helping you with the office and living space, but you gave back more than you'll ever know with your friendship and hard work. There was never any task you wouldn't tackle readily, with a smile. Everybody at the restaurant, everyone who cares about you, your family, is praying for you, young man. We're all praying for a miracle, so you hang tough," he whispered as tears ran down his face. "We don't want you to give up. Don't believe them, you can live," Jeff whispered as he faded back into the shadows.

"Oh God, Erik, where do I begin?" Margaret whispered. "I've been such a bitch to you these past years, and you just took it all in stride. I kept you from your daughter, chastised you at every turn." She sighed heavily. "And through it all you endured, never letting the bitterness show, even when Richard tore your life apart. Now, our daughter is gone. You sacrificed your life to try and save her. Erik, you shame me, I'm so sorry. I wish I could go back and do things all over again, take back all the hurt, tell you what a good father you've been to Brianna, let you spend more time with her and actually tell you what a good man you really are. I guess we just wanted different things."

Margaret paused and let out a heavy sigh. "I was angry. I wanted you to be something you weren't. But it seems that we always say these things too late. I'm saying all this now and you can't even hear me." She gently stroked the stray locks of hair that hung in his battered face. Margaret leaned over and gently kissed his bandaged head. She turned away and faced Shanda. "I'm so sorry, you two deserved some happiness. Stay with him, I'm sure that's what he would have wanted." Margaret Pendelton, the ex-Margaret Knight, said a final goodbye and silently walked away, regretfully closing a chapter in her life.

Jeff came over to Shanda and placed a gentle hand on her shoulder. "She's right. He'd want to spend his last moments with you. I'll sit here for a while if you'd like."

"No, that's all right, I'd really like to be alone with him, just hold onto his hand until it's over."

Jeff bent over and gently embraced her. "You brought him such happiness, there was a special spring in his step and a sparkle in his eye whenever the two of you were together. Always remember that."

"I will," she whispered as she took Erik's hand.

* * *

Shanda had been with him for nearly half an hour, holding his hand and staring at the digital displays and readouts of medical instruments that she really didn't understand. She only knew that the lines were getting flatter, and the beeps less frequent as the minutes passed. She felt such emptiness, sitting alone with him in the darkness wishing that there was some way to help him. She was so focused on Erik that she didn't respond to the tingling in her scalp until it was a constant eerie buzzing. She looked up into the darkness, toward the corner of the large room. She knew something was there.

"Who's there?" she whispered.

Silence answered.

"I know you're there. You can't hide from me. Come out."

She saw, deep in the darkness, a slim outline moving within the blackness. Shanda flipped the lamp on again, and switched the three-way bulb to its highest setting. There, sitting in the far corner, on a small chair, was the waitress from Madame's Restaurant.

"What the hell are you doing here?" she challenged.

"I'm watching over my brother, waiting for you to leave," she answered simply.

"You're lying! Erik has no sister," she challenged the young girl.

"None that he knows of. Erik has a small family, the human part of him just doesn't remember them," Alissa answered mysteriously.

"You'd better explain yourself, or I'll have security escort you out of here," Shanda replied angrily. How dare this girl torment her like this.

"Do that, and he dies, tonight, without fulfilling his purpose. Do that, and hundreds, possibly thousands, will die in the days to come, my sister," Alissa countered in a whisper, which Shanda could just barely hear.

"Now I know you're lying, I have no sister. What are you on, anyway?" Shanda asked bitterly.

"You have the gift, as your mother had, as her mother had, passed down from generations, over ten thousand years ago. I have the gift, only from a different source. Erik has the gift, one of many for a warrior, only far more powerful and potentially destructive than ours. His source was from a soldier, the most powerful soldier. The gifts were genetically enhanced in our soldiers. Do you want to learn the truth about Erik, the truth about you, me, and the things that are roaming throughout the town of Hopedale? Are you strong enough to handle the truth? If you're not, then you best leave because I have a job to do and I can't let you interfere," the young girl responded forcefully as she moved toward Erik's bedside.

Shanda responded to her advance by withdrawing a thirty-two auto from her purse. "I know how to use this, one of the benefits from knowing Erik Knight, so just stay where you are," Shanda warned in a lethal tone as she locked the weapon on the strange waitress.

Alissa paused, retreating three steps, never taking her eyes off the gun barrel pointed at her head. "This won't help him. If you really care about him, as you claim to, you'll step aside and let me do what I have to."

"And just what do you have to do?"

"Stabilize his condition, repair his body to the point where he will survive the mutation. As he is now, undergoing the change will kill him," Alissa answered. "I don't want to harm him, he's been through enough. I only want to help. Bring about what must be!" she added in an urgent tone.

"Can you really help him?" Shanda asked hopefully.

"Yes, but there are risks. If I don't give him this to stabilize him, he'll die before I can do anything." She held up a vile of blue liquid. "I can save him. He mustn't be allowed to die with his purpose unfulfilled."

Shanda focused her abilities on the young waitress. Their eyes locked briefly. She felt the desperation of the young woman, the overwhelming need to get to him, to heal him. She also felt a bond with her, a kinship that shouldn't be. It was a presence she had only felt with members of her immediate family. She broke her link with the waitress and looked back over at her dying lover. Deep down, something told Shanda that the girl could help him. Erik had no chance without some outside aid. Shanda figured she might as well let her try.

"Go ahead, what has he got to lose?" Shanda decided as she placed the pistol back in her purse.

Alissa uncapped the vial and gently poured the liquid onto a patch of exposed skin. The mysterious blue fluid was absorbed like a sponge drinking water.

"This will repair much of the damage done to his heart and lungs, accelerate the mending of his broken bones from weeks to hours, and repair the facial cartilage that's been ruptured. The elixir of life is one of many passed down to me and my kind over the centuries, and one of the few that I can make with ingredients found here," the mysterious waitress explained. "I only hope that I'm in time."

"What's in that stuff you just gave him?" Shanda stared at the dry patch of skin where the fluid passed into his body.

"Later," Alissa whispered. "Now, we watch and wait, and hope that the elixir is potent enough."

After fifty-five minutes of silence, the monitors registered a stronger heartbeat. His wavering pulse seemed to steady, but at a lower-than-normal rate.

"He should be strong enough to talk in another day or so. The mixture will continue to regenerate his essential life functions until he is strong enough to maintain them on his own. Then, it is up to the staff to complete what must be done."

Alissa pointed toward her large duffel bag. "In the meantime, I believe I owe you an explanation. My part of the bargain." The young waitress sat down and folded her arms. "Where to begin, probably with the closing of the Esper/Seelak War. That seems like the best place to start." Alissa took a deep breath and exhaled loudly.

"We're all products of a long-gone race of beings that inhabited this world for almost a thousand years. They lived alongside mankind, keeping themselves isolated, but still interested in us as an evolving species. You might say we're the reason for the continuing of the Great War; Humankind that is. You see, back then, there was a good chance that neither species would survive, theirs or ours. They were advanced, millennia ahead of where mankind is today. But for all their advancement, they were still plagued by war. Erik's lineage, your lineage, and my own are byproducts of that war, created to serve a purpose, created to right a hideous mistake, an error in judgment committed over 10,000 years ago." Alissa paused and sighed heavily. "I'm talking in circles, I apologize. But why bother talking when I can let you live it, are you willing?"

"Yes," Shanda answered, knowing exactly what her proposal meant.

Alissa walked over to her, and both placed their hands on each other's temples. There was a brief wave of discomfort as the two minds joined, and Shanda saw a part of human history contained in no history book anywhere on earth.

Chapter 12

The Esper/Seelak War

The large Esper walked into the settlement, nodding and acknowledging others as he passed. He stood easily head and shoulders above his peers in the council. His body, and the bodies of those in his sect, had been altered centuries ago. He and his kind were the culmination of thousands of years of genetic research on their home world. He was bred to be a soldier, his instincts, senses, and aggressiveness enhanced many times. His strength and martial skill was beyond the means even for his own people to measure. But for all his strength, he had the wisdom and compassion inherent in his species.

Those who made him realized that to make a compassionless soldier was to simply create a killing automaton, uncontrolled by a sense of right and wrong. He was intelligent, but not nearly as gifted as those of the Scholar sect. He knew of the healing arts, but not nearly as much as those of the Cleric sect. He admired those skills in the others who differed so much from him, and respected them for their unique abilities as they, in turn, respected him.

He approached the opening of a large cavern and entered, saluting the two soldiers who stood guard. As he made his way toward a large room, he was stopped by a telepathic thought.

"Jakor," the voice inside his head began, *"you return from negotiations with the Seelak, I trust the news you bring the council is favorable."*

Jakor smiled, something that looked peculiar on his chiseled silvery face. *"Sennek, my old friend, I have come to address the council. Come join me, and hear what I have to say."*

A smaller Esper materialized from seemingly nowhere to stand beside Jakor. The two exchanged a ritual greeting of friendship and respect and made their way to the Council Room.

"How goes your study of the species?" Jakor asked.

"As I feared, I, too, have news for the Council. I pray to our Gods that your news is better than what we have discovered."

Jakor nodded. His news was not good, but out of discipline, he would make his proclamation to the full council. He placed a hand on his smaller friend's shoulder as they both headed into the Council for session.

* * *

Jakor sat patiently, hearing the reports from each sect as they addressed the council. He understood most of what was being said, but some of the scientific data was beyond him. Sennek, who knew his friend's limitations, whispered telepathic explanations for his massive friend.

It was Sennek's turn to speak. He left his seat and approached the podium. The amplification light shone on him, and he began thinking to the representatives of their community of eight thousand, and the council of sects.

"My brothers and sisters, I have grave news. As we are all aware, over the past thousand years, we have been inundated by several new strains of virus that were hitherto unknown on this world. Over this time, diseases of all types have decimated our population. Every time we cure one ailment, a new virus or bacteria appears, and we must struggle anew to find cures. We have lost eighty per cent of our population to disease, and before this war, we knew the Seelak were experiencing similar medical problems within their population. Our medical resources are taxed beyond our ability to cope. This planet is producing bacteria and viruses specifically engineered to harm us. We now understand why. As in any body, this planet is fighting off an infection: Us."

Sennek paused as there were telepathic whispers amongst the council members and observers. *"We are an infection to this planet, a virus or bacteria that it is trying to rid itself. We now know why. We are, ourselves, infecting this planet with micro viruses, we are killing the species that this world has mothered and nurtured for hundreds of thousands of years. We are interfering with the natural evolution of this planet, as we suspected. We have examined some remains discovered from the last tribe of bodies we encountered. Their blood was contaminated with a virus inherent in our species and the Seelak species. We are killing this world, not just one species, but all species of this planet. We have seen evidence of depopulated forests around our settlement, no native wild life anywhere.*

"My friends, my peers, this world is at war with us as we are at war with the Seelak. This is a war we cannot win. We cannot defeat a planet. We can only find a small secluded place in the middle of nowhere, where our contamination will be kept to a minimum. We must let this world and its species evolve and develop. It is the way of things. We came here as guests thousands of years ago when, in ignorance, we destroyed our world. Now, we war again with the Seelak and we take another world to a course of doom. This cannot happen twice," Seenek remarked as there were now audible vocal and telepathic voices of amazement and panic.

"Order! There will be order in this chamber," a Senior Councilman shouted.

His cries were unheard. Jakor stood and faced the crowd. His hand fell toward the pouch that carried his Sentient Staff. He touched the liquid metal and it took its basic shape as a seven-foot staff according to its master's mental command. Jakor banged the staff against the floor and stared into the crowd with a war-like expression. The crowd was quickly silenced.

"Thank you, Jakor," the elder whispered as the massive soldier took his seat. "What you say, Sennek, is disturbing. Your sect has verified this?"

"Yes, Elder, all data and evidence have been provided to the Council through formal political channels, the data and conclusions are beyond reproach. It is regrettable, but what I say is truth," Sennek answered sadly.

"The Council will need time to review your data, Sennek. We do not doubt your words, we only wish to review all information."

"I understand, Elder," Sennek said with a bow.

"Jakor, you will address us," the Elder instructed.

Jakor took his place under the amplification light and spoke his news. "I have spent several suns under the banner of peace with our enemy, discussing much of what Sennek has brought to light, along with our territorial disputes. The Seelak care not for honoring the truce we made, which allowed us to construct our Worldship and bring us here so many years ago. They wish to go back to the ways of conquest. They believe we should eradicate the primate infection. They are angered over the death of their comrades from plague upon plague from diseases that are spread as the primates spread into other areas. They believe that by eradicating them, they will eliminate the diseases.

"This species covers the lands of this globe everywhere. The Seelak wish to commit genocide on an entire race of sentient beings – murder on an unprecedented scale. We must carry Sennek's research to them and hope that they can see for themselves the error in this course of action. With this new research to accompany what has already been presented, we have more than enough evidence to make our case. I will do this, Elder Council, upon your examination of data and with your permission."

"It shall be as you say, Jakor," the Elder replied. "We will send scientists to accompany you as well. No disrespect intended, but there may be technical questions above your level of understanding."

"Your words are wise, Elder. I see no disrespect. I will be guided by you," Jakor answered in the ceremonial form.

The elder nodded in approval. "It is you who honor us by your actions. We will reconvene in two suns."

A chime sounded, and the Esper population departed back to the day-to-day chores of their lives, each knowing that the next few cycles would bring about a drastic change to their small civilization.

* * *

Jakor spent the two days in the soldiers' compound, training and discussing battle strategy. The Seelak were a vicious enemy. They utilized the forbidden Netherspace technology, allowing them to traverse the inter-dimensional tunnels in this universe and seemingly pop out unexpectedly anywhere.

The tunnels between real space were, however, very narrow and hazardous. The dark matter that occupied that type of space readily spilled out into true space, disrupting the very physical nature of real space itself while the portal remained open. Small groups could traverse short distances at one time. If not for this fact, the entire Seelak military force could simply materialize inside their small city and eradicate everything in a single surprise attack. The only thing that announced their presence was the spillage of dark Nether matter into this universe while the porthole opened. It was as if the sun itself blinked out during Seelak sneak attacks.

Fortunately, Esper soldiers were trained to combat in these dark conditions, their eyes adapted to see in all spectra from the highest violet spectrum, to the lowest red spectrum. Netherspace portals served, usually, to allow the inferior Seelak army to ambush Esper soldiers and gain the advantage of a first strike. However, the Esper warriors were better trained than the enemy, and quickly turned the tables upon their attackers. Netherspace also served the Seelak as a quick, safe escape from combat.

* * *

Jakor reported back to the council after two days. There were several other reports given as he waited patiently for his turn. When his turn came, he approached the council floor and waited for instructions. The Council had selected three scientists to accompany Jakor. He was glad to hear that Sennek would accompany him. Something told him that this upcoming meeting would be pivotal to the future of both races.

"We have consulted with our enemy, and they have agreed to hear our scientists' evidence regarding the plagues decimating both our populations. We hold great hope for these talks. They are the last hope for our kind. We must make preparations to evacuate these settlements and resettle on a remote island away from the native species of this world."

"We will not fail you, Elder," Jakor pledged.

"May our Gods go with you," the Elder replied.

* * *

The small party of Espers made their way toward the Seelak encampment. Jakor carried the large statue of peace that advertised that their party came with only peaceful intentions.

After a five-mile walk, they were met by several Seelak. The Seelak were midnight black in appearance, in direct contrast to the silvery Espers.

"We greet you in peace under the statue of tranquility." Sennek extended his hand toward the leader of the Seelak delegation.

"We receive you in peace," the Seelak leader replied. "I am told that you have scientific information that you wish to present to us regarding the plagues brought on by these accursed ape-like creatures."

"We have," Sennek answered. "I am Sennek, of the Scientific clan of Esper. With whom do I have the honor of addressing?"

"I am Kalaak, also of the Scientific clan. Please present your evidence," the Seelak instructed, cutting across any dialogue the Esper scientist tried to establish.

"As you wish," Sennek replied, handing over several data crystals.

Kalaak took the crystals and placed them into his processing core. He studied the data and conclusions with several of the other members of their party. The Seelak team walked a small distance away after several minutes of reviewing the provided information. Both Jakor and Sennek could see animated discussions occurring from several of the enemy party.

"They're arguing over our conclusions," Sennek replied to Jakor.

The large Esper soldier grinned at his friend's statement of the obvious. "They will not accept your hypothesis." He looked down into his older friend's eyes.

"They must. There can be no other conclusion, the data can only be interpreted one way," the scientist insisted.

Jakor nodded, but he knew that the data could also possibly increase the enemy's position of mass extermination. "No one can know what the enemy thinks, old friend. Wait, one of them is coming back." The soldier gestured to the scientist.

The Seelak spokesman walked back toward the Espers. "We

have reviewed your data, and considered your conclusions. We agree with your data, and your analysis is well thought. However, we do not agree with your conclusions. Evacuation and isolation is not the answer, we must wipe out the primate infestation, totally and completely. A mere cleansing of our territories is no longer enough, we must unite and use our combined resources to wipe out the seed this world has planted everywhere. Then we can take over and make this world our own," the Seelak replied emphatically.

"No! No!" Sennek angrily disagreed, becoming emotionally distraught. "We cannot, we have no right to commit genocide against an entire species. It is not just the primates; it is every living thing on this planet that we are infecting and that is infecting our races. Destruction is not the answer. Killing one species will not save our people, you would have to kill every living thing on this planet," the Esper scientist pleaded. "Right down to the very core plants and fish that we use as a food source. Even the food we eat as nourishment will contain elements toxic to our people. If you waged the type of war you propose, you would sentence our species to starvation and eventual death as well."

Kalaak had folded his arms and shook his head. "You're proposing that we simply admit defeat and run away after a thousand of this planet's years? Abandon all that we have accomplished and isolate ourselves until this world eventually kills us? You ask the absurd, Esper. I cannot bring that kind of decision back to my people. Our Council would hang my head on a pole outside of our gates for even suggesting such foolishness." Kalaak paused, briefly looking back at his party before continuing. "Consider this: These apes are weak, even your scholars are many times stronger than this upstart race that has no real technology. Your genetically enhanced soldier over there." He pointed toward the titanic Jakor. "Could probably defeat thousands of them alone. Is he not engineered to be the strongest and most powerful of your race? Our soldiers and your soldiers could easily conquer this planet and eradicate this planet's infection. We could be the rulers of this world."

"Did you not carefully study the data?" Sennek pleaded.

"Did you not see that there are no other possible conclusions! We cannot murder an entire population, let alone several populations and different species. It is the planet waging this war, not the primates, nor the flying creatures or the crawling creatures. The ecological make-up of this world is rejecting us. You must see that truth. Why do you deny it?" Sennek asked, his emotional state becoming even more agitated. "We are the infection, not them!"

"You Espers are too emotional. That is your weakness, and will be your downfall," Kalaak remarked, gesturing. "Our only problem now, as we see it, is you. And we have finally found a way to rid ourselves of that problem."

From behind the Esper party, a portal from Netherspace opened. Darkness spilled into the area blanketing the natural sunlight. Two creatures emerged from the opening. The first was a formidable-looking Seelak, taller even than Jakor. The second was a monstrous creature that was like some cross between a native panther and a Slaka Dragon from their now extinct world. The creature was almost fifteen feet in height and over twenty-five feet in length.

"Meet the products of our scientific technology," Kalaak announced proudly. "Genetically engineered from our best scientist, me; programmed to hate Espers and designed to feed on emotion, the same types of emotion you Espers emit so readily. Prey." He gestured to the Esper party. "Meet your new predators, our key to winning this war, and exterminating the species of homo sapiens. Destroy them all!"

The creatures attacked, ripping two of the Esper scientists to shreds, gleefully feeding off their powerful emotions of stark terror and shock. The Esper emotion fed the genetically engineered monstrosities, making them even stronger. Jakor was struck by the larger creature, the powerful blow propelled the Esper warrior over a dozen feet. Jakor, however, was no normal Esper. His strength, speed, reflexes, and aggressiveness were far beyond normal. He reached inside his tunic and grabbed his Sentient Staff. The weapon expanded and responded to his mental commands. He was now enraged. The Seelak had broken a sacred truce and slaughtered members of their party.

Jakor attacked the large enhanced Seelak. His staff clanged

on the skin of the creature. Sparks flew as the sentient metallic weapon impacted with the creature's enhanced metallic shell. The shell cracked, and the creature retreated, and then turned to face him.

Jakor pressed his attack on the huge mutant Seelak. His silvery fists pummeled the armored creature in wave upon wave of sheer ferocity. The Seelak struck back. The power of its own blows was staggering. Its power was enough to kill an ordinary Esper.

Jakor withdrew slightly. He struggled to see where the rest of his party was. He was horrified to see the giant cat-like creature gnawing on what was once Sennek. Jakor howled with rage, his genetically enhanced aggressiveness and anger pushed him to attack. He leapt at the large cat, covering several meters with one bound, his fists raining dreadful blows upon its huge body. The feline roared with distress, and swiped at him with massive paws. Jakor was struck by one of the paws, huge claws left a large gash in his silvery metallic flesh. He responded by slamming his Sentient Staff down upon the creature's front leg and was rewarded with a loud snap as its leg broke from the blow. The creature shrieked with agony and limped away from Jakor. Jakor never saw the boulder that struck him from behind. The enhanced Seelak hurled it from a great distance. The force of the impact caused the Esper soldier to fall and lose consciousness. The Seelak was about to finish him when it was ordered by its creators to withdraw. Both monsters re-entered the portal and it closed behind them.

Kalaak knelt over the fallen Esper soldier and checked his vital signs. "He will live. Let him return to his colony, a disgrace, defeated. We have dishonored ourselves enough with this slaughter, I'll not kill a warrior like this. He deserves a better death. We will return to our people and prepare for the final battle of this war. We will not go quietly. We will conquer this planet and wipe out the ape-like species that grows here like a plague, spreading across this world like a diseased fungus."

* * *

Several minutes passed and Jakor slowly regained his senses. The boulder that fell him still lay perched upon his shoulders. He hefted his arms, propelling his massive frame up and tossed the 800-pound stone to the ground. He walked over to where the lacerated body of Sennek lay. As he studied the mutilated body of his friend, he let out a shriek of rage that was easily heard for miles.

"My dear friend, how could we have been deceived so, under the Statue of Peace?" he whispered. "They will pay for this atrocity, I promise you. They will all pay dearly," he added in a lethal whisper.

He recited the traditional burial prayer for the dead over each fallen body. He wanted to carry his old friend back and bury him properly, but knew time was of the utmost importance, and the time he had left was limited. His arrival, and the news that the sacred truce had been violated, would be the trigger for the Espers to arm for a final assault. The preparation for an attack on his settlement was probably already underway. His people needed to be rallied and forces marshaled immediately.

Jakor's anger ran through his body unchecked. He looked back over at the body of his friend and screamed a shout so loud that its echoes reverberated for miles. The massive silver figure walked over to the boulder that had struck him and pulverized it to powder with his fists. His anger slowly faded, only to be replaced with a deep remorse. He knew the days ahead would be filled with the horrors of war.

Jakor pondered the possible reasons that the enemy allowed him to live. They must surely know that he would return home and report the atrocities carried out against their party under the Statue of Peace. Jakor turned and headed home. He ran, faster than the fastest cat. He leapt over boulders and chasms, ignoring everything but the desperate urging in his mind to return home and report, to give his people time to prepare for the upcoming attack.

Jakor spotted the settlement in the distance and he urged his limbs to carry him faster. He sprinted by the armed guards, yelling to them to prepare for attack as he passed by. The sentries sounded a general alarm as he made his way into the Elders' chambers. The door to their meeting room was barred shut from the other side. Jakor drove his fist through the thick wood, forcing the doorway off of its hinges, propelling the splintered wooden barrier into the conference chambers. He did not waste time with the usual formalities, his words were simple as he faced the High Council.

"The Seelak have broken the Statue of Peace, our party has been murdered. Attack is imminent. We must prepare ourselves," he shouted telepathically, and then turned away.

"Wait!" one of the Elders yelled, using his voice instead of telepathy, which was always used inside the chambers. "How can this be?"

"We were lied to," Jakor answered. "This agreement to hear our data was nothing more than a prelude to a trap. They have created monsters to do their fighting for them. These creatures killed our scientists, nearly killed me. We were nothing more than an experiment to see if their creatures functioned properly." Jakor looked back at the Council members who sat in stunned disbelief. "We must prepare to attack our enemy, before they can attack us. We already are at a disadvantage. They are most assuredly marching as we speak." Jakor turned to leave the chamber.

Jakor was conferring with other members of his Soldier clan, preparing strategy and tactics, when the news came.

A Scout came into his shelter and reported. "They are coming, Jakor."

"How many?" he asked, still looking at a map of the area.

"All of them," the scout whispered.

Jakor looked up from his map in shock. "Not just the soldiers?"

"No, my liege, There were soldiers, scholars, and scientists from what I could make out. Their soldiers are larger, like us, so they are easy to spot. There are several soldiers in each group, but it appears the entire colony is marching out to do battle, plus some things that are larger than soldiers, unlike anything I have ever seen before."

"Yes, I am familiar with them." Jakor nodded. "Those will be the focus of our initial attack."

"You have come up with a strategy?"

"Yes, the Seelak are not the only ones who are capable of surprises. I have a few of my own prepared. They were foolish to leave the Worldship with us. There were many things that still have some power, even after these thousands of years. Come, let us go to the Council, quickly. We'll have barely enough time to deploy our forces before the Seelak come knocking on our gates."

Jakor addressed his five sub-commanders and his 750 remaining soldiers, along with the rest of the Esper population. The community had crammed into the central square, waiting for their instructions to defend their community and their lives.

"Our timing is critical," Jakor emphasized to the large crowd. "These creatures utilize Netherspace, like the other Seelak, and can disappear at any time, and re-appear just as quickly. It is imperative that those of you who will be firing the plasma streams hit as many of them as you can on your first shot. These weapons we've managed to salvage only have enough power for one or maybe two bursts, then its back to more conventional means. There is also no guarantee that all the weapons will function properly. We have repaired them to the best of our capability, but cannot test them without depleting their small remaining charges. As we all know, our reactor cores were fused when we crashed here, leaving most of our resources destroyed or contaminated. These were taken years ago and hidden in case of conflict with other native species." He paused, looking down at the sleek weapons. "Never did I dream that we would be fighting the Seelak again with them."

Jakor's plan was brilliant, but risky. He would have twenty of his best soldiers take positions in the hills surrounding a large open field. The presence of his small army would draw the enemy into the field. They would march directly toward the soldiers, anticipating a quick victory. The remaining non-soldier Espers would be hiding in various places along the wooded areas inside their own Netherspace portals, nearby, yet undetectable until needed.

As soon as the enemy soldiers completely entered the field, they would emerge from hiding and quickly take up positions behind the enemy. As soon as the soldiers fired upon the great beasts, they would emerge from the enemy's flank and attack.

The Seelak would be trapped, forced to fight a defensive battle. The soldiers would then cut a path through the enemy troops, effectively cutting their forces in half. Then, they would engage in hand-to-hand combat with whatever forces would be remaining on both sides.

This was risky, and would ultimately result in a blood bath, since the other Esper forces and Seelak forces that were not soldiers had very little military training or combat experience. Jakor assumed that the Seelak soldiers would be at the front of the army before they attacked, while the weaker non-military sects would be at the rear. By having the two non-military entities combat each other, he hoped to minimize their slaughter. Everything depended on the success of eliminating the creatures and most of their soldiers before they could jump into Netherspace. If the creatures jumped before the battle, all would be lost, and they would be hard-pressed to defend against both Seelaks and their monstrous creations jumping in and out of combat.

The Seelak perfected the use of Netherspace, while the Esper people had shied away from the dangerous life-threatening technology. The portals in Netherspace were easily lost from the dark side. If one lost site of the exit portal, one would be trapped forever on the other side, condemned to eternal darkness.

Every Esper in the colony knew that the fate of Earth's creatures relied upon the successful outcome of their race in this all-encompassing battle. It was worth the risk of hiding in this forbidden space just this one time. Jakor figured, as long as his people stayed by the portal and didn't wander the seemingly endless tunnels of that alternate dimension, they would be safe until their call to action came.

"Proceed, Jakor, the Council will be guided by your leadership during this time of great military crisis," the elder announced, waiting to hear the warrior's plan.

"We must deploy now. Our enemy is already moving into position to strike against us. We must set up around the perimeter of these small hills." He gestured toward a three-dimensional representation of the landscape. "We will draw them into the great opening with our small force. Everyone else must be concealed in the surrounding forest." He pointed to the surrounding growth. "We will have our armed soldiers at these high points. When the enemy has entered into the field, they will eliminate as many of the creatures as possible. The rest we will deal with. Under no circumstances engage the beasts. Let the soldiers do that. Fight the non-soldiers as much as possible, you will live longer," he remarked forcibly.

"I know many of you are not experienced in combat, I regret there is no time in which to even give you the most rudimentary instruction," he added. "Those of you who are armed with a Sentient Staff, listen carefully: The staff will respond to your mental commands. It will react to what your mind thinks and sees, so keep focused on your combat and the weapon will do most of the fighting for you. Good luck, and may our Gods preserve us. Let us go forth onto victory."

* * *

The Seelak army continued to march forward, a great black mass of bodies some ten thousand strong, including the dozen pairs of mutated abhorations they created to do most of their fighting for them. Each seven-foot-plus Seelak mutation rode atop a feline-dragon, gently caressing the great beasts as they plodded along the grassy terrain.

The great beasts sensed the upcoming conflict, as did their riders, though the riders seemed to relish the thought of vanquishing their foe, consuming every enhanced emotion of fear and terror the enemy would emit during battle.

In battle, all sentients had fear. These feline creatures could feed off that fear and become stronger. It was the intent of the Seelak that their creations rip their enemies apart, piece-by-piece, and feed off the terror of each soldier as they met their horrible death by dismemberment. The fact that there would be weaker, untrained opposition meant that the feed would be that much greater. The fear in an undisciplined mind was far greater than a mind accustomed to combat. The Seelak creations rode on with glee, anticipating a great feed to satisfy their never-ending hunger.

A scout approached the warrior leader and made his report.

"They're in the next clearing, waiting for us, but it is only a small force, comprised of only soldiers. The other sects do not come out to engage in battle."

The Seelak leader paused momentarily, and then began to laugh. "The fools are so honor-bound that they assume only soldiers will be fighting this last battle? This victory will be almost too easy. Let us go meet with these brave soldiers, have our beasts take lead. As soon as they enter the clearing, have them charge and attack. We will follow, at a slight distance, to clean up the remaining soldiers, then march on to their encampment unhindered," the leader instructed.

The scout lifted up a small golden horn and pressed it to his lips. He blew one shattering note, and the creatures advanced, moving very quickly. The scout waited thirty seconds and blew another note at a slightly different pitch. The Seelak Soldier clan began to advance. All others formed at the rear and began to follow suit.

The creatures entered the clearing and spotted their shiny enemies simply standing at attention, acting as if they had no care in the world. The feline beasts and their riders galloped swiftly across the half-mile that separated them from their prey. The soldiers followed behind their front troops, closing the gap between both forces.

When there were only a hundred yards between the two armies, the lead Esper raised his hand. There was no time to react or wonder what the gesture meant. In less than three seconds, ten of the twelve Seelak warrior pairs of mutants were vaporized, consumed inside bright balls of fiery plasma. The shrieks of pain were beyond anything either side could bear, as, piece-by-piece, the creatures' bodies were boiled and withered away. The other pairs vanished in a Netherspace portal, and re-emerged behind the Seelak army.

Ten more fiery bursts engulfed several hundred Seelak soldiers, consuming them entirely. The Seelak formed a defensive circle in the middle of the field, waiting for further onslaught. As was planned earlier, the Esper forces emerged from the forests, and hemmed their enemies in preventing any possible escape, save for Netherspace.

"We have been tricked," a remaining Seelak soldier cursed

looking at their leader as they watched the remaining Esper population swarm onto the battlefield.

"Treachery from those honor-bound Espers? I can't believe it!" The Seelak Commander saw his army's easy victory routed into an inevitable bloody conflict in mere seconds. "Our foe learns fast, consenting to use our old weapons to gain an advantage, as we planned to use our creatures. We have only two sets of creatures remaining, and many of our soldiers have been crushed, fried into non-existence," the commander observed. "Let's close with their forces. They won't fire and risk hitting their own people. Perhaps we can salvage a victory yet."

* * *

The battle was savage. The Esper soldiers clashed with the Seelak forces, staffs and blades whirred in streaks. The cries of the dying and wounded soon accompanied various battle shouts.

Jakor spotted a pair of mutant creatures decimating a group of untrained Esper philosophers, tearing them apart. He fought his way over to the group, and smashed his staff down against the feline creature's hind flank. The beast howled in pain and rage as it quickly spun around. It struck at the Esper warrior with titanic forepaws. Jakor stepped back, allowing the blow to whisk by him. He counter-attacked savagely, his staff a blur of motion. Both creatures were forced to withdraw from his furious assault. Each had suffered dreadful injury from his Sentient Staff.

The large cat leapt again, launching itself like a twenty-foot missile directly at Jakor. Jakor ducked to avoid the beast, but the creature reacted, raking its massive claws along his back as it sailed over the Esper warrior. The blood flowed freely from the deep gashes on his back, but he ignored the burning pain. The enhanced Seelak jumped off the feline's back and produced a black fighting saber from seemingly nowhere.

The cat backed away, sitting on its haunches. The Seelak gestured for Jakor to approach. He raised his staff and willingly obliged. The two combatants circled each other, testing each other's strength and skill with cautious strikes, neither one over-extending themselves.

Jakor swung his staff in a wide semi-circle designed to bring the end of his staff flush against the Seelak's side. The Seelak guessed his maneuver, and adjusted its guard accordingly. Both weapons met with a huge impact, sending showers of sparks over both combatants. Jakor recovered from the jarring impact and drove the butt of his staff into the Seelak's midsection before it could recover its guard. The creature folded over, but came up swinging the mighty sword in dangerous arcs that were designed to slice the Esper in two. Every time the weapons collided, more hot sparks flew from the alien metals.

Jakor changed his strategy, and willed his staff into something else. One end of the weapon formed itself into a large hook-billed blade, while the other end increased in thickness and density, providing stability and balance for the new weapon form. He swung the heavier weapon at his foe. The added weight forced the Seelak blade down again and again, doing what the lighter staff could not.

The Seelak tried to adapt to this new form of combat, but was unable to cope with the change. Its saber had small chips and burrs upon its once-sharp edge. It still swung the damaged blade, aiming for Jakor's head. It increased the ferocity of its attacks until Jakor was reluctantly forced back, step by step. The enhanced Seelak swung a massive overhead blow at the Esper, fully prepared for the impact of the two weapons. Jakor didn't block this blow, however. He expertly rolled to one side, avoiding the blow altogether. The force and momentum of the Seelak warrior's blow carried it forward, completely off balance. Jakor slammed the edge of his modified Sentient Staff upon the Seelak's armored back. The edged portion of the staff bit through the armored hide with a sickening crunch. The creature staggered, up-righting itself. It was bleeding profusely from the gaping wound, spilling blue ichor onto the green grass.

The Seelak charged again, and Jakor easily avoided the attack. The Seelak's intention, however, was not to attack, but to escape. It landed on the back of the large felinoid.

A sudden cloud of inky black surrounded the two creatures. They were preparing to escape into Netherspace. Jakor knew that if they teleported, they would most likely leave the area, and be a nuisance throughout their genetically enhanced lives, and would no doubt plague the race of simians that had evolved on this world.

He reached inside his tunic and produced a stun grenade. He had carried it with him for centuries, never knowing if the weapon still had potency. Jakor flipped the activator, and heard the whining chirp as its energy core built to a critical mass. He threw the grenade into the portal as it closed around the two beasts. He heard the sound of an explosion, and felt a mild concussion. He surmised that most of the force of the detonation was contained in the region of Netherspace. The portal was effectively destroyed, and normal space quickly filled in the void caused by the vanishing blackness. Both creatures lay in a twisted heap on the corpse-littered battlefield. That was the last of his surprise munitions. The rest of the battle was strictly hand-to-hand combat.

Jakor joined the other soldiers and clansmen, fighting, at times savagely, to defend the planet's new dominant species. After three hours of non-stop combat, the last of the Seelak warriors fell. The remaining Seelak reluctantly surrendered and were herded roughly into a makeshift prison camp. The two creatures that Jakor had incapacitated were locked inside the now abandoned and partially gutted Mothership, other warriors had brought down the other pair. The metal of that ship's hull could not be penetrated, and Netherspace portals would not function within the confines of the ship's interior.

The final battle for Earth had cost the Espers nearly all of their remaining population. A scant four hundred Espers survived the final conflict, while only slightly over fifty Seelak survived the hostilities. None of the Seelak soldiers survived. Jakor lost all but twenty of his soldiers. There were sparse few of each remaining Esper clan, and most of those that had survived the battle had suffered some type of injury. Even Jakor, with all his enhanced might, had sustained several deep lacerations that needed treatment.

The Esper warrior looked over at the battlefield and gaped at the endless sea of bodies that expired in this futile confrontation. "Such a great waste," he muttered to himself. "If only they had listened. If we had combined our talents, we could have survived, somehow. Why does it always have to end in violence with our two species? We built an entire Worldship together, a marvel of technology to take us hundreds of light years to this new home. Only by working together did we accomplish this, why must it always end in blood!" he shouted into the air angrily.

"Because there was no other way," a voice from behind answered.

Jakor spun around quickly and stood facing a Seelak captive being escorted by two guards. It was the scientist he had met with prior to the final battle. The elder Seelak had many cracks in its shell, and was oozing blue ichor from several wounds.

"Why is there no other way?"

"Because you wish to preserve the apes, and we wish to exterminate them. If we were to go along with your plan, we would be condemning ourselves to eventual extinction. That is not our way. To die in battle or die for a belief is far better. We believe we're right and you're wrong. Your way will get everyone killed. That is why we fight," the Seelak answered bluntly. "It is that simple, no cosmic mystery to unravel, soldier, an answer simple enough for even your limited intellect to comprehend. We fight to survive. But you have prevailed, we are all doomed," it added bitterly.

"There are always alternatives to bloodshed," Jakor replied, surprised at the blunt openness of the captive. "We had accomplished much working together. Together we could have found a way to co-exist on this planet with its native species."

"No, my warrior friend," the Seelak said sadly. "Your scientists have confirmed what we knew all along: This world is killing us, both our species, as we are killing the species of this world. There is no answer, only eventual death. We sought to prolong our existence by depopulating this planet. There was a moderate chance of success, but I'll tell you now, between victors and vanquished, I did not think we could succeed. But speaking out against our ruling caste would have caused my instant execution. I am not so foolish as to not value what little time I have left in my life."

"I'm afraid this battle has sealed both of our fates," Jakor remarked, looking over at the field littered with corpses from both sides. "There are too few of us now to accomplish anything. We are all injured to some extent. Many of our Scientific and Medical were slaughtered. This pointless battle has condemned both our races."

"If it means anything, warrior, I am sorry that it came to this end. I did enjoy my time among your people before the war, but one must do as is commanded in our civilization, whether it be deemed right or wrong."

"I, too, am sorry. I cannot say for certain what will happen to your people now," he added somberly.

"Our fate is now in your hands, warrior," the Seelak said. "You will decide if we live or die."

"No," Jakor disagreed, "not my fate, the fate of the Council, or what's left of it. I have no authority in those decisions. My function has been served. I have done my duty."

Jakor motioned the guards to take the prisoner to where the others of its kind were being held. The Council was even now debating the Seelak's fate. He would carry out their orders, and then they would decide how to survive the post battle. Jakor knew, as did the Seelak, that even in the midst of their war, they could only have minor skirmishes, with only the Warrior clans taking part. A full-scale confrontation would depopulate both warring factions due to their small numbers. They had proved that hypothesis today; evidence enough lay on the battlefield. Jakor took one last look at his fallen comrades, and enemies, and turned toward their encampment.

* * *

"They must be appropriately punished for their actions," a Council member stated.

"What point is there in punishment?" another challenged. "They are no more, and we are no more. Punishment is futile at this point."

The Council had been debating for nearly three cycles to decide the fate of the forty remaining Seelak survivors. The last of their beasts had recovered, and were being held captive within the massive hull of the incapacitated Worldship. Jakor sat in his customary location, sadly looking at the empty seat that was once occupied by his departed friend, and the nearly vacant hall.

He quickly noted that more Espers had died from wounds received in battle over the last few hours before this meeting. There were scarcely two hundred Espers in a hall meant to hold almost ten thousand, and those in attendance were far from perfectly healthy.

"Enough," the Elder Councilor spoke as he raised his slim silvery hand. "I have heard enough debate. Any more discussion is pointless." He began addressing the small crowd. "The Seelak shall be punished for bringing us to this end. Whether history deems us petty or wise for inflicting punishment is irrelevant, because we will pass, history will never know of our existence. The beasts that the Seelak created were engineered to feed off emotion. I gather the Seelak have emotions, though granted not as strong or prevalent as ours. Let those who remain share confinement with the monstrosities they created. Let them be the source of food for their own creations. The beasts will never be able to be fully satiated by them and will never fully recover, and they will be tormented by the beasts as long as they continue to live. We will entomb them in the hull of our Worldship. It will serve as their final prison and burial place for all eternity," he said in a ringing tone.

There was absolute silence throughout the chamber as the remaining Espers struggled with the horrible fate that the Council had prescribed for their enemy.

"Is that not excessive, Elder?" Jakor asked.

"What is the appropriate punishment for homicide, genocide, and the attempted destruction of an entire ecosystem, soldier?" the Elder countered.

"Surely, you are aware of Seelak society. Most fought unwillingly and were forced to follow orders or be eliminated. We have no soldiers or military minds in these survivors. They are a few working-class drones and some crippled scientists."

"Scientists who created genetic monstrosities to destroy us, Jakor," the Elder replied forcefully.

Jakor arose to his impressive height, his hand instinctively reaching to his staff. "I cannot allow this."

"You would dispute the Council which has ruled our world for over half a million cycles, warrior?" the Elder asked in a soft yet powerful voice.

The tension in the chamber was palpable. Several soldiers stood from their positions, looking to Jakor, ready to follow their leader's example. The fact that the other warriors seemed prepared to follow Jakor didn't go unnoticed.

The mightiest of all Esper warriors was silent. However, his body assumed an aggressive posture, and there were several gasps when he activated his Sentient Staff.

"Jakor?" the Elder whispered, his eyes never veering from the exposed weapon. "You have brought us this great victory. You saved this planet. Would you tarnish that by now rebelling against us? Would you now turn on your own people, your own culture? You would raise a weapon against your own kind?"

Jakor stared into the Elder's eyes, the warrior's own blue eyes burning like two hot young suns. The Sentient Staff deactivated. "No, Elder, I will abide by your words out of respect for this body, not because I approve of them." He placed the weapon back in its pouch.

"As you wish," the Elder answered, visibly relieved his authority would not be challenged. "The Seelak will be punished, those are the words of the Council. Are there any other objections?"

No others objected.

"Then, carry out the will of this governing body, for there are still more hard decisions to make."

Jakor bowed and departed with the other remaining warriors. He did not agree with the Elder Council, but it was not his place to argue. He understood the Council's anger and understood the crimes of which the Seelak were guilty, but to be entombed alive, as food for some laboratory creations, made him shudder. He silently wished that the grenade had had sufficient force to destroy the two creatures they captured. He knew that if Sennek were alive, he too would disapprove of the course of action being taken.

The warriors escorted their captives toward the towering

structure that was the Worldship. The craft was almost completely buried into the side of a large mountain. Only a small portion of its gigantic hull protruded. The captives were silent, yet hesitant, as they were forced up the ramp leading into the access bulkhead.

As they approached the entrance to the ship, the captives spotted the creatures being forced back, deeper into the ship, by five soldiers armed with Sentient Staffs. It was then the Seelak realized their fate. Widespread fear and panic overtook the small band of forty battered Seelak. Jakor and his warriors were hard-pressed to drive the reluctant prey into the bulkhead opening. He heard shrieks and several pleadings for mercy from their captives. Normally, he was immune to such things, but this time his entire being was wracked with pity as he personally drove several Seelak forcefully into the ship.

Only one Seelak went without hesitation, the one that Jakor had spoken with earlier. He had accepted his fate and walked into his doom with no trace of fear or reluctance. He turned toward Jakor and bowed slightly, then entered his final confinement.

He suddenly turned and looked up at his captor. "Can I know your name?"

"I am Jakor."

"I am Keelal."

"Keelal, this is not my wish. Now it is my turn to be sorry. This act shames me," Jakor confessed.

"Then we both carry the shame for the hideous acts committed by our races, warrior. Fret not, I'll lay no blame to you if you will lay no blame to me for these horrid acts committed by forces outside our control," the Seelak whispered. "It will be our little secret."

Jakor grinned. "Our secret then," he agreed sadly.

"Live well, Esper." Keelal turned and entered his first moment of imprisonment.

"We shall not, Seelak, for we are both doomed races," Jakor whispered.

The five soldiers retreated from the inside of the ship and closed the massive metallic door behind them. Jakor locked eyes on the seven-foot enhanced Seelak as it picked up its first victim. It gave Jakor a look of pure ice water, as if saying with its eyes, "This is not over. We will meet again." The door sealed and locked with a doom-filled clang.

"Place the warning markers," Jakor ordered.

Several Espers rolled a large chamber in front of the door and magnetically fused the chamber into place. The pillars on either side of the chamber were marked with both Esper and Seelak, as well as other mathematical symbols they had hoped future races, including the primitive species already inhabiting this world, would be able to identify. It was a clear warning not to disturb this chamber. Jakor watched with reluctant satisfaction as the final work was done to the warning markers.

"Bury it," he ordered.

On his command, the series of small charges set above the chamber detonated. Tons of rock and debris fell on top of it, completely burying the Mothership inside the huge mountain of rock and debris that had been created when the ship initially crashed into the giant hillside. Jakor studied the mountainous landscape that contained their ship and its new occupants.

He shuddered involuntarily at their fate. The beasts seemed to only obey the soldiers of their kind, and there were no soldiers left to command them. He could not imagine a more terrible fate than to be imprisoned as food for some genetic mutant monsters. He shook his silvery head, then turned his powerful shoulders and headed back toward their main encampment.

What will be our fate? They could no longer live in this world, and they had no more resources to leave the main landmass they inhabited.

Chapter 13

A seed of hope is planted

The sun was setting as Jakor settled himself in his quarters. This had been the most trying of times. The fighting was over and the prisoners entombed. There was little else for a soldier to do to occupy the time remaining.

Jakor was tired – a deep down tired from physical fatigue and mental anguish. There would be a black stain of guilt upon his race for what they had done this day. Whether History remembered it or not, Fate would not forget, and Fate had a way of making all who defied her pay and pay dearly.

He settled his massive frame on his spartan bed and closed his eyes. He relaxed each part of his body, allowing the deep sleep to take him.

"Jakor!" a voice whispered in his mind. *"Jakor, please reply,"*

The soldier opened his eyes and became alert. *"Who is contacting me?"* he replied, broadcasting a general telepathic reply.

"You must come to the Great Hall in the Council. We will meet you there."

Jakor stood, and made his way to the Council Chamber. He entered the vast hallway that was created from living rock, and made his way toward the Great Hall. He quietly entered the hall from a seldom-used doorway and studied the seemingly empty chambers. He could sense the presence of others, and knew that they were deliberately concealing themselves. Jakor walked into the open, stopping at the large podium.

"I have come as you requested," he began. "Why do you hide from me?"

"No one is hiding, Jakor, we are just making sure that you have come alone." The elder made his way down from the aisles of seats.

Jakor was shocked to see the Council Elder along with the two most senior members of their committee.

"Elder!" Jakor began. "Why have you summoned me in this way?" He was more puzzled than angry.

"There is one last great deed that we must accomplish, soldier, and it cannot be done without you. The four of us represent the highest members of our sects," the Elder explained.

"Mishall is the premier scientific mind left to us now that Sennek has expired, Kaylar is our finest cleric, and I am the most gifted in the scholarly pursuits. You, soldier, are the strongest, most powerful of us all. You are a product of a combination of all of us. We need your genetic traits, along with ours, to pass on to this race of beings dominating this planet. Our time must soon end. This world belongs to them now, not to us. But, we can leave some of them the knowledge of our race – in an indirect way – to use and hopefully to avoid the mistakes that we made."

"How is this possible?" Jakor asked.

"By utilizing a sentient micro virus," Kaylar replied. "We take our own genetic material and implant it into one of our engineered micro viruses. The virus will then be programmed to seek out certain host bodies that will be the most compatible hosts for our particular genetic traits. Those with enhanced knowledge and intellect will likely become hosts for the virus that contains the Elders or Mishall's genetic material, those superior in the warrior skills will be infected by the virus carrying your genetic traits. Only a scarce percentage of those who possess these traits will be ideal matches, but only the ideal matches will benefit from the gift. The virus will keep searching, moving from host to host until the perfect hosts are found."

"What then?" the soldier asked as his interest peaked.

"It will then combine itself with the host DNA and become a part of that being's genetic pattern, passing along the enhanced coding to its offspring for generations to come, ensuring that what we were will always be somewhere within the native species of this planet," Kaylar replied.

"I understand, but why would you do this? There is an unspoken reason, I wish to hear it," Jakor said almost too forcefully.

The Council members looked at each other guiltily and then the Cleric responded. "I have had a vision of the future, the distant future, Jakor. Our actions in the governing body will have hideous consequences on the simian species of this planet. The things we entombed will not die. I saw them sleeping a great sleep for thousands of years then being freed by some mishap, raining terror upon those of this world, unchecked, reproducing themselves, and eventually harvesting the simians like we would harvest the native fish in the nearby body of water." The cleric shuddered. "We have erred greatly, and only in this way can we try to atone for the harm we have sentenced upon those yet to come."

"I knew it!" Jakor replied. "I knew entombing those Seelaks was a mistake."

"Yes, it was." the Elder agreed. "We were angry, blinded by a need for vengeance upon the Seelak. Our thirst for vengeance blinded us to what we were doing. Only after, when our minds were quiet, did we understand the ramifications of what we had done."

"We can still free the Seelak, my men and I can have them free within the week if we work continuously. I will personally bury my staff into the creatures that took Sennek's life. I will do this gladly," the soldier offered eagerly.

"You will fail," Kaylor answered sadly. "You would only succeed in creating a landslide, killing yourself and the others who would tunnel with you. The explosion has unsettled the area around the ship. Any further disturbance would be catastrophic."

Only by having your genetic material in one of them will allow them any hope of survival. When the time is right, the virus will release the entire power of its coding into the simian host. It will become a hybrid species, utilizing the strengths from you and whatever strengths lie inherent within the host. It will be his job to right the wrong that we have committed. The role of the one carrying the Elder's genes will be to remember us, some of our history, to seek your hybrid out at the right time, and give him the instrument of transformation which will enable him to utilize your strengths."

"What is that instrument?"

"Your personal weapon, the Sentient Staff that acknowledges you as its only master. Your memories and your personality will be encoded into the virus. In this way, the staff will accept its new master," The cleric replied.

"How will this weapon be found?"

"Its exact location will be programmed into the Cleric virus. It will be found, I assure you," the cleric answered.

"Will you partake in this, Jakor, mightiest of the Warrior sect?" the Elder asked.

"I will." Jakor handed over the weapon that had been carried for generations by his ancestors.

"Come then, let us proceed." The Elder gestured.

* * *

It took the scientist several cycles to create the precise coding for each particular micro virus, and then another several cycles to implant the genetic material from each Esper member into each microorganism. When the work was completed, the cleric released their creations into the air, watching with some measure of satisfaction as the wind carried off the fruits of their labor.

"That is all that will be left of us," the Elder remarked sadly. "Let us hope that we have done our work well. The very life on this planet will depend upon it."

* * *

There was a swirling of purple and blue. Shanda was once again back in the hospital room. What had seemed to pass like days were only scant minutes. The bond with Alissa had been the most intense thing she had ever experienced. Both women removed their hands and quietly retreated into themselves momentarily.

Shanda looked up at the young waitress who was also collecting herself. "That's absolutely fantastic."

"Those viruses found homes in our ancestors, passing down the gifts from generation to generation, waiting for the proper time to be revealed. My gift was the gift and burden of this knowledge, and to bestow the Sentient Staff to its proper heir. My family has carried this object for generations." Alissa pointed toward the duffel bag by the corner chair.

"And that heir would be Erik," Shanda answered. "Erik has the genetics of that huge Esper in his bloodstream?" she said in disbelief.

Alissa nodded. "As I have the cleric's genetics and you have the elder's genetics. He will need your gifts at a later time; but now, he needs the benefit of what resides deep inside him. He must take up the Staff and end the Seelak threat once and for all."

"What finally happened to the Espers?" Shanda asked with a burning curiosity.

"They chose to terminate their existence and end the threat they were to humankind," she answered sadly. "The images of their deaths are too painful for me to recall. I only know that they met their end bravely and with great honor. The Espers never meant to harm us. It was anger, justified anger, which led them to imprison the Seelak survivors. They realized the consequences of their actions too late, as you saw."

"Now Erik has to clean up the mess," Shanda replied.

"Erik is a formidable man," Alissa answered. "But as you see, he's no match for a genetically enhanced Seelak. Once he transforms, the odds will be even. Between his native skills and Jakor's skills, there's a good chance that he will prevail in the upcoming battle." Alissa walked over to Erik's hospital bed and studied him.

The hideous tears in his flesh were no longer oozing blood, the bruises and contusions on his face were noticeably lighter, and his nose seemed to be undergoing cosmetic reconstruction at a cellular level. Shanda noted his heartbeat was stronger and regular. His breathing seemed less labored.

"Whatever you gave him seems to be working," Shanda remarked thankfully.

"Yes, though I never thought it would have to do so much, he was damaged very badly during this conflict. I regret not foreseeing this final encounter. Perhaps I could have prevented it."

"No," Shanda disagreed, "that's what makes him Erik. He always fights, no matter what the odds are. He was fighting for his daughter, and nothing would have prevented him from doing that."

Alissa placed her hand next to his temple and closed her eyes. "He is getting stronger, but there is still much more healing to be done. The elixir will lose potency within the next three to four hours. It should be able to repair most of the life-threatening ailments he suffered within that time. The staff will do the rest. When he awakens, his thoughts will be of his daughter, he will be panicked and irrational," she looked at Shanda. "You must tell him what you have seen, let him touch your mind, show him what I have shown you. He will believe you without question. He would have doubts if this came from me. He must take the staff willingly. It cannot be forced upon him. If the staff senses any reluctance, it will reject him. You must convince him that what we say is the truth. He trusts you more than anyone. If you tell him what I've shared with you, there's no doubt he'll accept it."

"I'll do what I can," Shanda promised as she stroked Erik's hair. "There's hope for you after all," she caressed his cheek.

"Come on." Alissa gestured toward a small couch. "We should both rest. The real battle will begin soon enough."

Chapter 14

The Pendelton House

Richard Pendelton sat with his wife and two police officers. They received an exhaustive briefing as to the efforts and actions being undertaken to rescue their daughter and the other abducted children.

Margaret graciously opened up her home to the other parents, offering the spacious dwelling as a sort of command post for the town officials and the families affected by the latest abductions. This made it easier for the authorities to make only one briefing and update to all the families together, and allowed the parents to draw strength and comfort from each other.

Richard had been remarkably calm when Margaret broke the news to him of Brianna's abduction. Part of him was glad Erik Knight would no longer be a thorn in his side, but he regretted the expiration of such a formidable foil. His best people could not keep a tail on him for more than five minutes, and deep down he had a healthy respect for the once powerful investigator. Knight was now in a coma and, from what he had been told, scant hours away from death.

"At least you went out in a blaze of glory," he mumbled to himself. "You'll be remembered as something of a hero, or at least be made a martyr," he added ironically. Richard lightly touched his wife's hand. "I'll be right back."

He stood and walked into his spacious study closing the door behind him and locked it. Everything was falling apart around him. He'd been the direct cause of multiple deaths, injuries, and now the abduction of four more children, including his stepdaughter. How many more, he wondered, were going to wind up paying for his company's mistakes, his personal errors in judgment. How much was it worth to keep things secret?

He stared long and hard at the telephone, knowing if he were going to activate his final scheme, things had to be put into place now. His operatives were standing by, awaiting his word. At his command, the gunship would launch, fully armed, to the excavation sight, and blast it and, Heaven only knew how many, innocent soldiers to Kingdom Come.

Richard went to the small bar across from his desk and poured himself a scotch. He drained the glass with one swallow and filled it again, emptying the amber liquid. The scotch burned as it traveled down his throat and sent a warm feeling throughout his stomach. He walked back over to his desk and sat in his over-sized leather seat.

He picked up the Nextel phone laying there and dialed the secure two-way frequency. "All ready?" he whispered into the phone.

"Roger! Go on your mark," the voice replied.

Richard picked up the phone and carried it with him over to the open bottle. He drained a third of the bottle, this time not bothering with the glass. He closed his eyes as the liquor numbed his senses. He looked down at the Nextel and keyed the transmitter. "Go."

"Roger, we are go for execution," the voice over the radio replied.

Richard sat back down at his desk and tossed the Nextel on the desktop. He just condemned four innocent children, including his stepdaughter, to death. They were more loose ends that needed to be cut in order to assure the company's safety.

Richard reached inside his coat pocket and took a blast of breath spray to cover the alcohol on his breath. He walked out to await the news and observe the upcoming events with his wife and the other parents. He headed back down the lavish foyer and sat next to his wife. Margaret took his hand and leaned against him for support.

"It's okay, we'll get her back," he whispered. "We'll get them all back."

The authorities were executing a full-scale assault on Hopedale Mountain. Over two hundred National Guard troops were, at this moment, converging on the desolate mountainside. Three air support helicopters would be flying cover for the troops. The troops would have heavy weapons and artillery to be used in blasting the creatures into oblivion. They now knew what they were up against. There would be no more surprise attacks and no more casualties. The authorities were determined to rid themselves of these things once and for all.

What had disturbed the authorities the most was the fact that these creatures deliberately attacked and abducted children. The attack they used required planning, and planning represented sentience and intelligence. Also, the deliberate thrashing they gave Erik Knight indicated a type of vindictiveness found only in thinking, aware beings. Wild creatures would withdraw from an aggressive confrontation. From the reports the authorities had reviewed from the surviving teachers, one of the creatures fought with Knight, and finally maneuvered him into a situation where the man could be eliminated. These were not simply wild creatures acting on instinct, but sentient thinking, malevolent creatures. This made them far more dangerous and a greater threat to the populace.

The authorities were still baffled as to why the things chose children. Though, deep down, they didn't want to know. They could only imagine what horrors the children were undergoing at this very moment.

* * *

Brianna awoke to darkness, finding brief solace in a small nap, she was only aware of the three other children around her. They had all been crying intermittently over the past several hours. She didn't know how long they were captive, her young body only knew sheer terror, as occasionally they spotted an ominous shape moving within the darkness, or heard the occasional growl of the large cat creature that carried them here. The children huddled together, trying to find some comfort in each other's company.

"Brianna?" a voice whispered in the darkness.

"Yes?" she answered.

"Where are we?" the voice asked.

"How should I know? We must be underground though, it's awfully cold," she answered as her body shivered.

"Do you think your dad will find us?" another voice asked.

"I don't know," she whispered. "I hope so."

"I'm scared," a young girl whispered as she huddled closer to Brianna.

"We're all scared," Brianna and another boy replied.

"Shhh, something's coming!" the boy whispered in a voice thick with fear.

* * *

The Seelak advanced on the group of young children, its enhanced vision picking them out easily in the darkness. It took special notice of Brianna. It knew this young primate was an offspring of the hybrid it killed. It could sense the Esper within her very makeup. It would savor the life force of this child the best.

The creature ignored the shrieks of terror as it approached the children, savoring their fear like one would enjoy a fine meal. It grasped Brianna by the scruff of her neck and held the young girl in midair. It delighted as she screamed in absolute terror. The other children tried to flee, but stumbled over each other in the darkness. They wound up curling up into little balls, tucking their knees into their chins and crying loudly in abject terror.

It casually tossed the hybrid offspring aside and gathered another, each fragment of emotion strengthening it further. It carried off this victim to its companion. The large felinoid played with the child like a cat would play with a mouse – pawing at the boy, letting him fumble around freely in the darkness for a brief moment, then swatting with just enough force to knock him over, but not cause serious injury. The felinoid played with its victim for almost ten minutes before it carried it back to where the others were huddled. The felinoid then disappeared into the darkness.

Brianna had been crying nonstop for fifteen minutes. Her jeans were soaked when her bladder emptied from fright. The other child who had been taunted by the feline creature fared no better. All the children had lost control of their bladders and bowels at some point. They weren't bothered by the discomfort or smell. Little by little, they were going into shock.

"Daddy, where are you?" Brianna mumbled over and over as she rocked herself back and forth.

The other children mumbled the same mantra, praying their parents would show up and take them away from this nightmare.

Brianna heard footsteps crunching on the floor toward them. She knew something was coming again. "Daddy!" she screamed. "Daddy, please come get me, I wanna go home!"

Chapter 15

Saturday morning, 5:30 a.m.

Corporal Novacs leaned against the bumper of the ten-wheel transport, sipping his second cup of coffee while the lieutenant droned on incessantly. He hated this part of any mission, the beginning – too much talk of planning and contingencies, the administrative things officers enjoyed doing, not the non-coms. If every officer had their way, there would be forms in triplicate for simply going to the bathroom.

He looked over at his sergeant. The man gave him a brief roll of his eyes, to which Novacs grinned quickly. He knew that the sergeant felt the same way.

The sergeant was in his late fifties, with silvery gray hair and eyes to match. He was one of the few men which everyone in Fox Company held in the deepest respect. It wasn't the respect born of fear, but a respect developed from a man who wasn't afraid of getting his hands dirty with the troops. The sergeant never shied away from any task, and would never order one of his men to do something that he would not or had not done himself.

After what seemed like hours, the lieutenant completed his briefing and walked off with the local politicians. The enlisted men, some 200 fully armed combat soldiers, gathered around the sergeant. There would be no daydreaming during this ops briefing. The sergeant was quick, blunt, and to the point.

"Okay, soldiers, we have an unusual job to do. We're hunting some sort of creatures that have already killed several police officers, military personnel, and civilians. The one man who seemed to know the most about these things is in intensive care right now, probably already dead, from what we were told of his condition," he began solemnly. "These things have taken four children. We're going to take them back. Is that clear, soldiers?"

"Clear, Sergeant!" came the unified response of nearly 200 voices.

"These bastards can pop in and out like some kind of ghosts, so everyone needs to watch everybody else's ass. We're going to divide into groups of ten men and all converge on the mountain at different points. Two men on each team; the point and the rear will be issued IR gear and starlight lenses in case we get caught in the darkness. They'll tell you where and when to shoot. I suggest you follow their advice closely.

"Our objective will be to cover designated swatches of ground until we converge at the uppermost point. We've got a hell of a lot of wooded ground to cover. Some of it probably hasn't seen the footprint of a man in hundreds of years. It will take us most of the day to get to our designated target area. It's my belief that we'll encounter our adversaries long before we even get close to our mission objective. Everyone, I want radio checks every ten minutes." He paused, staring at the map of Hopedale Mountain taped to the hood of their truck. Several convergence points were highlighted, along with the areas of creature activity. "There's something up there, somewhere, and I intend to find it within the next two days. You all have your assignments. Those teams accessing the woods via the lake, get to your boats. Land teams, organize your equipment and let's hit the woods. These children have been gone for almost an entire day. I want them back before nightfall. Are we clear on this, people?"

"Yes, sir," the two hundred voices replied in unison.

The soldiers broke into their smaller units and began deploying into the parklands. Those squads that were crossing the nearly two-mile-wide Hopedale Lake by motor boat would have a significant lead on the other teams that were groundbound. The military entrance into the woodlands looked like a massive ground assault. In all the town history of Hopedale, such an event had never occurred.

The Town Fathers and several local legislators from the district were on hand to monitor the proceedings. The politicians were only there for the face time in the press, serving their own political self-interests. They had no real interest in offering any leadership to the community nor comfort for the families affected by the current tragedies. The major in charge of the operation was reluctant to give too many details to them, or be anywhere near their presence unless it was absolutely necessary. He stood in the shadows as each politician gave interviews to radio and television personalities covering the operation. He smirked to himself as each politician lied blatantly as to their involvement with mission planning and coordination.

"Typical low-brow politicians," he mumbled to the captain who was next to him. "They aren't even qualified to pump gas, let alone represent people. Why do we keep electing jackasses into public office?"

"Probably because only an incompetent jackass would want the job," the captain whispered.

The major looked over at him and suddenly burst out laughing. "A point well spoken, Mr. Anderson." He slapped the man on his shoulder. "C'mon, let's get a cup of coffee. It's going to be a long day."

* * *

Corporal Novacs paused, swatting at a swarm of persistent gnats buzzing around his head like a floating black cloud. His team had been hiking toward the outer trail markers for almost an hour.

"I think these things like the repellent," he swore as he continued waving the insects away.

He took a brief look at his topographic map to get a quick lay of the land. The land inside the parklands was relatively easy hiking – several well-beaten paths in ever-expanding circular patterns around the large lake. However, the outlying woodlands were a much different story. The altitude lines on his map ran in several crazy directions and very close together beyond the park. This was a clear indication that he would be doing some fairly heavy incline hiking later on in the day as they left the outskirts of the park. Novacs reported his observations to the team leader who was busy radioing their position and location to the base coordinators at the roadside Command-and-Control center.

"There's no way in hell we can cover sixty-plus square

miles of woodlands in one search," Novacs grumbled to the private walking next to him. "Let alone one day."

"Hey, man," the private replied, "I just work here." The soldier paused then asked a question that was probably on everyone's mind. "Hey, Novie, what d'ya think is really out here, man?"

Novacs shook his head. "I really don't know, Sparks, you know as much as me on this one, bro'. We seem to be hired on as exterminators for some really big-ass roaches or something. Just keep your eyes open, though. The sergeant thinks we'll see these buggers as soon as we leave the parklands. Based on this map, and at our present rate of terrain cover, that should be in about fifteen minutes."

* * *

Saturday afternoon, 1:00 p.m.

The traffic in the Critical Care Unit had been exceptionally heavy during the night and deep into the morning hours. Something was happening to a patient that defied medical science. Several doctors and surgeons had been called in to study the phenomenon, but no one had been able to come up with a satisfactory explanation as to what was happening inside the body of Erik Knight.

"This is impossible!" the doctor swore as he checked his patient's vital signs again.

Erik Knight's body was remarkably different than when he was wheeled into the Critical Care Unit. The multitude of deep lacerations and bruises were nearly invisible, leaving behind surgical staples embedded in healthy tissue. The deep flesh tears upon his torso were little more than light pink scars, hardly noticeable against his flesh tones. It was as if someone had performed complete cosmetic surgery on his frontal facial structure. Where there once was a shattered mass of broken cartilage now resided a totally reconstructed nose and nasal passages.

Erik's unconscious body had been wheeled to x-ray when his monitoring equipment registered increased vital signs throughout the night and early-morning hours. Doctors watched in amazement as his once battered and broken body mysteriously mended itself.

"I don't know where to begin," the doctor said as he addressed Shanda and Alissa. "His bones are totally knitted, his heart's been beating on its own for nearly four hours, and his ribs magically fused and reformed," he recited in total disbelief. "And not only that, his lungs look like they've never ever been cut. We can't even find any lingering scar tissue that would indicate any trauma to the area, or in any vital area." The doctor glared down at his notebook. "His vitals are all different now. His heart is beating stronger and his tissues and skeletal structure seem to be thicker, stronger. The bone mass readings we took have to be wrong. Nobody has a bone density this hard. It's as if his skeleton were made of iron, not bone. This is the most bizarre thing I've ever come across."

"You're saying he's going to make it?" Shanda asked, getting her hopes up.

"Yes, we're going to want to keep him here to run some extensive metabolic tests and tissue studies to understand what's happening, but he's well on the road to a complete recovery," the baffled physician answered. "But not from anything we did. What happened to this man defies any medical phenomenon we know of. By all rights, Erik Knight should be dead." The doctor shook his head and left the room.

Shanda looked over at Alissa whose face seemed to reflect genuine confusion. "What's wrong?"

"He's healing much quicker than I expected, faster than a normal man."

"That's because he's not exactly normal, we both know that, but he has abilities even you don't suspect," Shanda boasted.

"I don't understand," Alissa replied.

"His body can already generate enhanced bursts of strength, his senses are far keener than any man's, and his fighting abilities are almost supernatural."

"How do you know this for sure?" she asked.

"I felt it in our link. I experienced all his gifts firsthand. I saw him fight at the park. He's already above normal. Why didn't you expect that? I thought you had all the knowledge of these people?" Shanda challenged.

"I have no answer, perhaps the virus did more than the Espers intended, possibly. There was no time to actually test their creations," Alissa replied somewhat defensively. "I never claimed to have all the knowledge of these people, just the task I needed to perform and some rudimentary skills, such as the potion we used earlier. Our minds could never hold the knowledge of that race. We haven't evolved to that point. That much, I'm sure of," she added.

"I'm sorry, I'm not accusing you," Shanda said in a much softer tone. "I guess I'm just nervous. It's just all so much to comprehend."

"I understand, sister." Alissa reached out and took her hand. Both women watched and waited in silence as more minutes ticked past.

Several minutes later, Erik began to stir. His eyelids fluttered then opened. He tried to move, but was restrained by the casts upon his arm and leg, as well as several tubes and monitors placed in and on his body. Erik struggled, battling the disorientation.

"Erik! Easy, you're in the hospital." Shanda placed her hand on his to lightly restrain and reassure him.

He tried to speak, but the wrapping around his skull prevented him from moving his jaw. His eyes seemed to come in and out of focus. Shanda could read the confusion and concern on his face as he slowly became aware of his surroundings.

She picked up on a great wave of grief and fear so strong that she was nearly overwhelmed by it. She looked down at him and saw his eyes were filled with tears. He remembered: His daughter had been taken. He remembered the events that brought him to this place. She had known Erik for many years, and had never seen such a look of total and complete despair on his face as resided there now. She gently laid her hand upon his head, caressing him. He looked up and groaned, a sound of endless agonizing torture.

"I know, my love, I know. We'll get her back. There are so many things you need to know before you can do that, so many things we never knew before," she whispered while drying the tears flowing down his cheeks like two rivers.

Alissa walked over to Erik's bedside. She gently placed two fingers upon his left temple. "He is much better now. The elixir has done its work. His body is much stronger. It will be able to withstand the changes it will undergo. His human form, as it was, would not have survived."

"Just what are you talking about?" Shanda asked, looking away from Erik.

"His normal human biology would not have allowed him to survive the mutation caused by the Sentient Staff. The staff will change him, make his Esper more predominant. As a mere human, though very strong, he would not have survived the transition. The elixir not only healed his torn flesh, but also enhanced him as it was designed. He is now more than he was, but not nearly what he will become – what he has to become in order to defeat both creatures." Alissa looked at Shanda with confusion. "You still don't understand, do you? Both those beasts are now at the height of their power. The armored Seelak is many times stronger than it was before. Erik fought it while it was at its weakest. It has gathered food and has no doubt already fed. As he is now, even with the enhancements the elixir has given him, he would be no match for one creature, let alone two."

Shanda suddenly became enraged. "You, you son of a..." she stammered. "You don't care a thing about him, or who he is. You only care about creating some sort of mutant Frankenstein's monster. I love him, and I won't see him hurt any further," she added in a voice filled with venom.

"You have a right to be angry, Shanda, but deep down you know this must be done. You have seen the truth. How can you be so stubborn after all that you have been shown? Erik must become what he must become. Neither my feelings nor your feelings have any part in this. Those creatures must be destroyed!" she added forcefully. "Not entombed or captured, but destroyed. Humankind does not have the capability to do so without tremendous collateral damage. Even if they detonated a nuclear device on that hill, the creatures would sense the threat and disappear through Netherspace, only to appear somewhere else and start the cycle over again. They must be contained here, now, while there's still time, before they can reproduce themselves." She walked closer to Erik and looked down at him. "And he is the one who must do it," she whispered, taking Erik's hand in an almost affectionate gesture.

Shanda knew the young girl was right. Despite her anger and frustration, she knew Alissa was telling her the truth, as far as she knew it. Shanda also knew, from her own latent abilities, there was more – something Alissa didn't know, that was yet to play out. She wasn't going to give up on Erik just yet. "You're right, and he'll change willingly, if only to get his daughter back." She walked over to his bedside.

Alissa looked directly into Erik's tear-filled eyes. "I know you feel sadness at the taking of your daughter. Do you want her back?"

Erik nodded his head.

"The doctors will try and keep you here. Will you allow that?"

He shook his head.

"You now have the strength to free yourself from the plaster restraints. Use that strength now, call upon it. This is your first test," Alissa prodded.

Erik glanced over at his right arm which was completely covered in a heavy plaster cast. His eyes narrowed, and the arm began to tremble slightly. Shanda saw the muscles in his shoulder bunch and contract as they worked in rhythm with his arm. There was a sudden loud crack as the cast began to splinter and crack. Erik's arm tore free of the plaster restraint, sending fragments of the cast all over the bed and floor. He flexed his leg muscles and easily shattered the cast on his left leg as well. He then took both hands and grasped the layers of bandages and plastic bracing wrapped around his head and jaw. With a small effort, he tore the material from his skull and tossed it to the floor. He slowly sat up on the bed and brushed the long stray locks of hair from his unshaven face. He wiped his eyes quickly and looked at Shanda.

"How?" he whispered. "I should be dead, or at least crippled after what those things did. How is it that I'm alive?"

"It's a long story, Erik," Shanda began. "Let me tell it to you the way I was told." Shanda reached for his hand. She gently touched the side of his head with her other hand. "My love," she whispered, "we were truly made for each other."

Their minds touched, and Erik relived the last days of the Espers and Seelak. He saw all that Alissa had shown Shanda, and shared Shanda's astonishment. Erik gasped in amazement as the two enhanced their link.

The shared link triggered the dreams that plagued Erik's subconscious. Shanda relived the battle through a different perspective, experiencing the combat firsthand, not simply as an observer, but as an active participant. She realized these were memories locked away deep inside her lover, memories now being released. She shuddered at the ferocity of the combat, and felt the enhanced emotions that were inherent in the race of beings called Espers. She recalled the feelings and attitude were remarkably similar to what she shared with Erik when he fought the thugs in her store.

Erik recalled the image of the massive explosion that engulfed the beings at the end, and shared Jakor's final plummet to his death. There was no fear as he fell, only a deep regret of what they had done and all that they would never aspire to.

The link between Erik and Shanda broke. Erik sat stupefied on the corner of his bed.

"I thought they were only dreams, bad dreams. Never in my life could I imagine there's a part of someone else inside of me," he whispered.

"We all do, all three of us," Alissa added as she walked toward the black duffel bag.

"This is unbelievable. I feel as if I'm still in a dream." Erik looked down at the fragments of shattered plaster on the bed and floor. "But it's not, is it? Those things have my daughter."

"Yes," Shanda whispered. "But there's more. I'll let her tell you." Shanda gestured toward the young woman.

Alissa went to the large duffel bag and carried it toward Erik. Something inside the bag began to moan and purr, like the hum of an electric generator. "I'm now fulfilling my purpose, Erik Knight. My family has carried this item for generations. It is yours. You now know the truth of who you are and why you were chosen. Will you accept the responsibility and obligations that go along with this property?"

"You know I have no choice," he said, slightly bitter. "I'll do anything to get my baby back, and you know it. But then, you've always known about me," he whispered as she approached him. He understood why Alissa turned up at Madame's, and why she started working there. It was to be near him.

"Be warned, once you take and activate the staff, you will be changed forever, no longer human, but not purely Esper, a true hybrid. You will stand alone among the race of men. Do you accept this?"

"Yes, anything to get my daughter back."

Alissa reached into the duffel bag and produced a dark satchel and belt. Wordlessly, she handed him the items. Erik studied the weapon resting in the satchel, it was barely over two feet in length, but instinctively he knew it would elongate and take the shape of whatever he desired. The staff seemed to murmur and vibrate with recognition.

Erik felt a strange comfort as he tested the object's weight and feel. The weapon purred at his touch like a content kitten. It acknowledged him as he gently stroked the silvery metallic object. Erik looked up toward Shanda, his eyes burning with a new fiery purpose, and a lethality she'd never seen in him before.

"The weapon accepts you, very good." Alissa remarked.

"Help me find my clothes. I'm going to get my baby girl," he whispered in a deathly quiet monotone.

Shanda quickly grabbed his clothing from the closet hangars and handed the articles to him. Erik dressed, and carefully placed the satchel holding the Sentient Staff around his waist. He tied the long hiking boots then put on his jacket.

"Now," he said, "let's get the hell out of here."

* * *

All three walked out of the Critical Care Unit and began moving toward the exit. One of the doctors recognized Erik and confronted him.

"Where do you think you're going?" the young doctor asked.

"I'm leaving," Erik replied as he headed toward the door followed by the two women.

"Wait a minute!" the doctor ordered. "You just can't simply walk out of here, we have dozens of tests that need to be performed. You can't leave," he added, directly blocking Erik's path.

Erik looked down at the young intern. His eyes were a flaming pupiless sapphire blue that burned with an inhuman intensity. "I have more important things to do today." He lifted the stunned physician with one hand and carefully moved him aside. Erik paused briefly to straighten out the wrinkle he put in the intern's lab coat, and then proceeded toward the exit.

Shanda stared at Erik as they made their way out of the lobby and into the parking lot.

"Are you all right?" she asked.

"Yes," Erik answered. "It's just that something's pushing me, urging me on, almost as if there's somebody else inside me, screaming to get to the surface. I feel a sense of unbridled anger, but I don't know why. I mean, I'm pissed at those creatures, but this is different, unlike anything I've ever felt before." The detective paused, taking a deep breath. "And the strength, I feel like I could pummel a mountain with my bare hands."

"Jakor," Alissa answered. "You are experiencing Esper emotion, or a small piece of it. Their feelings are much stronger than humans'. They were a passionate race."

"The thing in my dreams?" Erik asked

"Jakor, the warrior, it is his essence you carry. You feel the call of battle, the desire to carry out what has been programmed into your being," she explained as they entered Alissa's car.

"Once you activate the staff, all will be revealed to you. You will become the Hybrid," she explained.

"Whoa, lady," Shanda jumped in, "I thought he already was changed. He took the staff like you said."

"Yes," she said as she drove back toward Madame's. "The weapon has accepted him, but he has yet to activate the weapon and complete the transformation."

"What will happen to me, Alissa?" Erik asked.

"I don't know for certain. I only know you will become what you're supposed to become. I know nothing more," she added evasively. "You have accepted your birthright. You must activate the staff. It is the only way to save your daughter."

As they drove on, they passed a large convoy of military trucks and vans.

"The Army?" Shanda asked, looking puzzled.

"It looks like they've gone in with hundreds of people this time," Erik observed all of the troop carriers and assorted vehicles.

"They will be wiped out. They cannot overcome the Seelak and the Netherspace portals. The beasts have fed and are at their peak of strength. Those men will only make the beasts that much stronger," Alissa added nonchalantly.

She pulled the car over by the side of the road and turned off the ignition. "It's time, Erik, you must use the staff," she said forcefully.

"I know." He opened the car door.

The three got out of the car and walked toward the side of the road. The sun was starting to break through the heavy cloud cover.

Erik suddenly took Shanda in his arms. "I love you," he said simply, wrapping his arms around her. "I don't want to forget you, don't want to forget what I've found with you. I'm afraid of what this thing will do to me. I'm afraid it will take away my humanity, take away all that I am, everything that makes me a person."

"And I love you," Shanda answered. "You'll always be Erik Knight, the man I love, no matter what that thing does to you. It can't change who you are, deep down. Come back to me, please," she whispered as their lips met.

"I'll try, with all my being, I promise I'll try," he whispered.

Erik gently pulled himself away from Shanda and unsnapped the pouch that held the staff in place. The weapon purred wildly in anticipation. He looked down at the sentient object and suddenly felt a slight wave of apprehension. He looked over at Alissa.

"Will I ever be me again after this?"

"Erik, I honestly don't know. All I know is that you'll be different. My job is to get you to undergo the transformation no matter what, but I can't lie to you, I don't know what will happen to you. It's never been done before. I do know that if you don't do this, your daughter will die, those soldiers will die, and those things will simply heal any wounds they receive and continue to terrorize this place. They will eventually lay eggs and reproduce themselves, then there will be more of them, and they will continue to harvest us like cattle. Though I am a hybrid too, I don't wish humanity to be used as food for these creatures," she answered.

"Okay," Erik whispered. "Here goes!"

He pulled the staff from its pouch and held it out from him. The weapon instantly responded to its wielder and became a staff of almost six feet in length. Erik swung the weapon with deadly precision, making lethal swings and parries in the air. The staff made a whistling sound as it bonded with its new owner. Erik felt something akin to ecstasy as he swung the staff, faster and faster.

"For Brianna!" he shouted into the air, holding the staff over his head with two hands.

A sudden rush of raw power infused every fiber of his being. His skin began to change color, going from pink flesh to a silvery metallic sheen. The once-soft pinkish flesh morphed into a chrome-like hard, malleable metal coating over his body. His senses became far more acute. He could hear the buzzing of insects hundreds of feet away, smell the scents of different flowers and other odors in the air, and see distant objects as if they were very near. It was as if he were a part of the living planet, something the Espers were on their home world and wanted to be here. Only now, thousands of years later, through a human, could they accomplish that feat. The genetic gifts he had, that separated him from others, were enhanced a hundred-fold.

Sharp pains tore through his senses as his skeletal structure was modified further. He buckled from the agony, crying out in pain, but still clung to the staff. Enhanced bones became even stronger, denser in makeup than the simple calcium and mineral substance they once were. He could feel his body not only growing in size, but in sheer bulk and density.

His brain began to change. The transition activated all of his mind's potential. In a normal human, only twenty percent of the brain is ever utilized. Erik's mutation was unleashing the sheer potential of his brain. The virus coding triggered from the staff fired unused synapses, increasing his motor skills and reflexes to dozens of times the norm. He could sense thoughts all around him, feel the energy field of the entire living planet. It was as if he had been deaf and blind then suddenly had those senses activated during a rock concert complete with laser light show.

The sensory overload brought him to his knees drowning his personal identity among the hundreds of sensations going through his mind at once. He let out a loud scream as his mind and body endured the continuing metamorphosis.

The memories and lifetime experiences of the mightiest of the Esper warriors flowed into his consciousness. He relived an alien being's entire lifetime of experiences in mere seconds. He felt brief sorrow for the massive being as he saw through its eyes, its fall and death. He knew the name: Jakor. It burned itself into his memory. He was Esper, but he was also human.

The virus triggered in his system combined the diverse genetic materials from both DNA structures rebuilding him into something more, something greater than the sum of each individual part. The virus made him a hybrid – a living legacy to a race long-gone, their final soldier to correct a mistake left behind for thousands of years.

Shanda called over to him, but he was unaware of her presence, his enhanced mind was busy sorting and resorting sensory inputs, applying filters to reduce the stimuli until his newly enhanced nervous system and brain could adapt.

After several long agonizing minutes, the pain was gone. The Hybrid stood, the staff still firmly in his grip. He survived the mutation. He looked at his hands and wiggled his fingers. Small razor-sharp claws now existed where he used to have fingernails. He felt an extraordinary sense of strength, as if he could topple a mountainside by simply pummeling it with his silvery fists. He squeezed his hand into a fist and watched as the powerful muscle tissue writhed beneath a silvery sheen of metallic skin.

The man that was once Erik Knight was nearly a full head taller, and far more massive in physical proportion. Erik's human physique was that of a honed athlete, but the figure standing before them was simply awesome.

* * *

Shanda and Alissa were stunned. They watched wordlessly as the Sentient Staff completed its work. The Hybrid that stood before them was something neither was prepared for. Its eyes burned a fiery aqua blue, a seemingly endless sea of pale blue fire. The flesh was chrome in appearance, reflecting the sunlight and surroundings like an organic mirror. They both watched as the Hybrid studied itself, carefully examining the claws that had replaced its once rounded fingertips.

The Hybrid inhaled deeply, filling its lungs with air as its chest cavity expanded, the shirt and jacket that had covered its torso had torn to shreds when his physique expanded. The silver entity that was once Erik Knight tossed the tattered garments from its body. The Hybrid's body was ripped with muscle. The writhing of each mass of muscle tissue seemed to make the chrome color flesh flow like liquid. It studied its new body, carefully exploring each limb and contour with fascination. The Hybrid then looked over at the two women briefly.

Shanda saw that the face still resembled that of Erik. At least that hadn't changed. With the exception of the hair on his scalp, there was no other trace of body hair on its naked skin. It seemed to have a different look, a look that spoke of exceptional wisdom and knowledge, a look that seemed to transcend humanity, making Shanda suddenly look away. She could no longer feel the presence of her lover in her mind. The link they shared seemed to be destroyed by whatever manner of being Erik had now become.

The Hybrid looked back over at the two. They tensed. Alissa, too, realized the familiar sense of Erik Knight was no longer within this alien creature. It seemed to be something completely different, as far from human as the Espers and Seelak were. The Hybrid walked over to a nearby road sign and studied it momentarily. Then, with apparent ease, it ripped the sign from the roadside. It held the sign, along with the three-foot concrete slab that it was embedded in, over its head. Slowly and methodically, it bent the solid steel pole into a pretzel, and then straightened it back out again. The Hybrid carefully placed the sign back into the gaping hole and seemed to stare back at its arms again. The massive being held its hands out in front of its pupiless eyes, studying them in amazement. Both women could sense the thing's confusion. It seemed extremely puzzled by its surroundings.

The Hybrid looked toward the two women again, its haunting eyes analyzing each one of them. Shanda could sense its powerful mind studying her, trying to determine if she was a threat. She could also sense discord, as if she were reading hundreds of thoughts at a time, hundreds of voices, as if she were reading a crowded room, coming from the single mind. Shanda looked over at Alissa. The young waitress seemed very unsure of herself.

"What's happening?" she whispered.

"The transformation isn't complete yet. His mind is still being altered. I had hoped it would still recognize us, regard us." Alissa paused. "I may have been wrong in assuming that it would remember anything about its past at all," she added in a silent whisper.

"It has a name," Shanda whispered back, somewhat annoyed.

Erik, or what was once Erik, looked up toward Hopedale Mountain, and then back at the two women. The Hybrid seemed to shake its head rapidly as if trying to rid itself of something. There was a sense of concern. The Hybrid turned quickly back toward the mountain. Something seemed to be happening to the massive chrome being as the two women watched. He looked back over at the mountain, and then back at the two of them. For a moment, Shanda thought that there was a spark of recognition in those blue pupiless eyes.

The Hybrid looked down at the necklace around its neck. It carefully studied the small metallic objects suspended from the silver chain. It held up each object in front of its eyes, carefully studying each tag, almost gently caressing the stamped metal of each one. One of the tags had a small dent, and he stopped, and studied it intensely, pressing his chrome metallic finger into the indentation. For a long moment, the Hybrid's features softened, its metallic face seemed almost nostalgic. But as quick as the look appeared, it was replaced by a look of sheer unbridled rage, then worry.

Shanda and Alissa picked up the sense of alarm and concern. They were both overwhelmed by the extreme intensity of the Hybrid's emotions. The intensity was far above what either of them had ever experienced.

From somewhere deep inside the Hybrid, a thought was broadcast, so loud and so powerful that it screamed within both their minds. The great being's mind only projected three words, but words that spoke volumes to both women. They knew somewhere inside that newly formed creature was Erik Knight, alive and well. Shanda wept tears as the words were littered with the familiar presence of him, the bond that they had shared reestablished itself, only now stronger, burning like a beacon inside her: *Brianna! Daddy's coming!*

"He's still in there," she said as her tears continued to flow. "He's still alive."

"Yes," Alissa answered. "Love is a very powerful human emotion. It makes sense that it would survive."

"It's more than that," Shanda disagreed. "I could sense him … Erik. *Erik's* essence survived. I could tell it was him. He said 'Daddy' is coming. We both know that's not an Esper term."

The Hybrid roared, a sound so loud and powerful that it cracked the windshield of Alissa's car. Both women felt the presence of Erik Knight increasing within the Hybrid's make-up. As Erik's presence became stronger, the desire to find his daughter burned stronger within him. Enraged, the Hybrid pummeled a nearby wrought iron gate, reducing it to scrap metal. It took two steps toward the parklands, then leapt forty feet into a huge oak tree. It then moved through the treetops swiftly until it disappeared into the vast forest.

"It's begun," Alissa whispered as the two women watched the treetops and stared at the imposing outline of Hopedale Mountain. "May the Gods help us all if he fails."

Shanda walked over to the remains of the gate and studied the twisted slag of metal bars. She was quick to note that the bars were composed of two-inch iron pillars, and her lover had torn them apart as if they were made of soft modeling clay.

"I almost feel sorry for those things," she whispered. "He'll tear them apart."

"No", Alissa disagreed. "They are the equal of his strength, but they are two. They will fight as a unit. He will still be hard-pressed, and need every ounce of his strength and skill to prevail, if he prevails."

Shanda looked over at her in alarm. "I thought that all of this was done so that he could destroy those creatures?"

Alissa nodded her head in agreement. "Yes, but the outcome of any battle is never certain. Humanity has been given a chance. It all resides with him now."

* * *

Hopedale Town Forest, 2:07 p.m.

"What in the hell was that?" Novacs swung his M-60 in a wide semi-circle.

"Don't know, but I almost wet m'self," Sparks whispered as he closed the scant three meters separating the two men.

Both men had heard a loud bellow that reverberated throughout the woodlands. Novacs heard the other men in his group of ten whispering amongst themselves.

"C'mon, people, let's keep moving. Look sharp. We're well into the unmarked sectors of this little wilderness playground. I want a continuous 360-degree sweep, side to side and up and down. Reports say that one of these critters is fond of the tree-tops. Let's not get jumped," Novacs announced as he urged his team forward.

The group of ten men continued their sweep deeper into the wilderness area, each one privately trying to identify what manner of creature could emit such an unearthly cry. None of them hoped that they would find out.

* * *

Bravo group paused for a five-minute break. They had been one of the luckier groups who crossed the two-plus mile body of water by boat. After seven hours, they were almost half-way to their objective.

The woodlands at this junction were most inhospitable. Briars and small saplings littered the forest floor, providing a near impenetrable thicket of underbrush for the hapless soldiers. The mosquitoes and black flies hung around the men in a merciless black, blood-sucking cloud that, at times, almost obscured their vision. One other group had radioed that they had located an old logging road and were following the road into higher elevations.

Bravo group was heading right up the middle, forced to machete their way through the heavier sections of underbrush. They were averaging about a mile each hour since the ground inclined, it was slow moving, but standard practice when conducting a search. The fact that they had to cut their way through the thick brush didn't make their journey any easier. Each section of ground had to be thoroughly covered before they could proceed.

The threat of the unknown creatures also made each man extra cautious. Each soldier could feel it in his feet and thighs as they made their slow ascent.

* * *

Brianna and her friends lay huddled together in a tight ball, attempting to share each other's body heat. The children had given up on any hope of being rescued.

Brianna, deep down, wondered what had happened to her father. She remembered seeing him locked in combat with the man-like creature at the park. She feared that he had been killed, or else, why wasn't he here by now?

The children had managed to sleep for a few hours. Sleep allowed them a temporary escape from their terminally dark imprisonment. They could hear their captors moving somewhere in the darkness, sometimes passing close enough to make the children shudder in fear, other times, they only heard a distant rumbling.

* * *

The Seelak awoke from its slumber and stretched its black-armored limbs. It needed to move, to escape the darkness of this place for a while. It carefully checked the eggs in its nest before slowly approaching the chamber's exit.

As it quietly departed the cavernous chamber, its feline companion quickly accompanied it. Together they traversed the deep tunnel that led to the surface and to the light. Both creatures leapt into the trees, and began easily moving from tree to tree, covering several yards with each leap as they made their way down the steep incline of Hopedale Mountain.

The felinoid saw movement below, and dropped from the trees like a speeding arrow. The silence of the forest was broken with a sudden muted shriek. The creature leapt back into the treetops, carrying a live deer in its jaws. Both creatures took delight in tormenting the creature, tossing it back and forth between them, relishing in its primitive terror as it was propelled helplessly through the tree limbs. Then, as quickly as the game began, it ended when the Seelak lost its grip on the creature and it fell crashing to the forest floor. Both creatures paused, stared at the lifeless carcass, and then leapt higher into the trees.

They had been traveling through the tops of the massive oak trees for nearly half an hour, almost relaxing, enjoying the light and fresh air when the Seelak sensed a disturbance. Its genetically heightened senses caught the spoor of primates. As it tasted the wind, it quickly noted that there were too many different scents for it to easily lock on a single odor. The felinoid growled cautiously. It, too, had picked up the telltale scent from the midday wind currents.

Both creatures sat near the top of a gigantic white oak tree that was nearly a hundred fifty feet tall, and over six feet wide at its base. They sat nestled inside the tree limbs, utilizing the large green leaves as cover and looking down for any trace of movement or strange sound that would give them a clue as to the primates' location. For several minutes, they sat unmoving, listening and sampling the now tainted air. A twig snapping caught the attention of both creatures. They quickly moved in the direction of the sound.

Silently, they traversed the treetops until they could see

a group of primates off in the distance slowly making their way up the hillside. Both creatures tensed momentarily, then seemed to vanish into an inky liquid darkness. The darkness vanished, as did both creatures.

* * *

Richard Pendelton was tired. He had been up in his office all night and morning, getting e-mail from his corporate operatives informing him of the progress of his mission objective, and of the progress made by the armed bodies within the Hopedale parklands. Margaret had been on the other phone line getting calls from their family and friends.

Based on the latest communications, the teams should be encountering the creatures by now. So far, the soldiers were getting deep into the mountainside with no interference. Richard knew the Army now had three helicopters circling the search area. They had been informed the helicopters would be departing from Logan, but that bit of intelligence didn't pan out. Instead of tailing the helicopter group, his ship would have to arrive separately and head directly to the target.

Pendelton's Apache attack ship launched moments ago and was already en route, traveling close to 150 miles per hour. It would reach its destination within the next half hour or so, then the real fireworks would start. The Apache's orders were clear: Completely wipe out all traces of the tunneling and camp-site. The pilot had orders to exhaust all ordinances during this operation. Pendelton also was informed that the ship's M-61A Vulcan Cannon had been armed, and would shoot down the other Army helicopters if they interfered with the operation.

Richard was nervous, the kind of nervous that made the pit of his stomach ache, and tensed every muscle in his already aching back. He had a throbbing headache that settled behind his eyeballs and felt like someone was driving an ice pick through his skull. His entire life and future rode on this operation. Everything his family had built and entrusted to him was on the line right now – a massive financial empire that spanned two continents, several businesses and investments, as well as his own personal wealth and freedom. If he failed, he would lose everything. But if he succeeded, the cost would ultimately be his soul and his conscience, and at this point, he had chosen the latter. His soul – he really didn't believe that he had one. His conscience he could, eventually, learn to live with.

Thus, the choices were made. All that remained was to sit back and witness the unfolding of events and be there for his wife, once news of her daughter's demise was finally determined. Richard did care for the child, somewhat, but his darker self realized that she had to be sacrificed so his empire could survive, so that he could survive. To him, nothing else mattered.

* * *

Bravo group paused momentarily. Each man was busy adjusting various equipment and pouches. There were several sounds of Velcro refastening, and canteens being either opened or closed. Private Douglas noticed the sudden appearance of a dense patch of blackness, a black so deep that it seemed to dull the midday sun.

"Sergeant!" he shouted. "We've got company coming."

The ten soldiers snapped to attention, locking their weapons on the spreading blackness. The temperature around the soldiers dropped considerably, sending an ominous chill down the spine of each man.

"Fire!" somebody screamed.

The woods filled with the sound of heavy weapons fire. Yellow tracers hurled into the black abyss, intermixed with armor-piercing M-16 rounds and the more potent high-velocity M-60s. They heard something shriek with rage over the sound of their weapons as the men continued to focus their fire on the black apparition. Something moved inside the darkness, and the men could see sparks from bullet impacts.

"Pour it on!" the sergeant screamed.

They weren't aware of the second blotch of darkness that opened up directly behind them, so focused were they on their opponent ahead of them, until it was too late.

The felinoid killed three soldiers with one swipe of its massive paw, hissing with delight as it heard the sounds of its victims' bones snapping. As the soldiers turned to face the new threat, the Seelak warrior fully emerged from Netherspace and began its hideous attack. The darkened woods were filled with the shrieks of men being torn apart and the almost joyful cries of their attackers.

The remaining soldiers attempted to retreat and regroup, they were panic firing, spraying bullets in every direction. Several rounds struck both creatures, wounding them, but their enhanced energies kept them strong. The creatures were now at their full strength, more than a match for the remaining soldiers.

After sixty seconds of bloody massacre, the forest was quiet. The two creatures had suffered several wounds and were bleeding from gaping holes in their armored flesh. The Seelak warrior stood silently, glaring at the punctures in his armor. As the wounded creature rested, its enhanced metabolism worked to quickly restore him. After only another minute of inactivity, his wounds healed. The Seelak's body now showed no sign of battle damage. The felinoid's liquid black skin, too, had fully regenerated.

Both creatures leapt into the trees and began to look for further signs of the primates, leaving behind ten twisted, mangled corpses.

* * *

Captain Anderson looked over at the major, whose skin had gone pale as he reviewed the field reports. They had heard radio reports claiming to have heard the sounds of gunfire and unusual shrieks within the mountain. There had been several attempts to contact Bravo Company, the team furthest into the woodlands.

"We've lost contact with Bravo group," the major whispered to his subordinate. "Two teams have reported the sounds of weapons fire, but no one has heard jack from anybody in that group."

"It could simply be a defective radio, sir," the captain added comfortingly.

"It could be that they're all dead too," the major replied

darkly. "I'm diverting one of our choppers into their last known position. The other two will still be on station-keeping positions." He reached for his coffee cup. "I'm starting to get a bad feeling about this, Captain." He drained the remaining contents of his cup with one large gulp.

"Major Ross, Major Ross, sir," a panicked voice shouted from the Army Mobile Command Headquarters.

Ross walked briskly over to the man. "What is it, Corporal?"

"D Company reported they're under attack by something. We heard the sound of gunfire over the receiver, and then everything just went dead. Our equipment is fine, but we can no longer get a transmission from D Company's frequency."

"Do you have their position?"

"Yes, sir"

"Divert Eyes Two from station-keeping to that point," the major ordered, "and radio to the rest of our boys to keep sharp." Ross walked over to a large map of the area and studied the position of the remaining troops. "I want them in bigger groups. Have the groups that are in the closest proximity merge. These bastards are getting the jump on them."

The control center staff began issuing several commands to the remaining teams, ordering them to several coordinates to join with nearby groups and form groups of twenty or thirty men instead of ten.

"What now, Major?" a corporal asked.

"Now we wait, and hope that the larger groups are more successful. We also get confirmation from our airborne surveillance as to what the hell happened to those twenty soldiers."

* * *

The Bell Striker helicopter hovered fifty feet above the tree line, slowly moving through the last coordinates given for Bravo group. The pilot carefully guided the craft while his second strained through a pair of heavy binoculars, trying to penetrate the tree canopy.

The observer caught a glimpse of something: Sunlight glaring off something metallic. He instructed the pilot to circle around so he could get a better look through the opening in the trees. The helicopter moved forward slightly, then spun around 180 degrees. The pilot then pitched the craft forward 20 degrees, giving the spotter a clear view through the gap in the tree canopy.

The spotter glanced through his heavy binoculars, cursing as he surveyed the limited field of view.

"What do you see?" the pilot asked.

The spotter looked over his shoulder at the pilot and mumbled into his headset, "Bodies, mutilated bodies," he answered as he switched frequencies to the command centers. "Eyes One to Command, Bravo group has been wiped out. I repeat, Bravo group has been wiped out." The spotter switched back to the cockpit frequency. "Mark this location then get us the hell out of here."

The helicopter's powerful blades changed their pitch, lifting the airship higher into the afternoon sky. The craft banked sharply and headed back toward the command post.

* * *

The sparkling being of silver leapt from tree to tree, moving still deeper into the forest, propelled by an ancient knowledge. The Hybrid, Erik Knight, now knew what he was up against, and more importantly, he now knew where to look.

There was something at the higher elevations of Hopedale Mountain – something huge, buried for thousands of years. What he still didn't know was how these things had been freed. That was a question he'd answer as soon as he recovered his daughter.

So he moved, a sense of urgency propelling him, and as he moved, his own essence, his sense of humanity, fully returned. He was Erik Knight. He still retained his memories and his soul, but now he was more – he had the memories of another creature, another entire lifetime of emotions and memories along with his own. He experienced emotions he had no words for, feelings that he, before his change, wasn't capable of feeling. He had become what they had made him: one with the earth, one with their species, the strengths of both species combined into one being, a being which could claim kinship to neither race. It was a unique genetic construct designed for one purpose: Destroying two other genetic constructs, the byproducts of a long-forgotten war.

Erik paused in a tall tree, overlooking a large expanse of woodlands. He recognized the area, and spotted an old tree stand several meters away, still hanging in a tree. He was still adjusting to his new senses and new body. His mind successfully sorted out the extra stimuli fed from his heightened senses, and he controlled each heightened ability with his thoughts, calling up each gift as needed. His enhanced brain could sort, process, and filter all the external stimuli and respond accordingly.

He was having difficulty adjusting to his increased physical strength. He had over-shot several trees while leaping, only to come crashing into the ground, unceremoniously landing on his bottom. The unusually large oaks that predominated in this area provided a veritable highway system, making traversing the distance in the dense woodlands much easier than navigating the massive thickets and briars that occupied the dense forest floor. Erik had a new appreciation for the squirrels that adopted this method of navigating the forest.

He could feel the magnetic pull from the north, and he kept that sensation on his right side. He knew instinctively he was traveling due west, ascending Hopedale Mountain as he had done earlier with Steve. He easily leapt twenty feet, landing on the thick trunk of another oak. The claws in his hands and feet bit into the tree bark and provided a secure holding.

It was awkward to see his silvery flesh. He had to keep reminding himself this wasn't a dream. He wasn't going to wake up in the middle of the night. This was real. He had forsaken his humanity for the sake of his daughter and some alien race that perished thousands of years before he'd even been born.

He was truly alone, not only an outcast from his ex-wife, but also an outcast from the race that spawned him. There could never be a future with Shanda. He was a freak, an anomaly among nature. Who could love a near seven-foot chrome-plated humanoid?

Even if he did manage to rescue his daughter, and she were

still alive, how would she view her father now? *My dad, the "Bionic Tin Man."* Erik was tormented by these dark thoughts as he propelled himself still deeper into the woodlands.

Overhead, he heard the distinctive thrum of rotor blades. As he focused on the distant sound, it became louder and clearer. He saw in the distance ahead of him, from his high perch in the treetops, an Army helicopter circling an area three miles away. If not for his enhanced hearing and vision, the helicopter would have gone unnoticed. The helicopter pitched forward drastically and accelerated toward the East. Erik was heading in the general direction of the chopper, and knew he would pass through that area. Something was there, his insides told him, something that he knew he wouldn't want to see.

He moved quickly through the treetops, covering two miles in less than ten minutes. The trees in this area were not nearly as large, and it was more difficult to navigate them. He leapt from his perch in a smaller evergreen and touched down on the forest floor. He moved through the dense forest, leaping over saplings and briar patches as he moved closer to the position.

He picked up the scent. It was faint at first, but his senses amplified it to a powerful, overwhelming stench. It was a scent he had smelled before, in the jungles of Columbia and Peru, as well as the desert of Iraq. It was the scent of death and blood, the scent of butchered bodies and mangled flesh.

Erik freed the staff from its pouch, it responded to its owner by emitting an eerie whine as it elongated to a length of almost seven feet. He closed cautiously, expecting the worst. He then saw, at a distance, the gruesome carnage that was the result of the Seelak attack: Ten soldiers literally ripped apart. The ground was covered with blood and entrails from the soldiers. Black flies and maggots were feasting on the corpses whose limbs had been torn from sockets and tossed randomly about the scene of death. Erik could smell the traces of sulfur from gunpowder, and spent brass casings littering the ground.

As he continued to move through the area, he spotted the telltale bright glowing blue fluid from the creatures that had nearly killed him. He probed the fetid stuff with a metallic fingertip. He lifted the substance to his nose and took a quick sniff.

The blood scent imprinted itself on him now. His heightened sense of smell filtered out all other pheromone substances and locked on this particular spoor. He would track this creature like a bloodhound, after he got his daughter. It was obvious the creatures were out hunting the scouting parties.

Erik knew this would make his job of retrieving his daughter that much easier. He would not have to contend with the creatures during his rescue attempt. He only hoped that the remaining soldiers in the woods would not meet the fate of their fallen comrades.

He looked further to the West, up the sloping woodlands, and continued his long journey.

* * *

Major Ross had received visual confirmation from Eyes Two: D Company had been massacred. The tally so far was up to twenty soldiers, and still the creatures were at large.

The distance between the two groups of men was quite sizeable. Ross estimated that the creatures had to be moving at least thirty kilometers per hour to attack both groups within the time span the reports had come in. He had no idea how any creatures could move that fast in such dense terrain. His soldiers could barely walk through the denser portions of the woodlands and had to frequently cut pathways for themselves. He knew higher up the thickets would clear out, but his men had to get into the upper elevations without being massacred like sitting ducks. One of the larger groups was now navigating an abandoned logging road that led in the general direction of their search.

"I want voice contact with these groups every five minutes," the major demanded. "Can our choppers provide any air cover for those men?" he asked his subordinate.

"Negative, sir. The foliage canopy is too thick. We'd have sporadic visuals, even by the old logging road. That's why we can't use them for overhead recon either."

"Damn!" The major studied the groups on the map and adjusted the location pins to account for the new groupings. "We're getting massacred."

* * *

Corporal Novacs felt slightly better after joining up with the other patrol. They were now twenty strong, and moving along a relatively unobstructed log road. They were moving at a slow pace, several eyes and muzzles peering into the treetops, while others scanned the perimeter all around them.

Novacs didn't like this scenario. It went against all his battlefield experience. When the enemy has the knowledge of the terrain, ford up and take cover. Make them come to you. Novacs was a patient man. He knew these things would eventually seek them out, as it did the other two parties. Moving in the open, exposed as they were, was not very battle-savvy, but necessary when looking for a missing person. He felt naked and vulnerable.

Novacs glanced over his shoulder at Sparks. The young soldier was visibly sweating. "Easy, Bro'." Novacs whispered to his friend. "We'll get outta here if we can just keep our heads together."

Sparks grinned sheepishly, embarrassed that his discomfort was that visible. "I'm cool, man. Just keepin' mah eyes peeled for any unwelcome visitors," he answered in his heavy Southern drawl.

The woods around them echoed with the sound of wood crackling and splintering. The group looked about wildly before realizing that a large evergreen was falling directly toward them.

"Scatter," Novacs screamed as he saw the large tree plummeting earthward toward their position.

In his haste, Novacs lost his footing and fell face-first into the ground. As he spun around, he saw the main body of the tree as it fell upon him and several other men who were not quick enough to avoid it. Novacs shrieked with pain as a branch shattered his leg and pinned him beneath its awesome weight.

In the distance, he heard a shriek. He knew it was Sparks. Then, he heard a growl, a growl that made him forget his pain and replace it with abject terror. A pair of eyes peeked in through the boughs and branches to where he was. He heard the sniffing that the great cat-like beast made as it pawed the tree limbs, trying to get at him.

There was gunfire and darkness. He heard more screams and the sickening sound of bones being broken. He held on to his rifle, keeping the muzzle pointed outward, ready to fire upon any threat.

The darkness was like a thick veil of black. It was nearly impossible to see anything. There was an occasional muzzle flash that lit up the darkness followed by a bright line of tracers, then more darkness and mayhem. One of the soldiers, who had taken cover behind a large outcropping, managed to ignite a flare. He tossed it into the darkness and illuminated the hellish scene. Over half of the soldiers were dead, and three others were pinned under the large tree, but now their attackers were visible. Four M-16s fired in unison, scoring several hits upon their adversaries. The creatures hissed and shrieked with rage as bullets impacted against their bodies. The large cat rushed one of the soldiers, who continued firing up to the moment that the great creature swatted him down with one of its massive paws.

From his position under the tree, Novacs listened intently, as each separate sound of gunfire was eliminated with the death scream of a member of their party. Finally, there was only one left standing. Novacs heard the clicking of the M-16's trigger, but that was all. The poor soul had no more ammunition. He shuddered as he heard the soldier's cries of pain and torture. The creatures were playing with him, slowly torturing the man as if to satisfy some demented, masochistic need for inflicting pain and suffering. He heard the soldier gurgling, as blood slowly filled his lungs

Please, please no more. Just end it.

Novacs heard a sickening crunch of bone then the telltale thud of a body hitting the ground. Their party had been wiped out in a matter of minutes. Twenty men, armed with state-of-the-art rifles, had been literally decimated. *How could they live through all that fire?* Something in his gut told him he would be next.

He heard the creatures moving throughout the tree fall, dispatching his trapped comrades. He prayed they would forget about him, and move on to something, or someone, else. He heard a strange sound, and looked up. He saw blood-red eyes looking back at him from a tree limb, and saw an inky black claw reaching for his throat. Novacs reached inside his vest and pulled out a high-yield grenade. He pulled the pin and heaved the explosive in the general direction where the creature was. The thing retreated as the grenade hit the ground. The forest echoed the thundering concussion as the grenade exploded. There was silence, and then Novacs exhaled the breath he had been holding. Everything in the forest was quiet. The soldier silently rejoiced. Either he killed the creature or scared it off.

Something else was coming toward him, it was inky black and serpent-like. He tried to avoid it, but it coiled around him like a python, squeezing him and pulling on him. Novacs' leg burned like fire from the pain, and he screamed with agony. He felt his shoulder crack as the serpent continued to pull on him. Suddenly, with a sickening snap, Novacs was ripped from under the tree, his leg severed at the knee joint. The feline creature released him from the grip of its tail.

Novacs was rolling along the ground, his mind reeling from the utter agony of his injury. Dimly, he felt the icy cold grip around his neck. He forced himself to look into the fiery eyes of his captor – eyes that seemed devoid of any compassion or sense of mercy, eyes that seemed all too twisted and cruel. He felt the creature's icy grip increase around his throat. Novacs gathered up the last of his strength and spat into the face of the monstrosity that would surely kill him.

"Go back to Hell," he said as the creature ended his life with the simple squeezing of its claw.

The Seelak tossed Novacs' corpse and stomped it under its feet for several seconds, shattering the corpse into bloody hamburger. Satisfied it was no longer a threat, both creatures left the carnage behind and faded into the woods.

Off in the distance, a cardinal was singing, oblivious to the twenty mutilated bodies several feet below its perch.

* * *

Erik paused. He heard gunfire. He was able to isolate the number of different sounds even from this great distance.

It was at this point that he heard the explosion and the distant growl of the Seelak. Even at this distance, his hearing enhanced the sounds of the battle. He was torn inside: Part of him wanted to seek them out, hunt them down, and kill them; while his human half wanted only to free his daughter, take her from the hell she was in, and protect her. He knew he would do both, but doing so would cost more soldiers their lives.

Erik moved further up the mountainside, further than he had ever been before in his travels. This part of Hopedale Mountain rarely, if ever, had human visitors. It was the perfect place for the Espers' ship to crash land, as far away from anything as possible.

He leapt back up into a nearby tree, then catapulted ten meters to another tree limb. He moved further and further into the elevations until, at last after endless minutes, he arrived at his goal. He landed outside the campsite and slowly made his way through the vacated area.

He paused as he looked over the small tent city. "What in the hell was going on up here?" he asked himself as he slowly approached the encampment.

This was conservation land. There should be no signs of human activity anywhere for miles. He was amazed to see the various crates and packaging for large equipment, and what appeared to be a makeshift helipad. Something very big was happening here, something that shouldn't be happening at all.

He activated his staff, expecting his rivals to appear at any moment to challenge him and warn him off their territory. Like a silver ghost, he moved soundlessly through the groups of tents and equipment. He paused at one particular table. Insects were busy feasting on the remains of someone's dinner. Half empty coffee cups were scattered throughout the area, as well as a variety of assorted gear. He entered a large tent and carefully studied the radio equipment that was still activated, as if waiting for someone to use it. He carefully studied other objects and personal paraphernalia that littered the tent. It was at that moment when his eyes spotted the large coffee mug. He picked it up in his metallic hand, studying it carefully and noting the Pendelcorp logo proudly emblazoned upon the mug's face.

Rage shot through Erik's mind as he crushed the mug *into*

powder. Richard, you son of a bitch, you're at the root of all of this. Bits of the coffee mug fell from his now clenched fist. Erik picked up a large note pad and studied the contents. They appeared to be some sort of mineral and geological reports. Again, he noted the Pendelcorp logo proudly emblazoned upon each page. He took the book and tucked it into his satchel.

He quietly stepped out of the tent and began to check other areas of the large campsite. He found several crates with the Pendelcorp logo scattered haphazardly throughout the grounds and followed the trail of open crates for several yards. This led to a well-used footpath.

As soon as Erik stepped onto the footpath, his senses lit up. He could feel his daughter and the other children. He put his hand to the ground and listened with his Esper abilities as the earth told him in what direction his daughter was being held. Erik followed the path quickly and came to a massive opening that tunneled into the mountain. The smell of the felinoid and the Seelak warrior was overpowering, but he could also make out the distinct fragrance of his own flesh and blood, his daughter. He caught the scattered scent of other children, though one of the scents was not as strong as the others. There were also faint odors from several other spoors, but they were even slighter.

He stepped into the darkness, his eyes adjusting to the absence of light, seeming to shift to a different spectrum, allowing him to see near daylight quality. He moved quickly, deeper into the tunnel. Erik paused and touched the walls of the tunnel. He could tell by the texture that this tunnel had been dug by man-made equipment and was not a natural occurrence.

Erik had covered almost 400 feet when he began to catch a hint of death. The smell grew more and more pronounced as he moved deeper into the tunnel. The fetid stench of individual corpses assailed his senses as he came to the tunnel's end. He spotted five bodies, mutilated, and some sort of mining equipment.

As he studied the chamber opening, he had a vision of Jakor and the other Espers leading those creatures and their captives into the giant eternal prison. Then, another flashback of the explosion that buried this chamber. He studied the melted slag of metal that was once the alloy door sealed eons ago, keeping the captives permanently entombed. He looked back at the huge piece of equipment and assumed it was some type of beam used for drilling.

Erik peered into the opening, but found his way blocked by some sort of stone obstacle placed in front of the chamber entrance. Erik focused his senses, felt into the chamber, and heard the sound of faint breathing. He focused harder, and was able to discern heartbeats. There were five distinct signatures, though one was very shallow. He placed both his hands against the obstruction and pushed. Slowly, the stone barrier gave way against his strength. After he had pushed the obstruction about a foot, the sounds and the presence of the children were clearer. He heard gasps of fright and panic. The children had assumed that their tormentors had returned. He opened his mouth and shouted his daughter's name, yet no intelligible sound came out. Frustrated, he tried again. His throat was unable to create the words that his mind wanted to speak. Then he knew, he was now an Esper, think the words.

Brianna! his mind screamed. *Brianna!* His mind cried in anguish, longing to hear the voice that would tell him he was not too late.

"Daddy?" an unsure silent voice whispered in the darkness, as if addressing a dream.

I'm here, Baby. I've come for you. Daddy's here!

The feeling of joy was so powerful that it almost drove him to tears. Without thinking, he drew his fist back and smashed a blow into the obstruction that blocked his path. His hand smashed through the barrier, placing a gaping hole through the solid structure. He struck again and again, roaring in rage while pummeling the thick stone, reducing it to rubble. Erik held up his metallic hands to his face and looked at them, bewildered. There were no cuts, not even a scratch upon his silver flesh. He walked into the chambers, closing in on the source of his daughter's voice.

As he got closer, he heard the children shriek in unison. Erik spun, bringing his staff to the ready, preparing to strike out with the force of a hundred suns at the creatures that took his child.

"Daddy," Brianna screamed. "Something's here, something big with huge blue eyes."

Erik's heart sunk, his daughter had seen his eyes. To her, he was one of them. *Honey, you must listen to me. He's here to help you. He will not hurt you. Don't be afraid. Let him approach you, he will not hurt you! Do you believe me?*

"Okay," she whispered hesitantly.

Erik slowly approached the children. He felt their fear, heard their racing heartbeats as he came closer. Finally, he saw his daughter, clearly standing there in the darkness with the three other children. She looked up into his fiery blue eyes, struggling to control her fear.

Don't be afraid.

Her eyes bulged as she looked up at him, his luminous eyes reflecting beams of blue light off his silver skin. She reached out and he gently took her small hand in his metallic one. He felt her warmth, and then her acceptance.

"Daddy, what happened to your eyes?" she asked innocently. "Your skin, it looks and feels like metal. What happened to you?"

Later, he replied. *There is another child here, Bri. I'm going to get her. Don't move, I'll be right back.*

Erik carefully moved through the darkness, utilizing his enhanced senses like a bloodhound, he was able to track the other faint heartbeat. He approached the tiny body and picked the child up gently. Lisa Reynolds was alive, barely, but alive. He noted the bowl of water next to her and some dried foodstuffs from the camp. He studied the ground around her carefully. It was littered with her waste and vomit, and the child's clothes stank of it.

Erik then kicked the bowl and food away angrily. They had used her to feed upon, to gather strength. Erik shuddered at the thought. He remembered that the creatures fed upon fear, which was how they were designed, to feed upon the fear of the common Esper. But the Espers were gone now, and nothing was as palpable as the fear of a young child, afraid of monsters dwelling in the dark. Somehow, they figured that out and were using the fear of children to feed themselves. That's why they took his daughter and the others, as food. Erik headed back to his daughter, she too had been covered with the scent of her own body excrement, and he vowed to make these things pay dearly for what they had done to his child and the other children.

It all clicked into place: Pendelcorp was tunneling here. That explained the reports he found. The miners were looking for mineral deposits in this isolated location. They stumbled upon the Worldship, buried for all these eons, and broke into it. That awoke the hibernating creatures. The corpses he saw at the chamber opening were obviously what was left of the original mining team.

He would figure it out later. He had to get the children out of here. He carried Lisa Reynolds back to the other children, and began leading them out of the darkness.

Stay close. Keep holding my hand.

The children all formed a human chain, relying on Erik's sight to guide them out of the pitch-blackness of the chamber and tunnel. As he guided them, Erik spotted more human bodies. He carefully kept the children from stumbling over them as they headed out of the chamber and into the mining tunnel. He silently wondered what they were doing inside the chamber. *Later,* he told the PI that lived in his mind, his responsibility was to get his daughter and the others to safety.

It took nearly twenty minutes for them to traverse the tunnel he traversed in less than five minutes earlier. He had to keep reminding himself the children were weak from lack of food, and that it was pitch black and disorienting for them. Also, they were climbing up, and that made it all the more difficult for them. They frequently needed to rest. Erik saw, in the distance, the opening and the daylight. He knew there were things that he had to say, and say them quickly. His appearance would scare the children further unless they were prepared.

Brianna, children, when you see me, I'm going to look very different than I used to. Don't be afraid. I'm still Mr. Knight. I would never do anything to harm you. You must believe me.

The children mumbled as they slowly approached the tunnel entrance. Erik looked down at his hand and could see the sunlight already reflecting off of his silver skin. He heard several muted gasps as they slowly stepped out into the light. The children looked up at him in wonder as the light and the forest were reflected in his mirror-like silver skin. He looked down sadly at his daughter as she stared up at him.

Am I a monster to you, Bri? he asked her sadly.

Brianna studied him very carefully, touching the cold metallic flesh and tracing the outlines of his enhanced musculature with a tiny fingertip. She looked back up at him, and Erik smiled slightly. She grinned back as she took his hand again. "No," she answered with a compassion that belied her years. "You're my dad, and you came for me, for all of us, when nobody else did. You weren't afraid." She threw her small arms around his silvery body and pressed her head against his metal-coated torso. "I love you, Daddy, no matter what color you are," she whispered. "You do need to find some bigger clothes though," she remarked, studying his shredded jeans.

Thanks, Munchkin. Erik gently held his daughter in one arm while balancing the unconscious form of Lisa Reynolds on his other shoulder. He was thankful she had accepted him.

As he adjusted his grip on the Reynolds child, he heard the sound of rotors. Something was closing fast. The whine of this helicopter was different, it sounded bigger, more powerful, and potentially dangerous.

* * *

Major Ross was stunned to learn that another group of twenty men was now missing and presumed dead. He had given the order for his men to withdraw and regroup into one big offensive line. He gave them specific orders to fire on anything they deemed to be hostile. He had no idea how he would explain the loss of twenty per cent of his forces to his commanding officers. He still couldn't believe it himself.

"Major!" a voice shouted excitedly, "we have an unknown bogey entering our mission space, the signature is that of an Apache gunship. Our sensors are picking up active radar, sir. That bird is sweeping the area."

Ross let out a litany of swears as he ran to the radar screen. The blip was heading directly toward the mountaintop. "Warn that bird off, Eyes One and Two, close and intercept," he ordered.

"What the fuck else can go wrong today?"

* * *

The modified Apache gunship activated its new twin turbines and began a power ascent up Hopedale Mountain. The ship was following its preset coordinates. The pilot quickly noted two other helicopters left their positions and were attempting to intercept. The Apache pilot disengaged the autopilot and banked the craft savagely, pulling nearly two Gs as he banked the ship toward the first oncoming Bell Striker.

His radio blared with the calls from both approaching helicopters. The pilot flipped a red toggle on his weapons panel, and heard the whine of a sequential autoloader feeding the ship's main cannon. He painted the Striker with a laser sight, and the ship's onboard computer placed a targeting diamond superimposed on the cockpit glass around the closing Bell helicopter.

"Goodbye," the pilot whispered as his finger gently depressed the cannon trigger.

The Apache shuddered as hundreds of depleted uranium rounds and phosphorous tracers erupted from the six spinning cannon muzzles. The super hard rounds tore through the Striker's aluminum skin like a scalding knife through warm butter. One burst found the Striker's main fuel line, engulfing the ship in a ball of fire. The Striker fell to earth like a blazing comet then exploded upon impact with the ground.

The pilot noted that the second Striker had pulled away, and was now fleeing at 150 miles per hour in the opposite direction. The Apache pilot switched from guns to rockets and activated the ship's boosters. The attack copter accelerated rapidly, boring down on the unarmed Striker like a bloodhound chasing a rabbit. The Apache was closing, traveling at almost 300 miles per hour. The pilot bathed the hapless helicopter with active radar. The attack computer chirped, confirming a target lock.

"Splash two," The Apache pilot whispered as he freed two rockets from one of the ship's weapon pylons. He watched with satisfaction as the rockets streamed toward their target and impacted, blowing the Striker into hundreds of fragments of scrap metal. The Apache banked 180 degrees and resumed its preprogrammed course.

The Apache quickly closed on its preprogrammed coordinates. The pilot toggled his controls to the Typhoon missile console. The attack computer fed the missiles the proper instructions, and each missile gave an electronic hum to assure the pilot that everything was green for launch. The pilot looked at his flight computer, and was now within striking distance. He tapped the brilliant orange button on his control yoke and sent the first Typhoon missile speeding along its way.

* * *

Erik and the children heard the sounds of gunfire and several explosions. Erik knew that there was some arial combat occurring in the skies overhead. He leapt up into the nearest tree and climbed to the top. He had an unobstructed view of the Hopedale skyline from this altitude and his current vantage point atop the tree canopy. He watched with revulsion as the Apache gunship literally blew another helicopter from the sky. He watched as the attack helicopter banked leisurely and began to head up the mountainside, toward them.

This can't be good! Damn you, Richard, I know you're behind this, all of this. If we get out of this alive, so help me. Erik leapt from the treetop and landed gently in the leaf-covered ground. He quickly ran toward the children.

He had found a container of water and some boxes of granola bars abandoned in the campsite, and the children were eating and drinking hungrily. He had managed to get some fresh water into Lisa Reynolds, but the girl was unresponsive, probably in shock from her ordeal.

Erik deliberately kept a respectful distance from the children. They were still somewhat afraid of him. They wouldn't come right out and say it, but he could read their feelings and emotions. At least his daughter accepted him, and that was one thing he had to be thankful for. He bent over and gently scooped up the Reynolds girl. He had wrapped her in a blanket Brianna had scavenged from one of the tents.

The sound of the helicopter began to grow louder. Erik heard it long before the children did. Esper senses warned him of the oncoming threat. He didn't have to see the approaching ship to know that they were all in danger. He shouted a telepathic warning to the children even as he ran toward them. Somehow, through all the noise, he heard it, the sound of a missile being fired. A missile was being fired at them. Erik drew his staff and summoned the image of a massive shield. The staff flattened out into a thin disk four feet in diameter.

Get down, he broadcast telepathically to all of them.

Each child obeyed, and Erik quickly placed the makeshift shield over himself and the huddled children. *Cover your ears,* he ordered as the telltale whine of the missile grew louder.

The Typhoon missile streaked over their heads and headed directly for the mouth of the tunnel. The impact and detonation shook the entire mountainside. Erik pressed himself down further into the children as a massive plume of expanding fire and debris spread out from the point of impact. It took nearly all of Erik's strength to keep the force of the concussion from squishing him and the children into the ground. Erik heard the shield murmur and whine almost as if in protest to the force it was made to withstand.

He heard the roar of the gunship as it passed overhead. He lifted the shield and quickly checked the children. They were all huddled together in a tight mass. He scooped up Lisa Reynolds and guided the other children out of the now-ruined campsite. Again, he heard the thrum of a missile being fired, he covered the children and himself with the shield. The missile impacted closer this time. It was targeted for the campsite itself. The concussion plowed into Erik's protective shield, this time overwhelming him with its irresistible force. Erik groaned in agony as he forced his enhanced body to endure the force of the lethal explosion. The shield seemed to protest as it reflected the hailstorm of fire and debris caused by the missile's impact. Both Erik and the children were carried back several meters by the force of the impact, but the shield still held and nobody was hurt.

The Apache simply hovered over the area, as if surveying the results of its handiwork. Erik stood, still holding his shield low to protect the children. The campsite was nothing but a vast crater of fire and burning embers. He guessed the tunnel had been completely destroyed, forever concealing the bodies left there. The helicopter fired several rockets into the now-devastated campsite in some odd attempt to wreak even more carnage. Then it veered off toward the tunnel location. Erik counted twelve separate salvos fired and twelve successive impacts from the smaller, yet still lethal, rockets.

Everyone was quiet as they watched the huge gunship slowly bank around back toward the campsite. They were completely exposed. The ship paused roughly 100 yards from them. Erik could sense the astonishment as the pilot spotted them. *Children, into the forest quickly. Drag Lisa, but get out of here now.* Erik and the helicopter pilot continued to stare at each other across the vacant, smoldering dust bowl that used to be the Pendelcorp mining campsite.

The children dragged Lisa Reynolds behind them, each passing second allowing them to get deeper into the forest cover. Erik sensed danger, his enhanced vision focused on the massive chain gun suspended on the nose of the ship. The gun was pointing at him. He backed away, hoping he too could make it into the cover before the pilot overcame his surprise of finding people up here.

Erik deliberately kept his body between the children and the helicopter. He prayed they found a hiding place behind some dense tree growth. His enhanced body reacted before he was even aware. His shield lifted and his body assumed a defensive stance. The helicopter opened fire on him, and he felt the impact as the heavy rounds tore into his shield. The hailstorm of bullets lasted for ten full seconds. His shield deflected every round and burning tracer the ship threw at him. He could see the look of total shock and disbelief on the pilot's face.

He heard a high pitch whine in one of the Apache's rocket pods, and quickly continued a cautious withdrawal. He heard the light thud as two rockets leapt from its pylon and sped toward him. The rockets detonated against the shield, sending Erik hurtling backwards, landing in a motionless heap on the forest floor. The children shrieked in fear and ran, terrified, deeper into the woods.

The helicopter, its munitions spent, rose into the sky and departed, leaving the children alone in the middle of thousands of acres of woodlands.

* * *

Pilot Phil Rappola banked his Apache helicopter ninety degrees, and eased the control yoke back. The ship responded by gracefully lifting itself above the tree line.

He glanced back at the fallen man with wonder. "Where in the hell did you come from?" he muttered to himself.

He had never experienced anything like what had just occurred in the past few minutes. A man with silver body armor and a silver shield, Phil assumed it was some sort of military prototype battle suit. He had to admit it was impressive looking. The alloy in the silver disc had to be some unique titanium Kevlar composite to withstand the full onslaught of an M61A Vulcan Cannon. Even his high-yield, armor-piercing rocket was unable to pierce the odd metallic barrier. Phil would make some inquiries with his Black Market contacts and see if they had any knowledge of such unusual equipment.

He circled back over the body at an altitude of several hundred feet and spotted the children making their way back into the blasted clearing toward the fallen man. He was under orders to eliminate everything up here, but even Phil Rappola had lines he wouldn't cross, and butchering children was beyond even his mercenary ethics.

He radioed an all clear to his employer, utilizing the appropriate frequency, and then activated the ship's new dual turbines and left the region as fast as his helicopter could take him. He maxed the rpm's on the craft's two engines, reaching a top speed of over 350 miles per hour.

The Army wouldn't have had sufficient time to call in any further air support, and they would not risk the third Bell Striker hovering at a station-keeping position at the base of the incline. He left the area unchallenged, hoping and praying he wouldn't encounter an F-16 Fighting Falcon or an F-15 Eagle. His Apache was a formidable weapon against ground-based personnel and vehicles, as well as other choppers, but it was no match for the superior power and speed of a modern fighter plane. Rappola knew that there were fighter squadrons based nearby that could reach him before he could make good on his planned escape route. As fast as his ship was, it seemed to be moving too slow for his comfort at this point.

He'd been flying for several minutes, growing more at ease with each passing mile, when the guidance computer on the ship went black. He struggled with the controls, and to his horror discovered he was no longer in control of the aircraft. The ship changed its heading, as if acting on its own accord, and began to head out toward the Atlantic. Rappola tried a sequential restart of the navcomm computer, but got no response. He tried to reboot the flight control center, but failed in that task as well. The ship was flying itself, he was now a prisoner. Rappola cursed and swore savagely as he tried desperately to regain control of the ship.

He knew his only alternative was to eject. He looked into the evacuation cabinet of the helicopter, but found it had been stripped of all rescue and emergency equipment.

"Damn it!" he screamed, pounding on the control board in frustration.

He knew what was going to happen. He'd been set up. There would be no payoff, no big score. His reward for cleaning up Pendelcorp's mess was a one-way ticket to eternity at the bottom of the ocean. Rappola became irrational, and angry. It was perhaps his savage anger that caused him to draw his pistol and discharge several rounds into the helicopter's computer systems.

To his misfortune, his third shot shorted out the timing mechanism that would send a burst of electricity to the concealed charges placed on the gunship's fuel tanks. A spark of current was freed and traveled through the wires. The ensuing explosion rained down fiery bits of helicopter through the residential suburbs outside Boston. Rappola's anger brought his eventual death that much sooner.

* * *

Brianna hadn't moved from her father's side for five minutes. She had opened one of his eyelids, only to see that his eyes were now a dark inky blue, not the luminous fiery aqua blue she had seen earlier lighting up the darkness in the cave.

"Daddy," she whispered as she held his cold metallic hand. "Please don't die, don't leave us alone out here. Those things will surely find us again."

She felt a slight movement in the hand she was holding. The dark cold blue eyes slowly began to flutter, and as they blinked, they began to glow with aqua luminescence.

* * *

Slowly, the Hybrid, Erik Knight, recovered from the colossal blows that felled him. He groaned, his alien vocal chords making strange inhuman sounds as he sat up. He looked up at his daughter, and she offered him her hand, doing what she could to assist him as he slowly stood.

Erik had been in several full contact fights, fights for his life, and taken hundreds of blows and impacts to his body, but all of that paled in comparison to absorbing the impact of the two rockets that hit him. He glanced down at his right arm, the shield still in place, molded to his forearm. He knew if he were human, his body would now be scattered across the ground, charbroiled in little pieces.

He looked down at his daughter, saw the look of concern etched in her innocent face. *I'm fine, Munchkin. Is everyone in one piece?* The other children looked up at him with amazement and wonder

Each child either nodded or grunted.

Where is Lisa?

"Behind a big tree, over there." Brianna pointed.

Erik looked over what had once been a Pendelcorp base of operations. There was nothing left except a burning crater. The missiles used in the attack were devastating in their efficiency. Everything was wiped out, not even a shred of incriminating evidence remained.

They all walked cautiously back into the desolate campground. Nothing but scorched earth and charred, burning wood remained. Everything for over 100 yards had been blasted into a crater, with the exception of a small six-foot circle of land where Erik had used his shield to protect himself and the children.

"Why, Mr. Knight?" one of the children asked.

Erik looked down at the young boy, his pupiless blue eyes blazing. *To hide the evidence. Wipe out all the loose ends.*

Erik's staff resumed its standard shape, and he willed the weapon to reduce its size further. He placed the weapon back in its satchel. *"Thank You,"* he whispered to the staff in the harsh Esper tongue, not knowing if it understood or was capable of understanding what those words of gratitude meant.

As he secured the weapon in place, it purred, almost with affection. Erik glanced down at it then began guiding the children on the long walk out of the woods. He led the group to where Lisa Reynolds was laying and gently picked up the girl.

We've got a good hike in front of us. Let's all stay together. He started to escort them down the mountainside.

Erik paused. He heard the sound of rotor blades. Another helicopter was coming, the pitch of the engine was different and he knew immediately that it was not the same ship that had attacked him before. He and the children watched carefully, safely concealed behind some giant tree falls. The third Bell Striker touched down in the middle of the burned-out crater. Three soldiers disembarked and began surveying the destruction. Erik knew what had to be done. The helicopter could take the children down the mountain in scant minutes, where it would take him until early the next morning walking. Lisa Reynolds needed immediate medical attention and the soldiers could provide it.

Children, go to them. They'll get you to safety quicker than I can. Tell them Lisa is back here. I'll stay with her until they come over.

Three of the children broke from their cover and ran for the helicopter, shouting and waving their hands. Erik felt a huge burden lifted from him as the soldiers spotted the three children and quickly ushered them into the helicopter. Two of the soldiers turned and headed to where Erik and his daughter were hidden.

I have to go now, Baby. You'll be safer with them.

"No, Daddy!" she pleaded through tear-stained eyes. "I wanna stay here, with you."

You can't, I have to face those creatures, Bri. I have to stop them. I can't put you in that kind of danger. He pointed to the still sleeping body of Lisa Reynolds. *She needs you right now.*

Brianna looked up at her father, her little eyes still streaming with tears, and nodded.

Erik looked down at her and smiled. *You'll always be my princess.* He removed the dog tags from around his neck, and gently placed them on his daughter. *You were holding these for me before, please keep them safe.*

The footsteps of the soldiers were audible now, and Brianna turned toward the sound. When she turned back, her father was gone.

Erik watched from the top of a large red oak as the soldiers carried his daughter and Lisa Reynolds into the helicopter. He focused his vision on his daughter. He could see her looking into the forest, her fist clenching the dog tags. He saw her bid him a final goodbye as she was carried into the helicopter and the door closed behind her.

The Striker's rotors spun quickly, and the ship slowly eased from the ground, carrying its precious cargo to the safety of home. He knew what his next move had to be. Somewhere out in this expanse of woodlands, two creatures loomed.

He recalled the general direction of the earlier disturbance. He walked deeper into the woodlands. Erik leapt twenty feet up into an adjacent oak tree and perched upon a massive limb. He quickly spotted another tree limb some several yards away and leapt to that one.

Covering several yards with each leap, the Hybrid moved through the wooded canopy, hunting for a trace or sign of the two creatures that nearly killed him earlier. He vowed to himself that their next meeting would be different. The next time they met, only he would live to walk away. That was how it had to be, the very fate of humanity depended on the outcome of his private duel.

* * *

The cheers erupted like wildfire when word reached the command post that the children, including a child assumed to have been kidnapped earlier, had been recovered.

The major puffed away on a cigar, leaning back in his chair. He ordered a recall of all their men out of the Hopedale parklands. He was reading a report concerning the fate of the helicopter that had downed two of his ships. Something very big was going on up there, big enough for someone to risk blowing a 400-foot crater on the top of Hopedale Mountain to destroy any lingering evidence, then destroy a multimillion-dollar weapons platform to keep the pilot quiet. Ross knew there would be an extensive investigation as to what actually occurred, but he knew this would eventually be filed as an unsolved mystery.

The major found it difficult to believe the children could just wander out of the woods waiting to be rescued. There were definitely missing pieces of information. They would need to debrief each child, away from any other authorities, to find out what really went on up there. Ross figured within the hour he'd have all the information he needed.

He was thankful the children were safe, yet that didn't help their secondary mission objective: Destroy the creatures that inhabited the mountain. This piece of their mission objective was, thus far, an abject failure. Major Ross was a man who didn't take to failure.

Chapter 16

The small fires burned themselves out, and the dust and ashes finally settled around the top of Hopedale Mountain. The damage caused by the missile and rocket barrage was devastating. There was no trace that a campsite ever existed, and the ridgeline over the tunnel sagged slightly, indicating the tunnel had completely collapsed upon itself due to the devastating impact of the Typhoon missile.

An inky blotch appeared in the middle of the newly formed crater, and two creatures emerged from the spilling darkness. They took several small steps as the portal closed behind them. Each creature looked around, trying to understand what happened to the forest that was there only hours ago. The smell of soldiers was still evident in the soil, as was the smell of the children they had abducted. Both creatures made their way ominously toward the tunnel entrance.

They stopped, looking at the devastation where their tunnel once stood. The large cat-like creature sniffed the fallen dirt and debris, and began pawing at the rock and soil that now occupied the tunnel space. The cat began tunneling deeper into the collapsed tunnel, only to have its work filled in by a small cave-in. The creature shook itself free of the fallen debris and howled with frustration as it pawed its way out of the freshly fallen rock and earth.

They had lost access to their home, and the Seelak lost its eggs, eggs that would eventually fully crystallize if not attended. The Seelak was enraged. Somehow the primates were able to remove the cavern cover and free the small things.

It returned to the spot where it first picked up the scent of the soldiers. It sampled the air. There was something else, something it hadn't smelled for thousands of years. It moved to a small patch of unscorched earth, lying in the middle of all the destruction like a desert oasis. It inhaled the air molecules over this area, and knew immediately that its ancient enemy had returned. It knew the smell of Esper, but this Esper contained an all too familiar accompanying scent as well: The Hybrid. The Hybrid was still alive. Somehow, it survived the brutal thrashing they had given him. Not only was the Hybrid alive, but it had undergone a change. The smell of Esper dominated its spoor, no longer a trace scent in the background.

The felinoid smelled the same patch and growled, its growl growing into a full-blown roar of anger and frustration. It, too, recognized the enemy. The Seelak joined its ally in a howl of pure unbridled hatred and aggression.

The scents of the Hybrid and children confirmed something else in the Seelak's limited intellectual capability. One of those children was a hybrid offspring. The Seelak's imprinted genetic code triggered: Kill all Espers. The Esper must die, and the primates who destroyed its nest must die. It would kill the Esper's offspring, as its children had been killed, and kill anything that got in its way.

The Seelak wandered over to a nearby tree and ripped off chunks of bark and wood with one swipe of its razor-sharp claws. It gestured toward its ally, and they both headed off into the forest, back down to the town – back to spread death and dismemberment to those who had destroyed its home and its eggs.

* * *

Richard sat in his office in total shock at his good fortune. The first phone call from his Nextel wireless confirmed the total and absolute destruction of the tunnel and campsite. The call his wife had received moments ago was from the police. Their daughter had been rescued, and was ferried by helicopter to the command center outside of Hopedale Mountain. Margaret was gathering some things for their daughter, and the two were preparing to head for the Army operations base to claim their child. The third turn of good fortune Richard received was from a news wire. The helicopter that assaulted the Army air ships had blown apart and was scattered over several acres of suburban property. Apparently, the pilot had tried to interfere with the programming and caused the craft's destruction earlier than had been planned.

Despite that one miscalculation, everything went according to plan. Pendelcorp and its owner were virtually free and clear of any wrong doing, and could in no way be implicated in any of the mess that had occurred up in the high country of Hopedale Mountain. Yes, it was a good turn of events for Richard Pendelton: No guilt, no fines, no prison term, and no Erik Knight to interfere with his plans for his family.

Richard grabbed his overcoat and headed out the front door to be with his wife and daughter. The adoption could proceed on schedule now. Another loose end would soon be tied up.

The ride to the Army encampment was quick. Margaret was bursting with anxiety, only wanting to see her baby and hold her once again in her arms. Richard parked his Mercedes behind a large military truck and was immediately approached by two Army personnel. He identified himself and his wife and was immediately escorted to a large olive drab tent with a Red Cross symbol on the rooftop. As they walked in, there was Brianna, wrapped in an Army blanket, along with the other missing children. There were several doctors sitting by the children, and two army officers, one major and one captain.

"It was him," Brianna insisted as she addressed the major. "It was my daddy," she added emphatically, holding up the dog tags hanging around her neck.

"It really was Mr. Knight," the boy sitting next to Brianna affirmed. "I mean, he looked way different, but he talked to us, and told us who he was." The boy paused, his forehead wrinkling. "Well, it wasn't really talking, but we could hear him inside our heads."

"You're all very sure of this?" the major asked.

All the children nodded in unison.

"My daddy came back for me, for all of us, like I knew he would," Brianna announced with a note of finality in her voice.

"Bri," Margaret spoke softly, just loud enough for her daughter to hear.

"Mommy!" the young girl cried as she ran over to her.

"Oh, thank God, thank God you're safe, child," she murmured as she held her daughter tight in her arms.

Brianna looked up at her mother. "Daddy was there. He punched through the boulder and guided us out of the tunnel. You should see him, Mom, he's huge and all silvery. His eyes are like two big blue pilot lights. He saved us from the creatures, and then saved us from this big black helicopter."

Margaret looked down at her daughter with deep sympathy. "Honey, that just can't be. I saw your father in the hospital, just yesterday. He was very, very sick. There's no way he could have gotten up and walked out."

"I don't care what any of you say. I know what I know," Brianna insisted.

A corporal entered the tent, saluted the major, and gave the man a written report. The major studied the report and looked absolutely bewildered.

"I wouldn't say that exactly, Mrs. Pendelton." He continued studying the words on the report. "We contacted the hospital after hearing the children's story. According to the Massachusetts General Hospital, a critical care patient simply got up and walked out of the hospital early this morning. The patient was identified as Mr. Erik Knight. One of the interns claimed that Mr. Knight was in excellent physical condition when he made his abrupt departure."

"How can he be sure it was Erik?" Margaret challenged. "They said he was as good as dead. Dead men don't just get up and walk away."

"It appears that the intern tried to stop him from leaving. Mr. Knight picked the man up with one hand and casually placed him to one side," the major answered, reading from the report. "So, the intern got a very close look at the face and made a positive ID. There are four other witnesses to corroborate this."

Margaret shook her head. "Brawn before brains, that does sound like Erik," she whispered.

"See!" Brianna accused. "You wouldn't believe me."

"He was escorted by two young women," the major continued, "one who had been with him since he had been admitted." The captain then mumbled something about purple hair.

"Shanda!" Margaret and Brianna spoke simultaneously.

"What else did your father say, child?" the major asked intently.

"He said that we should go with the soldiers because Lisa needed medical treatment. He said that he was going to take care of those creatures," Brianna replied.

"Interesting," the major mumbled. "But how can one man hope to succeed where we've failed?"

"If you saw him, you wouldn't have to ask," one of the children spoke up. "The rock that those things put in front of their cave entrance had to weigh tons, and he just smashed through it like it was made out of cardboard. Plus, he's huge, bigger than the biggest body builder—"

"That's enough," the major snapped, cutting the child off in mid-sentence. As he turned back toward his men, Ross looked over at the Pendeltons and knew that soon this tent would be filled with parents. He gestured to the captain to follow him outside. "Stay with the children, Corporal," Ross ordered as he left the tent, his assistant right on his heels. Both men walked back to their command center.

* * *

Major Ross sat behind the small desk in the command tent and stared hard at his second in command. "What's your take on this whole thing, Bill?"

"I don't know, sir," the captain replied honestly. "But if somebody told me yesterday that we'd lose forty armed men to some strange creatures in some backwater hick town, I'd have said they were smoking crack."

The major chuckled as he considered what each child had said. "Every kid said the same thing: There's some massive cavern up there on the top of that mountain, and somebody just went through a great deal of time and effort to seal it up forever."

"I think it's safe to assume that whomever sealed the cavern up are the same people responsible for unearthing it in the first place. From the way the Knight child was talking, it seemed as though they were walking through a mining tunnel of some sort," the captain added.

" It wouldn't be too far a leap to assume whoever dug that tunnel freed those things from the chamber they were sealed in," the major replied, picking up where the captain left off.

"I agree." The captain nodded. "The question is who? From what our records show, that area is state conservation land. Nobody should be doing anything up there."

"True." Ross nodded. "But apparently, somebody wasn't paying attention to the rules, or felt they were above the rules. Either way, that's not our mess. I just want our boys out of there so we can regroup and get some more sophisticated tracking equipment. I'd like some IR goggles, and heat-seeking LAWS Rockets for the next group that tangles with those bastards." Ross noticed the captain shaking his head. "Okay, what's wrong, Bill? I know that telltale shaking of your noggin."

"What do you make of that whole Erik Knight thing? I can't make it add up. If he is alive, and the hospital claims he is, how did he get up miles and miles of woodland, before our men, and why didn't these things take him out the way they've been killing our boys?" he pondered. "And what's with him becoming all silvery? We can assume he was normal-looking when he left the hospital. I can't imagine somebody's skin becoming silver and growing in body mass as details likely to be omitted from a hospital report."

"I don't know," the major replied. "That's another mystery that we need to solve. I can't believe the children just simply made him up. Somebody had to have freed them from the mine. It's unlikely that they could have escaped themselves, and dragged the other child behind them in a pitch-black tunnel." Ross smacked his hands together. "No! Didn't the police reports say that Knight fought these things earlier, both in the woods and in the youth park, and then again at the schoolyards?"

"Yes," Bill answered.

"In those reports, didn't they all say the creatures had glowing eyes, like the children said that Knight now has?" the major questioned.

"Yes," the captain answered again.

"Then somehow Knight is tied into this whole equation, tied in directly with these creatures, maybe even infected by one of them during their previous encounters. That could explain his remarkable recovery and the mutated skin. If we can find him, we'll most likely get all the answers we need," the major added.

"Or," the captain countered, "Knight was never there. The children managed to free themselves and concocted the whole story."

"Do you think that that's likely, Bill?"

"No, sir. It's just another possibility. As long as we're postulating, we may as well throw out all the possibilities."

" I think they were rescued by Mr. Knight. As far as the silver skin and pulverizing tons of rock, I'll ascribe that to overactive imaginations. Somewhere out there," the major gestured toward the direction of Hopedale Mountain, "Knight is wandering around, looking for a rematch, no doubt. If we could just get him here, get our hands on him...."

"Excuse me, sir," the captain asked. "Just how are we supposed to find Erik Knight in over seventy-plus square miles of woodlands?"

"We won't have to," the major answered as he lit a cigar and began puffing on it. "He'll come to us, eventually. We have his daughter, and if Erik Knight wants to get her back, he'll have to come to us."

"What about the girl's legal guardians, her mother and stepfather?" the captain questioned.

"What about them? Their daughter has been exposed to some unknown creatures. God knows what kinds of strange bacteria or germs the children have been in contact with. They must all be quarantined in a biohazard facility as soon as possible. Extensive tests must be conducted to assure they are all safe. Her parents have been exposed to their daughter. If we have to, we'll lock them in a med lab too. We'll get our answers, Captain. One way or another, we'll get our answers," the major added with a dramatic pause. "Don't you think?"

"That's a hell of a shaky card to play," the captain responded to the major's underlying threats. "Pendelton is no ordinary yokel."

"True," Ross agreed, "but we've got the backing of an entire federal bureaucracy behind us. I don't want to keep them too long, just long enough to draw Mr. Knight to us." Ross paused. "If it comes down to that," he quickly amended.

"Major, what you're suggesting is a violation of several military laws pertaining to civilian relations and abuse of federal power," the captain responded in a curt military demeanor.

"Shove it, Bill. I lost forty men in this jerkwater town – forty good men, men with wives and families. That's a lot of condolence calls to make. I want to know why they died, for what reason, and exactly what killed them. I can't ask those godforsaken creatures, but I can ask Knight. I'll get my answers, I owe it to those men and to their families. To Hell with regulations. Am I clear, Captain?" Ross added, emphasizing his second's lower rank.

"Yes, sir, Major," the captain replied tersely, emphasizing his disapproval with his vocal tone.

"Look, Bill," Ross began in a softer tone, "I'm just going to bend the usual protocol slightly. I don't plan on trampling over these people, and I don't want to cause the child any more stress than the poor kid has already had. But an exam is required for all the children by one of our doctors. We owe it to our men to get to the bottom of this. I need you with me on this. Can I count on you?"

The captain nodded and sighed. "Yeah, I'm in. We do owe the families of our fallen something, and Knight seems to be the man of the hour today. Let's just hope he doesn't join the list of deceased before the day is over with."

Chapter 17

The last of the Army search party had reported in and darkness settled upon the base encampment. The Red Cross tent was now filled with parents and children, excluding the parents of Lisa Reynolds, whom the Army was in the process of contacting.

Lisa Reynolds had been taken by ambulance to the local hospital for treatment of shock and dehydration. Brianna Knight, with help from the other children, had told and retold the story of their experiences and terrors at the mercy of both creatures, and how they were rescued, to a captive audience of parents and soldiers alike. Included in the audience of listeners were Shanda Kerwin and Alissa Penney. Margaret vouched for both women when they arrived upon hearing word of Brianna's rescue.

Shanda sat by herself outside the tent, staring up at the dark morass that was the looming mountain.

"Can we talk?" a voice called out, breaking Shanda's solitude.

She turned to see Margaret Pendelton. "Sure." Shanda gestured the woman toward the bench she was sitting on.

"I know you've been questioned already, and I know you and your friend weren't exactly forthcoming with information. That's all right," she added quickly. "But now I'm going to ask you, between just the two of us – lover and ex-lover of Erik Knight – what happened to him? Was it really him up there? Is Brianna telling the truth? Or is she just in denial about her father?"

Shanda turned away from Margaret and stared back up at the mountain looming like an ominous giant in the darkness. She considered the question for fifteen seconds before answering. "Yes. It was Erik," she whispered. "What's left of him."

Margaret shook her head. "I'm sorry, you said 'what's left of him'?"

"I can't explain it to you. You wouldn't understand, nor would you believe it. He sacrificed all that he was to save his daughter. He sacrificed any chance we ever had of being together. I lost the man I loved," she replied bitterly. "I can never have him back the way he was. Right now, for all I know, he's engaged in some life-or-death struggle with those monsters alone up there. If he dies up there, he'll die alone, and if he lives through the battle and is victorious, he'll still be alone. If you believe there is a deity that watches over humanity, you'd better pray that Erik wins, because his death will herald the end of our race as we know it, and the end of humans being the dominant species on this planet. Those things will use us all like cattle," she concluded as tears streamed down her face. "That's all I can tell you, I'm sorry. Brianna spoke the truth. What she saw was Erik, what he's become, what he's always been on the inside."

"Dear God," Margaret whispered. "I'm so sorry." She put her arm around Shanda's shoulder as she wept.

The two women sat quietly, staring at the mountaintop nestled underneath the evening starlight. Shanda felt a faint tingling inside her head. Her body began to shudder involuntarily.

"Oh my God!" she whispered to Margaret. "Erik must have lost. Those creatures are here, nearby."

"How can you tell?" Margaret replied as she peered into the darkness.

Behind them, they heard several screams of shock and panic. Both women turned to see a patch of blackness, blacker than the surrounding night, spread throughout the Army encampment. A nearby soldier screamed with horror as a black claw reached through the darkness and took him by the throat. The sound of his neck breaking reverberated throughout the small area.

Both Seelak creations emerged from the portal and immediately began to close on the Red Cross tent. Somewhere, gunfire broke out, and rounds sparked and deflected off the Seelak's thick armored hide. Another soldier leapt in front of the creatures and opened up with his service pistol. He was struck in the shoulder with one of his gun's deflected rounds. The felinoid pounced upon the wounded man, and grasped him between its vice-like jaws. With slowly increasing pressure, the jaws closed. The soldier's shrieks of agony didn't end until blood sprayed out of his mouth from punctured lungs and severed arteries. The creature dropped the lacerated corpse and continued moving forward.

Several soldiers formed a hasty line in front of the advancing monsters, their various rifles and pistols aimed at the enraged creatures. The creatures rushed the line as the soldiers commenced discharging their weapons. Several rounds found their mark, but the creatures were now on top of them. The soldiers were slaughtered in less than a minute.

Shanda and Margaret retreated behind a nearby jeep, helplessly watching the carnage unfolding before them.

"They're hideous," Margaret whispered. "They can't be stopped. They're going for my baby again." She broke from her cover and ran toward the tent where Brianna and the other children were.

"Wait! You'll be killed," Shanda screamed as she followed the panic-stricken woman.

Margaret Pendelton stood directly in the creatures' path, blocking their advance. Shanda quickly joined the courageous woman.

"No!" Margaret screamed at the top of her lungs. Her voice trumpeted above all the other noise, causing a sudden hush of silence. "You won't take them again. You can't have my baby." Margaret ignored the pleas for her to run. She glanced over at Shanda and held her ground. Richard yelled for her to escape, but she gestured him away. "You've done enough damage. Go away, please."

The enhanced Seelak warrior approached the two women, his claws outstretched and reaching for the kill. The creature stopped dead in its tracks, its expressionless eyes seemed to widen slightly. The large felinoid growled and retreated two steps. It clawed the ground questioningly, tearing up the pavement with its large paws.

The women heard a sound behind them. An angry

hissing reminded Shanda of an enraged reptile. Her entire body tingled and goosebumps emerged. Both women slowly turned their heads and looked behind them. Standing like a titanic sentinel with its massive arms crossed, staff firmly grasped in one hand, and wearing an undisguised look of pure hatred, was Erik Knight the Hybrid.

The Hybrid stepped in front of the stunned women and dramatically dragged its staff in a line in front of them and the Red Cross tent, daring the creatures to cross. He swung the staff with blinding speed, performing complicated motions that were only a blur to the human eyes. The routine ended, and he adopted an aggressive combat stance, staff ready to strike. The staff seemed to whine and murmur in anticipation of the coming battle.

"My God, Erik!" Margaret Pendelton whispered, looking up at her ex-husband. "What happened to you?"

Erik glanced back at the two women, his aqua-blue eyes piercing the darkness. *Go, now.* The two words roared in both of their heads. Shanda dragged a reluctant Margaret back into a crowd of armed soldiers.

"Hold your fire!" Major Ross ordered as he calmed the nervous soldiers whose fingers had all found the triggers of their rifles and pistols. "The kid said he's here to do our job for us. Let's give him a chance." Ross peered at the massive silver being in awe as it continued to glare at the other two creatures. "What in the hell happened to him?" he wondered aloud.

The two creatures recovered from their shock. They were so focused on their destruction that they failed to notice the Hybrid who had dropped from the trees directly outside the encampment. The Seelak leapt forward, its arms reached out in an attempt to grasp its silver foe. The Hybrid responded with an overhead swing of his staff. The weapon murmured with glee as it was smashed upon the Seelak's black-armored shoulder. The Hybrid didn't pause after that strike. He swung the staff laterally in a 360-degree sweep and swept the stunned Seelak's legs out from under it. The creature fell, landing flat on its back. The Hybrid brought his staff down, aimed directly at its head. The Seelak quickly rolled its body sideways, barely avoiding the blow that shattered the pavement where its head had been a fraction of a second earlier.

The silver Hybrid kept attacking. The Sentient Staff impacted against black-armored hide, each blow sounding like a thunderous clash of metal upon metal, spraying sparks upon both combatants. Erik succeeded in driving the Seelak back away from the crowd and the tent in which the children were being kept.

The felinoid sprang from its position, covering nearly thirty feet with its leap. It had waited until the Hybrid was facing away from it before it attacked. The Hybrid sensed the oncoming threat and executed a one-handed cartwheel, allowing the cat-like creature to sail by him harmlessly, and slammed his staff against the massive creature's flanks as it passed.

The cat landed and swung around swiftly to face the Hybrid again. It leapt quickly and collided with the silver warrior. The impact threw the Hybrid back, and the staff fell from his hand as he grappled with the much larger creature. The felinoid raked its claws across the Hybrid's massive chest, causing an ear-shattering squeal as the claws scraped against metallic flesh. The Hybrid landed a massive blow into the creature's jaw, lifting the great cat beast off the ground. The creature recovered quickly and attacked again, using its fifteen-foot tail like a great whip. The Hybrid blocked each strike with his forearms, frustrating the beast.

Erik and the felinoid charged into each other, both roaring battle cries. Erik pummeled the creature with both hands and feet, while absorbing dreadful blows from the creature's dinner plate-sized paws. There was no finesse in this combat, each participant simply lashed out with mindless fury. The felinoid, driven by its genetic coding, and the Hybrid, Erik Knight, seeking vengeance for the abduction of his offspring. The large cat tried again to pounce on its smaller opponent. Though smaller, the Hybrid possessed greater strength, and was able to catch his opponent in midair. He lifted the twenty-foot feline over his head and tossed it like a rag doll into the concrete.

From the darkness came a loud groan. A trash dumpster flew toward both combatants, missing the felinoid, and landing directly on top of the Hybrid with a sickening crunch of collapsing metal. Everyone was silent, staring at the shattered hulk of metal. Both creatures approached the ruined dumpster and stared quietly. From inside the wreckage there came a loud roar of rage. A silvery fist blew through the wreckage and accompanied the roar. The Hybrid punched and clawed his way out of the battered hulk to face his opponents again. There was, however, a gaping wound across its chest that was leaking a dark red fluid. He ripped a piece of scrap metal from the wreck and hurled it back at the creatures, then another and another, causing both to reluctantly give ground.

Erik did the unexpected and leapt between both creatures, raining blow upon blow upon both startled monsters. Both the Hybrid's hands and feet were lethal weapons; a combination of human combat excellence combined with all the generations of enhanced Esper warrior training. The creatures, however, fought back savagely. They, too, were enhanced with the skills of their ancestry. After thousands of years, the Esper-Seelak War was reaching its final, yet to be determined, conclusion.

The combatants separated again. The Hybrid leapt backwards an amazing fifteen feet into the air, executing several somersaults landing gracefully several meters away from his opponents. Each warrior's body was now littered with several lacerations. There were several discolorations on Erik's forearms where he had blocked the whip-like attacks of the felinoid cat creature.

Erik saw his staff lying on the ground several feet away from him. With a simple gesture of his outstretched hand, the liquid metal object leapt from the ground and nestled itself in his outstretched palm. His hands closed around the weapon, and it gave off an eerie moan.

Shanda peered over at Alissa who was watching the battle with great intent. She made her way over to the young waitress. "Can you tell what's going on in their heads?"

"The Seelak were somewhat surprised, but they have been programmed to attack and kill Espers. Their minds and instincts are on total automatic. They are, however, continually being fed by the fear from those around them. It makes them that much harder to destroy."

"And Erik?" Shanda whispered intently.

"He is himself. He has adapted to the changes and his

essence has survived the mutation of his body. He is one being with two sets of memories." She peered up at her. "Perhaps this is what was intended all along."

Shanda focused her telepathy on her lover, straining to
find the right frequency that would let her into his mind. After
a few seconds, she was able to read him, feel what he was feeling, and see what he was seeing. She could feel his unbridled
rage toward his opponents, a desire for vengeance that burned
like a white-hot fire, but that rage was over-ridden by an almost
mystical sense of control, a feeling she had shared with him
earlier in their prior link, but now much more enhanced and
overwhelming.

The three adversaries collided again. The Seelak warrior
rushed into Erik, absorbing dreadful blows from his staff, but
it still moved in. With incredible speed, it swung its tensile tail,
thrashing it across Erik's torso. The sound of the impact rang
like a gunshot. Erik fell back, bleeding from the gaping wound
across his stomach. Erik responded by smashing the end of
his staff down upon the creature's black-armored shoulder.
There was a sickening crunch as the staff shattered the armor
covering.

The Seelak avoided the follow-up blow and used its tail
again, but this time Erik managed to grab the appendage with
his free hand. He yanked on the creature's tail mightily, lifting the black-armored creature off the ground. Erik utilized
this momentum and began swinging his larger opponent like
a bola. He spun himself around five times, using the Seelak's
own mass to increase the force of each spin. On his final rotation, he let out a cry and put all of his strength into hurling the
creature into the air with as much force as he possibly could.
The Seelak literally flew over fifty feet, smashing through an armored convoy truck and crushing the parked car it landed on.

Erik pressed his attack on his other adversary. He leapt
high into the air and brought his staff down hard upon the felinoid who had closed in for another attack. The beast fell back
before Erik's fury, but kept swinging its razor-sharp claws and
threatened to bite him in two with every snap of its powerful
jaws. Erik glanced over to where the Seelak was. It was still
stunned, unmoving from its place on the crushed automobile.

He did notice a small river of fluorescent blue dripping onto the pavement.

The Seelak was no longer an immediate threat. He had to destroy the felinoid now, before its partner recovered. He couldn't finish off the Seelak warrior just yet. As soon as he took his eye off the cat, it would pounce upon him again with tooth and claw, as well as its whip-like tail. Erik's forearms were already battered from deflecting the creature's earlier blows. The felinoid sensed its partner was out of action. It attacked ferociously, as any animal when threatened. Erik was put on the defensive as the large creature attacked with incredible strength and speed. Erik was barely able to deflect the blows that seemed to be coming at him continuously. Grudgingly, he was forced to give ground, driven back from the stunned Seelak with each fresh attack.

Erik timed a counterstrike, and landed a quick thrust into the creature's ribs. The cat responded by leaping directly on top of him, forcing him down into the pavement, and knocking his staff away from him again. The weapon shrieked at the separation from its owner, and laid out of reach, murmuring and buzzing its annoyance like an angry wasp. The beast sat on top of him, its large hindquarters pinning his legs underneath the cat with their sheer bulk and weight.

Erik had to use both of his hands to keep the large gaping maw from snapping his head off. As he struggled with the cat's jaws, it was using its forepaws to rip into his unprotected chest and shoulders. Erik felt his metallic flesh tear under the cat's great claws.

With one great effort, he managed to free his left leg. He slammed his knee into the felinoid's side with all of his strength and was rewarded with the sound of snapping bone. The creature yelped in pain as Erik landed another blow to the same area.

Erik was able to release his right arm from the cat's large jaws now that the beast was distracted. He brought the arm over to his side as far as it would reach, and then spun his torso, propelling the arm into a thunderous right hook that landed squarely on the side of the creature's head. The felinoid howled in distress as it pushed itself off of him, nearly crushing him with its great weight. The large claws scraped against his flesh, and the creature pulled away from the force of the blow.

Erik stood, blood flowing from dozens of deep gashes and puncture wounds. The felinoid was dazed, shaking its head, and limping badly on its left side. Erik could see three ribs protruding through its midnight-black skin from where he had delivered the blows with his leg. He also noticed a steady trickle of purple fluid from the great beast's nostrils. He knew that he had managed to puncture a lung with his strikes. Something inside him urged him to press the attack. He knew the creatures could feed off the humans witnessing the conflict. He had to strike a killing blow before it could heal itself or get any stronger.

Thoughts precipitated action. The Hybrid closed his eyes briefly, picturing a more lethal weapon, an edged weapon. He reached out his hand and felt something settle into his grasp and take shape in his hand. He looked down at the large two-handed broadsword nestled in his grip. He brought both hands to bear on his newly formed weapon and rushed his wounded foe.

The cat swung a large paw at his head in an attempt to decapitate him. The Hybrid responded by swinging the sword directly into the limb's path. The paw severed, the claws falling away and rolling to a stop several feet from the felinoid. The creature howled in agony as it fell over, losing its balance. Erik raised the sword and drove it point-first into the area where he had guessed the heart to be located. The silver blade sang an eerie harmonic as it effortlessly pierced the dark tough hide and severed bone and sinew. Erik pulled the blade free, ripping the side of the felinoid open during the process, and was covered in purple ichor hemorrhaging from the mortal wound. Blood and entrails spilt from its body and littered the pavement. The creature whimpered in its agony.

The Hybrid raised its silver blade and let loose one final blow, the blade severed the creature's spinal cord and separated its head from its torso. The jaws in the powerful head snapped once, then again as the fiery green light faded from its eyes. The decapitated torso flinched and fidgeted for several seconds before it, too, yielded to eternal silence. The head and corpse began to sizzle and bubble. The once-powerful body began to liquefy and dissolve into nothingness. Soon, the only evidence that the creature had been there at all was a large wet spot on the pavement and several traces of spilt blood from its earlier wounds.

Erik spun toward the fallen Seelak. The creature painfully rose from the wrecked automobile. Erik raised his sword in readiness, and approached the Seelak. The creature's black-armored exoskeleton was cracked and broken in several places. It turned and saw the approaching Esper and hissed a savage cry of fury. Erik was also severely injured. His limbs ached and his torso was on fire from several wounds. He knew that his human body would have expired long ago, even as enhanced as he was upon leaving the hospital. Alissa told the truth: He would not have survived this type of combat without undergoing the change.

It happened as Erik was only ten feet from his opponent. He felt an overpowering sense of dark bioelectric energy. He was not afraid, only curious. The Seelak began to tense and, as if by magic, the hideous damage began to heal. The gaping holes in its armor regenerated. The areas that had been crushed by the Sentient Staff re-fused together.

Erik watched in silent awe as the once-crippled Seelak warrior restored itself. He instinctively knew that the creature had been feeding on the fear generated by the spectators during his fight with the felinoid. It had gathered enough emotional energy to completely regenerate itself.

The Seelak warrior approached its silver opponent. Both adversaries circled each other like two great gladiators. As they studied each other, memories began to trigger in each being. The Seelak had flashes of combat with an Esper warrior similar to this one, yet slightly larger. It inhaled the scent of its foe, and caught the familiar essence of the Esper that had defeated it so long ago.

The Hybrid experienced nightmare flashes of a frail Esper being torn apart. The Hybrid's memory cried out in agony as the name Sennek burned itself into the chrome warrior's consciousness. Jakor's horrid visions of that terrible day rushed through the Hybrid's mind like an avalanche, unleashing a burning desire for personal vengeance, not only for the abduction of his child and the murder of his friend, but for another atrocity committed against the essence of a being who now shared a place in his mind.

The Hybrid sheathed his weapon and flexed the massive muscles beneath his armored flesh. The burning rage fueled his body, drowning out the aches and pains of his prior combat. His aqua-blue eyes burned with an even hotter intensity, while his body began to glow with a nimbus of the same light blue hue. He screamed a sound so loud and penetrating the sonic concussion blew the Seelak off its feet and shattered every glass pane within a half mile radius. The very ground shook as the echoes reverberated into the night.

The Seelak quickly righted itself and attacked its enemy. The Hybrid responded with an awesome punch that cracked the ebony creature's facial plating. The Seelak retreated, picking up a 3500-pound vehicle as if it were a bathtub toy and heaved it toward the Esper. The Esper warrior caught the vehicle in midflight as if it were no more than a feather and threw it back toward the Seelak, which easily shredded the car with its black claws. Both warriors silently closed the gap. Each one was preparing for the upcoming battle.

* * *

The crowd of soldiers and onlookers gasped in amazement as the two genetically engineered super beings began the final battle of the Esper-Seelak War of over ten thousand years ago.

"This is way out of our league," Ross whispered to Anderson as they watched the Seelak tear apart the hapless automobile.

"That car had to weigh nearly two tons, and they tossed it around like a Nerf ball," Anderson observed. "We never stood a chance."

"Nothing of this world possesses that type of raw strength, not even the largest African gorilla. This is something older than humanity, I suspect," Ross replied, mesmerized by the combat.

* * *

The Hybrid and the Seelak collided with a sound like two freight trains impacting. They grappled with each other, constantly adjusting their legs for balance, each one looking for that extra piece of leverage. The Hybrid shifted his mass, freeing up his right hand, and landed a massive right cross which drove the Seelak back nearly twenty feet.

The Seelak landed upright and sprang forward like a bullet, crashing into the Hybrid's torso. The Hybrid fell over from the impact, the Seelak landing on his chest. In a move of surprising agility, the Hybrid brought both his legs up and managed to get them around the Seelak's neck. With a mighty heave forward, he threw the ebony warrior off him, smashing its head onto the pavement. Before the Hybrid could react, the Seelak swung its tail, cracking the tensile appendage against the Hybrid's torso as both combatants rose to their feet. The blow opened up a deep wound that trickled a steady river of reddish blood. The Seelak pressed its advantage, continuing to lash out like an angry serpent with its whip-like tail. The Hybrid fell back, bleeding from several more open wounds.

Despite the Hybrid's greater strength, it was weakening from the extended battle with the felinoid and prior escapades absorbing the weapons of the attack helicopter. Inside the Hybrid's body, Erik's enhanced mind was working feverishly to find a successful plan of attack. He had the answer. The Seelak was constructed to battle Espers. It was prepared for all types of Esper martial tactics. But the Hybrid was also a human warrior, with native human skills. Erik Knight was an extreme fighter with few equals. That was the key to victory. In a battle where both beings are closely matched, one must change the odds, and the Hybrid was about to do just that.

Let's try some modern American kickboxing. The Hybrid's stance changed, becoming lower and more balanced. The Seelak attacked again. The Hybrid twisted his torso, leaning back over his rear leg. The tail cracked against empty space. The Hybrid shot forward, pushing off his back leg, and leapt high into the air. He mirrored the spinning kick he had used against the Seelak earlier in the park. Only this time, his body was hundreds of times more powerful. When his rear leg impacted into the Seelak's chest, there was a loud cracking sound and the Seelak was thrown back several feet into the air from the impact, to land with a heavy thud on the paved surface. It stood, blood and gore flowing from the gaping hole in its chest plates.

The Hybrid charged in, closing the distance between them in a heartbeat. He unleashed a complicated series of punches faster than the eye could follow. Each metallic fist impacted with a resounding thud, sounding like a jack hammer. The Esper warrior never let up, all of his remaining strength was going into this final assault. He circled his taller opponent, peppering the black creature with a series of left jabs and right cross punches. Each time the Seelak tried to respond, the Hybrid used evasive boxing techniques to avoid the Seelak counterstrikes.

The Seelak, however, was far from helpless. It was beginning to adapt to this new style of combat, anticipating what its opponent might do and doubling, and even tripling, its attacks in order to change the momentum of the battle. It clawed at the Hybrid and launched several more fierce strikes of its own that scored several cuts on Erik's exposed torso.

The two super-beings separated momentarily, sizing each other up and getting a measure of each other's remaining strength. The Hybrid began to move around, dancing and weaving, bouncing, pivoting on the balls of his feet, circling the Seelak. The creature was confused, watching curiously. The left jab that impacted with the side of its face came totally as a surprise. When it tried to respond, the Hybrid ducked the blow and danced out of the way, closing the space again, quickly hammering the creature with another swift left jab, right hook, and uppercut which knocked the Seelak off its feet. The creature regained its footing and attacked with all its remaining fury. The Hybrid did not retreat. It continued to rain blows upon the creature like a heavy weight prizefighter. The Seelak's strikes were either deflected or dodged.

Enraged, the creature attacked again. Erik stepped back, still jabbing at it with his metal fist, and confounding the creature.

The Seelak roared with rage and frustration. Try as it may, it could not adapt to the Hybrid's ever-changing martial tactics.

Erik attacked again. He moved in and slammed a solid right into the creature's black face. He followed that blow with an immediate left hook and palm strike. The Hybrid stood toe to toe with his larger opponent and rained blow upon blow, his hands causing showers of sparks as they impacted upon the Seelak's body. Each punch positioned his body to throw another different type of attack. He pivoted his hips with each blow, pushing off his back leg, which provided even more power to his strikes.

The Seelak was unable to cope with the tactics. It fell back dazed and frustrated. As it did, Erik stepped forward, never letting up. His punches were faster than could be followed, his hands and arms lost in a continuous blur of motion. The Seelak's splendid armored shell was now a dizzying array of cracks and splinters. It tried to swing its tensile tail in a desperate attempt to counterattack and buy itself time to recuperate.

The Seelak extended its tail like an edged weapon. The creature began to whirl itself around like a top at dizzying speed. It closed on the Hybrid, striking the silver warrior across the forearm. The impact cut the Hybrid's limb almost to the bone. The Esper was forced to withdraw, cradling its damaged limb. It reached into its satchel, its fingers touching the staff. He willed the weapon to take its prior shape, the lethal battle blade. The Seelak growled with pleasure upon seeing the damage inflicted upon its opponent. The creature began to spin again, closing upon its wounded challenger.

The Hybrid raised his weapon, favoring his good arm. As the spinning whirlwind of a creature approached, the Hybrid swung the sword into its path. There was a brief sound as the sword and tail impacted, severing more than half of the tensile appendage. The Seelak shrieked in agony as blood spilt from the lethal wound. Before the creature could do any more, Erik took his weapon in both hands and lunged forward, driving the point of the sword straight into the hole in the Seelak's damaged chest plating. The sword seemed to whistle even louder as it crashed into the shattered black-armored shell and pierced it.

The sword penetrated the Seelak's chest, and the point exploded out the creature's back. The Hybrid hefted the black monster over his head. The Seelak shrieked with outrage and agony as the Hybrid held it, impaled helplessly in the air. The Hybrid swung the impaled creature in a counterclockwise motion. The centrifugal force wrenched the creature free of the blade when he stopped the motion. The Seelak warrior was propelled over twenty feet straight up into the air from the Hybrid's unorthodox maneuver. It seemed to take an eternity for the creature to come back to Earth. The onlookers watched in silence as it fell earthward.

For Steve, my daughter, and Sennek! His voice screamed in the minds of the human observers.

There were several gasps of shock as the Hybrid swung a mighty upward blow with his sword into the creature as it fell past him. The metal blade of the sword cut into the falling body, slicing it evenly in two pieces with a sickening crunch of severed armor plate, sinew, and bone. Erik looked down at the pieces of the creature. Its arms were flailing on one half, while its legs and tail twitched and jerked from its lower half. Like the felinoid, its body began to bubble and whither away.

The Hybrid, Erik Knight, stood quietly overlooking the rapidly dissolving body. The great sword he held loosely in his right hand melted back into a small cylindrical shape. He placed the weapon in the pouch at his side, and turned to face the crowd of onlookers.

He was severely beaten, bleeding from several gaping wounds and punctures. His breathing was labored and heavy. His body was beginning to succumb to the wounds and blows sustained in combat.

Erik stared into the crowd, seeing the faces of his daughter, girlfriend, ex-wife, and others whom he did not know. He desperately wanted to communicate with them, talk like a human. He moved his silver-hued lips, trying to make words, but succeeded in only making more hissing sounds. The battle-weary Hybrid took a step toward the crowd, and several people backed away nervously. The nervous military had several M-16s pointing at him.

Erik took another step, but stumbled as exhaustion finally overtook him. He fell to his knees, catching himself before collapsing face-first into the pavement. The Hybrid needed to heal itself. Instinctively, the ability resided within him. The ability to harness the power of the living earth given to him from his creators, embedded into his new genetic structure.

Erik relaxed himself and let the reams of knowledge that were now a part of him take control. He felt the Esper part of his personality, Jakor, rising again, dominating what he was. He raised his arms skyward, summoning something. He felt his body tingling, generating some sort of electrical field around him. In response to his plea, the very air around him began to crackle with electricity. His body was immersed in a silvery blue hue. Jagged arcs of raw electricity struck him from the charged energy field encasing his body.

The energy fed his body, wounds were healing, and his torn flesh was restored. His body was hungrily absorbing the energy. He felt exhausted, strained muscles rejuvenate and re-vitalize.

There were no more bruises or lacerations, and the welts that had discolored his silvery forearms vanished completely. Within the span of twenty seconds, the energy had dissipated, and he was completely restored.

The Esper intellect inside spoke to him, as if the two per-sonalities were two separate individuals inhabiting one shell.

You fought well, Hybrid. You have avenged my brethren, re-stored honor to our race. and rectified our grievous mistake. Be as you were before you took up my staff. Our gifts are still here for you as our thanks. You are our legacy. You are and will always be the Hybrid, the best of both our species. Use these gifts well.

Erik opened his eyes and looked at his hands. They were changing from armored silver to pink human flesh again. The sheer massive bulk of the Hybrid was replaced by his more human physique. He was, as Jakor said in his mind, as he was when he left the hospital: Enhanced greatly, but still human.

Erik knew, all he had to do was will the change, and he would become the metal-coated warrior that was now his alter ego. The Sentient Staff was still at his side, just his thinking of the weapon made it hum and purr in its sheath. He reached over and gently tapped the exposed metal pro-truding from its case and felt a surge of bioelectricity flow through him. There were abilities and latent talents yet to be explored, but he had time now to become familiar with all that he was, all that he was supposed to be.

The human-looking hybrid looked back over at the crowd of soldiers, politicians, parents, and reporters, all of whom watched the remarkable transformation from hybrid to human. "It's over," he stated simply, relieved to be able to speak once again. "It's all over."

The crowd of spectators still stared at him dumbfounded.

Brianna, who had been watching the battle with the other children, broke through the crowd and ran to her father's side. "Daddy!" she screamed as tears rolled down her face.

The young girl ran to Erik and he knelt down, allowing her to jump up and wrap her arms around him.

"Daddy, you're okay!" she whispered as she held him tightly.

"Did they hurt you, baby?" he whispered. "I'm so sorry I couldn't come for you sooner. I'm sorry I let them take you. I tried to stop them at the schoolyard," he said, holding her tight.

"It's okay, Daddy, you came for me, just like I knew you would." She held up his dog tags to show him. "I never doubted you for a minute."

Erik wrapped his arms around his daughter, feeling the warmth of her tears as they fell upon his shoulders, and easily lifted her off the ground. His smile was enormous as he held his little bundle of joy in his arms. "Like I told you before, nobody messes with daddy's little girl," he gently whispered into her ear.

Brianna's cascade of laughter served as a beacon of light to drive away the darkness that had settled upon the sleepy community.

Margaret, Shanda, and Alissa carefully approached the two, not wanting to interrupt the moment between father and daughter.

"Erik," Alissa asked, "are you okay?"

Erik lifted his head, looking in Alissa's direction. He nodded slightly and acknowledged the other two women. "I'm fine." He hugged his daughter tighter. "Everything is fine now."

Shanda walked up to him slowly at first, then she ran the last several steps, hurling herself in his open arm. "I thought I'd lost you forever," she cried.

"I'm all right, baby, it's over," Erik whispered as he inhaled the scent of her hair and perfume. "I'm sorry for what this must have put you through. There was no other way. I didn't have a choice," he added in an attempt to explain and apologize.

Shanda gently touched her finger to his lips. "No, no apologies. You did what had to be done, what the Espers needed you to do. I'm just thankful you're back to normal."

Erik smirked, and Shanda sensed immediately that all was not normal. But at this time right now, she didn't care. Erik was back, Brianna and the other children were safe, and the creatures from another time were destroyed.

"How?" Alissa asked. "How did you change back?"

"It wasn't intended to be permanent, I guess," Erik answered simply, not wanting to reveal everything to her or anyone just yet. He needed time to evaluate what had happened to his body, and to study the new gifts he had been given.

"Mr. Knight," a voice called.

Erik looked up to see Major Ross and Captain Anderson approaching him.

* * *

"Mr. Knight!" the major repeated loudly. "Well done, Mister, well done," the major complimented.

Erik turned and faced the major. He looked deep into the major's eyes with his fiery gaze. Ross could feel the Esper's powerful mind reading him, studying him. At that point, the major knew he was dealing with intelligence and a power beyond anything that he had coped with before. It was obvious that Knight was still more than human, the flesh simply a façade of the powerful being still residing within.

"Thank you," Erik replied simply and evasively.

"We have several questions," Ross added uncomfortably, comprehending Knight had some ability to read minds. He tried to shield his thoughts from the Esper as much as possible. "Would you consent to a debriefing in our command tent?"

"No, thank you," Erik declined. "I want to take my daughter home, curl up on my couch, and pretend this whole nightmare never happened—"

"Mr. Knight," Captain Anderson interrupted, "we just need some more details of what actually went on up there. All we have are the verbal accounts of four children. Any light you could shed upon this would be greatly appreciated by military intelligence. For example," the captain continued, using a more reasonable tone, "are there any more of these things running around up there, or anywhere? Do you know who controlled the helicopter that destroyed two of our choppers?"

"As far as I know, those were the last of their kind," Erik answered truthfully. "As for the rogue helicopter, I only have speculation, but no real proof of anything, yet. But when I do, you'll hear from me."

"We lost over fifty because of those things, Knight." Ross commented.

"I'm truly sorry, but that's not my fault. They almost killed me too, on more than one occasion, remember?"

"I'm afraid I'm going to have to insist on a debriefing, Mr. Knight. Too much has happened today, and we need answers," the major pressed, blocking Erik's path.

Erik looked directly into Ross's eyes, his light blue eyes burning with aqua fire. The major felt those eyes threatening to burn right through him with their inhuman intensity.

"Major, it's over, I'm not going anywhere. You already know how to find me. Let's not start another fight so soon after I finished with one. You're tired and I'm tired. You have a great many dead soldiers up in those woods." He gestured, pointing toward Hopedale Mountain, "And there are many hungry wild animals out wandering at night, searching for food. Your men deserve better than to be gnawed on by some carrion eaters looking for a midnight snack." Erik walked by the major.

"We'll get them out," Ross replied in a whisper as he watched Erik walk away. The major noted the look of content and satisfaction as young Brianna Knight looked over her father's powerful shoulder. "We're not through yet, Mr. Knight," Ross mumbled to himself, "not by a long shot."

"Where are we going, Daddy?" Brianna whispered.

"Home," Erik replied as he carried his daughter toward Madame's.

Ross watched Shanda, Alissa, and the Pendeltons pile into

their cars and head toward the restaurant.

* * *

Jeff sat quietly at one of the booths, reviewing invoices and balancing ledgers from his business. His mind kept wandering back to the sight of his friend's broken body lying in the hospital bed on the verge of dying. He would occasionally look over into Erik's corner booth, remembering his young friend as he enjoyed his favorite meal, or dealt with clients. Jeff knew that was not how Erik would have wanted to end his life. He figured there was not much chance of finding young Brianna Knight or any of the other children abducted from the schoolyard. That, too, anguished his soul – four innocent children terrorized by those beasts.

The dark thoughts continued to depress him further and he pushed away his receipts and papers in disgust. He heard the chimes announce the arrival of somebody entering the diner.

"We're closed," he yelled moodily.

"Jeff?" Shanda made her way into the main area of the restaurant.

"Shanda?" Jeff replied. "Is it over, is he..." he paused, "is he dead?" he finished, struggling to force the distasteful words from his mouth.

"Uncle Jeff?" a little voice cried from the hallway.

Jeff's eyes widened, and he slowly stood from the table. "Brianna?" he said in disbelief. "Brianna Knight!" he whispered as he saw the girl walk into the dining area. Jeff ran to the child and scooped her up in his arms. "How is it possible?"

"Daddy came and got me, Uncle Jeff. You shoulda seen him. He was all silvery, like a big mirror, with glowing blue eyes," Brianna announced proudly.

"But I saw him, we saw him earlier," he stammered, looking at Shanda for help.

"It's true," Alissa walked into the diner with Margaret Pendelton.

"But how?" he asked.

"It's a long story," Shanda answered, looking over at Alissa who smiled briefly. The mysterious young girl seemed relieved the events finally played out to their proper conclusion and Erik would not be condemned to a life of isolation.

They all sat down and gave Jeff the quick version of the incredible events that occurred over the past two days. Jeff's jaw continually dropped bit by bit as the story continued, until his mouth hung open in disbelief.

"Where is he? Where is he now?" Jeff demanded.

"Right outside, waiting to talk to you," Shanda answered.

* * *

Jeff stepped out into the dark parking lot, peering into the darkness, as if not knowing what to expect.

"Erik?" he called out into the darkness.

Up here, in the big tree over the dumpster, a voice rang out in his mind.

Jeff was startled as he heard Erik's voice trumpeting inside his head. He looked up and saw a pair of glowing blue eyes looming in the tree. Erik gracefully dropped from the tree to land silently two meters in front of the startled man. Jeff looked at his friend in awe.

"You get used to being up there," Erik remarked as he studied his friend.

"My God!" Jeff exclaimed. "You look like you just came out of a show room, not a single scratch or mark on you. Far different from when I last saw you."

"Yeah, they fixed me up as good as new – better than new, you could say," Erik agreed.

"So I've been told," Jeff replied. "What happened to you, what did they do?"

"It's complicated, and I still haven't worked my way through it completely," Erik began. "I'm the byproduct of a genetic virus, a combination of human genetics and a breed of advanced beings known as Espers. When the Espers came to our planet, they were not alone. Another species called the Seelak accompanied them. They combined their technology to create a titanic vessel capable of carrying the remnants of their people to Earth. Their races had been at war for centuries, the conflict had made their world uninhabitable. They realized that both their races would die if they didn't cooperate and save themselves. They ended their war and put all their efforts into building a huge spacecraft that they called a Worldship, a ship capable of carrying them all to a new world.

"When they first arrived on our planet, they lived in peace, working together, but disagreement broke out between the species, and the Seelak eventually moved themselves to a new encampment away from the Espers. Both species did what they could to avoid Mankind, until it was realized that their species and the human species could not coexist. Native diseases began to plague both Esper and Seelak, while the bacteria that they brought with them proved deadly to the native life on Earth.

"The Seelak wanted to destroy all humankind, while the Esper preferred to isolate themselves and let this world evolve naturally. The Espers and the Seelak disagreement escalated into another war. This war proved to be the end of both species. The Seelak created creatures to feed off of Esper emotion, use them like food, but the Esper had created huge powerful warriors to aid them in their fighting, I'd call it a warrior caste for lack of a better term." Erik paused for a moment to let Jeff absorb what he had said.

"I'm following you so far, but how does all this involve you and whatever those things were?" Jeff asked.

"I'm just getting to that," Erik answered. "During the final battle, the Espers were victorious. Several pair of the Seelak creatures had been killed, only one pair remained, and that pair was locked inside their huge spacecraft. The Espers decided to lock the Seelak survivors into the Worldship with their creations, to serve as an alternate food source. From what I understand, Seelak emotions are not nearly as intense as Espers. Since these monsters were designed to feed off of strong Esper emotional energy, the creatures would be constantly starved, while the Seelak would be tortured for food for the remainder of their lives, trapped inside that large ship with their monstrous creations."

"That's horrid," Jeff remarked with a shudder.

"I agree, but their crimes were just as horrid and the Espers felt the punishment was fitting for their crimes. But what they didn't realize, until after they had completely buried their ship, was that the creatures would not die, they would enter a period of hibernation, and would eventually be released, which we both know happened," Erik said lightly. "The Espers created a series of genetic viruses to embed themselves into certain humans that had particular genetic traits. My body was host to the genetic coding of their greatest soldier, a being named Jakor. He was the mightiest Esper warrior ever created. His genetic codes have combined themselves with mine to allow me to combat those mutations when they escaped their confinement.

"Very few people have the genetic virus within them, in those very few, the virus will remain dormant. Shanda has Esper genetics, as does Alissa, as far as I know, nobody else in our area does. The three of us were all drawn to this area for a reason, the Espers knew this day would come, and made sure humankind would have someone to fight for them," Erik finished his limited explanation and awaited his friend's response.

"I don't know what to say," Jeff whispered. "That's the most incredible thing I've ever heard." Jeff looked directly at Erik. "And what about you, how does this affect you now? Are you still different? I mean, you look like the same man I've known for so many years."

Erik took two steps and turned. "I've been altered, incredibly. This shell of skin is just a disguise for what I really am, a large metal-skinned interspecies experiment. I have the knowledge of an alien being locked inside my head. I'm sharing my mental real estate with a being called Jakor. It's almost as if I've known him … it for years. His personality exists deep within me. He can speak to me at times. I can feel and experience things no human can, see things and sense things no one else can.

"When I was up on that mountain, it was almost as if I were a part of this planet. I could feel the magnetic pull of the poles. I could smell the scent of Brianna on the soil, feel her feelings." He paused, sitting on the steps looking up at the evening stars. "Then there's the physical strength. As I am, right now, I'm easily ten times stronger than I was before, and I was already lifting seven hundred pounds of free weight at the gym before all of this happened, thanks to the mutation from the virus. It seems that its abilities were more predominant in the perfect genetic match, me. It was hard enough keeping that feat secret. Imagine if I start lifting cars or trucks for exercise?"

Erik could see traces of doubt in his friend's eyes. He quietly stood and walked to a nearby car. He casually lifted the front end of the car four feet off the ground with one arm, and then carefully lowered the vehicle's front end to the pavement. He heard Jeff gasp in astonishment. He walked back to the steps and sat down. "If I make the change, become the hybrid creature that fought the Seelak, the physical strength is beyond anything I've ever imagined. There are abilities, senses, and power in the hybrid still remaining to be explored." Erik put his face in his hands and groaned.

"All of this scares me. I never asked for this, this isn't what I wanted for myself: To be a freak." He looked over at his trusted friend "I wonder, Jeff, am I still human, do I have the right to love that woman in there, knowing what I am, and what I'm capable of becoming?" he asked his friend. "Will she still be able to love me?"

Jeff approached his friend, placing an arm upon his shoulder, and stared up at the stars, following Erik's gaze. "Two interesting words," he began, "changed and different. Have you changed? Yes, you're stronger than you were before. You have senses and abilities others don't, and you can become a being with metal armor for skin. But from what I understood from Shanda and Alissa, and from what you've just told me, you all have unique abilities. You were all chosen for a reason. You told me that you've had a sixth sense, a unique ability since you were a child, that it set you apart. Shanda too has those gifts. It seems Alissa has those gifts as well. You were given those abilities for a purpose: To stop a dreadful thing from occurring and you did. But dreadful things occur every day. Why not use those gifts and stop more dreadful things from occurring?" Jeff asked, letting the question hang in the evening air unanswered.

Before Erik could reply, Jeff continued. "So, we both agree that you've changed, but are you different? You seem like the man I've known. You act like him. Your friends seem to think you're the same. Inside, where your heart is, you are Erik

Knight. Maybe you have a piece of this Jakor person in there, maybe he's there to guide you, help you cope with your new gifts. If these Espers were as advanced and as wise as the ladies claim, I don't believe that they would enhance an unsuspecting being without giving him some sort of user's manual or instructions. This extra set of memories and intellect is probably your instruction guide to help you cope and understand your abilities, and to use them wisely, which so far you've done."

Jeff sat next to Erik on the steps. "Changed, yes, but not different. You're still the same man, only better. As far as Shanda goes, she knows what she's getting and accepts it, or she wouldn't be here now."

"One more thing," Erik added.

"There's always one more thing with you, isn't there?" Jeff added in mock annoyance.

"The military knows about me. There is more than a healthy curiosity about what I did today and how I did it. They'll be here, probably tomorrow, for a grilling. I don't know how far they'll go, or what they'll do to get what they want. But I don't see it ending with just one meeting. And I don't think they're going to go away."

"What are you getting at?" Jeff asked intently.

"I got a quick read on the major who spearheaded the operation today," Erik began. "His interest was more on the line of 'Can we use this thing as a weapon? Can we make more of him?' than it was any relief that the situation here was over. I don't know how far they'll go or who they'll put at risk," Erik added, knowing that Jeff understood what he meant.

"I'm willing to take that chance. Besides, I don't think anyone in their right mind is going to pick a fight with you," he answered flatly, swatting at a persistent mosquito. "Look, I don't have metal skin, and unless you plan on changing now, I suggest we no longer provide food for the bugs and go inside. You have two pretty ladies waiting for you inside," Jeff stood up, heading for the door.

"Jeff," Erik said quickly as he stood. The older man turned. "Thanks."

Jeff nodded. "Welcome back, Erik. Let's go enjoy our company."

Both men went inside and did just that, talking and celebrating until very early the following morning.

* * *

The gathering finally ended around two o'clock in the morning. Jeff had called several staff over for the celebration. Alissa had spun a fantastic fairy tale of hospital mix-ups with patient records to minimize Erik's hospitalization for the co-workers.

Nobody seemed to care or pay much attention though. They were all happy to have Erik back where he belonged. Shanda and Margaret spent a great deal of time together with Brianna and actively kept the young girl mute regarding her father's recent experiences.

Erik sat back and talked with everyone and enjoyed the evening. It had been a while since he felt like he belonged anywhere, but he finally realized home was this small little diner, his tiny apartment, and one-room office. Everything that he needed, he had had all along: Friends, family, and people who cared about him.

Erik occasionally glanced over to where Richard Pendelton sat, alone in a corner booth, looking as out of place as anyone possibly could. Erik had unfinished business with him, but that would be done later, at the time and place of his choosing. Pendelton had put his daughter at risk, and was willing to sacrifice her life to keep some corporate secrets. Erik would make Richard pay for that, and it was an account he would settle very soon.

* * *

Erik lay awake in his bed, staring out into the empty darkness. Erik and Shanda had conducted their own private celebration when they arrived at his apartment, normally he would relish the time sleeping in her arms, but he kept having images of those creatures flashing through his head. Erik realized if he was having trouble sleeping, his daughter must be quite uncomfortable in the darkness.

Erik leaned over and gently kissed Shanda who was in a deep sleep next to him. He put on a pair of sweat pants and left the bedroom. He walked into the small living room, his enhanced eyes piercing the veil of darkness. He quietly tiptoed over to his wall safe and opened it. As he opened the door, he was greeted by an almost welcoming purr of the Sentient Staff. He gently grasped the flowing living metal and felt its warmth against his palm. He studied the object carefully for a few moments, listening to the purrs and whines of the metal as he brushed the metallic surface with his fingertips.

"You and I have some things we need to accomplish," he whispered to the staff, suddenly feeling foolish for addressing the weapon. The staff, however, seemed to comprehend its new owner and hummed with an almost human anticipation.

Erik left his apartment and walked out into the night. He stared up at the stars, wondering if the light from one of them was also shining on some other sentient being somewhere in the vast universe. He took the staff and willed the weapon to elongate. The staff obliged, sighing with satisfaction at being activated. Erik closed his eyes, and pictured himself, as he was earlier, a great being of silver, with glowing blue fireballs for eyes. He felt a slight tingle throughout his body, and when he opened his eyes, he saw silvery metallic flesh once again replace his frail human skin. He looked up at the nearest tree and easily leapt the thirty feet up to the nearest large limb. He began to move, silently and swiftly, leaping from tree to tree, seemingly the only creature stirring at such a late hour.

* * *

Brianna Knight sat in bed with her covers tucked close around her. She was absently squeezing her father's dog tags. The young girl witnessed the demise of the creatures at the hands of her father, but for some reason still expected to see the inky black Seelak and its huge cat-like companion appear from the darkness to take her away again.

She looked over at her mother who was sleeping soundlessly in the chair in the corner of her room. The more she thought about it, the more agitated she became. After five minutes, she felt the overpowering urge to look out her bedroom window. She crept from her bed, and peered out from the locked bay window into the darkness of the night. It didn't take her long to spot the silver being crouched on one of the large limbs of the tree outside her window, guarding her house like some armored sentinel. The silver being looked over at her, and its fiery eyes – eyes that lit up the darkness – winked.

A voice sounded gently in her mind. *Go to sleep, Munchkin. Nothing will bother you ever again.*

Brianna smiled, her childlike fears whisked away at the sight of her father. "Goodnight, daddy," she whispered as she climbed back into bed.

Within seconds, her body yielded to the much-needed rest and peace of slumber. The Hybrid stood watch for several more minutes, and then leapt into a nearby tree. He had several other children to visit this night.

* * *

Lisa Reynolds sat in her hospital bed with her parents. She was on her third cup of hot cocoa, and getting no closer to falling asleep. She felt tired, but every time she closed her eyes, the nightmare would continue. Her mother was shedding tears as she held her daughter, and her father cursed at his inability to help his only child.

"Momma," she whispered, "there's a voice inside my head, calling my name. It's calling me over to the window."

"You're imagining things, honey," her mother whispered.

"Just like I imagined those creatures," Lisa replied as she broke from her mother and ran to the window. She gasped, then smiled with delight, whispering to a voice only she could hear.

Her parents looked at her, and then joined her at her hospital bedroom window. On the rooftop of the adjacent building was the same large silver being with glowing eyes that rescued her from her horrible ordeal, and gently carried her from the cavern into the woods. She remembered his gentle metallic arms as she faded in and out of consciousness, while he carried her from her dark prison.

Lisa took this opportunity to thank her chrome-plated knight, and giggled as he bowed flamboyantly then brought his staff up in a kind of salute. The two talked for several minutes, mystifying both parents.

"Goodbye, Mr. Knight," Lisa whispered.

The silver being turned and leapt from the rooftop into a nearby tree, and the Reynolds family watched with fascination as he vanished into the dark night.

Andrea Reynolds looked at her daughter carefully, the terror seemed to have vanished from her face. She actually was laughing as she made her way back to her bed. "What did it say to you, dear, what did you say to it?"

"He came by to check up on me, to make sure I would be all right. He said he knew that I was probably still scared. He said his daughter was."

"His daughter?" Andrea asked, shocked. "Child, do you actually know who that was?"

"Yes," Lisa answered. "His name is Erik, Erik Knight. He's the one who came and got all of us yesterday. His daughter goes to school with me."

Lisa's parents looked at each other in total disbelief, staring out at the window, and then back at their daughter.

* * *

Richard Pendelton sat behind his desk, draining his second bottle of scotch. He glared up at the fancy gold inlaid clock upon his wall: 3:45 a.m.

He should be tired, yet somehow, he felt an unusual exhilaration. His men pulled it off. They successfully covered their tracks pertaining to the Hopedale mining operation. The cost had been high, but his stepdaughter was home, safe, rescued by her father. That, too, was unexpected. Erik Knight had survived, somehow transformed into some type of inhuman super being.

Pendelton knew, deep down, from their brief eye contact at Madame's, that Knight knew he was responsible for the tragic incidents of the past several days. To Richard's advantage, all of the potential evidence had been obliterated, or buried beneath thousands of tons of rock and earth, never to be uncovered again. The only evidence that Knight had was anecdotal, nothing concrete that his lawyers couldn't shred in a court of law. He knew, however, that Knight was far from stupid, and that the man was a vengeful sort. Knight would be coming for him. It wasn't so much a matter of *if* in Pendleton's mind, as a matter of *when*.

But that was another worry for another time. It was somehow comforting to have Knight still alive, a foil in which to continually match his wits and skill against. It had been almost too easy to destroy the man years ago. It would be far more challenging to accomplish the same task again. For Erik Knight was the ultimate loose end, and Richard Pendelton hated loose ends.

Richard received several calls from his associates regarding his company's current position throughout the early morning. All outstanding loose ends had been cut and any potential liabilities removed.

He finished off the dregs of his last glass of scotch and swirled the ice cubes around the glass. "To success," he whispered as he drained the last bit of liquid and crushed the liquor-soaked ice cubes with his teeth. *And to getting away with murder,* he added in his thoughts as he swallowed the crushed ice.

Epilogue

Six weeks passed since the dramatic climax of events in the sleepy suburb of Hopedale.

The military had done an excellent job of squelching any further outside media regarding the unorthodox occurrences. All photographs of the Esper-Human hybrid and Seelak encounter were confiscated for official government security reasons, leaving behind several furious press photographers and reporters. There were several small carefully planted stories pertaining to the incidents in the larger metropolitan papers such as the *Boston Globe*, but each story related the events and occurrences in humanistic terms, ignoring the actual facts.

People who actually witnessed the encounter rarely spoke of it. The parents of the children who were abducted were paid substantial amounts of cash from the government to say nothing. The Reynolds, who had no need of money, were compensated with lucrative government contracts to the family's business enterprises. The Pendeltons also benefited greatly by saying nothing more of their daughter's abduction. Two of the families had placed their homes on the market with the intentions of moving as far away from Hopedale as possible and starting over again with their new federally funded nest egg.

Erik Knight continued his small agency, operating out of Madame's Restaurant, and continued to fret over his finances. His relationship with Shanda intensified. An inseparable bond formed between the two, which Erik planned to cement with a diamond.

He occasionally felt the irresistible urge to head up into the mountain, where he would vanish for several days at a time in the woodlands with little notice. Erik liked becoming the Hybrid, and enjoyed leaping from tree to tree like a jungle animal. He could move through the forest like a phantom, unseen and unheard, unfettered by darkness or any other limitation that would beset a normal man. These private times allowed him to further explore his talents and abilities. To Erik, these times were as close to ultimate freedom as he could experience. As the Hybrid, he could sense the very essence of every living thing around him from the largest deer to the smallest fly. It gave him a new appreciation for wildlife and the wonders of nature.

It was at the end of one of Erik's forays into the mountain that he spotted Martin Denton's SUV parked outside Madame's. Erik walked into the restaurant quickly and was intercepted immediately by Alissa. The young waitress gestured to him as she walked toward him.

"Mr. Denton has been here for you for the past three days. I told him I would have you contact him upon your return, but he didn't want to wait," she whispered to him as he headed toward his office. "I keep telling you, Shanda keeps telling you, and Jeff has told you: When you get the urge to commune with nature, please bring along your cell phone so we can reach you in case of emergencies. Or," the waitress continued, "times like this when you have important people who need to contact you."

Erik looked down at the small woman and smiled brightly. "Yes, Mother." He opened the door to his office.

Denton was sitting on Erik's couch, examining a framed picture of Erik, Shanda, and Brianna. The attorney looked up, startled, and stood, quickly placing the frame back on the table.

"I was beginning to wonder if you were ever going to show up here again." Denton extended his hand toward Erik.

"Sorry about that, Martin, I wasn't expecting anybody this week," Erik apologized as he shook the man's outstretched hand.

"My boy, you need a pager, or a cell phone, or something," Denton added as Alissa cleared her throat and elbowed Erik in the side.

"So I've been told," Erik answered, looking at Alissa. "Repeatedly," he added, watching Alissa leave with a self-satisfied smirk.

Martin sat back down on the couch, and Erik sat at his desk. He looked over at the large man who always accompanied the older man and nodded slightly. The suit returned the gesture. The three men sat in silence for nearly sixty seconds.

"Erik, I'm going to get right to the point," Denton began.
"Please do."

Denton smiled. "You've been a consultant for our company for quite a while now, and have established an excellent reputation within the firm."

"Thank you," Erik replied, wondering where this was going.

"Our firm is looking to branch out, get into smaller markets, establish a more personal relationship with small clients. Only our operatives and agents aren't equipped to deal with the kind of cases that come up in this type of market. We're used to corporate investigations, political corruption, and cases of that nature. We want to broaden our base, so to speak, but don't have the in-house capability," the elder man stated.

"Are you trying to recruit me, Martin?"

"In a way," the older man answered. "Before you answer, please hear what I have to say."

"Please," Erik replied, gesturing for the man to continue.

"Let me start by saying that the firm knows you've undergone … how shall I phrase it, a change?" he stated delicately.

Denton reached inside his black attaché case and produced a sealed envelope. He tossed the envelope toward Erik who opened it carefully. The envelope contained a series of nine by fourteen photographs. They were pictures of Erik as the Hybrid. Erik studied the pictures carefully. They were various snap shots of his final confrontation. It was unnerving to see himself that way in photographs, and it reminded him that beneath his human-looking appearance, he was a being very alien to those people around him.

He looked over at Denton, his eyes desperate. "And what makes you think this is me?" Erik challenged.

"Keep going," the older man urged.

Erik came to the final three pictures that clearly showed the silvery being reverting back to its human form, his particular human form. Erik was impressed. Denton's law firm must be very powerful and influential to be able to keep these from the military and the government.

"I suppose you're not going to tell me how you got these," he said, chagrined as he placed the pictures back in the envelope and placed them on his desk.

"That would be betraying a confidence," Denton answered.

"Are you going to try to blackmail me with these? Is that why you're here?" Erik said forcefully as he stood up from his chair.

"No! My young friend, please sit down, nothing like that. I just want to be completely open with you, lay out all the cards on the table. The firm knows what you are, and I'm sure you've already guessed we're more than a law firm, but that's a discussion for later. We've discussed recruiting you before, but I've always advised against it. You're most effective as a rogue, and frankly, you wouldn't fit into the corporate structure of the firm."

"Thanks," Erik remarked dryly.

"I'm telling you nothing that you don't already know, young man," Denton responded. "But, there are things that you don't know, such as even now, there are several organizations within the government and military that have taken great interest in you."

"I've expected as much," Erik replied. "I didn't think they would just go away. But," he added, "I'm more than able to take care of myself. I have capabilities the military or government haven't seen, that your firm hasn't seen. I'll make them sorry if they come after me," Erik added in a deadly voice of steel.

"Which is exactly why they won't come after you," Denton responded. "They'll come after your pretty little girlfriend, they'll come at you from your daughter, they'll come at you from your friends, they'll come at you from your business, attacking everything that you care about, never confronting you directly, but always there in the shadows," the old man replied. "As strong and as powerful as we suspect you've become, you can't be in two or three places at once, can you?" Denton asked gently.

Erik sighed heavily. He hadn't anticipated having to protect those around him, only himself. Suddenly, he felt very stupid and very foolish. That feeling of helplessness began to settle in the pit of his stomach, the feeling that he detested most of all. He felt his eyes burning, and he glanced down at his hands, which were resting in his lap. The skin began to change hue. He felt his muscle tissue contract as the adrenaline in his body reacted with his genetically enhanced DNA.

"No," Erik answered with a savage hiss that made the older man shudder. "I can't be in two places. But if they hurt my daughter, or anyone close to me, I'll make the Seelak problem seem like a kindergarten picnic. I have the ability to wreak more havoc than just stirring up a small town." He looked up at the older man.

Two fiery aqua embers replaced Erik's blue eyes. His body seemed to swell as he raised a metallic fist. He grabbed two three-inch thick telephone books from his shelf and effortlessly tore the volumes in half with his bare hands. The act of aggression seemed to calm him and he felt the mutation lose its hold upon him. He looked down at his hands. They were flesh colored again, and the mild burning sensation that marked his transformation ceased.

He looked over at Denton. The old man was nervous, seeing pictures of a transformation and actually observing the phenomenon were very different. "I'm sorry, Martin, sometimes when I get aggravated, it begins to happen without my control. I didn't think about the others, I didn't think they'd be affected by this so soon. I figured I'd have enough time to sort through all the complications and work it all out beforehand," he looked at the older man. "That was pretty stupid of me."

"Nobody is perfect, Erik," Denton said, his voice warm with understanding. "Good people don't go after innocents, Erik, and you're good people. Unfortunately, there are those people in higher places that don't play by the same rules you do. That's where we can help you. We are the most powerful law firm on the eastern coast. We have connections in Washington, all the way up to the President. We can protect you, your family, and your friends. I know how you feel about being your own man, and I understand and respect that. I would have made this offer to you months ago if I thought you'd accept.

"Even without your new capabilities, you're an asset. Now you're not only an asset, but you're going to be a target for every black ops military program with a budget or government agency with some scheme that would benefit from your talents.

Sooner or later, they will come for you, and the government doesn't play fair. They'll use any method to take what they want, and they won't ask before they do it. Whether they go through your family or your lover, they won't stop until you capitulate. To them, you're an uncontrolled, unknown force – a threat to government security and, more importantly, a resource they wish to exploit."

"I have no wish to work for the government," Erik said forcefully. "Tell your black ops friends that, if I'm pushed, I will push back and they won't like it when I do. I can be just as dark and deadly as any government agency, Martin. If it comes down to a war, I'll give no quarter, government official or not. Bureaucratic bones break just as easy as anybody else's," the detective threatened. "If you really want to serve your Washington employers, you best tell them to back off and stay very clear of my world," he warned. "Or else."

Denton sighed. He'd anticipated Erik's stubbornness. "Let me finish, please. Think about what you're saying. Do you want armed agents raiding this place? Do you want the government issuing a warrant for your apprehension, if it comes to that? Maybe you can fight off the army and the government, maybe you're even more powerful than we suspect, but, Erik, you can't live in a vacuum, you can't spend every waking moment fighting the government," Denton implored. "Son, you're outnumbered by about a million to one. Also, how long until the Chinese, or the Middle Eastern factions get wind of what happened here? That's an entirely new kettle of fish. Do you really think you can take on the whole world by yourself? Is that what you really want: To spend the rest of your days fighting and fretting?" Denton asked in a reasonable tone.

Erik exhaled heavily as he considered Martin's words. The elder gentleman had an annoying way of putting things into perspective. Erik knew he was right. Alone he could probably engage any force, but he wasn't alone, he had a child and he had other relationships. As powerful as he was, he couldn't protect them all. Denton was offering him a possible way out, a solution to a problem he hadn't fully considered yet. Working for the government left a foul taste in his mouth. Taking orders and simply being a lackey wasn't his idea of a life, especially since he'd spent most of his adult life avoiding this type of situation.

Erik cracked his knuckles and shook his head, frustrated. He felt trapped, caged by events beyond his control. He had no way out. The government, apparently, would waste no time in coming for him.

"So, what exactly are you proposing?"

Denton smiled, obviously encouraged by Erik listening to reason so quickly. "If you join the firm, we'll make the appropriate contacts to see that you're undisturbed. Also, you get the benefit of a steady, rather large paycheck, whether you're on active status or not. You will no longer have financial problems and you'll have more time, effort, and equipment to help those that come to you, the little person who really needs the help," Denton added as a further enticement. "Hell, even if you don't join the firm, I'll do everything in my power to keep you appraised of what's coming your way. I like you, and I respect you." The old man paused. "I'd also like to consider you a friend as well as a business associate."

Erik was tempted, but also suspicious. The offer was nothing like he'd anticipated. In fact, it was almost too good to be true. "It's a very generous offer, but what's in it for the firm?"

"Fair question," Denton answered. "We get the benefit of branching out into human interest cases. I won't lie to you. There is a degree of self-interest here. We want to bolster our favorability rating in the marketplace. Branching out into smaller human-interest cases will allow us better position in public relations. The firm plans on growing into this market slowly, one man at first, then eventually grow that one man to a team leader of three or four investigators. We've gotten the reputation as a 'rich man's' firm. I admit we haven't done ourselves any favors with some of our clientele, but there are those on the board of directors who feel we could benefit from some good PR.

"Plus, there's the other side of the issue, the larger cases, the kind of things that we do in the dark for dear old 'Uncle Sam.' I already know you're familiar with those, because we've used your talents on these in the past. Only now, we see the ability to use you on more sensitive cases that would benefit from your unique talents," Denton answered honestly and bluntly. "I won't lie to you. Seventy to eighty percent of the time, you'll be doing your own thing, being your own man as you prefer, with the exception that our firm will be diverting a small number of small private clients to you, in addition to the clients you glean yourself.

"The other times, we'll need you – 'we' being the firm and the feds – on our more … sensitive projects. There'll be times when we may pull you from a small case to handle something of a delicate nature for us. We'll place an outside specialist to pick up your case load in your absence. You have the firm's solemn word that your clients won't suffer for your removal if that occurs."

Erik leaned back in his chair. Denton's offer was appealing. He refused an offer long ago, and it had cost him his marriage and nearly cost him his daughter. "You make a compelling case, Martin. As long as you can assure me that I'll still have my own business, and am my own man most of the time, I think we can come to an agreement."

"You have Martin Denton's solemn word." The man extended his hand.

"One thing first, something I've been sitting on and could use your help with."

Denton raised an eyebrow as Erik walked away from his outstretched hand toward his wall safe. Erik tapped several keys on the safe's code pad and the small steel door swung open. He reached into the wall unit and produced a black leather binder. He approached Denton and tossed him the binder. The old man opened the binder and leafed through its contents. He looked at the young investigator incredulous.

"Mineralogical reports, mining core samples from Hopedale Mountain," the elder lawyer remarked. "That's conservation land, nobody should be doing anything up there, let alone conducting a mining operation." He placed the folder on Erik's coffee table. "I gather you obtained this from the site during your escapade last month."

Erik nodded.

"Pendelcorp is a tough nut. If I recall correctly, the CEO is married to your ex-wife," Denton observed. "This wouldn't be a personal vendetta, would it?"

Erik looked over at the old man, his eyes burning. "Martin, if I wanted to deal with Richard, I'd handle it in a more subtle manner. This document puts his corporation at the site where those creatures were. I saw abandoned mining equipment in that tunnel, as well as several corpses. They unearthed those monstrosities, broke into their chambers, and unleashed them upon this town. They're responsible for the deaths of at least a dozen men up there, as well as indirectly accountable for the death of forty or fifty soldiers, and possibly two pilots and choppers. I don't have enough horsepower to go after Pendelton directly with this, but with your firm, and your reputation, you could begin the process of exposing those weasels. I'm not an attorney, so I don't know how to go about building the right kind of case against them. This is the kind of thing you specialize in. Can you help me?"

Denton leaned forward, picked up the bound pages, and leafed through the binder again. The dated reports and studies were incriminating, but the firm would need more to go on than one man's word and a binder. Plus, the government already released its report on what occurred up on Hopedale Mountain. Trying to prosecute this now would undoubtedly catch the interest of certain federal agencies that would rather the matter be kept quiet. Denton knew that to pursue this without further evidence would be pointless, and to hunt down further evidence would only involve the same bureaucracy that wanted this story buried forever.

"Let me be frank," he began cautiously. "In order to effectively build the kind of case you want, we would require more evidence to implicate any company in wrongdoing. Do you have any further proof? You said there were bodies up there, can they be recovered?"

"No," Erik whispered. "That damned helicopter blew everything to kingdom come. It fired some very powerful short-range cruise missiles and caved the whole tunnel in and wiped out the entire campground. The only thing up there now is a big smoking crater and some burnt trees and vegetation. The final rocket barrage scattered any smaller debris to the four winds. Whoever wanted that stuff eliminated was quite thorough," Erik lamented.

Denton tossed the black binder back at Erik. He caught the book and placed it back on his desk. "Without something further, I'm afraid that there's little we can do. If we start poking around with no specific direction, we'll alert every fed that wants this story buried. Also, if we wave that around, someone will get enough common sense to impound it via legal chicanery, and that will leave you with nothing. My best advice to you would be to hold on to it and wait. Time is the key factor right now. This is still too big a sore spot. Give the wound time to heal over before you start picking at it. The more you pursue this matter now, the more attention you draw to yourself and those you care about. I know it's difficult, but for now, let it go," the elder man confessed. "Look, Erik, I'm sorry. I know that's not the answer that you wanted to hear, but anything else would be a lie, and I won't lie to you."

Erik sat in silence for a few moments, considering the lawyer's words. "I appreciate that, Martin, really. It would have been very easy for you to feed me a line, but you didn't. That says a lot. I think we'll make a good team, assuming I will be answering to you when my services are needed."

Denton looked perplexed momentarily as he digested Erik's reply. He again extended his hand. This time Erik stood up and shook his hand firmly. "Welcome aboard, Erik. You've made the right choice, young man."

"I know," Erik replied. "I had an opportunity once that I let slip by, I won't make the same mistake twice."

Denton smiled. "I'll make the appropriate calls and inform the firm that you're on the team. For now, I'm happy to give you this as a token of our new business arrangement." Denton reached inside his jacket pocket and handed Erik a thin envelope.

He opened the envelope and was stunned to see a bank check for 50,000 dollars. Erik's jaw fell as he studied the number.

"Eliminate your debts, buy your young lady some luxurious gift, and give yourself a fresh start, Mr. Knight. Everybody deserves a second chance," Denton added as he headed toward the office door.

Erik watched as Denton and his guard drove away. He stared down at the large check. This would more than wipe out the string of debts he incurred over the past years and leave him plenty for his savings account. He pocketed the check and picked up the Pendelcorp mining report. He took the binder to his small copy machine and duplicated several random pages. Erik folded the pages and placed them inside his pocket and put the binder back in his wall safe. He grabbed his keys and headed out. If he hurried, he could still make it to the bank before it closed, and then to the jewelers. It was time to pay a visit to Richard Pendelton. The two men had several things that needed to be discussed. He may not be able to prosecute that pompous bastard, but there was still a way he could utilize his new arrangement.

* * *

Margaret Pendelton was relaxing in the hot tub when she heard the door chime ring. "Figures!" she whispered as she picked herself up from the comforting warm water. She covered her shapely form with a terrycloth robe and headed toward the door. She was surprised to see Erik. Her ex never stopped by unannounced.

"Hello, Erik," she began. "What brings you here?"

"I need a few words with Richard. He and I have some business matters that need to be discussed," he answered evasively. "It's quite important, and he'll be most interested."

"Come in," she replied, escorting him to her husband's office. Margaret knocked on the large door. "Richard!" she shouted through the thick wood barrier. "You have company."

Endless seconds seemed to pass before the large door opened and Richard stepped out into the marble-laden foyer. His eyes widened when he spotted Erik.

"Ah, Mr. Knight, what brings you up from the bottom feeders you're so fond of?" he asked condescendingly.

"I have some papers that relate to a case I'm working on. I'd like to get your opinion on them. I'm not sure what to make of them. I figured before I went to the authorities, I'd get a businessman's perspective." Erik paused momentarily. "Would you mind?" he asked innocently enough, doing his best to put Pendelton at ease.

"Why not!" Pendelton answered in a smug tone, gesturing for the detective to enter his office.

Margaret looked at the two men as the door closed, knowing something more was going on than either would admit.

"Play nice, you two," she said to both men as the door closed.

* * *

Richard walked over to his bar and prepared himself a large drink. He made a great deal of noise examining the various liquor bottles at his disposal.

"So much good vintage," he spoke aloud as he selected a bottle of gin. He began mixing himself a cocktail while studying Erik who was seated quietly in one of the spacious leather chairs facing his large mahogany desk.

Richard had finished mixing his gin and tonic, and sat behind his desk, leisurely sipping his drink. "I'm actually glad you stopped by." Pendelton couldn't help himself and decided to bait his favorite foil. "Margaret and I were just discussing the adoption proceedings for Brianna last night. I'll have my attorneys send you copies of the forms for you to sign. They're not very complicated. I'm sure you'll be able to figure them out by yourself." Pendelton awaited Erik's reaction of panic and outrage. The detective simply sat there, staring at him, his blue eyes burning with inhuman intensity. Pendelton cleared his throat and quickly changed the subject. "What did you want me to look at, and of what possible interest could it have to me?" he asked, looking away from Erik's stare.

Erik reached into a pocket and tossed the folded papers onto Pendelton's desk. The man picked up the bundle and began to leaf through each sheet carefully.

"Where did you get these?" he demanded.

Erik just continued to stare at him, his eyes burning a hole into Pendelton's guilt-ridden soul. "I was up there, remember. I'm the one who got my daughter and the other children back. I saw the bodies, I saw the base camp, and I saw the machine you used to free those creatures from their tomb," he answered very softly. "You're responsible for a number of innocent people dying, Richard," Erik accused. "Not to mention tunneling and mining in protected lands. That alone will cost your corporation some hefty fines, the prior will land you in the federal pen," Erik stated softly in a deadly whisper.

Richard controlled his emotions carefully, trying to keep some advantage. "This is all very interesting, Knight, but how can you tie this to me? Anybody could produce these documents with any commercial grade equipment. For all I know, you manufactured these yourself. From what I've heard, and what you said yourself, everything was obliterated up there, nothing remained," Pendelton countered as he took a long swig of his gin and tonic.

Erik grinned. "You're right, this alone won't convict you in a court of law, but I'm sure someone would find it very interesting. You, the man who claims to love his step daughter, can be linked to the very thing that endangered her life. Plus, if I told her what I found up there, who do you think she's liable to believe. Even if she doesn't believe me completely, which I highly doubt, she'll never trust you again, you'll never get the family you want, and she'll, in all likelihood, turn away from you completely." Erik paused. "I win, Richard. Game. Set. Match," Erik said in a note of finality as he reached over and took a sip of Richard's drink and then spit the contents back into the glass. "Yuck, how can you drink that stuff? It'll kill your liver."

Richard took the glass and walked over to his wet bar. He casually emptied the glass into the small sink and rinsed it. "You blue collar naïve," Richard began, "do you think you have what it takes to challenge me?" Richard screamed. "You have nothing but some pieces of paper, no real proof. Margaret will never believe you. She'll think you're out for vengeance, nothing more. Margaret is firmly in my camp. She likes the things I have to offer. She'll believe me. You see, lowbrow, what it boils down to is simply your word against mine. In that arena, I win; game, set, and match. Your puny act doesn't scare me one bit. You just try something, buster, and I'll have my lawyers sue your blue-collar, lowbrow ass into non-existence for libel. Margaret loves me. She'll listen to me, not you," Richard said forcefully, struggling to control himself.

Erik slowly stood up from his seat and walked over toward Richard. He stopped directly in front of the man's face, and looked him right in the eye. "Who said anything about Margaret?" he whispered in a deadly tone. Erik turned, heading back toward his chair.

Richard knew that the bond between Knight and his daughter was unbreakable. He was a silver-skinned God in her young eyes. Whatever he said, the young girl would take as gospel. She would never accept him if Knight spoke outright against him.

Richard acted impulsively, reaching out and grabbing Erik by his shoulder. As the detective turned, Pendelton threw his weight behind a solid right cross to his face. Erik caught the man's fist in midflight in a grip of iron. Slowly and continually, he increased the pressure on Richard's balled fist until his fingers and knuckles crackled. Pendelton winced in agony. Erik twisted his grip, forcing Pendelton to his knees.

"That was incredibly stupid, Richard." Erik applied even more force to Richard's hand.

* * *

Richard was gasping as waves of shear agony shot through him. "Please," he gasped.

Erik slowly eased the pressure. "See, you can be nice if properly motivated." He lifted Richard up from his knees with one arm and tossed him into his desk chair several feet away. Richard looked over at him with hate-filled eyes as he cradled his hand.

"You're a fool, Knight. You'll never be able to give your daughter the things I can and have given her. She likes the lifestyle she has here. She likes the luxuries that I, alone, provide her. You barely make enough money to pay your child support. You'll never get your daughter. No court in the world will decide against me. You can't even afford a lawyer. You may be stronger than I am, you silver half-breed freak, but I have the money and the power. No matter how physically powerful you are, you can't touch me. You're still the same impotent bum you've always been. When it comes to dealing with and wielding real power, you're way out of your league, little man," Richard remarked with a snide chuckle.

Erik raised an eyebrow and reached inside his pocket. He produced the deposit receipt from his bank check and the recorded copy that he requested. "Oh really. Meet my new employers. I just got my sign-on bonus," he responded, placing the papers on Richard's huge desk. Pendelton leaned over and studied the documents.

"No!" he whispered in disbelief. "It's not possible."

"Oh, it's very possible," Erik countered. "Let me explain it to you, wise ass: I work for the most powerful and influential law firm on the eastern seaboard now. I'll see your lawyers and raise you. I'm sure you're familiar with Mr. Martin Denton Esquire. He's my new boss, and he's expressed a great interest in seeing that nobody bothers me so I'm free to handle the new private clients group they wish to start up. I'll probably be leading a team of investigators in a year or two, plus doing all kinds of, shall we say, *confidential* investigations. Mr. Denton has taken great interest in your activities. In fact, we discussed you in great detail earlier today," Erik added, taking great pleasure in seeing Richard's face turn pale white. "We may not get to you right away, but we'll get there. I'll probably be leading the investigation myself."

Erik leaned over the huge desk, his eyes suddenly burning fiery aqua blue. "Bottom line, mister, is this: You'll not adopt my baby, you'll stay out of Hopedale Mountain, and you'll see to it that you become a model citizen from now on, because I'll be watching everything that you do." Erik paused then quickly grabbed Pendelton by the collar of his expensive Italian suit. "And if you ever, ever place my baby in any more danger, there won't be enough of your body left to feed an ant," he whispered in a low cold tone, shoving Richard back into his chair. "Oh, one more thing," Erik added quickly. "I'll be petitioning for increased visitations for myself and my fiancé. I do hope you'll be supportive."

Erik looked down at the expensive Mahogany desk and couldn't help himself. He pushed down on the thick surface. It creaked in protest then splintered, splitting evenly in half and toppling onto Richard's lap. "Better have the quality of your office furniture checked," Erik added as he turned toward the large door. "Don't bother getting up, I'll show myself out," he whispered as he opened the door.

He walked out to his truck, feeling better than he had in years. He finally got the best of Richard Pendelton – he would savor the man's looks of horror for years to come. Erik finally had the advantage over the scheming weasel. Though he couldn't nail him for the atrocities he caused, he could keep Pendelton in check from causing potential future problems, plus gain the leverage he needed to get his daughter back into his life on a more full-time basis.

* * *

Erik sat nervously at his usual booth, waiting for Shanda to walk in for their evening together. He nervously sipped his glass of water and noticed his hands were shaking.

Alissa walked over to him and whispered, "The mighty Erik Knight, who single-handedly stopped the Seelak on-slaught, isn't getting cold feet, is he?"

"No." He took another sip of water. "But he's getting aw-fully jittery. It would be a real let down to pop the question, pull out the ring, and then get shot down," he lamented.

"She loves you, completely, Erik, everyone can see that plainly, and you love her. Everything will go fine. Stop being such a big worry wart," the young waitress replied with a com-forting lilt in her voice.

Erik sensed Shanda's presence, and looked toward the door. Shanda walked in and smiled as she headed for his booth. She leaned over and kissed him as she slid into the seat opposite him. Shanda spent several minutes lecturing him about venturing off into the woods without bringing a phone or beeper, constantly holding his hand emphasizing how worried she had been during his absence. Then, in a sudden shift in direction, she began to talk about her day. Erik listened patiently for an hour as the two of them dis-cussed the events of her morning and afternoon. They were halfway through their meal when the conversation turned to his activities. Erik began slowly and carefully.

"I had a visitor this morning. His name is Martin Denton." Erik paused as Shanda recognized the name. "I've been doing freelance work for him for a few years now, and they've decided to open a private clients' group for low to middle income people, my clientele," he emphasized.

"And," Shanda urged, sensing a bomb was about to drop.

"And this," Erik answered, reaching into his pocket and producing the deposit slip and placing it on the table. Shanda's eyes widened as she read the figure. "My sign-on bonus," Erik stated flatly. "I now work for the largest law firm on the east coast, but still get to keep my office here and see my own clientele. They'll be referring cases on an as-needed basis, plus they'll be pulling me into some high-end corporate stuff when needed." Erik paused, trying to gauge her for a reaction. "It's a job with upward mobility and a bright future," he added.

Shanda shrieked aloud in delight and reached over the table, embracing him in a gigantic bear hug. "I knew somebody would recognize your talents, Erik! I can't tell you how happy I am for you," she said as she seated herself back down. "It sounds perfect." She took his hand.

Erik glanced up and saw Alissa and Jeff loitering near the adjoining room, as well as several other staff. He gestured them away with a look as he reached over and gently took her other hand in his. Shanda caught his glimpse and turned to see the group of busy bodies disappear around the corner. She looked at him perplexed, and Erik just rolled his eyes and sighed.

"Shanda," he started as he cleared his throat, "that brings me to the next thing: You already know how much I care about you." Erik paused, and noticed that her eyes had begun to water, and tears slowly began to stream down her cheek. "You were right earlier at the hospital when you said we were truly made for each other. I sincerely believe that. I want to make our arrangement something more permanent. I want you to be my wife. Would you marry me?" he asked softly.

Shanda tried to stop the tears, but she couldn't. "Yes, of course I will," she answered him softly, leaning her head into his and kissing him deeply.

Once they parted, Erik reached beside him and produced

a jeweler's box. He slowly held it up, his hands shaking, and presented it to her. He opened the box and took out a large diamond and sapphire ring. "I hope you like it, Mrs. Knight."

Erik gently placed the ring on her finger, and Shanda broke out into a full fit of tears as she got up from her side of the booth and fell into his arms.

Jeff, Alissa, and the rest of the staff at Madame's appeared from behind the wall of the adjoining room, clapping and cheering for the young couple. Jeff carried a large sheet cake, and placed it on the table in front of them.

"Congratulations, lovebirds," Jeff said happily as he pecked Shanda on the cheek. "You, missy, have your hands full with this wild mustang," he added lightly.

Shanda, who was sparkling and glowing with radiance, replied, "Oh, I think I can find several ways to keep our wayward boy home at night," she replied.

Everyone laughed while Erik blushed slightly.

Jeff shook Erik's hand. "You deserve all the happiness in the world. My best to you both."

"Thanks, Jeff."

"Now c'mon, let's eat this cake, I'm hungry," Jeff started slicing the delicacy for everyone.

* * *

Erik awoke suddenly, he glanced over at his clock: 3:25 a.m.

He could hear his staff calling to him in his mind. Deep down, he felt the urge to be in the woodlands again, under the pale moonlight. He cautiously peeked over at Shanda who was sleeping soundly beside him. The warmth and perfume of her body was difficult to leave, but he knew the nagging wouldn't end until he had been out into the darkness for at least an hour. He crept from the tiny bedroom into the living room and quietly opened the small wall safe. He reached in and took the satchel containing his staff and placed it around his waist. Erik then tiptoed outside and into the small rear parking lot in the back of his apartment. He lifted the staff from its satchel, willing it to elongate into its true form. The staff sang in an eerie harmonic as it happily complied with his mental command.

"All right, I feel the need to be out in the open too. Let me change and we'll tour the town for an hour or so," he said to the sentient weapon.

The staff seemed to murmur in acknowledgement as Erik allowed himself to become his Esper form. He easily leapt thirty feet into a nearby tree and began his preferred route around the small suburb. He leapt from treetops to rooftops then back into the larger white oaks around the Hopedale Park. Once at the park, Erik perched on a thick limb, fifty feet above the playground sand. His mind flashed back to the battle he fought here, reliving each blow as well as the horror of the mothers and children at the birthday party. *That's in the past. I have a whole new future to look forward to. I'll have Shanda and Brianna to share it with. Now, I can give my daughter some of the finer things that I could never do before.*

But deep inside himself, he heard Jakor's whisper. *He had given his daughter the most important thing a father could give a child: Love. That love for his child spurred him to achieve all that he now was. He was the Hybrid because of her, in order to save her. He would never have to doubt her love for him, and she would always know her father loved her unconditionally. That was more important to a child than any material possession he could give to her.*

Erik smiled. It was good to have that extra voice inside, a seventh sense to go along with the telepathy and empathic gifts he acquired throughout his life.

The Hybrid, Erik Knight, looked up at the full moon, its light reflecting off his metallic flesh, and savored one last moment in the night. He now wanted to be home, in his tiny little apartment in this sleepy little suburb, wrapped in the warm embrace of his fiancée. With a cautious leap, he began the journey home.

About the Author

Greg Ballan is a graduate of Northeastern University holding Bachelor's degrees in Marketing and Management. He lives in the real town of Hopedale minus the creepy aliens and monsters. Greg enjoys several outdoor activities such as hiking, archery and shooting. When he's not working his full-time job as a Financial Analyst or getting lost in some unknown woodlands, he's crunched over his laptop putting his warped imagination into words or penning a column about politics, hunting humor or his latest tale about avoiding housework and yardwork.